Sam Bowring is a television writer, playwright and stand-up comedian. He is the author of the Broken Well trilogy, as well as several books for children, including *The Zoo of Magical and Mythological Creatures* and *Sam the Cat*. He lives in Sydney, Australia.

sambowring.com

By Sam Bowring

THE BROKEN WELL TRILOGY

Prophecy's Ruin
Destiny's Rift
Soul's Reckoning

STRANGE THREADS DUOLOGY

The Legacy of Lord Regret
The Lord of Lies

The LEGACY of LORD REGRET

STRANGE THREADS BOOK 1

Published in Australia and New Zealand in 2012
by Hachette Australia
(an imprint of Hachette Australia Pty Limited)
Level 17, 207 Kent Street, Sydney NSW 2000
www.hachette.com.au

10 9 8 7 6 5 4 3 2 1

Copyright © Sam Bowring 2012

This book is copyright. Apart from any fair dealing for the purposes of private study, research, criticism or review permitted under the *Copyright Act 1968*, no part may be stored or reproduced by any process without prior written permission. Enquiries should be made to the publisher.

National Library of Australia
Cataloguing-in-Publication data

Bowring, Sam.
The legacy of lord regret / Sam Bowring.

978 0 7336 2812 2 (pbk.)

A823.3

Cover and map design by XOU Creative
Text design by Bookhouse, Sydney
Typeset in 12/16.5 pt Dante MT Std
Printed and bound in Australia by Griffin Press, Adelaide, an Accredited
ISO AS/NZS 14001:2009 Environmental Management System printer

The paper this book is printed on is certified against the Forest Stewardship Council® Standards. Griffin Press holds FSC chain of custody certification SGS-COC-005088. FSC promotes environmentally responsible, socially beneficial and economically viable management of the world's forests.

For Lornie.
It's been too long.

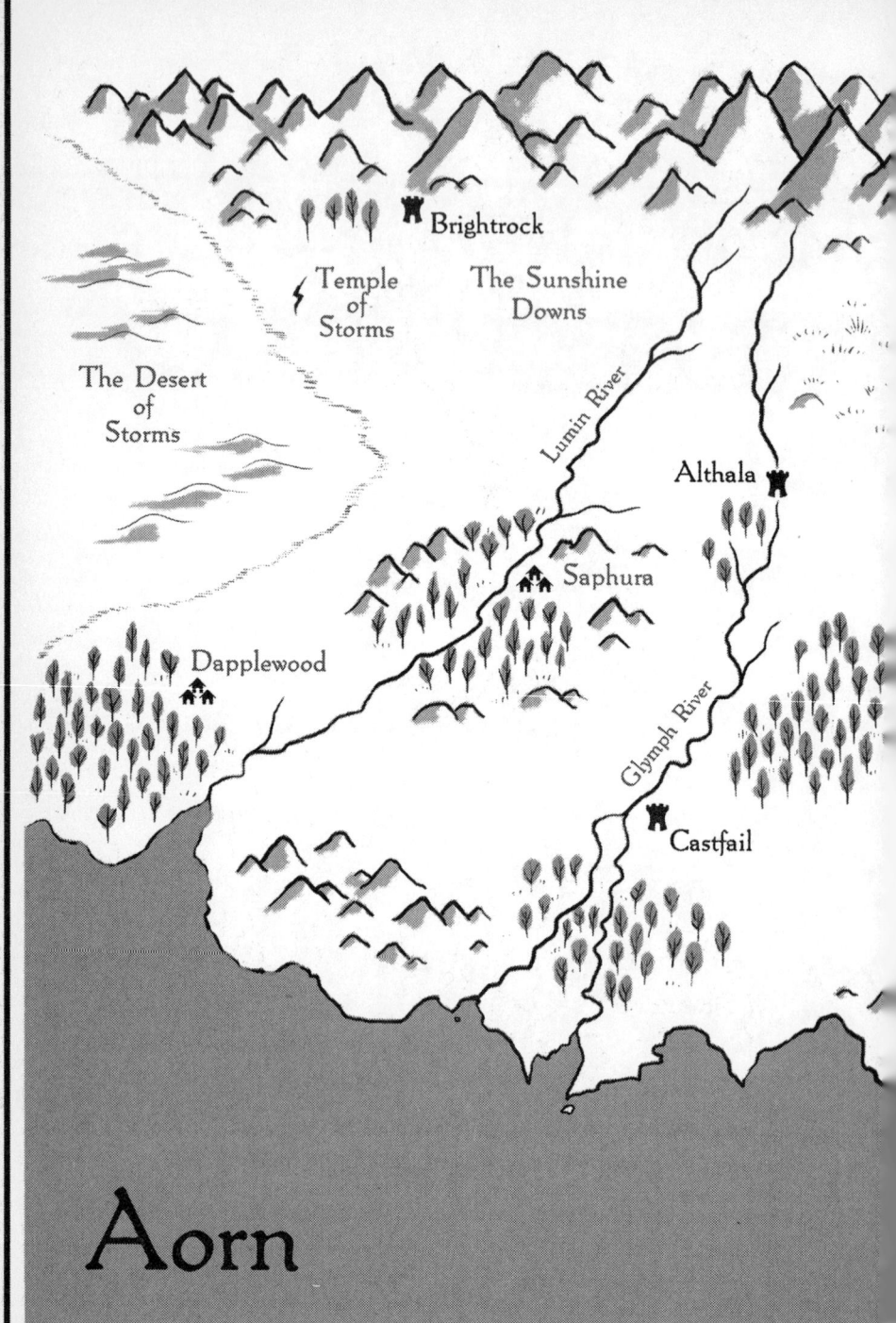

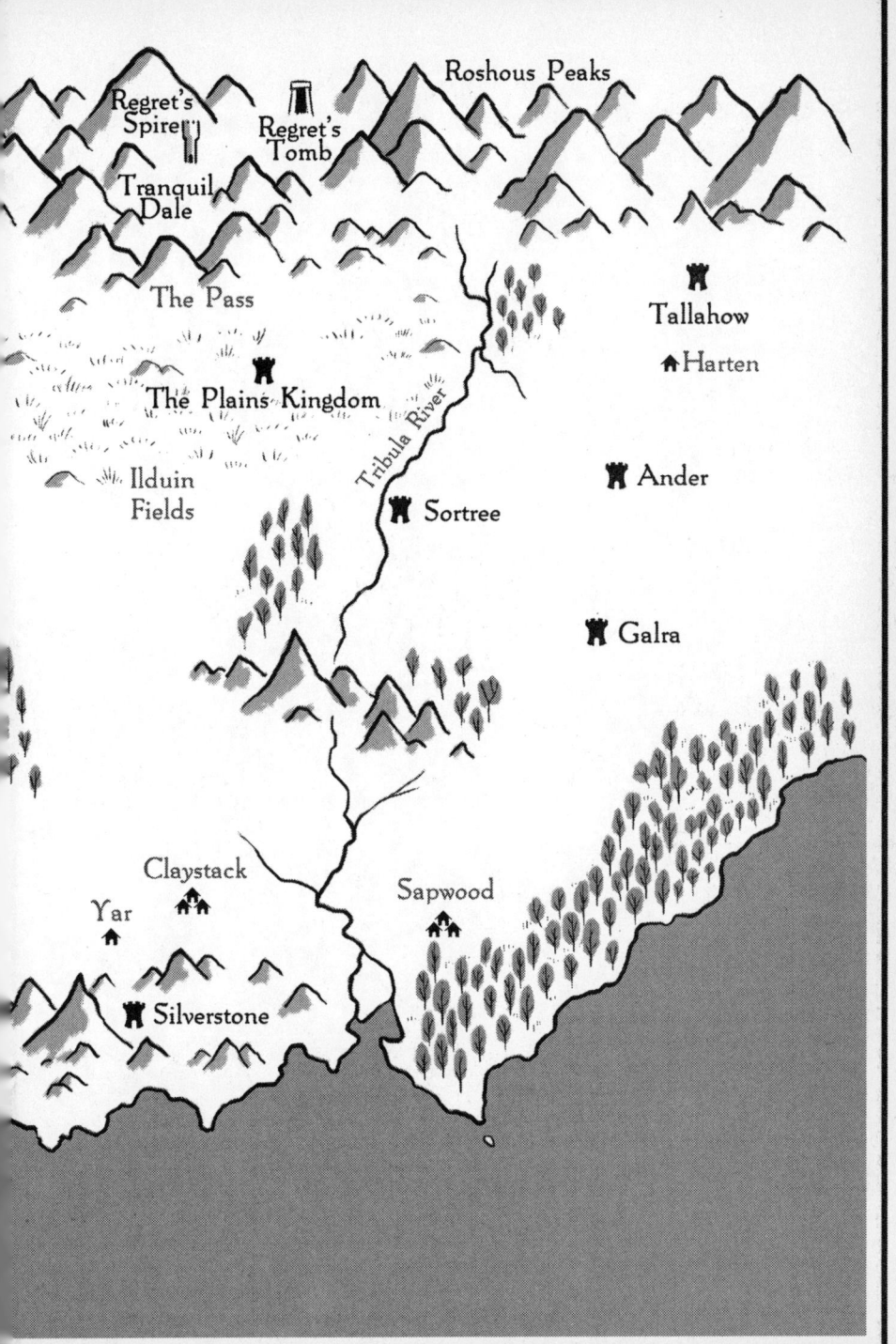

STATUE AND SONGBIRD

Rostigan would not have picked the day. Oh, there had been signs to worry him over the years, but no one thought they were ever coming back. Tales and memories, their names collecting dust on history's pages, and everyone happier that way. Why they would suddenly reappear – not one, or two, but *all* of them, at once . . . well.

A sunny day it was, even in the cave. Golden beams burst through holes in the roof, keeping the skitterers skulking in crevasses, wondering what had happened to their usual dank sanctuary. And Rostigan, having hoisted himself up onto a rock shelf below one of the wider openings, discovered treasure where the light fell. There, nestled between runs of moss and trickling water, craning upwards with speckled clover-like leaves, grew a patch of curltooth.

He breathed out slowly, almost doubting what he saw. A rare and vague warmth wafted up from the deep place, from the cavernous chambers and shadowed hallways of his self. It connected him to things forgotten – as if, for a moment, he stood atop the tall tower of his life, aware of every stone and stairwell under his feet, while he looked out on a starry sky.

He shook his head, lest reverie take him.

Reaching into his satchel for a small pair of scissors, he set about the delicate work of snipping the twine-thin stalks of the curltooth. He had to be careful, for his hands were big and rough, his fingers barely fitting through the scissor handles and apt to crush the tiny plants. Each stalk held a single leaf, worth a bag of gold at least.

I'll have to fix this spot in memory, he thought, though when he'd be along this way again, he did not know.

The very last stalk he left intact. It confused him to do so – it was not as if sparing it would encourage the others to grow back faster, yet somehow it seemed greedy to take them all. Already the amount of gold they represented would be too much for him and Tarzi to carry. *We'll have to trade up for gems,* he thought. *Why not take the last leaf too, then? A few extra emeralds and rubies will hardly break our backs.*

He left it nonetheless. The rest he wrapped carefully in a cloth, which he placed in his satchel among less precious bundles of black cress, ascenia, and scrapings of purple moss.

'What are you doing up there?'

Tarzi had appeared at the cave entrance. She was gripping a straining branch from a tree at the threshold, using it to hang into the cave, leaving only her feet firmly planted outside.

'Why don't you come and see?' he called.

She glanced around nervously. He knew she didn't like the skitterers, the way their armoured bodies rasped over rocks as they moved, or their myriad beady eyes.

'They won't hurt you,' he said. 'They're too scared of the light.'

He didn't mention that, when he'd first climbed onto this shelf, a skitterer had been scuffling about, pausing to watch him arrive. 'Hello,' he'd said to it, and it had come at him, long feelers spread wide to expose its moving mouth parts. Perhaps it had felt cornered – Rostigan did not think the others would do Tarzi any harm, but he also did not think she would enter the cave in the first place.

'I'm hungry,' she called.

'Don't you have songs to practise?'

'Hmph,' she said. 'Give me a title and I'll perceive every word simultaneously, like a scroll laid out from end to end.'

Rostigan sighed. 'Why don't you write some new songs then?'

'Perhaps if you stopped spending your time scrabbling about in caves, I might witness something worth writing about!'

'Well, you may get lucky – the skitterers might discover their brown little hearts and attack me.'

He closed his satchel and pushed off the shelf. As he landed heavily on the cave floor, a rock cracked under his booted heel, and alarmed clicking sounded from dark corners. Tarzi yelped, almost losing hold of her branch. She hauled herself back along it until she was upright, released it to whip away, and disappeared.

Rostigan chuckled and headed to the entrance, avoiding the place where he had cast down the body of the quarrelsome skitterer. Two others were already crunching on it, working inwards from the legs.

Squinting in the glare, he stepped outside. Low hills overlooked the beach, its white sand a furnace that warped the view of crashing waves beyond. At the top of the closest rise Tarzi stood facing away with hands on hips, a silhouette in the light, her tawny curls shining like translucent amber. Her pose suggested that maybe, if she stared it down, the sun might go away. She moved under the shade of a grey-barked tree where their packs lay, kneeling down to rummage through them. Rostigan arrived to find her pulling out food, looking hot and bothered – her skin dappled with sweat, most prominently at her temples and between her breasts, elsewhere making her blouse stick to her.

Such a beauty, my Tarzi, and not modest about it either.

She glanced up at him, a flustered look in her big dark eyes. 'Don't look at me like that.'

'Like what?'

'Like you enjoy seeing me distressed.'

'You're distressed?' Rostigan gave a surprised laugh.

'Besides,' she went back to rummaging, 'even if they'd attacked you, who wants to hear a song about some fellow fighting a bunch of beetles in the dark?'

Rostigan shook his head slightly. He wondered if she would ever accept that he was not the type to actually seek adventure – that his actions at the Ilduin Fields he had considered necessary, not desirable. To Tarzi though, he would always be the hero Skullrender, a name given to him at that great battle. And ever since then, try as he might for a quiet existence, there was always someone in need of help. Most recently they had come across a village that had been serving as an ongoing meal for a Worm of Regret, and Rostigan had been the one to venture into its foul-smelling lair – an unnatural lean-to in nearby woods, built of trees wilting inwards – and put an end to it. Such creatures had persisted since the time of Regret, but it seemed to Rostigan there had been more of them lately. Another sign, perhaps, of what was coming, though not enough to pick the day.

'Why,' he said, crouching beside her, 'you choose to follow around an old statue like me, I will never know.'

'You're not old. Or, if you are, it's just a touch – enough to make you look dignified.'

The stained knees of Rostigan's trousers and cave dirt encrusting his arms did not make him feel dignified. Still, he'd been told he was handsome enough times over the years to have come to accept it, despite the stony, angular face he saw in the mirror.

He drew the sword from his back and rubbed it on the grass, cleaning off skitterer blood.

'Look at this desultory collection,' Tarzi said disdainfully, sweeping a hand over the food she had unpacked. There was a small portion of bread, some dried crab meat, half a vial of sweet sap, berries that looked on the turn, a few sprigs of mint, and a rabbit she had caught that morning. They had been many days away from settlement, and it was beginning to show in their supplies.

'We're close to Silverstone,' said Rostigan bleakly, and her eyes lit up.

He knew she grew bored with their treks through the wilderness. It was her choice to be here, however, and she could leave whenever she wished. That was the original bargain, though if Rostigan was honest, its parameters had muddied over time. They had shared a bed almost from the start, wherever that bed might be, and so of course that tangled everything. And while there were days when he wished he was alone, and wondered why he'd ever agreed to let a minstrel accompany him – even one as enticing as Tarzi – there were others when he was inexplicably compelled to see her happy, and thus agreed to civilisation.

'Did you find anything in the cave?'

'As a matter of fact . . .' he said, reaching for his satchel. He retrieved the curltooth carefully – there was no wind, but he remained wary of a sudden gust – and unrolled the cloth before her. The blue-green clover heads had already begun to crumple, and he knew he should get them drying in the sun.

Tarzi scrunched her freckled nose.

'You don't know what this is?' he asked.

'Weeds?'

'Curltooth.'

Her scepticism changed to amazement. 'No!'

'Yes.'

'But folk say curltooth is no more!'

'So they do. And yet.'

She frowned. 'You're *sure* that's what it is? You've seen it before?'

The deep place yawned, threatening to swallow him. 'Once or twice,' he said.

'But then that's . . .' She scanned the leaves, counting up their worth in her head. 'That's a fortune!'

'Yes.'

'They say it only takes a crumb.'

'It's true.'

She poked at a limp leaf. 'We may never have to work again!' She seemed suddenly horrified by the thought, and Rostigan felt affection for her then, vulnerable as she was to her own self-created worries.

'The value of these,' he gestured at the wilting leaves, 'is their own. We could sell them, but then what? Someone else enjoys the luxury great wealth can buy, and we enjoy great wealth without the luxury? Doesn't that sound rather roundabout to you?'

'Are you saying . . . ?'

Rostigan smiled. 'Why don't you get some water boiling?'

For a moment she looked like she didn't believe him, but then pleasure flushed her cheeks. She leapt to her feet, gave a little clap, and shot off down the hill towards the beach, where a stone ring housed the smouldering remains of last night's fire. Rostigan followed slowly, and while she went about cleaning the pot, which involved a run over hot sand to the water and back, he laid out the curltooth in the sun. Normally he would leave herbs alone to dry without worry, but this day he sat down on a log to watch over them closely. As Tarzi built up the fire and boiled the water, tore up mint and skinned the rabbit, for once she did not seem to mind his idleness.

'Now,' she said, rubbing sludge off her hands into the sand, 'what shall we make?'

Rostigan had never cooked with curltooth before, though he'd seen it done. One thing he remembered about the cooks who wielded it – they were always judicious about the number of accompanying ingredients. Curltooth had no taste of its own, its quality being to enhance other flavours, and if a dish contained too many, the result could prove overpowering.

'Well,' he said, 'perhaps a rabbit-mint stew?'

'Seems a bland meal for such an occasion.'

'Songbird, we could have mint soup alone and it would make you quiver.'

She froze for a moment with excitement, then rabbit and mint went into the pot. With exaggerated ceremony Rostigan lifted a curltooth leaf, tore a tiny shred from it, and dropped it in also.

'Now what?'

'We wait, as with any meal. Come,' he patted the log beside him, 'you can rest in my shade.'

After a while Tarzi gave up peering into the pot as if she could actually see the magic taking place, and seated herself. He put an arm around her, but she was too restless, and soon got up to pace and fuss about in a way that had him worried she would kick sand onto the drying curltooth.

Once the stew was finally ready, her hands shook as she ladled it into two bowls. She gave one to Rostigan and waited expectantly, as if it was up to him to take the first taste. Shrugging, he scooped up a spoonful of rabbit and broth.

Perhaps it had been a while, but curltooth worked as well as he remembered. The mint twisted through his mouth in fresh green ribbons, and the rabbit was so alive on his tongue he felt like he was eating its soul. On seeing his rapturous expression, Tarzi could wait no longer, and took her first hesitant sip. The face she made Rostigan had seen before, but only in the heat of certain moments.

'By the tides,' she said, and nothing more for a long time. Together they ate slowly and reverently, and when there was no more they scraped the bowls, then licked them clean and fingers as well. Even the insides of their mouths they licked, eking wayward morsels from between teeth.

Rostigan realised he hadn't checked on the curltooth for a while, but a quick look showed it was all still there, some of it already brown. A jar would be better for it, now that it was in danger of crumbling.

'If you go and fetch the rest of the food,' he said, 'and a jar from my satchel, I will share a little secret with you.'

Quickly she obeyed, running up the hill and back with what he asked for.

'Now,' he said, as he took the jar from her and deposited the curltooth safely inside, 'some of the herb still lingers in your mouth. Why don't you try the berries?'

Eagerly Tarzi set about sampling the food they had left. Each new thing brought a moan and eyes rolling heavenwards, and Rostigan did not mind that she finished their stocks – he might have had a berry or two himself, indeed. Soon the last item remaining was the vial of sweet sap – which Tarzi unstoppered with a wicked grin and poured down her throat all at once. She sat up straight as if hit by lightning, her eyes even larger than usual.

'Everything all right?' said Rostigan.

'Wah,' she said, smacking her lips. 'That was . . . by the Spell . . . I tasted that down my *spine*.' She set the empty vial down gingerly.

He chuckled. 'Maybe we should hold onto this curltooth for a while?'

She nodded. 'Perhaps we could sell just one leaf? Imagine how much fine food we could buy with that much gold!'

'That we could.'

Her mischievous look came back.

'What is it?' he said.

'I just thought of something else that might benefit from such enhancement,' she said, and leaned in to kiss him.

As she closed her eyes the sky went black, as if the sun had suddenly winked out. For a moment everything lay in pitch darkness . . . and then, just as suddenly, the day blazed forth once more.

'What's wrong?' she said, opening her eyes, annoyed to find his lips unyielding.

'Nothing,' Rostigan said unconvincingly. Had he imagined the plunge into night? He knew he had not.

As he stared out at the crashing waves and sunny sky, he let his vision slip beneath the surface. Beside him, Tarzi became an interlocking series of circulating energies. Translucent bands flowed around each other within the shape of her, thickening in the cores – the red of her heart, the shadow of her spine, the rainbow sinkhole of her mind. Like all things, she was woven from threads born of the Great Spell.

Away at the shoreline, the waves were like a multitude of glowing paper-thin reeds thrashing against the sand, scattering amorphous fragments up the beach. Above the water, breezes ran in silver lines, only briefly visible, like fish turning on their sides to flash their scales as they swam by. Golden vines of sunlight reached from heaven to earth, a hundred thousand thick from his eyes to the horizon. He watched for any stir in that wavering forest, yet nothing but distant birds made it ripple.

He sent his gaze deeper, to where there was a sense of how things connected – land to sea, cloud to root, death to life, man to woman – a tapestry at the outer limits of his perception. Beyond it the threads were fainter still, only discernible at all because they were so large – shadows of the Spell's giants, moving beneath the veil of the world, impressions in the corners of his eyes. They were not clear enough to make out, thus giving no hint as to what had gone wrong. Trying to look at the Great Spell was like staring into a river – he could catch reflections on the surface, but the depths were impenetrable.

'Come,' said Tarzi, touching his cheek. 'We have been in the heat too long – let's retire to the shade.'

He allowed her to pull him to his feet, glad she had no inkling of what had just happened. But he had seen the world blink, and still would not have picked the day.

Later that afternoon they moved away from the coast, through a vale in which the trees stood politely to the sides. Soon the waves were a distant echo, muffled by wooded hills lying between. Moving around the base of such a one, they stumbled onto a cobbled road.

'Well,' said Tarzi, 'perhaps we're not as far from Silverstone as we thought.'

'No.' Rostigan stared gloomily at the road. No wonder

Tarzi had grown impatient – he must have dragged her along the beach for longer than he'd realised, to have arrived here so quickly. 'Perhaps we'll even reach the city before nightfall.'

The road led through uneven land, up and down hillocks choppier than waves. At the crest of one they passed a guard post – a rickety wooden tower with an unlit brazier at the top.

'Strange,' said Tarzi. 'That should be manned. Where's the guard?'

Rostigan shrugged. Scanning ahead, his far-reaching gaze caught movement in the lower distance. A figure ran along a row of rushes by a stream, wrapped up tight in a red cloak, face masked by a kerchief and a broad hat – a woman, maybe. She disappeared into the trees.

'I don't know,' he muttered.

'If I'm right, Silverstone is over the next rise.'

It's so quiet, he thought. *We should hear the city by now.*

On they went, up the next hill to the crest. From there they looked over the old floodplain valley on which Silverstone had been built. Named for the shining blocks used to construct it, the lavish city crept up into the hills themselves, all the way to templed peaks. Bustling with people, and famous for its bathhouses steaming with mineral salts found in these hillsides, it had always been a place of abundance.

'By the Spell,' said Tarzi, her jaw going slack. 'What . . . how can this be?'

A great field of exposed, empty earth lay in the very shape that Silverstone had been. Its edge wandered across the floodplain, up into the hills and back around again in a huge brown circle. It was as if every brick, every building, every person and thing had been lifted away, leaving nothing behind.

Rostigan felt heavy, sick confusion bitter in his mouth, as if the residue of curltooth somehow even enhanced the taste of that.

Was this his fault?

'Rostigan!' cried Tarzi, grabbing his arm. 'Where's the city?'

'Shh,' he said, holding up a hand. She fell silent, wondering what he listened for. Then she heard it too – a voice, female and lyrical, ghostly and distant. It was too soft to hear the words, until they stole closer like a breeze.

Pride, they say, before the fall
Yet Silverstone stands great and tall

And then a tinkling laugh, fading into the rustling grasses.

A strange feeling took hold of Rostigan. Was it horror, or relief?

'What was that?' said Tarzi fearfully.

'Get down.' He pulled her to the ground.

'Ouch!'

'We do not want to be written about from afar.'

'What are you talking about?'

Could it really be? How was that even possible?

He remembered the figure fleeing into the trees. Who had that been? Someone afraid of what they had seen here? Or her?

'Stealer,' he muttered.

'Stealer?' Tarzi echoed, dumbfounded. 'What are you talking about? She died hundreds of years ago.'

'Yes,' said Rostigan. 'And it was the knights of Silverstone who killed her.'

STEALER

Rostigan hoped he was drawing a particularly long bow, yet its arrow seemed to point a true target.

'Come, Tarzi,' he said, trying to sound certain as he collected his thoughts. 'You know the tales of her, probably better than I. Follow me – we stand out here like boils on a backside.' He began to elbow his way down the slope.

'Well, of course,' she growled, huffing after him, 'but as tales, not current occurrence!'

'Shh!' Their voices were carrying well over the eerily quiet hills. 'Here.' He crawled to some bushes by the side of the path.

Tarzi peered off through the leaves as if the city might reappear. 'I know people in Silverstone,' she murmured. 'What could have done such a thing?'

She turned back to Rostigan, who stared at her sombrely.

'Stealer?' she said, incredulous. 'You cannot be serious.'

'The floating voice,' said Rostigan. 'That's something

spoken of, isn't it? Stealer's echo, a mark in the air of what she had done? That she had *stolen*?'

Tarzi's expression remained dubious. It was not surprising, he supposed. He was not even sure why he tried to convince her – perhaps as a way of convincing himself.

'There are plenty of threaders,' Tarzi said, 'who can produce a voice from the air. Tide's end, I even know a ventriloquist or two.'

'And these ventriloquists,' Rostigan wet his lips, 'are they also able to remove whole cities from existence?'

And, he added to himself, *on the beach, you did not notice, but the sun blinked . . . a thing not seen since the days of Regret, and the Wardens.*

Should he tell her about that? He had withheld at the time so as not to worry her, yet now here he was trying to persuade her of Stealer's return, apparently based on nothing more than a hunch. His actions, he knew, had become somewhat contradictory. If he really wanted her to believe him, he should reveal what he had seen. Certainly the disappearance of daylight fit with histories which she herself recounted, legends known all over Aorn. She told them often – had done so, in fact, just before they had struck out on their latest sojourn into the wilderness, many nights ago . . .

Tavern-goers refilled their glasses and settled back to listen as Tarzi walked the tiles before the fire.

'Once,' she said, 'there lived a powerful threader, who would become known as Lord Regret, who ruled over the Tranquil Dale – back when it was a welcoming place, full of fine folk like you and me. Regret was a colourful fellow, thin as a stick, who liked to wear flamboyant robes and dye streaks in his wild hair. His bright appearance, however, hid a dark interior, and as time passed this became more and more apparent. Monstrously gifted, he could conjure rainbows or summon bones from people's bodies with equal ease.'

She made a snatching motion at a seated farmer, who flinched, and others chuckled.

'Worst of all, Regret learned – no one knew how, nor does to this day – how to manipulate the Great Spell itself! Not just the patterns born from it, which are the domain of all threaders – trees and cows and rainbows and bones – but the very fabric of existence, from which all things come. He set to work changing the world to match his twisted vision of it, born of delirium and nightmare. Starting with his own domain, he stripped his once-happy subjects of their humanity, turning them into pitiless creatures unbound from reason.'

'The Unwoven,' someone muttered, and others trembled.

'Aye, the Unwoven. But creating them was just the beginning. As Regret put his hand behind the world and wrenched at threads he found there, he injured deep and age-old patterns. Imagine it, my friends – the Great Spell, altered by a madman's will! All that sprung from it affected, a forest grown in poison soil, the repercussions felt all over Aorn. Children were born with limbs missing, plants that never flowered before broke out with aberrant blooms, and sometimes during the day, the sun would simply vanish, as if it were an eye that had shut.

'Regret was selfish, and insane, and did not care that his meddling threatened the nature of all things – revelled in it, in fact. Armies marched to try to stop him, but the Dale entrance was narrow and well defended by the Unwoven, who had an unnatural strength about them, and an unwillingness to die. They fought as if they loved their master, though to look upon them, one would not think them capable of love anymore. As Aorn's soldiers fell in their thousands, it seemed there was no hope of penetrating the Dale and that the world was doomed to be swallowed by Regret's chaotic ambition.'

'The Wardens came!' called someone excitably.

Tarzi arched an eyebrow, as if to say 'I'm telling this tale', and waited until she commanded silence once again.

'Indeed. Eight heroic threaders – the best Aorn had to offer – banded together to defeat the mad lord. They called themselves Wardens, and journeyed into the Roshous Peaks, a treacherous place at the best of times, now full of the creatures Regret had made. Taking this route, they approached the Dale from the north, away from its southern entrance where armies dashed themselves to pieces. From a high vantage they overlooked Regret's Spire, and saw that which now hung above it – a strange rent like a gaping wound in the sky, revealing the threads of the Great Spell for all to see. Here, then, was where Regret had torn open the veil of the world.'

Tarzi prodded the fire with a poker, releasing a spurt of sparks.

'The Wardens went to the Spire roof, to see if they could close the Wound. That was where Regret found them, attempting to undo his handiwork. And do you suppose he was happy?'

She cast the poker aside and outstretched her hands, as if to cast spells. Folk in the front row shifted uneasily.

'No,' she hissed, 'he was not happy! Decidedly unhappy in fact, and when Regret was unhappy, misery washed from him like a grey haze. He could make a person remember all the ill they'd done in their life – all the mistakes made, all the wrong turns taken – until they felt like naught but a pale imitation of what they could have been, had they but lived a little better.'

There was more than one shiver at the idea.

'Through such bleakness, the Wardens fought on. It is said the battle lasted for a day and a night, though for those involved, time passed differently. Regret had added to and rewoven his own pattern in unnatural ways, giving himself strengths he had never been born with – even transforming himself during the fight, into something like his own foul creations, with bat-like wings of human skin, and flesh for hair and glowing eyes.'

Rostigan, sitting alone at the back of the room, drowned a half-smile in his mug. The last time Tarzi had told this tale, Regret had become lizard-tailed with flaming fingers. He supposed she felt it necessary to add such detail, since little was known for certain about the fight itself.

'Standing together,' Tarzi continued, 'the Wardens managed to prevail. Some say it was Yalenna who finally burst Regret's heart in his chest, others claim it was Mergan, or that as a group they tore him apart, scattering him across the roof. At least one thing is known for certain – Regret was finally dead.

'What, though, of the threads he had stolen from the Spell, and made a part of his very self? To give himself strength, to gain unnatural skills? What happened to them, do you suppose?'

Tarzi focused on a cross-legged boy, staring up at her in wonder.

'They went *into the Wardens*,' she said, splaying a palm wide on the boy's chest, 'becoming a part of their own patterns! Worming inside, *altering* each and every one of them into something *other* than what they had been. None of them would ever age again – maybe because the threads they now carried were too important, too *permanent* – but that was not all that had changed. Strange new talents were theirs to command, and some of them, like Forger and Stealer, may as well have changed into different people entirely; depraved and bloodthirsty, maybe driven mad by their transformation, they were certainly no longer recognisable to their old comrades. Fortunately others, like Yalenna and Braston, remained as good as ever, despite what had been forced into them.

'The Wardens were saviours for a brief moment in time, but in the days to follow, the battles they waged against each other would draw in the rest of the world, and make Aorn's people wonder if they would have been better off under Regret. And, through the Wardens, his corruption lived on . . .'

'Are you sure?' Tarzi glanced at the sky, as if it might fall dark again. 'Maybe you imagined it.'

Rostigan barely heard her. Not even a trace of Silverstone's threads remained. It had not been ripped away, it had been *removed*.

'Rostigan?'

'No. I did not imagine it.'

'But what does it mean?'

'I don't pretend to know for certain, but if . . . *someone* . . . stole an entire city they may have punched enough of a hole in reality to send out ripples, maybe big enough ones to explain the flickering of daylight.'

Tarzi's eyes shone in fear.

'And I saw someone,' Rostigan added, 'just before. Cloaked, running away, and wearing a broad hat too.'

'Why didn't you say something?'

'I did not think it significant at the time.'

'I've seen paintings of Stealer. She always wore a hat.'
'Yes.'
'And covered her face.'
'This figure wore a kerchief.'
'That does not change the fact that Stealer was killed!' Tarzi rubbed her temples furiously, muttering to herself. 'Knights rode forth from Silverstone, dressed not in armour, but plain trousers and tunics. Riding mares unremarkable in nature or colouring, wielding dull and simple swords. And since there was nothing about them to turn into poetry, when they found Stealer in the woods, her quill could not save her. As she burned, all the things she had stolen were returned to the world.'

Rostigan nodded. 'That is the tale.'
'That is the tale from *three hundred years ago*.'
'Indeed.'
'Are you saying you don't think she really died?'
'No.'
'Then what?'
'I don't know.'

Rostigan did not voice that, for some time, he had been growing concerned about the Spell. It wasn't just the increased rumours of worms and silkjaws, or the battle at Ilduin, or even the moment of night on the beach . . . it was the sight of a falling leaf spinning too slowly, or an animal running backwards in a way that seemed impossible, or an odd scent wafting in the air, like earth burning. It was knowing that the Wound above Regret's Spire had never been closed and, more and more, it was a feeling he had.

He had not tried to explain it to Tarzi. She was young, and for her the world was as it had always been.

Looking about, he thought he spied the place where the figure had disappeared – yes, there, by a stream running into the woods. His head pounded – if Stealer really was loose again, there would be much grief for the people of Aorn. Even the other Wardens had been afraid of her. Immune to her gift they may have been, but she could still vanish castles from under their feet, armies from their fields. If Rostigan had a chance, here and now, to stop her before she did any more harm, before the world even knew the peril, before she could add new pages to her legend . . .

Now was the kind of time when he bemoaned Tarzi's company most. And, frustratingly, exactly the kind of time which she stayed with him to witness.

'I must track the woman I saw,' he told her. 'It's the only way to be sure. And, if it is Stealer, I must kill her.'

Despite everything, a wild excitement filled Tarzi's eyes. 'Imagine the song should you best her!'

'Do not wish such things upon the world,' Rostigan said darkly. 'Hope that I am wrong.'

―

It was growing dark and the stout trunks were thickly crowded, in places almost wall-like. Fallen trees lay at odd angles, pushed from the earth by the hungry roots of others, but without the space to fall.

Rostigan moved under a slanting trunk, Tarzi on his heels trying to remain as silent as he. She was fairly adept at it, he had to admit – as light on her feet here as when she sprung from tabletops performing stories – and yet there still sounded the occasional scrape of her boot on bark, or the crackle of leaves underfoot. It was dangerous – if the woman they pursued really was Stealer, the last thing he wanted was for her to hear them coming.

The trees gave way briefly to stony ground by the side of the stream. Rostigan entered the clearing carefully, but no one was there. Instead, on the opposite side of the clearing, a strange sight greeted him. Running in a straight line off into the dark was a passage between trees too uniform to be natural. Its floor was lightly churned, earth caving inwards where the roots of stolen trees had been. As Rostigan drew closer, a whisper wafted forth.

> *Standing in a wooden queue*
> *South to north, straight and true*

'She carved herself a path,' he said.
Tarzi bit her lip. 'At least it will make her easy to follow.'
'Only for me.'
'What?'
'Yes, songbird, time for you to roost a while.'
'How am I supposed to recount your doings if I'm not there to behold them?'

'Or indeed, if you are rhymed out of the world?'

'I wasn't making any noise!'

'You were doing well, but you must understand that this errand is madness. If Stealer really is somewhere ahead, there's every chance I won't return – and I won't risk you into the bargain. She adores beauty, they say, so you'd be the first to find your way onto the pages of her notebook. The greatest hope is to take her by surprise – something I can achieve more easily without you.'

Tarzi sighed and dropped her pack to the ground. She looked caught between being annoyed and slightly pleased with the compliment.

Rostigan went to the mouth of the passage. There were fresh footprints in the earth, mockingly petite. He glanced back at Tarzi – she had not protested overmuch, and he suspected she might still try to follow. Perhaps she would decide she could remain a safe distance behind him and observe any confrontation from hiding.

'Tarzi,' he said.

'Mmm?'

'In your stories, when someone is told to stay behind, they never do.'

She grinned. 'What of it?'

'Don't smile, girl,' he snapped. 'Stealer is no laughing matter. Her return could mark the beginning of a new chaotic age. Perhaps there is but one chance, one small and tiny chance, to stop her now before that happens. Is that worth jeopardising for a tale to tell drunkards?'

Tarzi's glare was icy.

'Promise me, *promise* that you will not follow.'

She sat down heavily on a log.

'Tarzi?'

'I promise!'

'A real promise, true? You will not sit for an hour, grow bored and creep along after?'

'Wind and fire! I promise, you insufferable man.'

'Good.' He turned away.

'What makes you think you have this small and tiny chance anyway? If it really is her, which there's no way it can be.'

'I have my reasons.' Rostigan took a deep breath, and entered the passage.

He went more swiftly than before, for he predicted Stealer at tunnel's end, and that was not yet in sight. Insects and worms that had made their homes in the earth around absent roots now wriggled free and exposed. The passage never deviated, and, as night fell, the wood grew blacker and blacker.

How deep have you gone? he wondered. *How far do you flee?*

He winced as his boot crunched a beetle.

Finally, ahead, he caught the twinkle of firelight. He slowed, stepping in shadows not found by the rising moon. Softly he approached the end of the passage, which he could now see opened up into a small clearing. He paused on the threshold, peering through gaps in the trees. There, on a rock before the flames, sat a lone figure.

She was the very image of her portraits. Small and slender in a scarlet cloak, under which other layers wrapped her tightly – gloves and leggings, boots done up to her knees, her shirt almost flat across her chest. Her kerchief was draped across her knee, but the broad-brimmed hat still hid her face. The quill in her right hand came down to meet the notebook in her left, and the point flew deftly across the page. There was a glimmer of threads streaming in from the air around her, only visible in the moment before they reached her. She chuckled, a wet sound, and a moment later her ghostly words floated out of the air.

> *Apples taste so fresh and sweet*
> *It's what makes them so good to eat*

In the dark Rostigan felt his heart grow cold. Had she really just done what he thought she had?

'See if you like that, Aorn,' she muttered to herself. 'So precious a simple thing, you probably didn't even know you had it, but you'll notice now it's gone, gone, gone . . .'

A night bird hooted on a branch above her. She glanced up at it, and Rostigan saw glittering eyes and a mouth that there was no mistaking. Jagged strips of flesh were missing from her lips, leaving the rest to hang like tattered curtains that permanently revealed her yellowed teeth.

As the bird stretched its wings, her quill descended toward a fresh page.

'Such whimsical destruction,' said Rostigan.

She started, her eyes snapping to where he lurked, quill hovering at the ready.

'Who's that?' she hissed through jiggling lips.

'Do you really need a bird in your collection, when you already took a whole city today, Stealer?'

She laughed. 'I thought I was forgotten after so long, but I do myself discredit.'

'Who else would purge Silverstone from the face of Aorn?'

'Yes, it was I – and, knowing that, you still sneak upon my fireside, bold enough to speak when most would flee? Do you fancy yourself protected, there in the shadows?'

'If you cannot see me, surely I am safe from being described.'

Her laugh was louder this time. 'Perhaps you've heard the tale of the knights who slaughtered me? It's given you false confidence. Do you really think there's nothing to be said about someone, just because they dress in brown trousers and only carry stupid blunt weapons?'

'Then how did they kill you?'

'We all sleep sometimes. It seems that men would rather remember themselves as gifted planners, rather than brutes who butchered a woman in her bedroll.'

'And why,' he said, 'have you returned?'

'Do you know, it is the strangest thing – I have no idea at all. Just woke up as if I never left, imagine that! I think it was even in the same place as where they killed me, though the landscape has changed a little so I can't be certain.'

'Aorn was better off without you. It will be again.'

'Oh yes?' Her eyes narrowed, and her quill darted across the page.

He makes a dangerous remark
This skulking fellow in the dark

Her words crawled up Rostigan's arms like ephemeral centipedes . . . and passed him by. Stealer's expression turned to one of shock. She leapt to her feet and bolted.

Rostigan had not expected her to flee. He bounded after her, his bulk a hindrance in the confines of the wood. She darted ahead, a flash of scarlet slipping between crowded trees. Gritting his teeth, Rostigan ignored the long scrapes of clutching twigs down his arms, the sharp branches that gouged him or flew at him in shards as he slashed them from his path. He heard her curse, and rounded a trunk to find her struggling with her cloak tangled in a bush. She ripped free and spun to face him as he advanced, her eyes widening at his raised sword.

'Wait, it's not fair!' she cried. Her hand flew up as she tried to undo the threads of his sword, but with a mental flick he batted her influence away.

'Don't you want to talk?' she said. 'I only just –'

He smashed the sword down between her eyes, driving bits of skull deep into her neck.

Rostigan carried the body back through the trees. She did not move, yet he thought there was life in her still – that, if left alone, she would eventually heal. Wardens had always been considered something close to immortal.

He arrived at her campsite, where the fire still burned. It had done the job once – no reason to think it would not again.

'Tarzi!' he bellowed, down the long passage.

She must be a league or so away, but he was sure she would hear him through the still night. She would want to look on the body, to see the mouth that removed all doubt, and thus have something to put in her stories.

'Tarzi!' he shouted again. 'It is safe to approach!'

He propped Stealer against a rock in an affectation of recline, taking care to remove the notebook and quill from her person. From either side of her split skull, her eyes suddenly became aware. They flickered to him, full of hate, and she gurgled somewhere down in her spliced throat, below the mess of her ruined lips.

'Patience,' he said.

He turned away, inspecting her notebook. Her writing was spidery yet legible. There was a verse about a guard in a guard post, followed by one about Silverstone, one that had created the passage in the trees, and finally, one about the taste of apples. The rest of the pages were blank.

He crouched down before her. 'What business do you have in the world, Stealer? Why have you returned? How?'

She could not answer.

After a while he heard Tarzi approaching, and went to show himself at the mouth of the passage.

'Rostigan?' she called nervously.

'It's me,' he said. 'Come and see, for I would not leave you with nothing for your songs. Come and look upon Stealer while you can.'

Tarzi entered the clearing, her face going white at what she found there.

'That's her?'

'Yes.'

'*Stealer*? Not some . . . I don't know . . . imposter, following in her footsteps?'

'If so, they did a good job replicating her likeness. Not that you can really tell now, I suppose.'

She clutched his arm. 'She's looking at me.'

'Do not fear, she cannot hurt you. I thought you would want to see her before I consign her to the flames.'

'But how did you best her?'

'I was lucky. I was able to circle around to where she sat and strike before she knew I was there.'

Tarzi stared a moment longer. 'It's really her, isn't it? That mouth . . .' She trailed off, looked away.

Rostigan felt like a cur who had dragged home a dying bird to its owner. 'Enough?' he asked.

'Enough.'

'Very well.'

As Stealer's eyes flashed in protest, he lifted her up under the arms and draped her across the fire. The gurgling in her throat grew louder, her fingers waggling spasmodically to a whir. Rostigan quickly gathered armfuls of dry brush, which he dumped around her.

'Must be terrible,' he said matter-of-factly as he worked, 'to go the same way, again, so soon.'

The fire began to belch blackly and soon all movement stopped. Fat sizzled on crumbling bones.

'Let us away from here,' whispered Tarzi.

Rostigan ignored her, waiting for something she could not see. He wanted to make sure Stealer was gone for good.

With no flesh to reside in, the threads of Stealer's pattern began to unwind, losing their – her – shape. Soon they were as wavering and random as the twirls of smoke they danced between, and fading quickly. Rostigan sent his gaze deeper, chasing after them, and they rekindled briefly to his vision . . . but, just as on the beach, there came a certain depth past which he could not see. Stealer's threads disappeared beneath the veil of the world, back into the Spell, and were gone. Only one bundle remained, like an ethereal tussock of twitching blue seaweed, which snapped off from the rest to bounce along a narrow plane between the layers of existence. Rostigan grimaced – it seemed these threads could not penetrate the veil, something he had feared but not expected. He felt certain they were the ones stolen from the Great Spell, gone to Stealer through Regret, and now, seemingly, they could not return to where they belonged.

Before he could ponder anything much, the bundle rushed directly towards him. He started raising a hand to ward it off, but it sped up and slapped against his chest – no, not his chest, the centre of his *being* – worming its way into his pattern. Although the sensation was not quite pain, it was tumultuous nonetheless, as parts of him disconnected and reconnected to make room for the new addition. He felt lines travelling up inside him toward his mouth, where his lips began to tingle.

No, he thought, fearing the splitting of his flesh.

He reasserted himself, concentrating hard on keeping his own threads in place. Rejected from his lips, the lines curved downwards on themselves to hook into the greater bundle. This itself seemed unable to settle, as stronger, more sedentary structures refused to budge in its way.

You can't go where you want, can you?

The bundle spread out into him nonetheless, seeming to make secondary choices. Meanwhile he stood rigid, unable to move or gasp as he suffered an interior rearrangement of the self, until he might even have blacked out on his feet.

'Rostigan?'

Tarzi touched his shoulder. How much time had passed? It did not feel like mere moments, yet nothing in her manner suggested he had been standing there long. She was nervy, but her furtive glances were being directed at Stealer's remains.

'Can we go?'

Rostigan was no longer aware of the new threads moving inside him. Sickeningly, he suspected they had meshed with his own until they were not sensed as foreign. Did he feel different? He was not sure. When the Wardens had absorbed Regret's stolen threads, it had changed them both in ability and personality. Formerly good people have been driven to commit unspeakable acts of evil, seemingly without reason other than for their own greed and enjoyment. Did *he* now possess some overwhelming need to plunder the world's beauty, as had been Stealer's favourite pastime? With relief, he decided he did not think so. For one thing he had avoided being inflicted with a gruesome dripping mouth, so maybe he had escaped the rest as well? Patterns were not all the same, and he had denied the bundle seating itself as it had wished.

He struggled to hide his concern as Tarzi led the way out of the clearing.

'So,' she said, after a while, seeming happier now that they were away from Stealer, 'Silverstone should be returned now, yes?'

Rostigan grunted noncommittally.

'By the Spell,' she went on, 'that was really something. I can't believe it Rostigan – you actually killed Stealer!'

'Yes,' he managed, in a cracked voice.

They spent the night in the clearing by the stream, where the ground was flat and dry. Rostigan lay awake trying to work out what had happened to him. Perhaps he had just imagined it – perhaps Stealer's threads had merely wafted his way as they rejoined the Spell, and it had only *seemed* like they had gone into him, when in fact they'd gone right through him – but no amount of wishing could make him believe it.

He rose and went to the stream with Stealer's notebook and quill. As he sat by the water, a lone fish broke the surface, maybe trying to swim to the bright face in the sky. He frowned, quill poised above paper – he had never been much good at rhymes. After some thought, and having decided the quality of the verse did not matter, he set down words.

The moonlight dims
as the little fish swims

There was a soft *plip* as water rushed in to fill the space left behind as the fish disappeared. The words he had written whispered out of the air, and his heart fluttered to hear them spoken aloud in his own voice. He glanced at Tarzi but she was sleeping peacefully.

In disgust he threw the notebook and quill into the stream, though he knew it would not make any difference. They were common objects, nothing special, just a record of Stealer's trophies. It was to Rostigan the fish's threads had come, never travelling through any quill or being captured on any page. He could form the stealing words however he wished – on paper, sketched in dirt, in his mind.

He almost marvelled that an understanding of Stealer's talent came to him so naturally. Would have, if he had not been so repulsed. At the least he was thankful that he felt no satisfaction at the theft.

Morning came, and they made their way back through the wood, out onto the hills. As Tarzi raced up to the crest that overlooked Silverstone, Rostigan saw hope fall from her face, and guessed the reason why.

The city had not returned.

THE TEMPLE OF STORMS

Yalenna opened her eyes. Her cheek was pressing against white stones, so smooth they almost seemed soft. She ran a finger over them, beneath the cocoon of her own snowy hair.

She sensed people nearby and, glancing through her tousled strands, saw bare feet going about their business across an open area. On her other side was a marble statue set into the wall – a young woman with a serene face staring into the distance, her long tresses spilling freely down her back, wearing a robe clasped at her shoulder with a lightning strike brooch. As Yalenna saw it, she became aware of something jagged digging into her own shoulder, crushed between it and the floor. She pushed up on her hands, curling her feet beneath her, and saw the same lightning strike clasping her own robe.

She was awed and perplexed, though her surrounds were familiar – she was in the Temple of Storms – and yet there had never been a statue of *herself* here.

'Storm's end!' came a voice nearby.

It was a man also in a white robe, who stared from her, back up to the statue, then at her again. Others nearby were stopping too, men and women in the same temple garb, edging closer and whispering excitedly.

'She looks just like her!'

'Wind and fire, it cannot be.'

'The Spell remembers all patterns. All things are possible to return.'

'Nay, it must be some ruse, some trick.'

'I say it is a miracle. I say we are blessed.'

Some of them began to drop to their knees, while others peered on, uncertain.

Yalenna frowned in confusion, not because of the gathering crowd, but because she was finally beginning to wake up.

She should not be here.

She had *died* here.

Years after the Wardens had toppled Regret, and those corrupted by the task had been laid to rest, she and Braston had realised that they themselves spread the corruption too. Not in the same violent, chaotic way as some of the others, not in a way that drove them to destroy . . . yet they destroyed nonetheless, slowly and surely, simply by *being*. The powers granted to them should not have been, and their continued use damaged the very nature of the world. Now she could feel it happening again.

Blessings began to seep from her. Tiny whorls of bundled threads *breathed* from her, floating off to find people to sink into and entwine with. Perhaps the person blessed would go on to find their true love, or win at cards, or be visited by fine pigeons every morning for a week. There should have been no harm in spreading such good, yet she understood too well that it changed things in ways the world had not expected. Maybe the man who found his true love would abandon his wife, leaving her forever heartbroken. Maybe the loser at cards would grow angry with his opponent's run of luck, and drunkenly draw his dagger. Maybe a pigeon's chicks, unguarded in the nest while their parents were away, would be carried off by possums. Her blessings, she knew, affected the course of lives. She could not stop them, however, and did not even choose the nature of their expression unless she put her mind to it.

It had not been easy for her, or Braston, to learn that their gifts were actually harmful. It was with a grim acceptance that they had decided, for the good of the world, to leave it. Thus, once the other Wardens had been dealt with, her last memory was of lying down here, her belly full of quiet poison, drifting off peacefully while her worshippers wept around her.

Yet here she was again.

How long had she been gone?

Her first thought was that, in her unconsciousness, she'd healed herself against her own will . . . but that would mean only hours had passed, and she did not recognise any of these faces. Also, the statue of herself loomed overhead, its gaze calmly incinerating all hope of such a simple explanation. The sight of it confounded her, like a dream image she could not make sense of.

One of the bolder acolytes, a young brown-haired woman, came forward. 'Excuse me, but are you . . . do you need help?'

'No,' said Yalenna. As she rose to her feet there came a murmur of adulation from the crowd. She massaged the cheek she had awoken lying on, trying to focus. 'Who is in charge here?'

'I am the . . . er . . .' The girl faltered, her hazel eyes cast downwards for a moment. Then she found her backbone, and stood up straight. 'I am Priestess Arah.'

Yalenna was surprised. Then again, she supposed, she had been no older herself when she had become Priestess. Even now she probably looked the same age as Arah, as she had done ever since the change.

'Make way, make way!'

An older man with frizzy hair shoved through the crowd to Arah's side. He stared in amazement at Yalenna, his eyes flickering from her to the statue behind. Then his gaze narrowed and he reached toward her, his influence closing over her pattern. As it tightened, instinctively she flexed, soundly rejecting his invisible grasp.

'Harren!' said Arah. 'What are you doing?'

'She must be someone in disguise. And yet,' his eyes pierced her as if he searched for some hidden truth, 'she has substantial power, to break free of me so easily.'

'I *am* Yalenna,' she said, bristling at the note of defensiveness that crept into her voice.

'Did anyone see her arrive?' demanded Harren, of those gathered. 'Surely someone must have?'

Heads shook, looks bounced about, but no one replied.

Harren refocused on her. 'How did you get here?'

Yalenna found she did not like his prodding, his questions . . . his *impudence*. In that moment, though, she could not force out the answer.

I do not know. I do not know.

'I knew it was a sign,' Harren muttered. 'When the sky went dark did I not say, it is a sign of things gone wrong?'

That got Yalenna's full attention. Her eyes must have blazed, for Harren's fingers gave a twitch in readiness as if he feared she would assail him.

'What,' Yalenna said, 'do you mean by that?'

'Pardon me?' said Harren carefully.

'What happened to the sky?'

Three hundred years.

Yalenna sat quietly reeling from the discovery that she had been . . . dead? – or simply gone? – for that long.

'Have you come to . . .' Arah paused, managing to look vulnerable in her intimidating large marble seat, 'to lead us again, my lady?'

They were in an airy chamber at a stone table, beneath a high domed roof. Yalenna remembered the room well;

she had given many audiences here herself, and little had changed since. Despite her own worries, the uncertain look on Arah's face moved her to compassion. The girl must only recently have been made Priestess, and well did Yalenna remember the courage that took. Yet to Arah, it probably seemed like the task she had built herself up for was about to be taken away.

'I'm not here to supplant you,' Yalenna said. 'You were chosen by the elements, were you not?'

'Yes, my lady. Of course.'

'Then you are Priestess, as has always been the way.'

Harren, who stood by Arah's shoulder, looked irritated by the exchange.

'There is nothing you can tell us,' he said, 'about how . . . why . . . you have returned?'

His tone implied he considered his question dubious.

'Nothing but guesswork,' said Yalenna. 'My threads should have rejoined the Spell when I sacrificed myself.' *That had been the entire purpose of doing it.* 'Tell me, good Harren, have you heard of anything like this happening before?'

He frowned. 'Not specifically. Not with individual people, anyway. Some have conjectured about reoccurrence – a plant or animal thought lost to the world has on occasion reappeared, as if the Spell decided its pattern should be reinstated. But we cannot know for sure if that's what really happened. It may simply be that a thing was not seen for a time, staying hidden in the quieter corners of the world, until it could re-establish itself.'

Yalenna sighed. 'Tell me, then, about the failing daylight.'

'It was just as described in the legends of Regret . . . and the Wardens.' He eyed her closely, maybe waiting for her to slip up in some way, to reveal some lie. 'The day fell dark for a few moments, as if a hand had closed over the sun.'

'So, the corruption persists.'

'It is hard to say. There are sometimes things about the world that seem . . . odd. Yet never to the same extent as during the rule of the Wardens.'

'Braston and I *killed* the Wardens, including ourselves, in order to give back what we had taken. Did it work at all? Is the Wound closed?'

Harren and Arah glanced at each other.

'We aren't sure,' said Arah. 'No one gets into the Tranquil Dale and lives to report back.'

'So the Unwoven still reside there?'

'Yes.'

'Even after all this time? No one has tried to finish them? Or cure them?'

Harren scoffed, and Arah shook her head.

'It's suicide to enter that place. There are occasional rumours that the Wound has been seen, mainly from Plainsfolk foolhardy enough to venture into the Roshous Peaks. If it's there, it is low enough in the sky to be blocked from outside sight by the surrounding mountains.'

Yalenna felt sick. 'It was all for nothing. I convinced Braston to end his life for no reason.'

'I would not say that,' said Arah. 'With the Wardens and their magic gone, most of the corruption ceased – the earthquakes, the strange births, the skies.'

'Yalenna and Braston's sacrifice,' said Harren, 'is remembered as an act of great compassion.'

Yalenna noted the non-committal use of her name.

'That may be the case,' she said, 'but our ultimate aim was to heal the Spell for good. We hoped, when we released our threads, they would go behind the veil and the Wound would close.'

'Maybe that's why you're back?' said Arah. 'To finish what you started? The Spell surely *wants* to be healed. Maybe you're being given a second chance?'

Yalenna stared at Arah uncertainly. Young she might be, but there was something about her sincerity and innocence that made Yalenna fear her explanation was the truth, or came close to it. The Spell was ever mysterious – who knew what it could do?

'Let us not run a hundred leagues with this, Priestess,' Harren said to Arah. 'We do not know for sure that this is really Yalenna.'

'Still your tongue,' said Arah. 'You examined her yourself and found no trace of disguise.'

Yalenna was glad to see strength in the girl. Perhaps Arah did not recognise it in herself yet but to Yalenna it was clear as day. Harren, for his part, looked momentarily taken aback.

They heard the sound of running feet, and a young man burst through the room's marble archway. He came up short, blinking around, excited yet also intimidated.

'Er . . . pardon my intrusion . . .'

Harren seemed grateful for someone to snap at. 'Don't stand there like a slack-jawed ninny, Kor. What is it?'

'I . . . er . . .'

'Step forward!' barked Harren. 'Speak clearly! Has a message come?'

Kor bobbed his head. 'Yes, master . . . my lady . . . ladies.' He swallowed. 'From Althala. It says . . . it says that Braston has returned!'

'Braston?' Yalenna was incredulous. Why hadn't she thought to ask about the others? Then again, she had suffered quite a shock and did not feel in full command of her faculties. Yet if Braston had come back, maybe others had too? Cold thoughts froze her, visions of Forger, Stealer, Despirrow and Salarkis birthed again into the world.

Harren, after his initial surprise, advanced on Kor. 'Are you sure? What were the exact words?'

Kor cringed a little under the scrutiny. '"Let it be known,"' he said, '"that this very morning, King Braston returned to Althala from the dead, to reclaim the throne and lead his people once again."'

Harren rubbed his chin furiously, whispering something to himself. Then he grabbed Kor by the front of his robe. 'This message – what of its angle, its trajectory? You're sure it came from Althala?'

'Yes, master! From the castle itself.'

Harren turned slowly to Yalenna with a look of grave concern.

'My lady,' he said, 'I have been reticent to trust but surely you must understand why. Or perhaps this is some strangely elaborate hoax, designed for a purpose I cannot guess at.'

'I assure you,' said Yalenna, 'it is no hoax.'

'Out, Kor,' said Harren, waving the young man away. He returned to the table, to sit beside Arah this time, albeit in a much smaller chair.

'What can it mean?' said Arah, asking the unanswerable for all of them.

Yalenna barely heard her. 'What of the other Wardens?' she asked. 'Has there been any news of them?'

'What?' Arah's face was pale. 'No, we've heard nothing on that count. The Spell would not punish us with *their* presence, surely?'

'What about Mergan or Karrak? At the time of my death, they had both disappeared. Did they ever show themselves again?'

'No, my lady.'

Dead, she and Braston had decided, after searching for a long time. Neither of those two had been in the habit of vanishing without a trace. Karrak would not simply up and leave his empire, his slave trains, his skies full of crows. And Mergan would not forsake the friendship he had shared with her and Braston. Perhaps they had killed each other – a theory certainly borne by their mutual animosity – but, if they had indeed died, did that mean they were back now too?

'I must go to Braston.'

Even as she said it, she realised she did not have the strength. She was hungry, tired, and her head felt full of dead leaves. She had intended to threadwalk – a rare skill possessed by only the most powerful of threaders – but did not think she could summon the necessary concentration.

'What do you need, my lady?' Harren asked. 'We could have some of the temple guards accompany you, or –'

'I need nothing,' said Yalenna, 'though I thank you for the offer. I do not think, however, that I can leave this very instant. I should perhaps spend the night, take some food and rest.'

'You shall have everything you require,' said Arah. 'Though if you would like to stay a little longer, maybe even address our acolytes? I know it would mean so much to them – your memory is a great source of pride for the temple.'

'No, no.' Yalenna shook her head, Arah's request making her stomach turn. Earnest faces, looking to her for wisdom? *What could I say to them when I've no idea what's going on?*

She would not leave Arah with nothing, however, she decided. Although not one to use her powers lightly, she did not think that a little more threading would greatly affect whatever was happening in the wider world. She reached to touch Arah's hand, and the girl tensed, but did not withdraw. Yalenna shaped a blessing for her, and released it into her pattern.

May you know your own strength.

'There,' she said warmly, finding there was still joy in giving. 'You are blessed, Priestess Arah.'

Harren watched intently, and for a moment his face softened, revealing a certain fondness for his young leader. Yalenna found herself forgiving his reservations – perhaps she would have reacted the same way had some long dead person appeared on her temple floor for no apparent reason.

'And you, friend Harren,' she said, blowing him a little something too.

May birds never release their contents on your head.

Harren's eyebrows shot up – he had no way of knowing what she had given him, but seemed quite pleased nonetheless. 'Why,' he said, 'thank you. But, my lady, I would council you to be judicious in using your magic.'

'It hardly matters now,' said Yalenna. 'I cannot stop the blessings that spring from me. The most I can do is shape them to my choosing.'

Harren nodded. 'But you are exhausted, my lady. Perhaps it's time for you to rest?'

'In good time. First you must tell me more about what has happened in Aorn, in my absence.'

The Temple of Storms was built on the very edge of a vast expanse of desert, where runs of grass sent hopeful expeditions out into the sand. It was as peaceful a place as Yalenna remembered, where threaders who specialised in working with the elements devoted themselves to living in harmony with the Spell. For a moment she looked back at the bulbous white buildings, imagining her life as it might have been had she continued on as Priestess. She would have taught acolytes to wrestle the wind, channel the sun, send rain where it was needed – to work always with the Spell, using its gifts for the betterment of humanity. It would have been a worthwhile existence, and long finished with by now. Instead, Mergan – her old master from the threading school at Althala – had turned up shortly after she'd been made Priestess, and asked her to accompany him in ridding the world of Regret. How things had changed for her that day.

'I can make my own way from here,' Yalenna said, turning to her companions.

Arah looked crestfallen, but Harren was more stoic. He had proven a reliable font of recent history, speaking to her well into the previous night – until she'd *had* to lie down and black out – although it seemed that, on the whole, little had changed while she had been gone.

'I wish I could stay,' she told Arah. 'Really, I do.' She clasped the girl's shoulders, and kissed her on the brow.

'The artisans did a good job,' said Harren, 'of capturing your beauty, my lady.'

Yalenna smiled. 'You know where I travel to,' she said, 'if you need to send me word.'

She left them to travel eastwards across the patchwork of sand and grass, towards more fertile land. She wanted to be free of onlookers, and walked until there were trees between her and the temple. Kneeling in the shade, she tried to clear her mind, but struggled to focus. She found herself returning again and again to the same intrusive memory, ancient by the world's standards, yet vivid to her . . .

On the roof of Regret's Spire, the mad lord's unseeing eyes seemed to watch her as his red mop rustled about his head.

Yalenna could not quite believe that he was dead, though she and the other Wardens, now spread out around her, had fought so hard to make him just that. He had been bent on breaking the world, for lunatic reasons he would take to his grave, and they had stopped him – so why did she feel so despondent in victory?

'Up, Yalenna,' came Karrak's voice. She raised her head to see the raven-haired prince extending a hand towards her, soft concern in his eyes. Above him the Wound was open, its edges red-ragged and pulsing. Exposed beyond lay that which should not be seen, the workings of the Spell itself, like giant multicoloured veins made up of tightly woven smaller threads. Here and there these threads were frayed, akin to the split fibres of a rope, where they had been torn at, and stolen from, by Regret.

How had he mustered such audacity? Even as mad as he had been, surely any mind would tremble, any ego falter, in the face of such monumental thievery?

'Don't let his magic fester,' said Karrak, helping her to her feet. She shook herself, as if she could so easily discard the lingering bleakness Regret had left her with.

A cold wind blew through the great valley, reaching them on the Spire roof. It carried the sound of battle from the southern end, where the Pass between mountains into the Dale was heavily fortified against the armies of Aorn.

'Someone should tell our people,' Yalenna said, clutching Karrak's arm to steady herself, 'that they need not fight anymore. The Unwoven too, for their master is no more.'

'Regret's minions may carry his stain for life,' said Karrak dourly. 'The best to be hoped for is that they won't pass it on to their children. Or that they won't live to have any.'

Yalenna stared out at the distant figures. Had she been naive enough to hope that Regret's demise would change them back into the folk they had been before?

'Wardens,' called Mergan. The grey-haired threader was standing in the centre of the roof, the others scattered about him in varying degrees of dazedness. Salarkis was on his knees, weeping softly. Despirrow stared off at nothing, his once-proud robes now dirty and crumpled. Little Jillan was biting her lip so hard she drew blood. Braston leaned heavily on his sword, as if it were all that kept him standing.

'Pull yourselves together,' said Mergan. 'Our task is not complete. We must attempt to heal the Wound.'

Despirrow shot him a worried look. 'But how? Only Regret knew how to manipulate the threads of the Great Spell.'

'We must try as best we can,' said Mergan. 'You can see where threads have been torn out – they must be rewoven into their rightful places.'

'But where,' said Braston, 'have they gone?'

Suddenly from Regret's corpse, a series of strange bundles rose. They were unlike any human threads Yalenna had seen before, and failed to fade away like the rest of Regret had. Spilled loose from his disappeared framework, they drifted outwards, gaining speed.

'Mergan,' she gasped, pointing.

Mergan spun about as something like a lattice of string hit him in the head, and flew backwards off his heels. Nearby a blue tentacled thing whizzed along the stones, and Yalenna flinched as it leapt upwards, but it did not leap at her. Instead, it wrapped itself around Jillan's leg, whose eyes blanked as it sunk in, and she buckled to the ground. Everywhere pieces of pattern whizzed, and Yalenna stumbled as Karrak suddenly pulled away from her.

'Don't let them enter you!' he cried, but a moment later he shuddered as a black curl planted in his chest, worming its way inwards.

Yalenna had not seen whatever it was that found her, but something had, that was certain. She remembered a perplexing kind of pain as her pattern was invaded, which quickly led to blurriness. Then Mergan was beside her, croaking something. She tried to pay attention.

'Salarkis,' he said.

She followed his gaze, and lost a breath as she took in her comrade's new body.

'What happened?' said Salarkis, gazing upon his stony hands. 'My word. I feel as if I can finally do it! All those failed lessons Mergan, but I think I can finally threadwalk!'

He grinned, revealing sharp teeth like those of an animal, and the next moment began to unspool. He was threadwalking, faster and more easily than Yalenna had ever seen.

'Stop!' said Mergan. 'We need to stay together! We need to understand what has happened to us.'

Salarkis, however, disappeared. Beyond where he had stood, Forger tittered in amazement.

Braston, on his feet, was stooping over Jillan, who was trying to hide her face.

'Jillan?' he said. 'Are you all right?'

'Don't look at me!' she cried, with a strange gurgle. Shielding her mouth from view, she dashed to the Spire stairs, and down.

'Wait!' cried Mergan. 'Jillan!'

Jillan did not turn back.

Yalenna, who could feel herself changed as well, began to see the blessings wafting from her, though she did not yet understand what they were. Fearfully she looked to Karrak for support, and found his eyes cold and steely.

'Karrak?'

But he was not truly himself anymore. He was the man who would become known as the Lord of Crows, and she would learn that his appetite was ever for war, to feed the skies with the bodies of the slain. In the coming days he would kill his father and brother, take the crown of Ander for himself, and raise legions bent on turning all into his slaves. People would look towards his growing empire as they would a terrible storm on the horizon, though Yalenna did not know so in those moments, in which she only sought comfort from a friend.

None of them had been the same after that day. With no other place to go, the threads Regret had stolen from the Spell made the Wardens their new homes. Five of the eight were touched by violent, chaotic aspects, their patterns twisted in terrible ways that drove them insane and filled them with malice. It was the beginning of a new conflict, which would last until only Yalenna and Braston were left standing.

She remembered how, upon killing another Warden – Forger had been the first – she and Braston had remained on guard, expecting Forger's Spell-born bundle of threads to rush upon them out of the rest of his fading pattern. They had planned to deflect it as best they could, in the hope that it would somehow join the rest of him in slipping behind the veil. The bundle, however, had never come. They had assumed that it had done what they wanted, thus coming to believe that murder of their owners was the best way of restoring stolen threads to the Spell. And, in the end, knowing that she and Braston were corrupted also, Yalenna had convinced him the only way to close the Wound for good would be to end their own lives.

Yet here she was. And every time she tried clearing her mind, Regret's eyes stared back at her.

'Damn you,' she whispered. 'Get out.'

No one had bothered to at the time, but now she imagined herself running a palm over the dead man's eyes to close them.

What had really happened to the threads of dead Wardens? They obviously had not sunk under the veil, else she would not now be back, and breathing out blessings into the bargain. Had the threads gone so deep that they had faded from perception, yet somehow not been able to make the final crossing? If that were the case, why had they behaved so differently on the Spire roof?

The Great Spell, she knew, did not function under a set of rules – at least none that anyone had ever been able to ascertain. It was a fluid, changeable force, and perhaps over the years it had tried different ways to retrieve what had been taken from it. She had a vision of her own Spell-stolen threads straining to pass through the veil, like something too big to fit through a sieve, while the ones that she had been born with – the ones that were really *her* – wavered beyond it, still attached and anchored, wanting to disperse in death and yet not able, until the Spell somehow reversed the flow, and spat her back out in entirety.

She shook her head. How could she tell what had really happened? She would probably never know. The Spell worked in mysterious ways.

She took a deep breath and turned eastwards. Summoning a picture of Althala in her head, she concentrated until her pattern began to thrum. Her vision suddenly broke into line, sliding apart in different directions – and then she was undone, no longer aware, a collection of threads whizzing along faster than any regular person could travel.

Sometime later she tumbled out of the air, reforming in farmland pastures with a gasp, just outside the walls of Althala.

THE LORD OF PAIN

Forger stared up into the sky, his view framed by towering blades of grass. He blinked.

'What?' he said, and sat up.

He had awoken on dirt, though the particles were much bigger than they should have been. Not to mention the pebbles, which were the size of melons.

'Except,' he picked up a pebble and considered it, 'they aren't the size of melons.' He rose and looked about the forest of grass surrounding him. 'Because a melon would be the size of a castle!'

He dropped the pebble and kicked it away to thud flatly against a stalk. It was like kicking a heavy rock, and it hurt.

'Ah!' said Forger, rubbing his foot. His grimace twisted into a grin. 'I'm alive!'

He patted himself and found he was wearing his usual garb; brown straps holding together a collection of odd little patches of leather scattered about his body. Then he patted his bald head.

'So I'm me,' he mused. 'But I'm small.'

A huge ant appeared, and Forger gave a yelp of alarm. He went to the ground, grasping about for a sharp pebble. The ant paid him no mind, and cantered off amongst the stalks. Forger watched it go with wide eyes, ready to attack with his pebble . . . then rocked back and howled with laughter.

'Scared of an ant! Me!' He wiped tears from his eyes. 'Right. Now, by blood and fire, what predicament am I in?'

The last thing he remembered was Yalenna and Braston, killing him. That was the only way they had been able to do it, the cowards – together. He remembered a kidney exploding in his side, while they fought on with faces set serious in concentration, not even taking any pleasure in their success. What a waste.

That had been in a little cottage.

'Hmm.'

He found a second sharp pebble and approached a blade of grass. Jumping up it as far as he could, he stabbed the pebbles into its soft flesh like daggers.

'Right,' he said. 'Up, up, up!'

Using the pebbles arm over arm, he began to stab his way higher, climbing the stalk with tiny muscles bulging. As he reached the top, the stalk began to bend beneath him, and he took a moment to steady himself. Around him stretched a sea of grass, and off in the distance stood monumental trees and an enormous cottage.

'Are you the same?' he asked it. 'Or is this,' he gestured around himself, 'the exact spot where I died? And *my* cottage, glorious crypt that it was, has since rotted away? Because,' he froze his gesturing hand and stared at it hard, 'it is obvious much time has passed.'

After Regret, Forger had learned miraculous things about his changed self. Pain made him stronger, whether it was pain he caused, or pain he took away. It had been pleasantly surprising to realise that this did not disturb him. Gone were the foibles of his human days, when the world's troubles weighed upon him heavily. Blissfully gone was the tendency to make every problem his own, to *care* and *fret*, as if compassion were some kind of currency and he aimed to grow rich. What a relief it had been, to be done with all that! He had gone on very happily to feed on humanity's misfortune wherever he found it, or created it. Something else he had learned, however – if he did not feed, he grew smaller, weaker.

So how long had it been?

'Cottages,' he muttered. 'What does it matter, what cottage is what, or where?'

The stalk gave in and he tumbled downwards, bouncing off other blades to land back on the dirt.

'Piss and fire,' he growled, sitting up to rub his bruises.

Behind him a patch of earth rose slightly, and eyes glistened in the shadows beneath. The trapdoor spider burst from its tunnel and seized him around the waist, dragging him backwards into its lair. The trapdoor fell back neatly in place, indiscernible from its surrounds.

Off in the distance, a child from the cottage began to play, his merry laughter echoing through the grass. A breeze rustled the stalks, and spots of light flitted about.

The trapdoor flew open with a force that sent it spinning, and a howl of rage issued from the tunnel. A hand reached out to clench the ground, and Forger hauled himself out of the darkness. He grunted, scratched and bleeding, and pulled on something with his other hand that did not want to leave the hole.

'Oho!' growled Forger. 'Not so keen now, eh?'

From the dark he dragged the spider forth by its front leg. In terror it tried to break free, but Forger heaved until it was bodily out of the tunnel. Ignoring its clicking jaws and flailing legs, he sent gestures at the surrounding grass, ripping sinews from the stalks and floating them to the spider. It felt good to be threading again, even on such a small scale. He set the sinews tying knots about the spider's limbs, which he then directed to root it to the ground. Soon the spider was pinned flat, its soft belly rubbing against the earth as it tried to rise.

'Want to return to the darkness, don't you?'

Forger gave a wave upwards and the grass bent away, dappled light replaced by blazing sun. He moved in front of the creature, squatting to stare into its multiple terrified eyes.

'Now,' he said, 'pain is what I need. Luckily, you have it to give.'

He ran a hand over one of the splayed legs, ruffling coarse bristles. Hair covered the spider, up its legs to its head, and all over its plump abdomen.

'Lots of hair,' said Forger.

He began to pluck.

For most of the morning he laboured on the spider, joyously drinking in its torment. He was deliberate and measured in his work, making sure he gripped bundles of hair for long enough before pulling them, that the spider knew what was about to happen each and every time. Eventually it was almost bald, its quivering flesh peppered by blotches of sticky blood. And Forger, having fed for the first time in three hundred years, grew until his head was just above the grass.

'That's better.' He sighed contentedly. 'Getting too big for an intricate project like you,' he told the spider, and turned away, leaving it staked out in the sun.

Pushing grass aside, he made his way towards the cottage. Two little boys were playing under a tree, their mother looking on from the porch, smiling at their silly game. It was like some hybrid of tag and wrestling, and also involved sticks somehow.

'How nice,' said Forger. He ducked his head beneath the grass, careful to stay hidden as he approached. The tree the boys played beneath was an easy climb, and up he went, keeping to the side facing away from the house. Once he reached the higher branches, he climbed around until he gained a good view of the boys. They raced about, but always eventually returned to the shade – all he had to do was pick the right moment. In the meantime he set about untying the threads that kept a heavy branch in place, until all it would take was a final tweak.

He did not have to wait long. The boys fell beneath him, a heap of gasps, grunts and chuckles. He gestured at the branch, snicking the last thread. With a crack it plummeted, and his timing was good. The boys were on top of each other, and the branch fell on top of both, crushing them to little-boy jam.

The cry from the mother came as expected, full of horror and disbelief – not quite what he needed, yet. She raced over and, with strength that belied her frame, wrested the branch off her sons. As she fell beside their broken bodies, Forger sensed hairline splinters running through her heart.

No, she mouthed silently, no sound escaping her throat. She pawed at her children, as if by rearranging their limbs back into normal positions, she could restore them to life. Her pain began to reach Forger, sharp and clear – a soul pain, the purest sort, and oh, it was good! She rocked as her tears flowed, and Forger grew stronger with each racking sob. She would not get over this quickly, he knew, and maybe there was a father about too, who would soon discover this pain himself. With any luck, Forger could lurk about this house until he was well satiated.

He realised he was growing heavier, perhaps too heavy for his current vantage. The branch beneath him cracked and fell, and he gave a little squeak as he went tumbling after, to land on his feet beside the mother. She flinched, blinking at him rapidly. He must have grown, for although she knelt and he stood, they were eye to red-and-weepy eye.

'There goes that idea,' he said.

Somehow she associated him with what had happened, and reached for his throat with a shriek of rage. Forger flicked his fingers at her feet and rooted her in place. Quickly he decided that, although less thorough than what he'd intended, there were faster ways to eke more pain from her.

'Who did I think I was fooling?' he asked. 'I don't have the patience to sneak about unseen while you mourn! Ha.'

He gave a wave, and, directing her body for her, sent her stumbling towards the cottage.

'Stop!' she cried. 'Stop!'

He considered the dead children for a moment, then floated their corpses after her.

'I think we shall prop up your boys at the table,' he told the hysterical woman, 'so they can watch what I do to you.'

Bouncing up the porch steps, he opened the cottage door and stood aside, hand held out in a gesture of welcome.

'Come on in!'

The lurching woman screamed at him without words.

'Really,' he said, 'can't you understand? I'm just trying to be happy. Why don't you want me to be happy?'

And he took them all into the house.

PRESENT TRUTH

Rostigan drew deeply on his pipe, filling up his lungs with smoke. He enjoyed the bite of it, strangely, the hot prickle of damage done.

Nobody bothered him here, sitting in a dark corner of the busy tavern. His stern face and heavy sword usually made sure of that, but tonight people were skittish, distracted by all they had heard over the past few days. This town lay in the plains some leagues from Silverstone, and enough travellers from that direction had given accounts of the missing city to leave the townsfolk frightened.

'I'm telling you,' said a farmer at the nearest table, 'it's just not natural.'

'Oh, *thank you* for that, Borry,' replied a pock-marked man. 'A whole city up and vanishes, and you declare it's not natural? What insight! It's a wonder you're just a common farmer and not some famous, wealthy scholar.'

'Settle down Tanis,' said a woman, 'there's no need for that. We're all worried.'

'I'm not worried. Has any of you actually *seen* Silverstone?'

'That's the whole problem,' said Borry. 'It can't be seen!'

'I mean, coal and ash, has anyone here actually verified the truth of these claims? It could just be some traveller spreading lies as a trick.'

'But it weren't just one. It was –'

'At least three,' said the woman. 'Different ones too, not travelling together.'

'You mean,' said Tanis, growing ever more exasperated, 'that they didn't *arrive* together. Maybe they met on the road beforehand, and said to each other, "Let's conjure a tale before visiting town one by one, so the poor fools don't suspect that we're lying sons of goats. What fun it will be to scare whatever semblance of wits they may or may not have right out of their hollow heads!"'

'You believe what you want,' said the woman. 'I saw the look in one of 'em's eyes, and I'm telling you, he believed what he saw. Said there was a voice in the air, just . . . hovering.'

'Haw!'

As the conversation grew louder, it attracted attention from other tables.

'I heard that too,' put in someone. 'Ghost words, no one there to speak them.'

'And what about rumours from the north?' asked a younger man. 'I was in Yar today, and there's talk going about that Braston rules again in Althala!'

'Aye,' said Borry. 'I heard that, Klion.'

'Indeed,' said Tanis, thumbing towards Klion. 'You heard it from *him*.'

'And Yalenna, too – they say she came back to life in the Temple of Storms!'

Rostigan, regrettably, did not think the rumours were false. He knew for certain that one Warden had returned from death – and if she had, why not others?

Borry, it seemed, echoed his sentiment. 'Wardens,' he muttered, shaking his head. 'The Spell's upped and brought 'em back, that's what I reckon. And if it's done Braston and Yalenna, well, why not also . . . but, ah, I don't want to say.'

'We all know who liked to leave words hanging about in the air,' said the woman.

'I don't believe this,' muttered Tanis. 'You're talking about children's stories!'

'Horse shit,' said Borry. 'Spell's done it before. What about feverblossom? It disappeared for a hundred years, and now it's everywhere in the west, thicker on the ground than grass.'

'And wildercats,' added the woman. 'And harp flies.'

Tarzi returned to the table with two mugs of ale and sat down despondently. 'Innkeeper doesn't think it's a night for minstrels,' she said. 'People are too worked up.'

Rostigan puffed on his pipe.

'You're all idiots,' Tanis declared as he rose, sounding more afraid than convinced. 'Why go putting such ideas in people's heads? Eh? To what purpose?' He stalked away toward the door.

Tarzi lowered her voice. 'We should tell them she's dead. It would put their minds at rest.'

'No,' said Rostigan, 'it wouldn't.'

'Why not?'

'They won't believe it. If she's dead, why hasn't Silverstone come back?'

Tarzi frowned. 'How should I know?'

I could tell you, he thought. *Her corrupted threads live on in me.* But how could he make her understand, without telling her everything? Even then, he was not sure himself why he'd inherited Stealer's power. All he knew was that Silverstone was hidden away somewhere inside him, along with everything else Stealer had written of during her short return. If he died, would all be restored? Or would the threads move on again, into a new host?

Tarzi made up her mind. 'The important thing,' she said, 'is that she won't be bothering anyone anymore. And while you may be content to sit there and stare into your ale, I for one will not stand by and listen to these folk needlessly scare themselves silly.'

She twisted off her seat to plant her buttocks on the tabletop, facing away from him, towards the farmer Borry and his friends. In a loud clear voice, 'It was Stealer who took Silverstone,' she announced.

The entire tavern fell to a hush. Rostigan felt anger pulse, that she would go against him like this . . . but then again, he never had ruled her, and so he did not stir. It was too late anyhow.

'What makes you say that, miss?' said Borry. 'You heard the words?'

'I did,' said Tarzi. 'I was there myself, two days ago. My companion and I found the city gone, and in its place was Stealer's voice, hanging in the air.'

Over behind the counter, the innkeeper – a fat man wearing a sweaty apron – put down a mug heavily. 'I told you,' he said, wiping his hands as he moved around the counter, 'this is not a night for minstrel's tales!'

'This is no wild legend or bawdy song,' Tarzi replied calmly. 'This is present truth.'

'Let her speak!' someone called, and other voices rose to agree.

Begrudgingly, the innkeeper receded.

Tarzi slid off the table and moved before the fireplace. 'Not only that,' she continued, as all eyes followed her, 'but we saw the culprit herself, fleeing into the trees!'

There were surprised murmurs.

'What did she look like?'

'How did you know it was really her?'

'I'll tell you what happened,' said Tarzi. 'You see, as fortune would have it, my travelling companion is none other than Rostigan Skullrender, champion of the Ilduin Fields.'

Eyebrows went up as folk reconsidered the stranger in the corner, and the heavy sword resting beside him. Rostigan held their collective gaze stonily, smoke seeping around his face, and no one stared openly for long.

'We tracked the mysterious figure into a dark wood,' Tarzi continued, 'through which she made herself a path by ripping the very trees out of her way!' She made violent motions, pulling up imaginary trees as if they were carrots, and her listeners tensed. Despite himself, Rostigan was amused.

'But it seems even the worst of Wardens need their rest,' said Tarzi. 'As night fell, Rostigan walked the dark corridor, and discovered the spot where Stealer was camping. You can imagine how quiet he had to be, to sneak up on the likes of her! He snuck from shadow to shadow, circling her campsite for an age, knowing that even the tiniest sound – brushing a bush or bumping a beetle – would bring her wrath upon him. While he moved he stole glances, saw her telltale cloak and hat, and her dripping, gaping mouth.' Tarzi pulled a twisted face that wasn't much to do with what Stealer had looked like, yet it scared her audience nonetheless.

'They say hers is the mouth of death!' breathed Borry.

Tarzi nodded. 'Nonetheless Rostigan kept on, slipping quietly through the trees. And, once he was close enough, he slowly raised his great sword . . .' Tarzi raised her hands above her, '. . . and brought it down to smash her skull!' She heaved her make-believe blade with such force that people at the closest table flinched. Back behind the counter, the innkeeper rolled his eyes.

Rostigan knew it was not yet quite the exciting tale that Tarzi wished for. She would, no doubt, embellish it further with each retelling.

'But this alone did not end her,' she went on. 'Thus Rostigan cast her on the fire, just like the knights in the old story. She kicked and howled, and burned as anyone would, to ashes and dust. I saw it and I can tell you – she will trouble the world no more!'

The expressions in the crowd were mixed – some relieved, others sceptical.

'Is that true?' A bearded man, emboldened by drink, gestured at Rostigan. 'You vouch for her tale?'

Rostigan tapped out his pipe, irritated to be drawn in, inevitable as it was. 'Yes.'

'You really are Rostigan Skullrender?'

He inclined his head.

'Then where,' said someone else, 'is Silverstone?'

'Did it come back, after you killed her?'

'It can't have – the minstrel said this was two days ago, but we've had other reports since then.'

'We did not see Silverstone return,' confirmed Tarzi.

This met with mumbles of dismay.

'Then how could it have been Stealer?' asked the bearded man. 'All the stories say her death brought back her victims.'

Tarzi spread her palms. 'As I told you, this is not a legend. I can only say what actually happened.'

The mood was confused after that. Had things been set to rights? Did the threat remain, or was it dealt with? If it had even existed in the first place?

Rostigan sighed and swigged his ale. He'd warned her.

'Sure you're not just spinning yarns, minstrel?'

'You think she's having us on?'

'Probably hoping for some coin.'

Rostigan's chair scraped loudly as he rose, causing all to fall silent.

'I *am* Rostigan Skullrender,' he said. 'And I don't pretend to understand how the powers of Wardens work. Are *you* a great expert, sir,' he addressed the bearded man, 'in the ways of ancient threaders?'

The man, uncomfortable at being singled out, shook his head.

'I thought not. I'll tell you something I do understand, however – death. And I promise you this: Stealer is dead, by my hand.' He let this sink in. 'Yet you are right to be troubled, for she was only one of eight. If others have returned as well, we may all face great peril.'

'Are you travelling to answer King Braston's call?' came a voice from the other side of the room.

Rostigan was caught off guard. The speaker – a threader, he realised, with some trepidation – stood by the door, having only recently arrived by the look of his damp hair, for the night outside was speckling rain. With relief Rostigan noted a badge on the man's breast shaped like a scroll. It was the traditional mark of a messenger, and threaders who specialised in the mundane function of sending and receiving airborne words were not usually potent in many other ways.

'That's him, from Yar,' the young man called Klion whispered. 'He's the one who's been telling people about Braston.'

'What call?' said Rostigan.

The threader arched an eyebrow. 'Has the message not arrived here?' His gaze settled on Klion. 'You – I told you to bring word to your mayor.'

Klion gulped. 'I . . . er . . .'

'Don't mind him, sir,' said Borry. 'He's a little slow.'

'Would that I had realised. Ah well, I suppose I was right to come here myself.' The threader cleared his throat. 'Word has gone out that any able and willing are welcome to swell Althala's ranks. Braston warns that other Wardens could be at large, and we may even see a return to the bad old days of war with Karrak and his cronies.'

There were fearful mutterings at that.

'Also,' said the threader, 'Braston means to do away with the Unwoven once and for all.'

The mutterings grew. This far south, people had probably never seen an Unwoven, which did nothing to soften their reputation.

'Why seek them out?' said an old man. 'Let them alone, I say – what does it matter to the rest of us if they keep to themselves in the Dale?'

'Keep to themselves?' said the threader. 'Tell that to the Plainsfolk, who suffer increasing numbers of Unwoven raids. They steal the bodies of the slain, then take them back into the Dale for some fell purpose. Have you heard nothing of this?'

'The Plainsfolk choose to live where they do,' said the old man. 'It's not our fault what happens to them.'

'The Plainsfolk,' said the threader, 'stop the Unwoven spilling forth to harry us all. You should show some respect for those who buy your safety with their lives. The threat is real, and must be dealt with, but the Plainsfolk cannot storm the Pass alone.' He looked to Rostigan. 'You fought the Unwoven once before, Skullrender?'

Rostigan nodded.

'So,' said the threader, 'will you answer the call again?'

Rostigan opened his mouth, but no words emerged. Oh, he did not want this, yet he felt it happening nonetheless. He wished that he was back in the wilderness, turning over rocks in search of purple moss.

'Of course Rostigan will go to Althala,' announced Tarzi, her eyes shining in the firelight. 'And,' she swept the room with her gaze, 'if there are others among you who would not see ruin visit Aorn, I urge you to join us. We will be leaving at daybreak on the north road.'

There sounded a few affirmative answers, but Rostigan knew that a new day and sore heads would make liars of most of them. Still, he was surprised by Tarzi. This conscientious side of her he had seen only once or twice before. Perhaps he viewed her too unkindly – just because she liked attention and making gold, did not mean she was a selfish creature.

'If the Wardens really have returned,' she continued, 'then danger threatens us all. You know the tales of what damage they did as they fought each other. Even now, Karrak may be somewhere raising an army of his own. Unless we wish to become fodder for his crows, we may have to fight.'

Rostigan, again, was surprised. He had not thought Tarzi appreciated all the implications of what had been happening, but that had been short-sighted of him. It was her business to know history and legend, so she was necessarily well versed with what may be coming.

'What about the good Wardens?' said Klion. 'Surely they will save us?'

'Oh yes?' said Tarzi. 'If that's what you believe, then by all means stay here and do nothing. Let me tell you this, however – even good Wardens need help. Why else would Braston ask for an army, if he could handle everything by himself? Make no mistake, fine people – complacence is tantamount to downfall. Silverstone is gone! Will you let that loss stand alone as a terrible tragedy, or become the new way of the world?'

Across the room, the threader gave a little smile. Rostigan could see the man was impressed – certainly he could not have said it better himself.

'All right,' said the innkeeper, once more coming around

his counter, 'I think you've terrorised my customers plenty for one night.'

'It isn't me,' snapped Tarzi, 'from which terror originates. I trust that *you* won't be joining us on the road tomorrow, good innkeeper? Where instead? Sleeping peacefully, like a hog in a hoghouse, unaware that you will soon be sent to slaughter? Happy in your ignorance, your denial?'

The innkeeper's face went bright red. 'That's enough!'

'*I* shall join you.'

This from a muscular young man with bronzed skin and a healthy spark, a farmhand by the looks. At his words, the friends he sat with bobbed their heads.

Rostigan knew the type. Bored with their decent lives, they would find the call to any adventure appealing. Armies were built on such headstrong young folk, who did not understand that glory was a word used long after the fact.

'And I, miss,' said Borry, 'though I may be too old for such an undertaking – at the least I shall bring you supplies for your trip.'

Other voices rose and soon the room was full of them. The innkeeper may not have succeeded in shouting down Tarzi, but as people began to discuss all that they had heard, she was, in a way, dismissed by the collective. Many of them now clustered about the threader, peppering him with questions. Meanwhile Tarzi moved back to sit with Rostigan, not meeting his eyes immediately.

'Are you angry with me?' she asked.

Rostigan removed the pipe from his mouth. 'A little,' he said. 'But . . . well, what does it matter?'

'And about going to Althala?'

As he scratched at the tabletop, a splinter broke free to drive up under his fingernail. Wincing, he pulled it out.

What other choice?

'Of course,' he said, and sighed.

SKULLRENDER

That night it took Rostigan a long time to find sleep. It wasn't because of Tarzi continuously stealing the sheets, then depositing them back upon him in a tangle, for he was used to that. Rather, it was news of the Unwoven stirring, making him wonder if they might soon leave the Dale on mass, as they had done once before. And, as he drifted in and out of wakefulness, he saw golden fields of grass shining in the sun, and felt a warm breeze on his face that was almost comforting.

~

They said there was nowhere flatter in Aorn, and Rostigan had travelled widely enough to believe it. Stretching from the foothills of the Roshous Peaks, the Ilduin Fields were a great expanse of hard ground and tough yellow grass. It was hot there also, damn hot, and he sweated constantly under his steel.

'There's the Pass,' said Loppolo, King of Althala.

Away in the distance, a V-shaped break in the mountains marked the entrance to the Tranquil Dale. In the centuries since Regret had turned his people into Unwoven, and despite their lord's long absence, they had never forgotten his order to guard it. Unusually, however, in recent days, a great many of them had spilled from the Pass to camp on the Fields, beneath colourfully inconsistent banners. It was a sight not seen in living memory, and no one felt it boded well.

'Why now?' said Loppolo. 'The Unwoven have always kept to themselves. Well, the odd raid, of course, but nothing on this scale.'

'For no good reason,' replied Rostigan.

'Have they rutted themselves out of space?' mused Loppolo. 'Can the Dale no longer support their numbers?'

Around the young king stood his officers, and a greater army of thousands. How strange it felt for Rostigan, to have deliberately sought Loppolo out and convinced him action must be taken. The king had proved stubborn at first, disbelieving that reports of Unwoven leaving the Dale were anything to be concerned by. 'Let the Plainsfolk deal with them, as they always have,' had been his answer. Rostigan, however, was greatly concerned, for any mustering of Regret's creatures surely meant trouble for Aorn. Thus he had broken his own rules, allowing himself a small lapse. It was surprising how readily it had come back to him, once he set his mind to it – he'd imagined his abilities in some dusty chest sunk to the bottom of the deep place. Yet, standing in the Althalan throne room, surrounded by lords and ladies and soldiers, even unsuspecting threaders, he had quietly woven threads into the words he spoke, to ensure they settled into minds as truth. Nothing monstrously manipulative, he told himself, just a few light touches to make certain that Loppolo was clear on the weight of the situation . . . and trusted Rostigan absolutely.

'There mustn't be more than a few hundred of them,' said Loppolo. His tone did not, however, imply this made things simple. Rostigan had counselled him on the journey here, ensuring he understood that Unwoven did not die easily. Their strength was greater than their bony frames suggested, and not much save a blow to the brain or heart would bring one down.

'The Plainsfolk arrive,' announced Tursa, one of Loppolo's advisors. Sure enough, several hundred soldiers in leather armour on horseback were joining the main force. A smaller party broke from them, led by a large man with a red forked beard.

'Ho, Althalans,' he called. 'Hail, King Loppolo. I thank you greatly for coming to our aid.'

'Your people should not stand alone, King Hunna,' said Loppolo, 'against such a vile threat.'

Hunna nodded. 'Often we have fought them in smaller numbers, but I've not seen anything like this before. Something has brought them out of the Pass – but what dark calling, I can't imagine.'

'Look!' said Tursa. Away on the Fields, a solitary figure was riding from the Unwoven camp towards them. It carried a white flag, which it waved back and forth over its head. Once the figure reached the halfway point between the armies, it halted, and planted the flag in the ground. Then it drew its sword and flung it away.

'By the Spell,' said King Hunna. 'I have never heard of Unwoven wanting to talk before.'

Rostigan frowned. Neither had he.

'I shall go,' he said.

'The kings should go,' said Hunna. His appraising eyes travelled over Rostigan, but failed to find any mark of rank or station. 'Who is this man?'

'I am Rostigan, my lord. And the kings should not go, in case this is a trap. You know how Unwoven are.'

'He's right,' said Loppolo quickly. 'Rostigan should go.'

'Then I should go with him,' said Tursa, shooting Rostigan a suspicious look. The advisor had been uneasy with him ever since he'd appeared in Althala out of nowhere and immediately acquired the king's ear.

'I make no guarantees as to your safety,' said Rostigan. Tursa, a rotund fellow with no combat experience, visibly thought twice about his own suggestion, yet evidently did not want to seem a coward by backing out.

'Though I would attempt to protect you,' Rostigan added quietly, 'if it came to that.'

Tursa opened his mouth, but said nothing, and a moment later nodded.

'We shall have representation too, then,' said Hunna. He gave a wave, and a younger man appeared beside him. 'This is Captain –'

'No,' said Rostigan. 'I beg your pardon, King Hunna, but the Unwoven and Plainsfolk are old enemies. Better to send removed parties, or else risk confusing things.'

'And I beg *your* pardon,' said Hunna, 'but I won't be given orders in my own lands by a man I do not know!' He gave Rostigan a hard stare. 'However . . . your words are not without wisdom. Things between us and them have been running a little wild of late. Besides, I doubt that thing,' he stuck a thumb towards the waiting figure, 'has anything real to say.'

'We shall see,' said Rostigan.

The yellow grass crackled under hoof as Rostigan and Tursa rode out to the Unwoven. Drawing closer, they saw it was a male, sitting astride a silver horse. His skin was pallid grey and incredibly smooth, yet taunt, the outlines of muscles and veins showing through. His shirt hung off him like a rag, though in contrast his trousers and boots were sturdy and well made. His limp hair was streaked with dull and faded red dye.

As they pulled to a stop, Tursa a little further back, the Unwoven gave them something that was not quite a smile, more a stretched display of jagged teeth.

'Greetings,' said Rostigan. He thought about introducing himself, but Unwoven did not use names, so he opted not to confuse things. 'We are representatives of Althala.'

The red-streaked Unwoven sniffed the air. 'What's that?' he said, the voice too deep for the emaciated head it came from. 'Can you smell it?'

'Smell what?' said Tursa. Rostigan raised an eyebrow at him as if to say 'do you really want to draw attention to yourself?' and the advisor fell silent.

'Can we smell what?' said Rostigan.

'Earth, burning,' replied Redstreak. 'And sometimes,' he flicked out a ghastly white tongue, 'like something is wafting through a crack.'

Rostigan frowned. 'Do you follow the scent?'

'No. But it makes us remember.' Redstreak blinked, focusing on them again. 'What are you doing here?'

'I thought you wished to speak with us?'

'Not at all. I was just taking my flag for a walk.' The Unwoven snickered. 'What point is there in talking to you and you, untarnished by his touch?'

'That's a joke – it's *you* who are the aberrations!'

This time Rostigan didn't bother shooting Tursa a warning look.

'How sad it must be,' remarked the Unwoven, 'to dwell inside your skin-bag with only ignorance for company.'

'Regret is dead,' said Tursa. 'He was just a man.'

'Quiet,' snapped Rostigan, but the Unwoven's face

already twisted in hate, dozens of lines wrinkling the once-smooth skin.

'I will find you,' said Redstreak, jabbing a finger at Tursa, 'in the fray.'

'So you do wish to fight?' said Rostigan.

'Yes!' The Unwoven shrieked joyfully, as if this was an idea just occurring to him. 'We shall fight! And after that, we'll keep going, and fight others too. And after that, fight more others too!' On another face, in another place, his would have been a true and happy smile.

'So why,' said Rostigan, 'did you wish to speak with us?'

'I told you, I don't.'

'You threw away your sword,' said Tursa.

'I didn't like it anymore. When I come for you, fat man, I won't need a sword. I'll rip your head off with my hands.'

'I won't listen to these . . . these foul lies!' exclaimed Tursa, and clumsily wheeled his horse around to gallop away.

Rostigan sighed. 'Why did you have to go and scare him like that? He just wanted to look brave in front of the army.'

Redstreak stared at him uncomprehendingly.

Rostigan leaned forward in the saddle. 'Tell me something, my fine friend. I wonder if Regret's Spire still stands in the Dale?'

'The Spire? Yes, it stands. It will always stand.'

'Of course. And is there anything in the sky above it?'

Redstreak blinked. 'A smell though the cracks. A sack of grace flung upstream, leaking into the flow.'

'Anything you can see?'

Redstreak's eyes flashed fervently. 'Red,' he whispered.

The word was like a weight upon Rostigan. The Wound was still open, just as the rumours always said, but he had still managed to hope that, after all this time, it would find some way to heal. He stared off at the colossal Peaks, as if his gaze could penetrate them, and see what they shielded from view.

'More cracks soon, warrior,' said Redstreak. 'And us to help spread his touch.'

With that he laughed, and rode away.

'I knew it,' said Hunna in disgust. 'It merely wanted to waste our time.'

'Why?' said Loppolo.

'Why do Unwoven do anything, when the only good thing they could do is slay themselves?'

'They do not think like you or me, King Loppolo,' said Rostigan.

Across the way the Unwoven were forming up, some on horseback but most on foot.

'They're coming,' said Tursa, his face pale.

From the Peaks beyond the Unwoven, a series of white shapes suddenly rose into view, like distant puffs of smoke. They ascended quickly, hard to make out in the brightness of day.

'My king, look!' said an officer, pointing. 'What are those?'

'Silkjaws,' muttered Rostigan, dismounting from his horse. With such foes on the way, it would be prudent not to sit on high.

'S . . . silkjaws?' stammered Tursa. 'But there are so many!'

All at once the Unwoven gave a collective howl and charged. Meanwhile, as the white shapes flew closer they became clearer – silent monsters wheeling in the air.

'Stand firm, Plainsfolk!' shouted Hunna, riding to his soldiers. 'We are no strangers to silkjaws, nor they to our swords!'

Yes, thought Rostigan, *but hunting down a single 'jaw for stealing sheep is not the same as this. I would not have guessed they even existed in such numbers.*

'Your threaders, King,' he told Loppolo, 'are our best defence against those creatures!'

Loppolo nodded determinedly. 'And archers with flames!' He began shouting orders as soldiers fanned out around him. Towards the back of the army, a couple of deserters broke loose.

As the enemy drew closer above and below, Rostigan knew there was no more controlling the situation. He had done what he could by getting an army here in time – the only thing left was to stand beneath the breaking wave, and hope it did not knock him down.

'At 'em!' came Hunna's bellow, and the Plainsfolk rode forth, spears held out before them.

'Charge!' called Loppolo, almost too late, for his soldiers barely achieved running speed before clashing with the Unwoven.

Everything descended into chaos.

From his back Rostigan unsheathed a broadsword most would need two hands to wield. Before him an Althalan twisted away with blood spraying from his neck, vividly painting the yellow grass. Another soldier swiped at the grinning Unwoven who'd dealt the blow, cutting a long gash down its arm. White blood oozed from the wound, too slow and sticky to spurt. Grinner laughed harshly and lashed out with his injured arm, landing a blow that broke the soldier's nose back into his skull.

'Go for the heads!' shouted Rostigan, as he dashed at Grinner. He brought his sword down in a overhead sweep and, with a confident sneer, Grinner held his own up to block the blow. Their swords met, and there was a very brief moment during which a look of confusion began to form on Grinner's face, and then both swords drove down deeply into his head at cross lengths. Like a partially attached quartered melon his head flopped to pieces about his neck, and Rostigan gave his body a heavy kick to send him away.

Something kindled in the deep place – a little flame in the void, burning brightly. Rostigan was instantly wary of it, for it gave out a glow of warm satisfaction. So long since he had felt such a thing, he could not bring himself to douse it. Instead he cradled it like a treasure, making sure to keep it small and contained. He would not allow it to grow, to consume him.

A scream sounded nearby as a Plainsman was torn from his horse by a swooping silkjaw, borne into the air leaving a trail of misted blood. A second 'jaw crash-landed nearby, bowling over a couple of soldiers. It scrabbled to stand up bat-like on the elbows of its wings, swinging its long head about, searching for targets with hollow eyes.

Of all Regret's creations, Rostigan disliked silkjaws the most. Everything about them was wrong. He was not sure they were even truly alive, for they carried nothing of flesh about them. Instead, the bones that gave them shape were bound together by sheets of coarse white silk, which stretched and contracted like fibrous muscle. They had no voices, and the only sound they made was the occasional rustle or clack of bones. The 'jaw on the ground opened its mouth, elongating the strands that held it together, giving a clear view of fangs embedded along misshapen jawbones. It gnashed so hard it drove the points through its own snout, and didn't appear to feel a thing.

A soldier leapt at it, slicing the silk along its wing, and it snapped down over his head and shoulders, biting savagely. The act looked like a semblance of feeding, but there was no stomach in the creature's empty body. Instead, blood soaked its white silk, and it shook its prey to absorb as much as possible.

A red silkjaw was a happy silkjaw.

A flaming arrow thudded into its side, but failed to set it ablaze, for the soaked strands were already too damp.

'I told him threaders work best,' muttered Rostigan, as he turned away. He could attack the silkjaw himself, even slay it – but it would be a laborious matter of cutting and slicing until the beast was a pile of bone and fluff. His time was better spent on the Unwoven, for he could kill them far more quickly.

He strode headlong into the thick of it, where bodies already grew plentiful underfoot. Unwoven had begun to spread out, and many of them now faced multiple opponents. Rostigan chose the ones who moved about with greatest ease, who batted away swords as if they were switches – until they met him, of course. Always he went for the heads, for there was no helmet, no shield, no weapon that could stand in the way of his sword. His bouts were swift and methodical, and again and again he crunched through skulls with powerful downward blows. Soon he took hurts of his own, and in places his armour dinted painfully inwards. He knew that he was bleeding at his side, that shards of metal were sticking in his flesh.

In the sky, silkjaws fell apart as threaders undid the magic that bound them together. One dove towards him even as its wings unspooled, bones falling free of the tatters. He sidestepped as it ploughed into the ground, and lifted its head almost piteously as its last fibres dropped away. Plenty of the creatures remained airborne, though – taking them apart, Rostigan knew, was not swiftly done, nor every threader's talent. Some of the threaders were employing fire instead, sending up thin snakes of it from torches, and arrows flamed upwards too. Here and there white shapes suddenly blazed, as 'jaws flared to cinders.

Some ways behind, Loppolo roared encouragement as he waved his sword, thickly protected by soldiers and threaders, and no enemy came within spitting distance of him. Then a sudden series of silkjaw dive-bombings thinned his guards, and Rostigan saw Tursa knocked from his horse. The king's steed cantered sideways as his soldiers jostled to enclose him once more, the group moving away from Tursa. Dazedly the fat advisor lifted his head from the churned earth.

Redstreak strode out of the tumult wearing a rabid grin. Tursa saw him and started, a terrible fear shining in his eyes. Redstreak moved towards him, flexing his hands and rubbing them together. Tursa looked around desperately.

'Rostigan!' he mewled. 'Help me!'

Rostigan was already running at Redstreak, whose head snapped about to see who was coming. Deftly, Redstreak slipped around what would have been a tremendous blow, which, in missing entirely, sent Rostigan staggering forward. Redstreak danced around behind him, and Rostigan felt iron fingers close upon his throat. He twisted, swinging Redstreak off his feet – the Unwoven weighed little for all his strength, and held on tight.

'I don't know what you are, warrior,' came his voice in Rostigan's ear as the grip contracted, 'but I bet you die when your head comes off, just like everyone else.'

Rostigan saw spots before his eyes, and awkwardly plunged his sword over his shoulder. Redstreak shifted his weight, pushing off Rostigan's hip to clear himself of the blow.

'Oh, hold me,' chuckled Redstreak throatily, swinging about Rostigan as if his neck was a beanpole, pulling him off balance this way and that. 'Embrace me, why won't you love me?'

Rostigan dropped his sword as his hands went to his throat, trying to prise the fingers loose. In the deep place, his little flame snuffed out.

'Your flesh is strong,' said Redstreak, digging in his jagged nails. 'But I think I can do it. I think I can!'

Rostigan tried to gasp for breath, but no air entered his lungs. The pressure increased, grinding the bones in his neck, and he fell to his knees. Where the flame had gone out, the deep place yawned wide, and he saw his life unfurl like a great scroll. He'd bested opponents worse than a single Unwoven before. Unexpected – was that not the very nature of death?

Is this where it ends?

Strangely, he felt something like relief.

Redstreak gave a grunt, and suddenly the constriction around Rostigan's neck went away. He sucked in air and rolled, coming up to see Tursa backing away with a sword that dripped whitely. Redstreak was staring at the advisor malevolently, one of his arms severed at the elbow.

'Can you do it with one hand?' Tursa snarled.

Redstreak reached out with his good hand to grab the elbow of Tursa's sword arm before the man could strike.

'Can you?' Redstreak said. He squeezed with a force that brought the sound of cracking bones. Tursa instantly lost all colour and dropped his sword.

From behind, Rostigan caved in Redstreak's head.

He wrenched his sword free of the toppling corpse, and rubbed his bruised neck with a grimace.

'Thank you,' he croaked to Tursa, who was cradling his jelly-limp limb with a kind of strange fascination.

'Did you see what I did? I chopped off his arm!'

'That you did. Now listen to me, Tursa – you get yourself back to the king, you hear me? Tursa?' He gave the man a little slap, and Tursa jolted, finally looking at him. 'Back to the king with you, yes? Maybe one of his threaders can fix you up.'

Rostigan turned back to the battle determined to make up for lost time. Although the Unwoven fought furiously, there were fewer of them now, for they had never tried to stay together. Each time one of them fell, more soldiers were free to help surround those who remained. Many of the silkjaws still airborne were at least partially undone, flapping wildly to compensate for trailing wings or dangling bones. Others were redly saturated, and these were the worst, ripping and tearing through groups of soldiers, resistant to fire, yet threaders attacked them wherever they landed, hands raised to send out myriad gestures. The best thing to do, Rostigan decided, was to hasten things as much as he could, in the hope of saving that many more soldiers. If there were enough left unscathed, maybe they could press on to the Pass.

He pushed aside others to get to the fighting, still avoiding confrontations with silkjaws when possible. Each time he reached an Unwoven, down it went with his sword in its head. As the sun moved across the sky, enemy numbers dwindled, yet still they fought on. There was no trace of fear on their faces as they stood ever-increasingly alone, no heed paid to the swathes of fallen comrades about them, no glancing around for a way to retreat – only laughter and hatred.

Rostigan made for the last one he could see, but it was dead before he got there. As it fell, the remaining silkjaws rose into the sky toward the Roshous Peaks. Rostigan stalked across the Fields in the glow of sunset, ignoring the cheers that broke out around him. Small patches of yellow grass that had escaped the stain of blood lit up like pools of gold in the dying light. Threaders moved amongst the bodies, looking for wounded amongst the dead.

Rostigan found Loppolo talking earnestly with his officers. Nearby, Tursa sat cross-legged and whimpering while a threader made motions over his damaged arm. Hunna rode up, the white smears of Unwoven blood along his horse stuck with bits of silk.

'By the Spell,' he said, as he dismounted, 'I am thankful, Loppolo, that you were here with us.'

'Aye,' said Loppolo. 'Though the cost has been great.'

'Better these here and now,' said Rostigan, 'than multitudes later, oh king. The sacrifice is worthwhile.' He glanced between the two leaders. 'I wonder, my lords, if we dare push our luck?'

'What's that?' said Hunna.

'With so many Unwoven warriors fallen, the Dale will be poorly defended. Imagine how they will sing of you both, should you rid Aorn of Regret's people for good!'

Loppolo looked like he didn't understand, while Hunna stared in undisguised astonishment – then threw back his head and bawled laughter.

'Have you gone mad, fellow?' he said, slapping Rostigan's shoulder. 'You want to take this battle-bruised bunch to the *Pass*? I admire your mettle, as do all who saw you fight this day – my soldiers are already telling each other stories of *Skullrender* – but if you think they will up and follow you into that place after what they've just endured, you have lost your mind.'

Rostigan wondered if one more time would hurt. A few carefully chosen words to convince Hunna of the idea's worth, accompanied by a little threading to ensure they took root, and perhaps they really could cleanse the Tranquil Dale . . . yet he had already broken his rules once, and did not want it to become easy for him. Besides, he had to admit, looking around at the bloody, battered soldiers still standing, that maybe Hunna had a point.

Circling crows were beginning to caw, their voices seeming to signal an ending.

'Enough then,' he said.

JUSTICE REBORN

Considered by some to be the greatest city in Aorn, Althala was certainly the biggest and the richest. Streets were paved with white cobblestones, buildings were solid and opulent in design, and everywhere storefronts spilled colourful produce out into thoroughfare displays. People moved in thick streams, happy and nodding to one another as they went about their business. Everything was clean and well presented – drains in the sides of footpaths channelled rain and refuse into underground caverns below the city, and even the occasional beggar was surprisingly well groomed. If it was anything like Yalenna remembered, a beggar would need a special licence from the city, which would only be granted if they were debilitated somehow. Others claiming poverty would be given two choices: leave Althala, or work in city-run farmland on the fertile plains to the east.

Today, however, it wasn't the beauty of the place that fuelled the bounce in various steps, as Yalenna quickly learned.

'I hear Loppolo's steaming,' she overheard a rotund woman say to a cloth trader.

'I warrant that's true,' replied the trader, holding out a length of blue silk for inspection. 'He knows he's at risk of falling into Braston's shadow, and disappearing entirely.'

The woman chortled as she pawed the silk. 'Very nice. Oh, but it's marvellous, isn't it? I can't believe it, I still can't! If you'd told me last week that I'd see the Lord of Justice himself return to life and reclaim the kingship – that I would stand in the castle square and *see him wave* – I would have thought you mad. And yet!'

'It certainly is amazing,' said the trader. 'Now, can I cut you off this much?'

Yalenna moved on, somewhat troubled. She understood the people's joy – she was looking forward to seeing Braston herself – but she did not like the news that he'd supplanted the rightful king. How had it happened? Willingly she hoped, akin to Arah's offer to step aside as Priestess. But even if that were the case, and talk of Loppolo *steaming* was just idle gossip, Yalenna felt Braston had made a big mistake. While it had been difficult for him to abandon his people – the hardest part of killing himself – he must know, *must* know, that he simply had no right to pick up where he had left off. Perhaps to him it seemed like no time had passed, but that was no excuse.

Pausing to eavesdrop on the woman and trader was the only delay Yalenna allowed herself. With the density of the population here, the blessings that seeped from her were finding many homes.

May you always smell clean.

May you never catch a cold.

May you discover hidden talents.

While there was a time when she would have taken pleasure from this, the bleak truth of it was that her magic constantly damaged the Spell. Without the ability to reign it in, being close to so many people made it all the worse.

She moved towards Althala Castle, its great white spires visible for leagues around. She navigated the streets easily enough, finding it remarkable how little had changed. She recognised plenty of municipal buildings, and wondered if the School of Threading still stood. That was where she had been placed as a young girl, all but abandoned by her merchant father. Thankfully, Mergan had recognised her great talent, and she had lost herself quickly in her new life. She did not deviate to go looking for the school now, however, her purpose overriding any sentimental urge.

Soon she came to the immense public square lying in the castle's shadow, an empty space under high balconies punctuated only by a few ornamental trees. She headed for the castle entrance, where Althalan guards, dressed in silver armour over red garments – something else that had not changed – manned either side of a grand archway.

'Excuse me, miss,' said a young man politely – a captain, by the look of his shoulder plumes. 'May I ask what business you have in the castle?'

'My name is Yalenna,' she said. 'I seek my old friend Braston.'

The captain gaped in surprise and looked her up and down again. She was still dressed in her white robe, her snowy hair flowing freely down her shoulders. It had always been considered an unusual colour, but not so rare that it made her instantly recognisable. Still, coupled with her name, and the robe, and who she asked for, she could see him sorting through the implications.

'Er . . . the, the *Priestess* Yalenna? You claim?'

'That's right.'

The other guards were grouping around, ogling her with various degrees of curiosity and suspicion. The captain glanced sidelong at them – some of them were older and more grizzled than he – and tried to look less flustered.

'How can I trust you're really her?' he said.

Little bundles of threads spilled from her, sinking into the guards. If they could see what she saw, she thought, there would be no doubting her word.

She tapped the lightning insignia that clasped her robe together. 'Does this not carry weight in Althala anymore?'

'Forgive me, miss,' said the captain, 'but there are other priests and priestesses who bear the same symbol.'

'I have a simple solution,' said Yalenna brightly. 'Take me to Braston and he'll tell you who I am.'

'If you're really her,' put in an older guard, 'why don't you give us a blessing?'

'I already have.'

The man frowned. 'What is it, then?'

Yalenna shrugged. 'I'm not sure, good fellow. I do not shape the nature of what I impart, unless I choose to. Would you like me to find out what it is you've received?'

She extended a hand at him, and his went to his sword. She ignored the action, instead searching his pattern for any new insertion. *There* it was, still wriggling into place.

'Ah,' she said. 'Anything you plant will blossom and thrive, even in the harshest soil.'

The man looked bemused, while the others chuckled.

'Off to try your hand at some gardening, Das?' asked the captain, and chuckles became laughter.

Blessings, Yalenna reflected, were sometimes wasted.

'What about me?' asked another guard. 'What did I get?'

She found herself growing impatient. 'I am not here for your amusement!' she snapped, which made them all jump a little. Forcing her voice back to an even tone, she said, 'Captain, please, take me to Braston. What is your concern? If I'm not who I say I am, he has nothing to fear from me.'

The captain thought about that for a moment, muddling through it a little confusedly – then gave up, and nodded. 'Very well. I will take you to the king.' He gave a little bow. 'I am Captain Jandryn. You lot,' he added, as some of the others made to move with him, 'stay here.'

Some of them looked disappointed.

Jandryn led her, not through the arch, but back into the square, towards other surrounding buildings that were part of the castle complex.

'Where is he?' said Yalenna.

'Althala jail,' replied the captain.

I might have known, she thought.

~

Here the stone was not as white as elsewhere in Althala, and there hung a certain smell in the air – sweat, and other unpleasantness resulting from human confinement. Rows of doors with viewing panels lined the corridors, some of them open to reveal empty cells. Some of them looked only recently vacated.

Ahead Yalenna heard voices, and a hearty laugh that felt like a warm blanket on her soul. Whatever madness it was that had returned her to the world, she was not in it alone. He was here too.

When Mergan first brought the Wardens together, she had not known Braston well. He had visited the School of Threading once or twice, and she remembered shaking his hand as a nervous young slip of thing. Later, once she had been made Priestess, and ruled in her own right, they had exchanged a missive or two, their interactions always very polite and reasonable. It had not been until they had journeyed together to the Spire, and afterwards spent the better part of a decade hunting and killing the remaining Wardens, that they had grown truly close. After all, they had been all that stood between Aorn and disaster – especially once Mergan had disappeared – and had needed to constantly support and trust each other.

Perhaps it was because of that trust that she now felt a little nervous, wondering how pleased he would be to receive her. After all, she had been the one to convince him to take his own life. She had needed to be staunchly adamant and convincing in her arguments even while harbouring her own doubts . . . which, it now turned out, she had been correct to have, for their deaths had seemingly solved nothing.

She had persuaded him to kill himself *for nothing*.

She rounded a corner and there he was. Muscular enough for two men, his barrel chest stretching wide the V-shaped neckline of his shirt, he stood at least a head above the others in his entourage. Every hair of his golden beard was perfectly in place, and his golden eyes twinkled merrily as he regaled his audience with some tale or joke. As she swished around the bend into his view, however, she ensured they would not hear the end of it.

'Yalenna!' he exclaimed. His face lit up in a way that assuaged her worries, and it was a release to smile at him fondly. He, on the other hand, was having none of her restraint, and bustled towards her, careful not to knock anyone else over in what for him were tight confines. He seized her under the arms and she laughed as he lifted her up in an enormous hug to swing her about.

'Braston,' she said giddily, once he set her down, 'you never did that before!'

'I'm happy to see you!' he said, beaming. 'By the Spell, if you weren't here, I don't know what I'd do!'

'It looks to me,' she said wryly, 'like you know exactly what you're doing.'

'Oh, this . . .' he glanced about at the guards, jailer, and nobles who accompanied him, now watching them together in open fascination. One of the guards held a brown-clothed prisoner with chained hands, who looked terrified.

'Just apportioning a little justice,' said Braston. 'You would not believe the state of this place!'

To Yalenna the jail looked cleaner and kinder than some she had seen in other cities, but she held back comment.

'I hear you're raising an army,' she said instead, though it came out a little sharper than she intended.

Braston grunted, and lowered his voice. 'I'm sure you know we're not the only Wardens to return. Stealer too, I think, for Silverstone has disappeared without a trace. I've also heard of goings-on in the Sunshine Downs that seem to have the mark of Despirrow about them. And if those two are back, and us as well, I can't see much reason to hope that the others aren't here. Even now Karrak is probably scheming with Forger, raising up their own forces. We'll hear about them soon, no doubt, and I do not wish to be slow to react. I wish to *pre-empt*!'

Yalenna stared into his earnest eyes. It had always been easier for him, she knew, to face a foe that he could see, could fight. Already he was focused on taking down the others, as he had been all those years ago – yesterday.

'Also,' he continued, 'have you heard? The Unwoven

have not been dealt with yet. They have begun sending hunting parties out of the –'

'You must realise,' she interrupted, 'that what we were trying to achieve when we ended our own lives has failed.'

Anger flashed across his face, and she forced herself not to look away. He, however, seemed more eager to forget her mistakes than she was, for he smoothed his expression, and took a deep breath.

'But Yalenna,' he said, '*they* are the more immediate threat.'

'Maybe so. But we cannot –'

'Cannot what?' He took her hands and squeezed them. 'Use this time we've been granted against all expectation? Do some good while we're here? Yalenna, I do understand that there must be some mysterious reason for our return – or maybe it's not mysterious, maybe the Spell simply wants us to exist! But even if it's something less pleasant than that, we don't yet know what it is. Am I supposed to stand idle while Karrak rebuilds his empire?'

'Of course not, but we must choose our actions carefully. I have already heard that you deposed the King of Althala.'

'I would not say deposed.'

'Wouldn't you?'

Braston grimaced. 'But the people, Yalenna, they were so glad to receive me! I appeared on the very throne where I died and, after the initial shock, you should have seen how they fell at my feet, how they praised the Spell for such a miracle! They would not have it any other way than I be king again.'

'And you, Braston – would you have it any other way? What if we discover that our purpose lies elsewhere? What if we must perish once more? Do you not think it affects the kingdom to have its rightful ruler cast down? I'm sure the people would still have been glad to see you whether or not you became their actual ruler. Instead you have changed the natural order by assuming control.'

Braston shook his head. 'You are too harsh. I made the same sacrifice as you, yet the Spell has brought us back. And certainly I don't intend to rush to death again, however keen you may be to do so!'

Yalenna prickled at the accusation, though part of her was strangely thankful that he at least acknowledged the tension between them.

'I should not have abandoned my people in the first place,' he muttered. 'I'm simply back where I belong.'

'We don't know that.'

'There!' Braston brightened. 'At least you're open to the possibility! Come, will you join me? I should get back to my task.'

Yalenna knew he needed time to adjust to any idea he did not like, and was especially stubborn when it came to mistakes he had made. Certainly she did not feel in the best position to talk him around immediately, given how wrong she had been herself.

'What are you doing?' she asked.

'Seeing prisoners.'

As they returned to the group, the shackled man cringed in the guard's steady grip.

'Take this fellow, for instance. A murderer who killed a man in a drunken bar brawl. Now look at him.'

The miserable prisoner stilled as all eyes settled on him.

'The man he killed was his friend,' said Braston. 'They knew each other from childhood.'

Tears began to etch their way down the prisoner's cheeks.

'Yet I can read his threads,' said Braston. 'His sin has cost him greatly, and he'll never again repeat it.' He nodded to the jailer. 'Unchain him.'

As the jailer lifted his keys, disbelief showed on the prisoner's face.

'But lord,' he whispered, 'I don't deserve to be released.'

'The words of someone who does,' said Braston, and the nobles in the group cooed to each other at his wisdom. 'If you cannot face your friends and family, you are welcome to join my army. Take him away.'

The man bowed and murmured thanks before a guard ushered him on. Braston smiled at Yalenna, and she tried to return it. She knew they had to be careful about using their gifts, yet Braston's came as naturally and unstoppably to him as hers did to her. He saw the tapestry of relationships around every person, how they were connected to the world – and if there was injustice there, done to or by the person, he could always sniff it out. Laudable as his intentions were, it made her uncomfortable to see how eagerly he embraced his powers.

He moved to the next door, where fingers gripped the bars of the panel.

'Let me out too, lord,' came a plea from within. 'I've atoned for my wrongs, I swear!'

Braston peered into the cell. 'A petty thief,' he said.

'That's right lord, nothing too bad! I only took a bit of fruit, the odd trinket – got to feed the family, you know how it is.'

'And a liar too,' said Braston. He slid the panel closed upon a howl of dismay.

'Should have known better than try to deceive the Lord of Justice,' murmured one noblewoman to another. She glanced curiously at Yalenna, who gave her a slight nod, and she blushed.

May you derive satisfaction from completing simple tasks.

'Are you really her?' the noble asked. 'The Priestess Yalenna?'

'I really am.'

'And have you come to join Braston?'

Yalenna quirked an eyebrow. 'I suppose you could put it like that.'

'My goodness. And since you're here, does that mean that we are blessed?'

'You are.'

The women glanced at each other in awe.

'By the Spell, my lady, what have you given us?'

'You'll have to discover that for yourselves.'

The women excitedly began discussing what unknown gifts they now possessed.

Yalenna sighed.

'Not sure about that one, lord,' the jailer said.

Braston was staring through the panel of the next cell door. 'Open it.'

With resignation the jailer obeyed, and Yalenna moved to Braston's shoulder to look inside.

The cell was filthy. Excrement smeared the walls around an empty bedpan. Sheets lay in a heap on the floor, the mattress frayed as if someone had been chewing it. The prisoner himself sat in a corner facing away, muttering as he scratched his scabs and ensured there would be new ones. As the door squeaked his head turned to reveal a sallow, unshaven face.

'Look,' he whispered, 'at all the nice warm goodies.'

'He's not right in the head, lord,' said the jailer. 'Ain't nothing to be done for him either.'

Braston stooped to enter the cell, and the man snarled, flecks of spittle dotting thin lips. He did not rise, but twisted to flatten himself against the filthy wall. His eyes darted frantically about the people watching him, finally settling on Yalenna.

May you always be true to your heart's desires.

'Such a pretty mouth,' the prisoner leered. 'I'd like to use it as a bedpan.'

The nobles gave exclamations of disgust.

'Mind your tongue!' barked the jailer, but Braston held up a hand for silence. He studied the man, seeing things that no one else could, and eventually gave a sad sigh.

'He's committed terrible deeds,' he muttered, almost to himself.

'Yes, lord,' said the jailer.

'No hope for redemption, either,' said Braston. 'Yet to keep him here, like a sick animal, for the rest of his life . . . isn't justice. It's cruelty.'

He approached the quivering prisoner, one hand held out as if to calm a frightened dog.

'Much better for you,' said Braston, 'to know peace.'

The man gave a squeak and tried to scrabble away, with all the effectiveness of a spider in a jar.

Braston drew the sword from his belt. 'I suggest you look away, gentle ladies,' he spoke over his shoulder. Not bothering to see if they took his suggestion, he raised the sword, and the prisoner let out a panicked shriek.

'Kinder,' said Braston, and plunged the sword through the man's breast, pinning him to the wall. The blow was true, and it did not take long for movement to cease. Braston withdrew the blade, letting the body crumple to the floor. He turned and moved out of the cell, everyone backing out of his way, the ladies glancing nervously at his dripping sword.

'Make sure he gets a proper burial,' he told the jailer.

'May I have a moment?' said Yalenna.

He nodded and they stepped aside. 'I'm sorry you had to see that. Justice is not always –'

'Please, Braston,' she cut him off, 'I am not one of your dainty sycophants. The only thing that offends me is what a terrible waste of time this is.'

Braston frowned. 'There are people who have been in this place years past their due, one way or another. How can I expect others to follow me if I can't even keep my own house in order?'

'I hardly believe that the Spell brought us back so you could grant rest to a few ne'er-do-wells.'

And it's not your house, she added to herself.

'But *I* cannot rest,' Braston said, 'with this place thrumming on the edge of my thoughts – it's too close to the castle. So many untidy threads clamouring for attention!'

She arched an eyebrow. 'I don't believe that. We are ever and always surrounded by injustice, and you *can* ignore it when you choose. We have more important –'

'I realise we must talk. I do. Tonight? Once I have carried out my task here?'

He turned and singled out the captain who had brought her here, loitering with the others.

'You, sir!' he called, pointing with his blade. 'Captain Jandryn, is it?'

'Yes, lord.'

'Escort Lady Yalenna to the castle. Make sure she's appointed fitting chambers, and that her every wish is met.'

'My only wish,' hissed Yalenna, 'is to work out what we're supposed to do!'

Braston affected not to have heard.

～

As she passed through the castle's archway entrance into a wide blue-stone hall, Yalenna found her annoyance growing. She did not want to sit in some chamber waiting for Braston to decide that he was ready to speak with her – yet she needed him, or, if need was too strong a word, then at the least she very much wanted his help.

'What of Loppolo?' she said suddenly to Captain Jandryn.

'Pardon, my lady?'

She couldn't blame him, she supposed, for not following her train of thought.

'What has happened to the rightful King of Althala?'

He blinked, obviously uncomfortable with her choice of words.

'Well, he . . . is probably in the throne room.'

'Oh? Does he still sit on the throne?'

'No. Er.' The captain glanced about, but there was no one to overhear. 'In truth, my lady, there is some confusion.'

'I have no doubt. I wonder if you'd take me to him?'

Uncertainly the captain nodded. 'As you wish.'

As they moved down the hall, Yalenna ignored groups of people whispering to each other and drifting along behind her. Word of her arrival, it seemed, had not taken long to spread.

They arrived in the immense blue marble chamber of the throne room. An interlocking line of diamond-shaped tiles made a path that wended its way towards the distant dais and throne, through a collection of fountains. Artificial streams populated by colourful fish ran here and there, sparkling in the light of high-set windows. Little birds flew about, their chirps magnified as they echoed off walls, and servants moved between scattered courtiers. It was as luxurious and grandiose a place as Yalenna remembered.

'This way, my lady,' said Jandryn. Everywhere people stared, and there was more than one finger pointing at her. Ahead a sizeable group collected around one of the fountains, all feathers and headdresses, frilled coats and silk slippers. In their centre a man reclined lazily on a bench, eating a piece of cake and looking bored. When someone whispered to him however, he glanced her way and came swiftly to his feet.

'My Lord Loppolo,' said Jandryn, bowing. 'May I introduce the Lady Yalenna?'

Loppolo bowed so deeply that his brown ponytail dangled from the back of his head. He was a pleasant enough looking fellow, beyond middle age but with a softness to his features, who wore many layers of differently toned clothes.

'My goodness,' he said. 'Welcome indeed, Priestess, to my . . . well, to *the* throne room, I should say.'

'Thank you, Lord Loppolo.'

'Such a . . . well now, I'm not sure if it's good fortune or not that brings you to our midst?'

'That is a question indeed.'

'Indeed.'

Loppolo wrung his hands, for a moment unsettled. Yalenna realised she was not quite sure herself what she wanted to achieve here. In her peripherals she sensed people coagulating about them, many probably hoping to catch a stray blessing. Some already had, her cloud emanating as abundantly as ever. Some of the smaller bundles even found homes in the birds flitting about, or the fish in the streams.

May you set achievable goals every day, went to a minnow.

'I understand,' she lowered her voice, 'that you were king until recently.'

'Oh, yes,' said Loppolo. 'Til very recently, my lady. A good king too, if I may say.'

His companions, some of whom were more hard-eyed than he was, murmured their agreement. Looking at them now, Yalenna wondered whether Braston's description of everyone collapsing to their knees when he appeared was entirely truthful. There were plenty of portraits and busts of him about the castle, so she did not think recognition had been a factor – but maybe fear had been. Who would stand against the hero-King of Althala, back from the grave?

'But,' continued Loppolo carefully, 'I can't argue with fate's deliverance, nor deny Braston his old seat. Not when his return from death must surely have been willed by the Spell itself.'

Yalenna was careful not to contradict this. Best that she and Braston presented a united front, even if she did not agree with his actions so far.

'So what now?' she said. 'It mustn't be easy for you to remain here in your old throne room.'

Loppolo nodded thoughtfully. 'I won't pretend it is. Going from being the exalted King of Althala, to suddenly . . . well. Normally succession follows a death, even exile from time to time, and perhaps those would be less perplexing ends.' He forced a smile. 'Not that I wish for them, of course. This way, I can remain a lord, and continue serving the people as best I can.'

The man was obviously struggling to justify what had happened to him, and Yalenna felt a compunction to shape a blessing for him – not randomly this time, but one of her choosing. She was not quite sure, however, what was appropriate. Perhaps it would be easier to see if she agreed with what was already in place? Sending her influence into his pattern, she sought the threads he had received from her – and smiled.

'May you always have happy dreams,' she said, passing her fingers through the air as if she bestowed the blessing by choice.

Loppolo looked surprised, then gave another quick bow.

'I thank you, Priestess.'

'And now,' said Yalenna, 'I find myself tired. I appreciate you speaking with me, Lord Loppolo.'

'Of course. And I hope to see you again soon, my lady.'

'Captain,' she turned to Jandryn, 'I would appreciate being shown to my quarters.'

'This way, my lady.'

Loppolo stood watching them go. Once they were out of earshot, he clicked his tongue thoughtfully.

'And what use,' he said, 'have I for dreams, I wonder?'

Several of his companions sniggered.

GIVE AND TAKE

Forger left the cottage the next morning feeling like a new man. He was taller, for a start, almost tall enough to pass for normal. He knew he wouldn't keep growing at such a rate, that after a while the growth would become more internalised – a growing of *power*, indeed! – but it was nice to know that no trapdoor spiders were going to burst out of the ground and try to eat him.

He closed the door on low sobbing. Quite a puppet show he'd performed last night – he the master, the boys his marionettes. *Look how they play, Mother, rolling a ball to each other across the floor. Oh dear, it's rolled into the fire! No little man, don't reach in after it! Dear oh dear, look missus, how his little hand is scorched, look, right down to the bone. That will teach you to reach into the fire, little man . . .*

And when the father had eventually come home, well, they had all had dinner together, hadn't they?

'Pass the salt,' he chortled, remembering. A boy with knife and fork in hand-and-melted-hand, his mouth dumbly opening and closing, and Forger doing a high-pitched attempt at his voice. 'Pass the salt, Father, pass the salt. Would you pass the salt please? Father, look at me – would you pass the salt?'

He spied a large tub of rainwater, and stood over it, splashing blood off himself. He might, he decided, have to dress differently to appear normal. His patchwork leather clothing would probably draw attention, and he wasn't sure he wanted that yet.

'Not until,' he muttered, 'I know what the blazing piss is going on.'

Three hundred years, he had learned during the night, since he had died. He thought about the very moment of his reawakening – staring up at towering grass was his first new memory, but it held no clue as to why he had been returned to the world.

'Oh well,' he said. 'First things first.'

He wanted to get to Tallahow – where he had trained as a threader and which had eventually become the seat of his power – but didn't think he was strong enough yet to threadwalk. *Besides*, he contemplated, *might be nice to see some of the land – see what has changed!*

Pleased with that merry thought, he turned back to the cottage. He would take some of the father's clothes, and perhaps there was even some coin lying around.

There was also the final question.

Banging through the door, he re-entered the cottage.

'All right, you two. I have one more thing to ask.'

Bound to a chair by rings of warped metal that had once been a teapot, the woman's head remained downturned, while at the head of the table the man raised his red-rimmed eyes.

'It's a question for each of you, and I suggest you think carefully about your answer. Do you understand?'

The man gave a jerky nod, and the woman whimpered an affirmative. They had learned the price of not responding.

'Very well, here it is: do you wish to die, or,' he moved towards the woman, who flinched, 'live with pain,' he slipped his fingertip under her chin and made her look at him, 'or live *without* pain?'

They were confused, suspicious of a trick. Really, where was the trust these days?

'Decide quickly,' he said, 'or I'll decide for you.'

'Live . . .' The man had trouble speaking with his jaw swollen.

'Yes?' said Forger. 'With pain? Or without?'

'W . . . without,' the man managed.

The woman began sobbing again.

'Honestly,' said Forger, 'it's a simple question.'

'And for her too,' said the man.

'All right, Father answers for you both. A shame, really, after building all this. It's like kicking over a sandcastle, isn't it? Oh well.'

He made a motion as if gathering something up, and, just like that, took their pain away. They blinked their last tears as he gestured at their bonds, the metal unclasping to drop away.

'Now,' said Forger, 'make sure you clean those cuts and scrapes, else they might turn bad. And get those bodies out of here before they fester.'

'Of course,' said the woman, rising. 'I'm not an idiot.'

Forger laughed. 'Sorry, my dear, I shouldn't tell you how to keep your own house. In fact, I should really get out of your way, and on mine. Oh, but I need some clothes, and a pack – fetch those for me will you, Father?'

'I think you'd better just leave,' said the man, glaring around his cottage angrily. 'You've already caused us enough trouble.'

'Oho! Don't think that just because you no longer feel pain doesn't mean I can't give it all back.'

The man baulked at that, at least. 'Very well,' he said dourly. 'I will get you something. It might be a little big on you, though.'

'Not for long, I hope.'

Soon Forger was walking away from the cottage, dressed in brown trousers and a loose cloth shirt, whistling cheerfully and leaving behind a couple who no longer cared that their children had died.

⁓

Forger wandered along the road, taking in the lush green landscape. He passed other cottages, and many a field of crop or beast. No doubt there was a township around somewhere, though he did not come across it. Whenever he saw people, he gave them a friendly nod and a tip of his new hat, of which he was very proud.

Then, all of a sudden, someone was walking beside him who hadn't been there a moment before.

'Hello, Forger.'

Forger lit up with pleasure. 'Salarkis! My goodness, I'd hug you if I didn't think it would bruise me. I was just wondering if I was the only one.'

'You aren't.'

'But you seem very serious, my dear. Aren't you happy to see me? Are you not pleased to live again?'

Salarkis shot Forger a look which was hard to decipher, given his pebbled eyes. 'I haven't come to talk,' he said. 'Not yet. I just wanted to see if you were here too.'

He began to unravel.

'Wait!' said Forger. 'Salarkis, don't go! Which of the others are back? Have you seen Karrak?'

It was too late. Cursing in frustration, Forger turned back to the road.

Where had he been on Salarkis's list? Who had the other Warden visited first?

⁓

As a mortal, Salarkis had never been able to threadwalk.

In the change, however, he acquired the talent, becoming the best threadwalker Aorn had ever seen. For the other Wardens such fast travel remained a difficult thing that required time and concentration, but for Salarkis it was as easy as flinging fish off a cliff. Not only that, but all he needed in order to find someone was to know their name. And there were other things he could send after names he knew too. Knives, blades of any kind – told a name by him, they would fly in search of its owner, no matter the distance between. He could not harm other Wardens that way, at least – there were strange limitations on what they could and could not do to each other, which Forger found rather tiresome – but he could track them nonetheless. No Warden hid from Salarkis.

'You're the brightest light in a sea of sparkles,' he had once told Forger, by way of explanation.

Forger kicked a stick along the road. 'Who have you seen, damn you?' he muttered.

Why the unfriendly tone in Salarkis's voice? They had always done well together, hadn't they? Made for an excellent pair of tricksters!

Admittedly they had never been as close as Forger and Karrak – dual kings of Tallahow and Ander, their cities twin centres of an ever-expanding empire. How wondrously cruel they had proved together, once they had realised their new common interests – how much fun they had had! And then, for no good reason, suddenly and without explanation, Karrak had completely disappeared. Even his crows he'd left behind, circling Ander as they called for their master – and Forger had called for him too, in his heart.

Forger had, in fact, become obsessed with finding Karrak, and had ranged far and wide but never once caught a whiff of him. Distressingly, Salarkis could not find him either – how Forger had shivered to hear that Karrak's 'bright light' had gone dark. He suspected that Yalenna, Braston or Mergan had killed him, but never figured out which of them it had been. Maybe all of them, together.

Then Yalenna and Braston had come upon him, that night he'd spent in a little cottage not far from here.

'*What did you do to him?*' Forger had roared above the howling wind, a thousand shards of broken wood narrowing to points in a swirl around him.

'*Nothing!*' shouted Yalenna. Forger suspected a lie, and sent the shard swarm whizzing at her. She had swept her arms forward, channelling the wind to blast them back at him.

'Ah yes,' Forger said, finally kicking the stick away. 'Of course I could not see the cottage – we destroyed it to pieces!'

There came a clip-clopping on the road behind, and he glanced about to see a horse pulling an empty cart, being driven by an old man. The man pushed back his hat, revealing a kindly face and proud moustache, and Forger had fun tipping his own hat in return. He liked the man right away, if only because of the distraction he provided.

'Where you heading?' the man asked.

Forger gestured up the road. 'Tallahow.'

'Me too. Want a ride?'

Forger grinned. 'That would be marvellous.'

'Name's Hanry,' the old man said, holding out his hand to help Forger up.

'Ah . . .' Forger wasn't good with lies. 'I'm Hanry too, actually.'

'Really?'

'Indeed.'

'I haven't met another Hanry in a good long while.'

'Well it's a good strong name, not to be given out lightly, eh?' Forger winked, and Hanry chuckled. He took up the reins and they rattled onward.

'So,' said Hanry, 'is Tallahow home?'

'I think so.'

'You think so?'

'Well,' said Forger, 'I've been away. I'm not sure how much it's changed since I was last there.'

'How long you been away, son?'

Forger didn't think Hanry would believe three hundred years – he almost could not believe it himself, found it incredible to think about. If the Spell had wanted the Wardens back, why had it taken so long going about it? Then again, maybe such a time frame wasn't long at all to the Spell.

Forger had been in his mid-thirties when the change had stopped him ageing, and with that in mind he tried to think up a believable answer.

'Over ten years,' he said.

'I suspect you'll find it much the same, then,' said Hanry. 'Ten years isn't much to a place like Tallahow.' He winced a little and his hand went to his stomach. Forger watched the movement with interest.

'You're in pain,' he said.

'Mmm?' said Hanry. 'Oh. Yes, trouble in my gut. Reckon I got a death lump. Not too bad most of the time, but . . . well, it ain't getting better, let that be said.'

'That's bad luck.'

'I'm not complaining, I've had a pretty good run. Managed to avoid any wife or children, unlike most fellows I know.'

Forger chuckled.

'Got family yourself?' asked Hanry.

'Me?' Forger found the idea confusing. A few skerricks of memory wafted through his thoughts, but failed to settle. 'Not really. I have a friend or two who are very dear to me. One of them I haven't seen in a while.'

'Oh?'

'He's like a brother, though not by blood.'

'I understand.'

'He went missing, though, and I haven't been able to find him.'

'Hmm,' said Hanry. 'Chance he's in Tallahow?'

'Maybe,' said Forger.

Where would Karrak go first?

'Well, I hope you find him.'

'Thank you.'

They crossed a bridge over a lively stream, where a father was teaching his son to fish. Fleetingly Forger toyed with the idea of sending the son plunging under the surface, but he resisted. He was having too much fun playing the part of the simple traveller, and so he simply tipped his hat.

'How far is it from here?' he asked.

'Oh, not too far. Should be there before nightfall. Assuming night doesn't suddenly fall in the middle of the day.'

'What was that?'

'Pardon?'

'What did you say about night falling in the day?'

'Don't you know, son? Didn't you see it for yourself?'

'I'm sorry, Hanry, but like I said, I've been away.'

'But this happened all over Aorn. For just a moment, it was as if the sun just up and left. The next moment it was back, everything normal again. Spooky, if you ask me.'

Forger frowned. 'So there's a problem with the Spell.'

'That's what some folks say. Others think it has to do with the Wardens, Braston back from the dead and who knows which of the others.'

Forger held his excitement in check. *Braston?* That was a name Salarkis certainly wouldn't visit first, which meant there was at least one other, and if there was one other, well hang it, Forger may as well go ahead and believe that they had all returned.

'Karrak,' he whispered.

'Oh!' Hanry shivered. 'There's been no talk of Karrak. Don't wish him upon us.'

'Apologies,' said Forger. 'It's just . . . well, I've always been curious about his legend. They never found out what happened to him, did they? In the years after the Wardens died?'

'Reckon from the sound of things, people were simply glad he was gone.'

'Yes, good riddance,' agreed Forger. 'A horrible bastard he was.' He tipped his hat to a lady on a horse going the other way. 'Tell me – is there any news about the other Wardens?'

'Some whisperings – oh!' Hanry gripped his stomach again, a line of sweat breaking along his brow.

'You should really see a threader about that,' said Forger.

'I mean to,' replied Hanry. 'Why do you think I'm going to Tallahow? I just hope they'll help me.'

'Why wouldn't they?'

'Oh, you know, from what I hear the ones good at healing are always in demand. They may not have time for a worn-out scrap like me.'

'They'll heal you,' said Forger. 'They'll want to – it's in their nature.'

'I hope you're right.'

The rest of the journey passed pleasantly enough. Forger looked about avidly, despite the fact not much had changed – or maybe because of it. The sun shone brightly, and the road was full of people to greet and tip hats at. Hanry told Forger rumours he'd heard about Yalenna and Stealer, and they spoke of other things as well. Forger learned that Tallahow's ruler was now a Lady Elacin, who had a reputation for being hard and shrewd in court, but generous with her people. Apparently hers was a recent rise, a troubled succession debated by some, and heads had rolled because of it. Intermittently Hanry was troubled by his guts, and after a while Forger offered to take the reins so the man could rest.

'Not much to it,' Hanry grumbled as they switched seats. 'Not much exertion in yanking a bit of leather every now and again. Doesn't change how I feel one way or the other.'

'But it's only fair I get a turn!' said Forger. He had never driven a cart, he realised – such a common thing, when he had done so much that was uncommon. It was strange and fascinating, and he slapped the reins down hard.

'Whoa, there,' said Hanry. 'We're like to lose a wheel if you rile them to that speed.'

In the late afternoon they drew close to Tallahow. The city was built on a gently tiered slope that ran up to the vertical cliff face of the eastern Roshous, against which lay Tallahow Keep. Grey walls surrounded the city, and a healthy stream of traffic ran to and from the western gate. They slowed as they joined the queue, and Hanry craned his neck to see over those ahead.

'It would be faster to walk from here,' he said, 'should you wish to.'

'That wouldn't be very polite,' said Forger. 'I'll keep you company until we cross the threshold.'

Hanry grunted. Forger could tell the pain was making him grouchy. It would be easy to reach into the man and intensify it . . . but not only would the resulting screams draw attention, he also found he did not want to.

'Listen, Hanry,' he said, lowering his voice. 'You've done me a favour and it's only fair that I return it. Can you keep a secret?'

'Unless I've a few ales in me.'

'I'm being serious.'

Hanry nodded. 'You can trust me.'

'It's for your own good, believe me.'

'Very well.'

'In that case, I'll tell you this: I can weave a thread or two myself.'

Hanry was surprised. 'You're a threader?'

'I can't heal you,' added Forger quickly, 'but, if you wish, I can ease the pain.'

A hesitant hope showed in Hanry's eyes.

'It is important that you still seek a true healer,' said Forger. 'What I can do will make you feel well but the lump will still be there, eating you up. So you must promise that you won't forget your reason for coming here.'

'I promise,' said Hanry.

Forger nodded and passed his hand over Hanry's belly. He drew the man's pain into himself, finding more there than expected. Hanry had been good at hiding it.

'By the Spell,' said Hanry in amazement, patting himself, 'I didn't believe you could really do it!'

'Remember, you aren't cured.'

'If all you have given me,' said Hanry, 'are some peaceful months before the end, then that is a great gift, fellow Hanry.'

'And yet you will still seek the healers?'

'I will. Wind and rain, I thank you.'

Forger smiled. 'Well, good. And now, with my debt repaid, perhaps I will walk on ahead. I am keen to find my friend, you understand.'

'Of course,' said Hanry.

Forger stepped down from the cart. He was a little confused about why he liked Hanry enough to bestow such favour upon him. There was something about the man though, or maybe not even about him specifically, but . . . had Forger known another Hanry, once?

It matters not, he thought. *I do whatever I like!*

'The best of luck to you, sir,' said Hanry, offering his hand, and Forger shook it.

He moved on, joining foot traffic past the line of waiting horses and carts. As he passed by grey-steeled guards watching over everyone, he tipped his hat once again.

Inside the walls, the streets were paved with darkly shining stones, and the tightly clustered houses were neat and orderly. Most people headed off down the slope to the city centre, but Forger made his way upwards, towards the keep. He turned into a street full of regal buildings with an official look to them, and came to a spiked gateway that led into the cold bare space of the keep courtyard. It was all wonderfully familiar.

The keep itself loomed overhead, squarish and flush with the cliff, carved of the same stone, staring at him with many windows. Wide stairs ran up to thick double doors, and two guards watched him suspiciously as he trotted up them. There was a smaller open doorway inset in the bigger ones, and he made to go through it.

'Oi!' The taller guard stepped in front of him. 'Where do you think you're going?'

'What's your business?' added the other.

'Why,' Forger said merrily, 'I'm here to reclaim the seat of my power.'

Swords went up, levelled at his chest.

'Must be a mad man,' said the tall one.

'Aye. I've a cousin like that. Some days, he thinks he's a bird.'

The tall one grinned.

'What kind of bird?' asked Forger.

The short one glowered at him. 'Do you know how dangerous it is to walk up here and say stupid things to us? It isn't funny, friend.'

Forger stroked his jaw. His power might still be growing, but he would have no trouble crushing the guards' hearts in their chests.

'What was that man saying?'

Two figures in silver robes emerged from the doorway – threaders. The one who had spoken was a cold-faced woman of middle years, staring at him suspiciously.

'Er . . .' said the short guard. 'Nothing, ma'am. Just something crazy – he's not a real threat.'

'Something about reclaiming Tallahow,' said the male threader. 'Unless I imagined it?'

The tall guard faltered under his piercing gaze. 'No, sir.'

'Take him to the dungeon,' said the woman.

'What?' blurted the short guard. 'I mean, excuse me, ma'am, but I think he's just a little touched.'

Forger imagined the looks of terror they would all have if they knew who he really was, and chuckled. In such a circumstance they certainly wouldn't be talking about him as if he wasn't there! It made him feel like a predator lurking in bushes, watching prey that was blissfully unaware of his presence.

'It may be the case,' said the woman, 'but Lady Elacin doesn't take chances. Besides, if he is insane, he may be repeating something he heard from somebody else.' She gave an impatient wave. 'Come on, get him inside.'

Now that there were threaders present, Forger considered attacking unwise. Maybe he could best them, maybe not – but he did not think there was any harm in waiting until he had grown a little more.

'Sorry about this, fellow,' muttered the tall guard, as he set about binding Forger's wrists.

'Don't worry,' said Forger, 'I'm just happy to be home!'

He was marched into the keep, through the lower floors towards the dungeon.

'Oh!' He stopped by a wall on which a tapestry depicted a bloody battle scene. Althalans and Plainsfolk were fighting Unwoven on a great field of yellow grass. 'That's new. What battle does that show?'

'Keep walking,' said the male threader, giving him a shove.

FEATHERS OF STONE

The muscular youth from the tavern the previous night – his name was Cedris, he'd informed them eagerly – stayed true to his word. As Rostigan and Tarzi arrived at the edge of town at daybreak, a group of young people were waiting there to travel with them. Cedris was a popular figure, it seemed, his friends keen to follow him.

As they set off, Cedris was already talking loudly and bravely in a way that Rostigan instantly found tiresome. It *was* a good thing, he supposed, that there were others to galvanise people to action, and that it didn't have to be him. What surprised him was Tarzi's hand in it, her determination to bring others to the cause. Ahead of him, she and Cedris spoke about how they would spread the word at the next settlement they came to, and rally more to Braston's army. A part of Rostigan wondered if Tarzi's motives were so golden, or if what she really sought were more stories. Maybe she even thought Cedris worthy of making them? The younger man would probably prove a willing subject, and for a moment Rostigan found himself imagining her following him instead. Jealousy flared, but he snuffed it out and let its ashes rain down into the deep place. If such a thing happened, the fact was, everyone would be better off. Rostigan would be free to start his search again – not that he had ever really stopped, but he did not relish the idea of breaking Tarzi's heart. She was good to him and he was fond of her, even if he did not truly love her. He would not see her hurt if he could help it, and she did seem to relentlessly adore him . . . why was that, anyway? What had he ever done to deserve such a thing?

His mind turned to the task at hand. *To travel to Althala and join Braston's army.* The thought almost made him laugh. And yet, for the first time in a long time, he was a little nervous too.

It was good to feel something.

'I know that look,' said Tarzi, falling back from the others. 'You're foreseeing trouble.'

'I always foresee trouble.'

'I know.'

Fortunately, for some days, there was no trouble at all. They walked in fair weather, stopping at towns where Tarzi and Cedris encouraged others to join the group. Rostigan found taverns to sit, drink and smoke in until inevitably Tarzi showed up to perform. Word, it seemed, had spread everywhere about the miraculous return of legends, and voices of doubt were fewer and further between. The

Wardens' reappearance had become accepted as fact, and everyone wanted to hear stories about them – their lives and adventures, their downfalls and deaths. Tarzi spun her tales with even more gusto than usual, and was effective at inspiring more folk to journey to Althala.

One day, as they were walking side by side, she gave Rostigan a friendly nudge.

'Come, my statue – why the dour face? You've been wearing it for days. Don't you think it's good to be doing something?'

Rostigan grunted.

'Better than scrounging for herbs in the wild,' she said.

'I like scrounging for herbs.'

She chortled. 'I know, I know. Speaking of which, you still have that curltooth, don't you?'

'Lower your voice if you wish to speak of it.'

'We, er . . . I wonder if we might sell a little? Could we? We need more supplies to keep this lot on the march. Some of them didn't bring much but the shirts on their backs.'

Rostigan gave her a flat stare. 'So I'm funding an army now?'

'No, no . . . it's just . . . well . . .'

'Piss and flame, you really believe in this, don't you Tarzi?'

She looked startled, and he realised he had spoken with fire in his voice.

'Sorry, songbird. It's just I haven't seen this side of you before. You know, wanting to give away gold and such.'

'I think you have,' she said, slightly offended. 'Not the gold part, but . . . well, what about at Sapwood? Who was it who pushed you to kill that Worm?'

'Pushed me? I was always going to kill that thing.'

'Were you, indeed?'

Cedris sidled up – as much as such a broad-shouldered fellow could sidle. 'Are you speaking about a Worm of Regret?' he asked eagerly. 'I hear they can rear taller than houses.'

'Yes,' said Tarzi, not removing her glare from Rostigan. 'Rostigan slew one some time back.'

'By the Spell, tell us the tale then! It would make a welcome change from hearing about Wardens all the time.'

'*Apologies* if I have been boring you, Cedris,' said Tarzi.

Cedris blinked. 'No, no, I did not mean that as it sounded. Please, I just think –' he turned as he walked, addressing the whole group, 'that I, for one, would enjoy hearing the exploits of the hero who walks among us!' He nodded to Rostigan, who in that moment realised he was not being thought of as some piece of driftwood dragged along in the wake of others. Was that how he'd been thinking of himself?

'Come, Tarzi,' he murmured with a smile, 'keep your followers happy.'

Tarzi gave an exclamation of vexation. 'There was a big Worm,' she said. 'Long as five horses stood nose to tail, with black skin and rotten little eyes. It wound tunnels under the village of Sapwood, feeding on happiness and leaving the people there empty of all save a sense of regret – barely able to go about their day, struck down by melancholy over past misfortunes. But luckily Rostigan came along, and killed it. The end.'

She gave a half-curtsy and folded her arms.

'Sometimes Tarzi doesn't feel like telling stories,' said Rostigan.

'I can see that.' Cedris made an exaggerated backing off motion.

Rostigan found himself chuckling, and a scowling Tarzi moved away from him.

Cedris took her place. 'So,' he said, 'you'll tell me, though, won't you – what was it really like to kill a Worm of Regret?'

Rostigan pursed his lips. 'Messy.'

―

Later that day they came to a fork in the road. A signpost stood there – to the east was Ander and straight ahead, Althala. Beside it on a pedestal stood a strange statue carved of black stone.

The figure was man-like and naked, half-crouched as if to spring, hands outstretched with sharp fingertips, its inhuman smile full of fangs. Its body was covered by overlapping scales, smooth where its manhood should be, and a tail curled around its leg, ending in a tuft of feathers. Feathers also stood in place of its hair, sticking out all which ways like some kind of wild crest.

'What's this?' said Cedris, going to stand before the statue. 'This shouldn't be! Last time I passed this way, a statue of King Ulden stood here.'

Tarzi frowned as she considered the statue – she had described the figure enough times to know who it was.

'Salarkis,' she said.

'Salarkis?' repeated Cedris, aghast. 'So someone's replaced Ulden with this . . . tribute . . . to a corrupted Warden? Who would do such a thing?'

No one answered. Rostigan kept still, watching the statue.

'We should topple it!' called a young man with a shaved head.

Angrily Cedris pushed against the statue, but it was far too solid and heavy. Some of his friends joined him, and they all heaved together, to no avail.

With a grunt of disgust, Cedris backed off. 'Come on everyone,' he said. 'We'll warn the people at the next town that some demented sculptor is vandalising their roads.'

The group moved on, though Rostigan dallied. As the feathered Warden continued to stare ahead at whatever he was planning to spring at, Rostigan looked behind him into the bushes. There the legs of poor King Ulden poked out from the vegetation, his feet cracked where they had been wrenched from the pedestal.

Rostigan frowned, and went after the group.

Some half a league onwards, Cedris gave a cry of dismay. Ahead, by the side of the road, was another statue on a pedestal. This time Salarkis was down on one knee, his finger beckoning, his fangs revealed in a fearsome snarl.

'I can't believe it!' said Cedris. 'This one was Queen Jilwyn. Who would do this? The detail is so fine – it has to be the work of some insane threader!'

Fearful looks shot about as the group imagined such a thing.

Rostigan approached, taking out his sword. He turned it slowly in his hand, almost as if he showed it to the statue . . . then, with a mighty heave, he swung it against the Warden's leg. The blade rebounded with a clang, leaving the stone unmarked.

'Do not blunt your weapon, Skullrender,' said Cedris. 'This will take time to pull down. We must tell them about it at the next town.'

On they went, and Tarzi slipped her arm through Rostigan's, sending an uneasy glance back at the statue.

'At least we know it was really stone,' she said.

No, thought Rostigan. *Stone would have chipped.*

When they came to the third statue, it looked like Salarkis was shrugging.

'Just move past the damn thing,' muttered Cedris.

In the afternoon they arrived at a sleepy little town in the midst of well-tended fields. Tarzi and Cedris immediately went to find the mayor and tell him about the statues. It would help in their recruitment efforts, Rostigan supposed, for if anyone here thought themselves remote enough to avoid the Warden's influence, this was proof they weren't.

Meanwhile, he had his own task – having finally bent to Tarzi's plaintive requests, he went looking for a local herb merchant. There were some wooden stores along the main road through town, and locals with carts of produce. He passed such a one, and overheard an exchange between a trader and an old lady.

'This apple tastes like clay,' said the lady.

'Looks fine to me,' said the trader, turning it in his hands. Where she had bitten it, the flesh was a healthy glistening white.

'Try some,' she challenged.

The trader shrugged, took a bite, and screwed up his face in distaste.

'See?'

'I got these fresh from the farm this morning,' he said confusedly, picking another from the cart. Tentatively, he took a nibble. 'This one too . . . what's wrong with them?'

'I want my coin back,' said the old lady.

Rostigan spied a store with thick purple curtains and a sign that read 'Borgan's Herbs and Potions'. *Trying too hard to seem arcane*, he thought as he went to the door.

Inside, shelves lined the walls, stocked with jars well spaced out to make them look more plentiful than they actually were. As the door banged behind him, a man – Borgan, Rostigan assumed – emerged from behind a curtain to favour him with a smile and take an alert position behind the counter.

'Good day, sir. Are you looking for anything in particular? I have some fresh ascenia, excellent for burns or bruising.'

Rostigan scanned the sad looking jars. 'I am neither burned nor bruised.'

'Ah, but you never know – next time you *are* burned or bruised, you might wish you had been more forward-thinking!'

'If I had been forward-thinking,' said Rostigan, 'then I would not be burned or bruised.'

By the look of the shop, he suspected there was little chance Borgan had the sack of gold lying around necessary to buy even a single leaf of curltooth. And, assuming he didn't, there was no reason for him to know that Rostigan carried a kingdom's ransom worth of the stuff.

'I was actually wondering if you'd be interested in purchasing some stock.'

'Ah,' said Borgan, less enthusiastically. 'Well, that depends. What do you have?'

Rostigan dumped his satchel on the counter, and began to fish out bundles for Borgan to pore over. The jar of curltooth, however, he palmed and slipped into his pocket. With it safely hidden, he pushed the satchel towards Borgan. Maybe he could earn enough from his more common findings to tide Tarzi over.

'Hmm,' said Borgan, regarding Rostigan with slightly more respect as he pushed some of the bundles aside. 'I'll definitely take the purple moss – running low on virility potions. Not the ascenia – as you may have garnered, I have enough trouble shifting the stuff. Is this milkweed?'

'Yes.'

'Wonderful. Haven't had any in stock for a while.' He gave the pale stalks a sniff. 'How long have you been carrying it?'

'A few days.'

'Hasn't gone green yet,' said Borgan approvingly. 'Oh, and black cress, yes, and . . . no, I don't need any halia.'

Rostigan remained silent as the man fussed about, sliding bundles from one pile to another.

'There,' he said finally. 'I don't suppose you'll take trade for these?'

'Do you have any food or weaponry?'

'I have a flash potion or two, handy for blinding an opponent . . .'

'Weapons of the more pointy variety, I was thinking.'

'Mmm.' Borgan tried to remember whether or not he had a stockpile of swords out the back. 'Can't say I do.'

'I'm afraid it will have to be coin then.'

Borgan cleared his throat. 'Very well. Let me see now . . .' He sized up the bundles he'd chosen, produced a piece of paper and quill, and started tallying. 'I'll give you . . . let's say two silver for each bundle, four for the milkweed . . .' His glance asked if this was acceptable, and Rostigan nodded. 'Give me a moment,' said Borgan, and disappeared behind his curtain.

He re-emerged with a cloth bag and began to count out silver. It wasn't as much as Tarzi wanted, but it would have to do. The 'troops' could eat hard-bread if they weren't paying their own way. Once they reached Althala, it would be Braston's responsibility to feed them properly.

As Borgan laid the last coin on the counter one of the shop's windows broke inwards, the glass splintering. There was a whizzing sound and Borgan gave a yelp. His hand went to his chest where, embedded through his shirt into his flesh, there quivered a thin sliver of metal.

'Wind and fire!' With a wince, Borgan drew the sliver out easily – it was the length of a pin, only the very end dotted with blood. 'What is this?'

'Something from the window?' said Rostigan dumbly.

Borgan came around the counter and went to the door. Outside, there was no one on the street.

'As if I don't have enough problems without unruly children bursting my windows!' He turned the sliver for inspection, hand shaking a little. 'But it doesn't look like anything from my building.'

Rostigan shrugged.

'Well,' said Borgan, 'the mayor will hear of this!'

Rostigan pocketed his earnings and allowed himself to be ushered out of the store.

What are you playing at, Salarkis? he wondered.

He sat on the tavern porch, puffing on his pipe. It was a peaceful spot, at the end of the main street on the outskirts of town. As the sun set, he found a melancholy stealing upon him. There seemed much to do, when all he wanted was to sit in peace. Instead, when he closed his eyes, he saw the white walls of Althala looming ahead.

Tarzi, Cedris and some of the others arrived, moving past on their way into the tavern. He gave Tarzi a nod and she plonked down next to him.

'How did it go?' he asked.

'The mayor waits on a rider to return and verify what we reported,' she replied. 'Such a strange thing – who would erect monuments to Salarkis?'

Rostigan gave his shoulders a slow roll.

'Are you going to come in?'

'No, songbird. I shall take in the air.'

She lowered her voice. 'Did you sell any curltooth?'

'I sold some of the other herbs. The local merchant could not afford such treasure.'

'Are you sure? Maybe he had a cask of coin buried out the back, left to him by his old grandmother.'

'Such an inventive mind. You should find work as a storyteller.'

'Rostigan, this is serious. We have to get as many people as we can to Althala.'

'Why is that your responsibility?'

'Because I'm a part of the world! If it fails, where will I go? Who will I drink with, Rostigan, who shall I sing to?

Who shall I lie in bed with at night with? Nobody, and nothing! Have you not seen the sky this evening?'

She pointed up at something Rostigan had been trying to ignore.

In the sky around the setting sun, among the wash of oranges and reds, darker patches could be seen, like huge, distant bruises – or as if the sun was a lantern glowing behind a sheet stained by dirty smears. Perhaps, if he hoped it, Rostigan could imagine they were the beginnings of night, somehow come ahead of greater darkness. Or . . .

'Maybe clouds,' he said.

'They aren't clouds, and you know it. The Spell is ailing. Don't *you* feel compelled to do anything? Aren't you supposed to be a brave warrior?'

Rostigan felt his face darken. 'I'm coming with you, aren't I? You never really asked if I wanted to, and nevertheless, here I am. Just don't expect me to help stir up villagers to go and get killed.'

'Of course not,' said Tarzi. 'That would require some hint of emotion, some passion on your behalf!'

She watched him carefully, as if searching for that which she'd accused him of lacking.

Rostigan took a long draw on his pipe.

'You're a strange man,' she said, rising, and went into the tavern.

Night soon swallowed the bruises in the sky. Inside, Tarzi began speaking, and all else fell to a hush. Although her purpose these days was to do more than simply entertain, she still gave a good performance, twisting words and adopting voices, bouncing about taking on characters. Sitting alone in the dark, Rostigan listened with half an ear. He didn't really want to, yet he found her words infiltrating his calm. Eventually he turned to look through the window behind him. Tarzi was in her usual place before the fire, adeptly commanding the room's attention and speaking with great gravitas. In the deep place, Rostigan knew that she rivalled the minstrels of the greatest kings.

'Before he fought Regret, Salarkis looked like any man,' Tarzi said. 'But afterwards, of all the Wardens, his appearance was the most changed. The threads that came to him from Regret, were akin to those the mad lord had used to create his monsters. Salarkis became like a monster himself, with hard scales for skin, sharp teeth, and stone feathers for hair. Rar!'

She lunged at a child on the floor, who squealed with delight.

'He also received special talents – he could travel quickly, and find someone just by knowing their name. What's *your* name, sir?'

The fellow she had singled out shifted uncomfortably in his seat. 'Tavan.'

'Well imagine, good Tavan, if you somehow earned yourself note in Salarkis's eyes. Maybe he would come to get you himself . . . or maybe he would simply speak your name to a blade and release it. Even if you were far away, the blade would fly, fly, fly until it *crashed through the glass . . .*' She spun and flung up her hands at a window, and Tavan almost jumped out of his seat, 'and deep into your breast!'

People chuckled at Tavan's fright, and he blushed.

'Well,' he mumbled, 'see how you like it, if someone says that to you!'

'Salarkis,' continued Tarzi, 'could kill anyone in the world, and he didn't even need to be there. Not his fellow Wardens, of course, or no doubt he would have sent knives to Yalenna, Braston and Mergan. Instead he acted as a messenger between the others, and delighted in joining their destruction. When Karrak attacked Galra, the city's king chose not to ride out with his army, but instead cowered in his throne room. Salarkis spoke his name to an axe and sent it over the castle walls, through a balcony door, down a hall, up some winding stairs and *then*!' She smacked her hands together. 'It burst into the throne room and spun towards the king. They say it struck him with a force that slid his throne to the wall, smashing seat and ribs with equal ease.

'Oh, they knew good times together, Karrak and Forger, Despirrow and Salarkis. Armies marched, rivers ran red, and Karrak's crows grew fat on gobbled eyes. But, one by one, Salarkis's comrades fell, or disappeared, until he was the last one left. He fled, and Yalenna and Braston hunted him a long time, sometimes together, sometimes apart. Eventually it was Yalenna who found him, in the wilds of Dapplewood, near the village that had been his childhood home.'

There came a sigh from the seat beside Rostigan. He froze, hairs prickling along his arms. No one could have taken that position without him noticing. Slowly he turned, as Tarzi's words still reached his ears.

'Little is known of their meeting. When Yalenna returned from it she claimed that she had blessed Salarkis, and that she had killed him.'

In the shadows by Rostigan, barely reached by the flickering light from inside, a figure reclined as if he had been there for hours. Scaly arms lay along the arm rests, his tail idly flicking the floorboards between his legs. He smiled at Rostigan, fangs gleaming behind the dark lips that framed them, and he tilted his head towards Tarzi inside.

'She's a pretty one,' said Salarkis. 'What's her name?'

For a moment Rostigan dared not breathe or move. Then, slowly, he set down his pipe.

'That was you,' he said, 'back on the road. Those statues.'

Salarkis gave a little bow in his seat.

'To what purpose?' asked Rostigan. 'Why show off like that? What point in sticking the herb vendor with a needle?'

'Just trying to get your attention,' said Salarkis. 'A little harmless fun. Besides, you're a fine one to talk about purpose – you who did whatever you wanted, who tore down kingdoms simply because they were there, Karrak.'

'Hush! Do not call me that.' Rostigan glanced back through the glass. No one was watching, but if someone came to the window, or stepped outside, and saw him talking to *Salarkis* . . .

'Let us go from here,' he said, rising.

'I want to hear the end of my story.'

'It's over,' said Rostigan, moving down the porch steps. 'You're dead.'

Without looking to see if he was being followed, he moved around the side of the tavern and headed out into the fields. There was a ripple in the air and a heavy crunch on the grass as Salarkis appeared beside him.

'I see your manners have not improved,' Salarkis said.

'What do you want?'

'Why, the same as you, no doubt. To know what is going on!'

'I do not care a speck,' said Rostigan, 'what is going on. It has nothing to do with me.'

'How can you say that, when we have all of us come back from the dead?'

Rostigan sighed. He supposed it would have been too much to ask for, for even one of them to have remained at rest, yet if anyone could tally them, it was Salarkis.

'I did not,' he said, 'come back from the dead.'

Salarkis was surprised. 'You didn't?'

He glanced back at the tavern, and Rostigan could see him having thoughts. It was irksome.

'You did not want me to speak your name where it might be heard,' Salarkis said slowly. 'Those people back there – they are not under your sway?'

'No.'

'They do not know who you are?'

'No.'

'You never died?' said Salarkis. 'You have been alive since . . .'

'Yes.'

'But where did you go? You disappeared! Not even I could find you, and I know your true name, no matter what false word you presently offer when it's asked of you.'

'Rostigan.'

'Rostigan,' snarled Salarkis. 'Why couldn't I find you?'

'I didn't want you to.'

'I found you today.'

'I'd forgotten to guard against the likes of you, sometime in the last three hundred years.'

'How? Please tell me, or curiosity will eat my brain.'

Rostigan supposed there was no harm in elucidating – it was not as if knowing how it was done would render the technique inert. 'I shrouded my pattern with the borrowed threads of dead crows,' he said. 'Dimming my "bright light", as it were, disguising myself as one of the flock.'

Salarkis remained confused. 'But where did you go? Why did you leave us?'

Rostigan snorted disdainfully. 'Were you such kittens, meek and mild, that you needed looking after?'

'You wound me, old friend. Why won't you explain it to me?'

'It's nothing I chose to share with you then. What makes you think I wish to now? I was living peacefully – nothing more or less – before you all came back. Now the sky is bruised, apples have no taste, and doubtless stranger things are on the way. The corruption is renewed, because of all of you.'

'You had no hand to play?' said Salarkis. 'You share no responsibility?'

'I've held my power close these many years. Unlike you, and the others, using it with reckless abandon. Sending pinpricks into innocent shopkeepers – is that worth another mark in the sky, Salarkis?'

'Innocent?' Salarkis shook his head. 'This from the slave lord of Ander? The man who chained mother to babe to hammer, so she had to hold both as she smashed rocks in the quarry? Yet he uses this word "innocent" at me, over a little jabbing?'

'I'm not that man anymore.'

Salarkis bore his fangs.

'Don't pretend you don't understand,' said Rostigan. 'It was happening to you too, before the end. You were remembering who you used to be, growing uneasy in your scales. You began to think Forger was going too far.'

'Shut up *Rostigan*.'

'Why else did you let Yalenna bless you? She found you, yes, but what of it? You could have escaped.'

'She caught me by surprise.'

'Did she? Or did you want what she offered?' Rostigan began to move back towards the road. 'You must have, else she would not have been able to force it on you. Do you still want it?'

'What makes you think I don't still have it?'

That caught Rostigan off guard. 'Do you? I did not think a blessing would survive death.'

'The rest of my pattern did, so why not a blessing?'

'That isn't an answer.'

'You're right.'

Rostigan frowned. 'What are you going to do?'

'I haven't made up my mind.'

'Have you seen him?' He might have to give a little here, he thought dully. 'Forger?'

'Briefly.'

'What was he like?'

'The same.'

'I would . . . ask . . . that you not tell him where I am. Or any of the others, for that matter. You're the only one who can find me.'

'Though will I be able to again, after today? You have a way of hiding which you may deign to remember the use of.'

'I told you, I do not use my powers anymore. I'll be on this road, walking along it, like a man.'

Back toward town, the light of the tavern on the outskirts twinkled.

'What road is this, anyway?' said Salarkis.

'From Silverstone.'

'Or, to put it another way, *to* Althala.'

'To many places,' said Rostigan.

'Either way,' said Salarkis, 'why would I strike a bargain with you? What do you have to offer me, besides distemper and accusation?'

Rostigan felt in his pocket, where a certain jar still nestled. He drew it out, undid the top, and carefully plucked out a single, crackly leaf.

'Curltooth,' breathed Salarkis. 'I haven't been able to find any since –'

'No,' said Rostigan. 'Folk say it has gone from the Spell. I found a little, however, after many years of none at all.' He twisted the leaf. 'I will give you this now if you agree to my request . . . and another later, if you do well by me.'

Salarkis smiled. 'Like old times, then? Offering scraps from your table, in exchange for my compliance?'

'Do you want it, or not?'

Salarkis held out a palm, into which Rostigan placed the leaf. Delicately, careful not to crush it in his scaly fingers, Salarkis picked the curltooth up and, to Rostigan's surprise, placed it straight into his mouth.

'What are you doing? You're meant to have it with food!'

Salarkis grinned. 'I prefer to reawaken the taste of every meal I've ever tasted.' He began to work his jaw, crushing the leaf to tiny fragments, working them into the corners of his mouth.

Rostigan thought he heard something, and glanced towards the town. Figures were moving along the road, getting closer, some of them holding lanterns.

'Rostigan, is that you?'

It was Tarzi.

'Tide's end,' he growled. 'Salarkis, they must not see you. You –'

It was too late. Salarkis, rocking back on his heels, moving his tongue around his mouth in pleasure, gleamed as light found him.

'Look!' shouted Cedris, holding a lantern aloft. 'By the Spell, it's him! It's Salarkis!'

Ruefully Rostigan made up his mind. 'I must attack you now, Salarkis,' he said quietly. 'Apologies.'

He drew his sword and swung hard against the other Warden, hurling him from his feet. Salarkis rolled, giving a stifled grunt of surprise as he also tried to keep his mouth closed to preserve the precious curltooth. Using his tail for support, he sprung back to his feet, his face furious.

'You will pay for that, warrior,' he muttered from between tightly clenched teeth.

'Get back!' shouted Rostigan, waving his sword. 'Get away from here, vile creature!'

'It wasn't statues on the road!' said Cedris. 'That's why the mayor's rider didn't find anything when he went back. It must have really been him!'

Salarkis smirked. 'What a smart fellow you are!' He threw his hands up in supplication to the sky, and did his best imitation of Cedris. 'Oh, what travesty, that someone would do this to our precious statues? Who, who could it be? Some crazy threader, maybe?'

Rostigan's sword came at him again, and he bounced backwards out of the way. Meanwhile Cedris and some of the other young folk fanned out on either side of Rostigan.

'We're with you,' said Cedris.

'You have to wedge your blade between his scales!' called Tarzi. 'It's the only way to drive through into his flesh.'

'Well,' said Salarkis, turning on Tarzi, 'somebody's been reading their bedtime stories. And who might you be?'

'You really think I'd tell you my name?' said Tarzi, though her voice faltered as she was singled out.

'Funny girl! You think I *need* your name to kill you? I can clamber through a stranger's window and stab her the old-fashioned way, should I wish to. I was just being polite.'

Whether or not it was part of a performance, Rostigan did not like Salarkis threatening Tarzi. He howled in earnest and ran at him, and they crashed to the ground together. For Rostigan, it was like falling on a sack of rocks.

'We struck a bargain,' he hissed into Salarkis's ear. 'Leave.'

Salarkis caught Rostigan's hand and bent his fingers back until there was a snap. 'This isn't over,' he said.

Rostigan fell to earth as the stony body beneath him vanished.

'Where is he?' shouted Cedris. 'Spread out! We must find him!'

'Desist,' said Rostigan. 'There will be no finding him.'

He hauled himself to his feet, wincing as he pushed his fingers back in place. It wasn't a bad hurt, and the bones would probably mend overnight – a petty slight, maybe, to remind him he was not in charge. Or maybe to maintain his disguise convincingly? Salarkis had not spoken his true name, after all, and had, when it came down to it, gone along with the charade.

'Is it bad?' asked Tarzi, gently touching his damaged hand. 'We should see if the village has a threader.'

'No!' said Rostigan, more harshly than he'd intended. Then, 'No, songbird. I'll be all right.'

'What did he want?' said Cedris, still clearly agitated and wanting something to swing his sword at. 'Was it revenge for killing Stealer?'

'I don't think so,' said Rostigan, trying to think fast. 'I suspect he was just out causing mischief, and I happened to bear the brunt of it.'

'Does he know your name?' said Tarzi worriedly, looking around as if knives might flash out of the dark at anytime.

'No,' said Rostigan. 'He did not seem to.'

'Strange that he found you out here by yourself,' said Cedris. 'Or did you –'

'Come,' interrupted Rostigan. 'Let us get back to the tavern. I am sore and in need of ale. We can postulate there about the motives of corrupted Wardens.'

Without waiting for answers, he stalked off down the road.

REGAINING STRENGTH

Forger sat in his cell, listening to a man scream. The novelty of his capture had almost worn off, and he was growing restless. Already he had played a guessing game as to whom the various bones scattered about belonged to. Some of them were so old, it was possible they had been people put down here by Forger himself.

A roach ran across the grimy floor and his fingers clamped down upon it. Idly he began to pick off its legs, feeding on little morsels of its pain. That was the thing about pain – the size of the victim did not overly matter. Pain was pain, pure and simple.

'That said,' Forger whispered to the panicked bug, 'the greatest pain comes from intelligent things, since they know what's being done to them, and have the faculties for mental anguish also.'

He rubbed his thumb and forefinger together, squashing the roach's head.

Opposite the row of cells, empty but for him, was a warmly glowing recess in which Tallahow's torturer went about his work. The man was called Yoj, and his subject, Forger had gleaned, was a noble called Artanon. Artanon was suspected of some kind of foul play that had earned him the ire of Lady Elacin. He was strapped into a metal chair, his arms running with a hundred tiny cuts, his face bruised and mangled, his fingernails burnt.

'I . . . don't know anything,' he half-mumbled, half-dribbled, even as the torturer picked up an iron rod and rested it in a brazier of coals.

'Threver says you might,' said Yoj.

'Might? Might!' wailed Artanon. 'That is not grounds for this!' His wail took on a different timbre as hot iron touched his skin.

Forger watched with interest. It was a tantalising thing, seeing another pain-giver work. He could not benefit from the results, since he was not their source, yet he had an appreciation for the art. Yoj was methodical and impassive, excellent qualities for any torturer worth his salt.

'And you need salt,' Forger told the dead roach, 'for rubbing into wounds.' He flicked it away, wiping sludge from his fingers.

It was time to make a move. As far as he could tell there were no guards besides Yoj, and the threaders who had brought him here hadn't been seen again.

Artanon passed out, and Yoj gave a little sigh.

REGAINING STRENGTH

'My turn yet?' called Forger. He rose from the shadows in the back of his cell, moving up to the bars.

Yoj glanced at him and scowled. 'You're just mad,' he said. 'Anyone can see that.'

'Aha! And what is madness, save a different way of thinking? By whose standard,' Forger ran his hand levelly through the air as if over an invisible tabletop, 'am I to be judged?'

Yoj ignored him, setting his iron in an urn of water, where it hissed and steamed.

'The threaders who sent me here,' said Forger, 'seemed to think I might know something. And I do!'

'Just be quiet, and you might avoid any hurt.'

'Neither of those things seem possible. If you were me, you'd understand.' He moved along the bars, knocking an old shin bone against them.

'Stop that!' said Yoj.

'Tell me,' said Forger, still banging away, 'is the infirmary in the same place?'

'You've spent time in the infirmary, have you? That does not surprise me.'

'Is it in the same place?' repeated Forger.

'The same place as what?' said Yoj with annoyance.

'The same place as it used to be.'

'Listen here, you're not going to the infirmary. Someone is going to come for you soon, to check the soundness of your mind. It is they who'll ask you questions.'

'What about you? You seem good at asking questions.'

'You don't have anything to tell me.'

'How do you know?'

'Because only a mad person would try to rile a torturer.'

'Shows what you know,' said Forger. 'As it happens, very soon, I'm going to topple this Elacin and make her eke the filth from under my toenails with her tongue.'

Yoj, who had been wiping his hands, put down his cloth and turned around slowly.

Forger gave him a big smile. 'Don't you believe me?' He set his hand on the cell door and surreptitiously fiddled with the lock's threads. It clicked open audibly, and Yoj's eyes slid to it immediately.

'You stay right there,' said Yoj, slipping a dagger from his belt.

Forger gave a little wave and took away Artanon's pain. Although the man was unconscious, the tautness left his posture, his head slumping in relaxation.

Yoj did not notice. 'Now,' he said, edging towards the lock, 'you leave that door closed and you won't get into more trouble. It's just an old lock that's come undone, so don't do anything stupid while I lock it again.'

'Is the infirmary,' said Forger slowly, 'in the same place?'

He gave Yoj all of Artanon's pain.

The dagger slipped from Yoj's fingers as he staggered forward on wobbling knees. He collapsed against the cell door and tried to grab the bars for support. Forger opened the door, pushing Yoj backwards to the floor. He stepped out of the cell to stand over the stricken torturer, whose frantic eyes were now full of terror.

'It's not your fault,' said Forger. 'I know that. You don't know who I am.'

'Puh . . . please . . .' managed Yoj, as he tried to crawl away. His arms, though undamaged, rippled with the fire of a hundred cuts.

'Answer my question,' said Forger, and kicked him in the stomach.

'Wha . . . what question?'

'Think, man!' shouted Forger. 'I've asked you ten times already! If you make me ask again, I'll feed you coals from the brazier!'

'It's in the same place!' cried Yoj. 'The same place!'

'See?' Forger kicked the man again. 'It's not that hard to be nice.' Stepping over Yoj, he went towards the stout dungeon door.

'Wait,' came a soft voice. Artanon was stirring in his seat, and though a patchwork of wet and dry blood crisscrossed his chest, and he had trouble speaking through puffy lips, he was no longer in any discomfort.

'What?' said Forger.

'Unbind me, sir, I beg you. You said you wanted Elacin dead? Well, so do I.'

Forger was goggle-eyed in amazement. 'You actually *were* plotting to kill her? My, you did hold out. I admire your strength of will!'

'What? No.' Artanon spat out a shard of tooth. 'I was never part of any conspiracy. But I'd say what she's done to me is reason enough to hate her, wouldn't you?'

Forger laughed. 'My goodness! She *made* herself an enemy? That truly is amusing. Very well.'

He gestured at the straps holding Artanon and they popped undone. Shakily, Artanon stood – although he couldn't feel it, his body was still very weak. His ruddy face twisted in hatred as he picked up a hammer and headed for Yoj.

'No!' said Forger, knocking the hammer from his grip with another wave. 'Your quarrel is not with him.' He opened the door, and stood aside expectantly. 'He was just doing what he was told. Leave him be.'

Artanon glowered at Yoj a moment longer, then grunted and moved past him. Forger waited for him to go through the door, then followed him out and shut it firmly behind. They stood at the bottom of a dark, narrow set of stairs.

'I've set you free, oh limping wolfhound,' Forger said, 'but now you're on your own.' He bounded up the stairs towards the fresher air of the castle proper.

'But . . . wait . . .' said Artanon, hobbling after him.

Forger laughed at his optimism, and trotted off towards the infirmary.

Forger caught a few odd looks on his way through the keep, but nothing he wasn't used to. Servants gave him a wide berth and courtiers wrinkled their noses at the smelly, dirty, plain-clothed man who strode so boldly along their majestic corridors.

'Has there been a dungeon break?' a noble scoffed to his lady friends, and they laughed behind their hands. Forger knew it was just a rude joke, that the noble did not realise he spoke the truth, yet he yearned to turn and teach them a lesson.

'Focus, my dear,' he told himself. He did not want to get bogged down, not when threaders could be waiting around any corner. He needed more strength before he was truly himself again, and he meant to get it.

In his days as Lord of Tallahow he had travelled this path often enough, and was pleased to find he still knew the way. The infirmary was on the keep's ground floor, quite near the dungeon as luck would have it – and quickly he reached the archway that led into the long, well-lit room.

There were threaders here, of course, moving from bed to bed, tending to the sick and injured. They did not worry him much, however, for they were only healers, who tended to be more skilled at restoration than destruction, so he liked his chances against them. For a moment he thought of Hanry, but his friend would not be here. This place was for soldiers, servants, nobles and other occupants of the keep. Doing a quick scan, he counted three healers, though there could be more through other arches that led to private rooms and operating chambers.

He reached out his influence to the nearest healer and felt about inside her pattern. She stopped what she was doing and frowned, obviously sensing the invasion. Quickly he gathered up a handful of the threads inside her foot, and wrenched. There was a crack, followed by a wet sucking sound, as her ankle popped out of her like a bloodied, misshapen plum. As she squealed and fell, people sat up in their beds, trying to see what was wrong. The other two threaders came running over and crouched down beside her asking what had happened. With tears in her eyes as she clutched her bloody foot, the injured threader stared around trying to work out where the attack had come from. Her gaze settled on Forger, and he gave her a wink. Then he took hold of the bed they were all clustered at the foot of, and, patient and all, sent it hurtling over them, rolling them to a ball of flesh and broken limbs under its juddering legs, to smash against the opposite wall.

Quickly he set about his task. It was easier, he had reasoned, to give people pain when they were already in it – gouge the right spots, crack the right bones, apply the right pressures, and what had merely been discomfort could be quickly turned to agony. Not to mention that this lot were in no shape to offer much resistance.

He ran from bed to bed, using his hands to harm while also sending objects flying – scalpels and scissors whisked about so randomly they even nicked him a couple of times. Mainly they found their intended targets, however, and slashed at faces or stuck into eyeballs.

A soldier ran towards him, apparently unhurt save for a bandage on his arm, and as he passed a mirror Forger gestured at it, ripping it inwards to prickle the fellow with glass. He turned back to the young man who squirmed beneath him, digging in further with his thumbs. Death showed a moment later, but the prize was won – for all their brevity, the youth's last moments had been pain clear and true. Moving on, he waved at a heavily bandaged patient, and the bandages twisted to constrict too tightly, refreshing old blood stains. At the next bed an old woman fumbled with the corner of her sheet, as if it was the only obstacle between her and escape.

Pathetic.

He pummelled her extremities, knowing she was only good for a few sound hits. Power began to course through him, straining against the inside of his skin as if his muscles grew too big.

He continued through the room as fast as he could, leaving behind splattered walls and slick floors. Each attempt by those who tried to rise against him was more laughable than the last. A couple more threaders appeared from other rooms, and these he aimed to kill quickly, finding it gratifying to see how easily he unspooled the spells they hurled at him.

'Barely a tickle,' he grunted, as he felt one of them trying to slow the blood that moved through his veins. In return he summoned all of hers, and it sprayed out of pores all over her body.

Before he knew it, he had reached the end of the room. Looking back, he saw a couple of patients he'd missed fleeing under the archway, their bed robes flapping behind them. He took a moment to drink in the scene. Some of the pain he had caused was ongoing, and continued to feed him as its sources moaned in tangled bedclothes.

'Ah,' he said, wiping his mouth as if he'd just taken a satisfying swig of water. 'That's better.'

Forger strode through the keep towards the throne room. He stood taller now and flexed his bulging arms with pleasure. The patterns behind things were clearer to his enlivened eyes, the threads that made up the world were his to twist and knot as he saw fit. The feeding frenzy at the infirmary had been just what he needed.

Guards began to swarm. There seemed to be confusion over who or what the threat actually was, and he saw several groups rush past in parallel corridors. Inevitably, however, some came upon him – evidently a dirty, blood-stained man was worth asking a few questions.

'You!' demanded a guard, braced by several other fellows. 'Who are you? What is your business in the keep?'

Forger grinned, and gave a little wave. A slight rearrangement, and suddenly the guard's nerves felt as if they were on fire. The pain spread through their number like flash contagion, and they screamed, ripped off their armour and fell to the ground to roll around, as if that was a way to smother the myriad pinpoints of agony.

'You are *my* guards, really,' he told them. 'That's why I won't damage you properly. You'll live through this, if your minds can take it.'

Forger knew the noise would bring others, so he quickly moved on. He noticed a tight servant's stairwell curling upwards, and darted into it.

''Scuse, miss,' he said, sliding around a serving girl carrying a teapot on a tray.

Several openings and levels later, he found himself at the top of the keep. Feet pounded the stairs beneath and he knew that he was being followed. He ran out into a sweeping corridor of grey stone lined with long windows that overlooked Tallahow.

'I like what you haven't done with the place,' he chortled.

Ahead, blocking the throne room doors, guards clustered to cut him off as others spilled into the corridor behind.

'There he is!' came a shout. Weapons were drawn, crossbows notched, and he slowed to a jog. Several silver robes were also present in the mix, including the two threaders who had accosted him at the gate. He reached out for the woman, intending to constrict her heart to a pip, but instead, as he tried to grip her threads, she solidified herself against his influence. She was strong and focused, and he found her pattern difficult to alter. As she pushed him out, for a moment he felt the clothes covering her, which she was not concentrating on protecting. With a snicker he ripped them from her, leaving her completely naked. She gave a gasp as she stared down at her exposed breasts and, in that moment of humiliation, he lifted her, unaltered body and all, and flung her through a window.

'He's a threader!'

'Kill him!'

He dove beneath arrows as soldiers rushed towards him, preceded by the first threader attacks. He unspooled a few spells before his fingers suddenly flopped limply, his bones melting to milk. Cursing, he reasserted his pattern, thickening his bones once more, brushing aside the influences that worried at him. He roared as he sent out more pain, giving the charging guards the same fire as those below.

Shards from the smashed window flew at him – 'That's my trick!' he growled. He caught some of them in the air and burst them to sprinkles, but several planted up and down the length his body. Angrily he brushed them out, blood welling in the punctures. The guards were now flailing and wailing, running about and crashing into each other. Threaders advanced amongst them as best they could, and he saw one stoop to a writhing man and pass a hand over him, dispelling his pain. The next moment a floating fully armoured guard crashed into Forger, knocking him from his feet. The guard was still alive and thrashing wildly until Forger grabbed his head and twisted with all his strength.

'Someone threw a guard at me!' he said incredulously as he rose.

It was the male threader from the gate, watching him meanly with fingers twitching. As he stared the man down, more attacks pinched at him from other sources, easy enough to fend off – but this fellow, Forger had a feeling, was the one to beat.

At once they both attacked, reaching for each other's hearts. Forger felt his tighten in his chest, as if an ethereal hand had squeezed it. Meanwhile he squeezed back, and sweat showed on his opponent's brow. The man's heart was like a palpating rock, and Forger could not get a grip strong enough to crush it. He slipped his influence behind the heart, and the threader's eyes went wide as he sought to counter, but Forger grasped his spine. He ripped it upwards, suspending the juddering body for a few last moments as it slid out of the man's neck into the air, until it broke free and the threader folded backwards like paper.

The remaining threaders were no competition. Flinging them from windows or popping their internals, Forger pushed his way through staggering guards as he moved to the throne room doors.

'I am Forger,' he bellowed as he burst them open, above the chorus of suffering behind him. 'Lord of Pain! Unrightful Lord of Tallahow Keep!'

He slammed the doors, jamming them tight so they became a solid wall.

The room was deep, its walls lined with mounted weapons. At the far end guards clustered around a dais upon which stood a grey velvet throne, and a middle-aged woman with dark curly hair, wearing a glossy green dress. More guards spilled in from a side entrance, though Forger did not see any threaders with them.

'You must be Lady Elacin!' he shouted.

Elacin watched him cautiously, wetting her lips as he approached. The nearer he drew, the more her guards bristled.

'Weapons down!' she barked. 'Stand aside!'

She moved through the surprised guards, making her way down from the dais to arrive before Forger at floor level.

'What's this?' said Forger. 'You do not wish to fight me?'

'We had no idea it was you, Lord Forger,' Elacin said, forcing a smile. 'Though we had heard tales of the Wardens' return, we did not . . . dare hope . . . that you would come to reclaim your old throne. But now you are here, and it's obvious that only fools would stand against you.'

'But you have not ruled for very long,' said Forger, somewhat plaintively. 'Only a year or so, I've been told. Surely you wish to hold on a little longer?'

'I would rather not rule, than be dead.'

Forger found himself at a loss. He had expected simply to kill this woman, then torture the guards for a bit until they learned to obey him. Now he had to decide what to do with her.

A man appeared at Elacin's side, old and grey in a simple brown robe.

'I am Threver, my lord,' he said, bowing. 'Advisor to the rulers of Tallahow for many decades. Perhaps I may be of help in assisting your return?'

Forger glanced between Threver and Elacin uncertainly. He flexed his hand – and saw with satisfaction that it was now almost big enough to crush a child's head. He was nearly back to his normal size. No wonder they were so scared of him!

Guards continued to funnel through the side entrance, and he noticed one limping yet shouldering through, a lurching effect that created a small stir among the rest.

'What do you suggest then, Threver?' he said.

'A peaceful handover.'

As if in refute of these words, someone fell against the other side of the sealed throne room doors, screaming in agony. Forger chuckled and gave a wave, withdrawing his influence from the afflicted guards outside. Right away, the screaming died down.

'There is no need,' continued Threver, 'for further bloodshed. Except, of course, to kill Lady Elacin.'

'What?' she blurted.

Threver ignored her, focusing on Forger. 'My lord, there must be no question over who is in charge. The people will be confused as it is, and Elacin alive would only foster debate and possibly lead to internal conflict.'

'You're a cold one, aren't you?' said Forger admiringly. 'Though I find your worries somewhat misplaced. I intend to reclaim my empire, to wage war upon the greatest powers in Aorn. Absolute loyalty is what I demand, and if I don't receive it, well, you've seen what I can do. Do I appear to be someone concerned with *politics*?'

'My lord, I only meant –'

'Lord Forger,' Elacin cut him off, 'I could be of service to you. I could –'

A crossbow bolt thudded into her chest, knocking her off her feet. Forger twisted to see who it was – and found the limping guard with crossbow dangling, laughing as he tore his helmet off.

'Artanon,' sighed Forger.

'There you are, bitch!' howled Artanon. 'Consider yourself lucky that your end was so swift!' He did a mad little dance with the crossbow, as if it was a partner. Guards watched him, ready to move but unsure if they were supposed to.

'Does my lord,' said Threver, 'wish that man seized?'

Somehow Artanon had notched another bolt. 'And you!' he shrieked, loosing it from an unsteady grip. The bolt flew at Forger, sank into his side, and his own pain blossomed.

Artanon moaned. 'By the Spell, forgive me! I did not aim for you – I meant to hit the brown-robed rat! '

'Dim comfort,' growled Forger. He gritted his teeth and yanked the bolt out. There were no threaders he would trust well enough to heal him, so he knew he had some wincing days ahead.

'I think,' he said, 'that you have earned your pain back, Artanon.'

He gave a nod and Artanon swayed on his feet, burbling.

'Seize him!' shouted Forger, and guards rushed to obey.

THE LORD OF CROWS

As the man who had killed Stealer and now fended off Salarkis, Rostigan had to be extra dour to avoid being asked questions by excitable young people. Meanwhile Cedris and Tarzi did a good job of keeping everyone moving along the road to Althala, the group larger after every town or village. Rostigan was not sure if Braston's call to arms was pre-emptive, overzealous, misguided, wise or even hypocritical. Obviously Braston considered it inevitable that his enemies would raise forces of their own, and certainly there was real fear from the populace on that count. Legends told of a time when the corrupted Wardens had all but swallowed the east, its people either destroyed or absorbed into a great marching front. The Lord of Justice tapped into that dread, his messages cropping up everywhere through the lips of threaders, encouraging all to stand with him against the coming storm. The only clouds Rostigan saw on the horizon, however, were not even clouds at all, as Tarzi had been quick to point out. The unnatural stains in the sky, which continued to appear around sunset, could only be blamed on the presence of the Wardens' themselves, twisting the world by existing in it, and using their Spell-stolen magic – and that included Braston himself. *Why*, thought Rostigan, not for the first time, *would the Spell bring back those who damage it with their very presence? Unless the ultimate purpose is to heal the Wound for good, and it matters not if there's some suffering in the short term. It's like a fever growing worse before finally breaking.*

And perhaps Braston's efforts to unite Aorn's forces were not entirely misguided. Even though Rostigan knew that he himself, at least, no longer represented the threat he once had, the Unwoven certainly needed to be dealt with. If nothing else, that was something an Althalan army might be able to do.

Tarzi used the money he'd made selling herbs to buy supplies and keep them all going. The thought that he had funded this group was enough to make him grimace. It put him too much in mind of a time when he had raised forces of his own, a time now hidden away deeply inside him.

He had been almost forty when Regret's stolen threads had changed his pattern. Things before that point were hazy, for he had been another man entirely – a good Prince of Ander, from a loving family, who might have led an unremarkable life had it not been for Regret. After suffering the change, all chances for that life were gone.

It was difficult to recall everything from his centuries in the world – to bring all relevant experiences to the forefront of his mind, especially those he had deliberately buried. But now, with would-be soldiers marching around him, and other Wardens roaming Aorn, he could not help but dwell on who he really was.

Karrak. The Lord of Crows. A dread figure of legend, a man without remorse, fear, or empathy. Reviled in his time and after by the free people of Aorn, he had brought ruin wherever his gaze fell, and ruled his own roost with uncompromising cruelty. While the other Wardens had been somewhat capricious in the chaos they caused, he had always maintained a steady focus, unrelenting in his aim to descend the world into war. Recently he had heard folk speaking his name in hushed tones, wondering if he too had returned, if the horizon would soon darken with the cawing cloud that heralded his approach. What would they think if they knew he actually marched alongside them?

Looking around at the group, he found he did not care. They did not know him. They did not know how far he had come from being Karrak.

Or how far I have fallen.

It was only Tarzi, newfound determination and all, whose heart he would not see shattered. He found himself imagining the horror in her eyes, the disgust that would fill her as she realised who she had shared a bed with all those nights, and all those playful, lazy mornings. Would she spurn him, or accept and understand?

I am Rostigan, he told himself.

It was a hollow assertion. Rostigan was just a name he used, and only for the last few decades. There had been other names before that, famous names, warriors of note in history's pages. Every time he had become known for some great deed, he'd eventually had to disappear and reinvent himself, lest people question why he did not age. It was not difficult, as long as he avoided any permanent residence. Old warriors, it seemed, were meant to fade away.

He sighed. It would not be the worst thing, for Tarzi to hate him. He knew she was not the one he searched for. She deserved better, someone who could love her as much as she loved them. And Tarzi was not *her*. In all the days since first seeing *her*, he had never found *her* like again.

He'd been sitting on his war stallion, both of them adorned with tortured pieces of metal armour. His guards clustered about him – brutes one and all, fiercely loyal, for he rewarded those society usually shunned, raising common thugs to captains. As for the rest of his army, they required a more constant effort to keep in line. Sometimes he gave deserters to Forger, to make examples of, and by the Spell they were grand examples. Karrak was more than capable of his own sadism, though, and also had a way to make his soldiers believe they fought on the side of right. With a little threading, he could make the words that left his mouth seem more real than they actually were, implanting them like belief in the minds of those who heard them. Lord of Crows, they called him, and Lord of Lies.

In fact, he watched over the results of just such tampering now. An influx of slaves in wagon cages were being driven along the ridge of the quarry in which they were destined to die, in stony land stripped of vegetation just outside Ander. King Alcrane of the Plains, it seemed, had got into a bitter dispute with Queen Cordahl of Sortree, each believing the other to be plotting conquest. The rest of the world had not understood why these formerly peaceful neighbours had clashed, especially when there was so much else to be concerned about. Nobody knew that Karrak had visited both Alcrane and Cordahl, and filled their minds with hatred and untruth, turning them against each other. They had fought until Karrak's words finally faded from them, and then they had cried together over the mutual desecration caused . . . just in time for Karrak to lead his forces against what remained of theirs and crush them with a finality that saw the Plains Kingdom and Sortree firmly under his jagged thumb.

'Come,' he said to his captains. 'I wish to inspect the new goods. See if there are any tasty morsels.' They laughed, and he led them towards the wagons.

Crows clustered in the bare branches of the few lonely trees that remained, or flapped down into the quarry to perch on rocks. They were a constant threat that kept slaves working – anyone lying down on the job ran the risk of losing an eye. There was more that one hollow socket down there in the dust and grit, serving as a reminder. Some of the birds preceded Karrak as he rode along the slave train, inspecting the sorrowful faces that peered out of cages. Usually this kind of thing warmed him, yet today he found the experience strangely empty. He'd already seen it many times – maybe too many, for the expected satisfaction did not come. It made him angry and he snarled, sticking his sword randomly through a wagon's bars. There came an answering cry inside, a thump and a child began squealing.

'Lucky dip,' he told his captains, wiping his blade, and they laughed.

They always laughed.

Two figures stumbled along behind the wagon, tied to it by their wrists. An older man, whose rangy hair and beard were streaked with dried blood, and a slip of a woman, her eyes so crinkled with worry that they drew in the freckles from her cheeks.

'This looks promising,' muttered Karrak.

The man – her father, he guessed, by the similarities in their features – almost fell, and she shoved her bonded wrists under his arm to lend balance. Suddenly a crow swooped upon him, beating its wings about his head and stabbing at his face. He cursed and struck out, powerful even with his hands tied, and sent the crow to the ground, to lie with one wing flapping uselessly.

'Well,' said Karrak, sliding from his horse, 'time to teach this new lot the pecking order. Stop the wagon!'

The driver obeyed, and the wagons following also drew to a halt.

'Look at me,' said Karrak, bringing his sword up under the man's chin, forcing him to raise his head. Fearful eyes met his, though there was anger there too.

'Who am I?' said Karrak.

The man ran his tongue over cracked, parched lips. 'Karrak,' he croaked. 'The . . . wretched . . . Lord of Crows.'

'And what have you just killed?' asked Karrak.

Without waiting for an answer, he slid the sword into the man's throat. The daughter screamed as blood poured down her father's chest and he pitched into the dust.

'Let that be a lesson to you!' roared Karrak, his voice booming along the wagon train. 'I am your master now, these crows worth more to me than you!'

'Damn you,' cried the woman, tears clearing the dirt from her hate-filled eyes. 'You are nothing but a disease, come to blight the land.'

'Watch your tongue,' said one of his captains, stepping forward with a raised hand.

Karrak blinked . . . and he saw.

Never before, or since, had patterns aligned like they had that day. A rush of imagery filled his mind, showing him how things could have been, if he had never been changed on the Spire roof, never inherited Regret's stolen threads – showing him the life that had been his to lose, an alternative to what it had become.

He would have kept on being the good Prince of Ander, would never have murdered his father and brother for the throne. On a diplomatic mission to the Plains Kingdom, he would have met King Alcrane in a different way, met his family, including his niece – a dainty girl with freckles whom he would have adored from the moment he'd seen her. He'd have found an excuse to speak with her after the official meeting, and then again the next day, lingering after negotiations had been amicably sorted. Alcrane would have watched with amusement as a royal union blossomed, giving his blessing when it was publicly declared.

In those few moments of seeing his lost past, Karrak felt something he had never known. What an amazing phenomenon it was, to care so much for someone else, to be so invested in their wellbeing, and to have someone care about him that way too, to know such togetherness and abiding friendship. The way it made him light, made him float . . . this thing was called love, he knew, and what miraculous wealth it was.

There followed a glimmer of the real past, of the night just gone – the wagon driver cackling as he raped the woman who would have been Karrak's wife, in the dirt.

Karrak came back to his surrounds as one of his captains backhanded her across the cheek. The captain gasped as Karrak's sword crunched through his spine. In a rage Karrak spun on the wagon driver, who froze like a mouse in lantern light. He brought the sword down so heavily on the man's head it sank all the way to his stomach.

Through swimming vision, he saw that his other captains were fearful, some backing away, others fighting the urge. What was he doing? He clutched his brow, trying to make sense of it – what madness had he just experienced?

'Bring her to the castle,' he growled, gesturing without daring to look. 'Unharmed,' he added and, trying not to shake, pulled himself up onto his horse.

Karrak sat in his chambers at the top of Ander Castle, the pipe in his hand long ago smouldered out. Some nights it pleased him to sit here in his armchair, staring into the fire, drifting off to sleep. There was no sleep to be found this evening, however. Not when he could all but sense her locked in a room far below, a bright glow on the edge of his thoughts.

She would never love him now, he knew that for certain. He had destroyed her home, murdered her father, and was the root cause of violation done to her. She had fallen for a Karrak in another life, a man who was not him and never would be.

What do I care? he wondered, turning the pipe to tip ash on the armrest. He could order her brought to him and do whatever he wished with her. He could speak to her, warp her mind with threaded words until she really believed she loved him – but that, he knew, would not evoke the feeling he'd had, which now haunted him. Oh, how he wanted it back, as much as he'd once wanted battle, and control and domination. All his jewels, minions and castles now seemed like hollow trophies. He had eaten the finest food, bedded the finest women, watched kings kneel before him and beg for their lives . . . and yet, for all of that, this one simple thing, this basic human experience, available to all from the lowliest peasant to the highest lord, was not available to him.

He pondered his alternative self – a smiling man, benevolent and charming. Was that who he had been? He had always seen his transformation as a glorious gain, of newfound direction and aspiration to greatness. He had never questioned the fact that ever since the change, he had been driven to *grind* and *burn* and *kill* and *conquer*, consumed by a hatred for weakness and vulnerability which gave him the strength to achieve what meeker, kinder men could not. Now he wondered if he had actually been robbed.

What if he deigned to become something like who he should have been? Surely that man was still somewhere inside, hidden amongst the anomalous threads that altered his pattern. Yet, even if he could discover him and bring him to the surface, it did not matter.

She would not love him, ever.

I should kill her. I am the Lord of Crows, not to be brought down by a lowly slave.

He rose, but the action was without conviction. He knew he could not destroy her. Even if he killed her body, her memory would live on forever.

He slumped back into his seat.

Was it the work of Regret? Some curse upon him, a leftover of the battle on the Spire? Something that had waited for the perfect moment to maliciously show him the path untaken? It certainly was in keeping with Regret's style, and Karrak did not think it unlikely, though such conjecture did little to reduce the impact of the result. Maybe it was even a sending from the Great Spell itself, as if it sensed the right of things across a great crevasse, as threads that should have found each other flapped loosely and untied.

Had she been *meant* for him?

He stood again and began pacing to ward off panic. If they had been meant for each other, had he no chance to ever rediscover that feeling? Now that he knew what he was missing, he could eat curltooth stew for the rest of time and it would never come close to satisfying him. Would the Spell ever deliver him another of her quality, or was he entirely removed from its tapestry – an aberration, a glitch, a wine stain in the corner? What if his true self was long dead, and he was nothing more than a distorted shadow? It had never crossed his mind before that *nobody* could love someone like him.

'Everything is not preordained,' he said, trying to believe it.

If he tried to *become* like the man he should have been, would he be rewarded? What if he reinvented himself, gave up this empty illusion of control in the hope that, one day, he might find her again?

He had the rest of time to try it.

A good man, he thought. He knew what such a thing looked like – he had put the mask on himself when it had suited his purposes. Could he put it on long enough to make the world believe that he was good?

Not from this starting point. He needed to begin anew. And he would lose her in the process, but it was the only way to find her again.

'What are you moping about, brother?'

Karrak spun about, for he hadn't heard anyone enter. There stood Forger, a full head and shoulders taller than he, dressed in his patchwork ensemble of leather. Looking at him now, he seemed both familiar and unfamiliar. Forger was his cohort, his confidant, a companion ruler in neighbouring Tallahow. They called each other brother – but now Karrak thought of his real murdered brother, and wondered who this strange creature was. Someone as twisted and broken as he?

Forger held out a bottle. 'I thought you'd want to toast your success!'

Karrak wished he had not come this night, yet he could not tell him to go away. Especially, he could not say what was on his mind. It would be seen as frailty, and rightly so.

'Of course.' Karrak waved at Forger's armchair, next to his own. It was larger than most, having been made specifically by the castle's master craftsman.

Forger sank into it, took a big swig of the bottle and handed it over. 'A clever piece of work,' he said, 'turning Alcrane and Cordahl against each other.'

'Yes,' said Karrak. 'Weak-willed mortals that they were.'

Forger chuckled. 'You're so morose. Looked like you were pacing a trench in the floor when I came in. You must learn to savour these accomplishments.'

'Indeed,' said Karrak, and took another swig.

'Look at me, for example,' said Forger. 'I'm blistering with power, and could have more, yet I've grown this big, and maybe it's enough. Any more and I wouldn't be able to enjoy the world, for I could no longer fit through its doors, let alone into its women! So instead I inflict a level of pain upon my people calculated to maintain my strength, and do not seek for more or less.'

'What are you saying?' said Karrak incredulously. 'You are content?'

'Perhaps. What more could a man want? Wine, maidens, a choice of castles, a chorus of suffering in his name . . . oh, I know, *they* are out there, working to take it all away. So mean, they are! Yet that's part of it too – without a little struggle a man would grow bored, don't you think?'

'You wish for conflict?' said Karrak, drinking more wine.

'Not really. But you do.'

'What?'

'Well, look at you. Since the moon was last full, you have conquered two kingdoms. Walls that stood for centuries have been ground to dust, yet I find you listless. For you, it is not enough to have *conquered*. You need to be conquer*ing*. You're like a hunter after the fox – the thrill is in the chase, but in the end what do you have?'

Karrak smacked his lips. 'What do I have, Forger?'

'A dead fox. The thing that made it enticing to you – its speed, its cunning, the challenge it represented, is gone. That said, I suppose there are ways to keep yourself entertained in the meantime. Punishing slaves, keeping the army focused. Killing your men today.'

Karrak scowled. 'You heard about that?'

'I'm not being critical, brother. I've been known to do some harm myself. Just strikes me as odd, when I know how hard you've worked to hone your captains' loyalty, to then punish them for no good reason. The mood amongst your closest will be confused, whence previously they felt exempt from your temper.'

'I do not care a jot how they *feel*.'

It was true. He did not care what anyone felt, not even Forger. No one except himself, and now her. But caring about her was almost the same as caring about himself, because she was something that he wanted. It still came down to his own selfish core.

With that realisation came decision. If all his trappings and influence and power, did nothing to satisfy him anymore, they were just a waste of time. Having earned them for himself, it was his right to leave them behind.

'You have been hanging onto that bottle for a while,' observed Forger.

Karrak took another swig and passed it over.

Forger raised it to the fire. 'To our continued success!'

'I thought you claimed to be content,' said Karrak, moving to a cabinet where more bottles waited.

'That is not to say I don't enjoy a good fox hunt! We just need to find a new fox. Like, oh, I don't know . . . the west?'

Karrak considered Forger, languishing there, jolly and tipsy and too big for his skin. He did not want to fight the man, as he would surely have to if he tried to release his slaves and give everyone their kingdoms back. Forger would see such acts as betrayal, and then Karrak would not be free.

The ground began to shake, glasses in the cabinet vibrating. Karrak reached to steady a bottle, waiting for the rumbling to pass. After a few moments, it did.

'Because of us, Yalenna claims,' said Forger. 'That's why they want us dead.'

'It's one of the reasons.'

'Do you believe it, Karrak? The streaks we now see around sunset, the quaking ground, the melted trees, the leaves that spin and never stop, never touch the ground . . . It's not our fault, is it?'

'Perhaps.'

'Aftershocks of Regret, that's all.'

'But we took the threads, my friend. From the Great Spell.'

'Yes! And look how great we have become!'

'Indeed,' said Karrak, unstoppering another bottle.

Once Forger had gone to collapse in his chambers, Karrak looked at himself in the mirror.

'Good,' he said, mulling the word over, seeing how it tasted on his tongue.

It was a question, to himself. Could he be good?

'Well,' he said, 'I'm bored as it is. Might as well give it a try.'

He shed his armour without ceremony, letting it clank to the ground around him. At his weapons rack, his hand lingered for a moment over his usual sword, but it was showy and distinctive enough to be recognised. Instead he chose a plain broadsword, strong and nondescript, and slid it into the scabbard across his back. From the cabinet he took a bag of gold, finished the remaining wine in two big gulps, and smashed the bottle in the fire. Then he went out the door.

In the kitchens, servants were startled by his presence.

'Forget I am here,' said Karrak, spinning threads into their minds, and they stopped their cringing and left him be. He set about packing himself enough food for a few days.

As he walked the bright, colourful corridors of Castle Ander, he wondered if he would see them again. Maybe all he needed was a couple of days to think, and realise what was really important. The lump-like feeling in his chest would fade. Was that why he did not dismantle his empire? Or go to a window and tell his crows: *disperse*.

Did he safeguard against the possibility that this was naught but a brief and stupid mistake?

His breath shortened as he approached the room where she was being held. There were two smirking guards at the door.

'She's been cleaned up for you, lord,' one said.

'Go to bed,' said Karrak, and the guards stiffened, and nodded. 'And kill yourselves,' he threaded, as an afterthought.

Was that *good*? he wondered, as they marched off. Aorn would be rid of two violent men, Karrak's army that little bit weaker.

He opened the door and went inside. She jumped up from her pensive spot on the end of the bed, her hair still damp, her shoulders speckled with moisture. Karrak found himself turning cold at the abhorrence in her eyes, a foreign feeling he did not care for.

She could still be his, he told himself. He could make her think she loved him. They could live in the castle together, she his doting wife.

'You're going to cast a spell on me, aren't you?' she said accusingly.

Karrak gritted his teeth. *It wouldn't be the same.*

'While my mind is still intact,' she said, 'I want to tell you that . . . that . . . ah! I cannot even find the words to describe what a loathsome burden you are to the world! No worse a monster ever slithered from its mother, would that she had birthed you off a cliff! And one day, *one day*, someone will succeed in killing you.'

Her ire was astounding.

'I saved Aorn from Lord Regret,' he said, wondering at the fact that he was driven to defend himself.

'And how would you save a baby from drowning? By throwing it to a slavering wolf?'

Karrak took a step forward, and she flinched.

'What makes you think,' he said, 'that I'm going to place you under any spell? Perhaps I won't do you that kindness. Perhaps I like my women unwilling.'

She paled at that, and he chastised himself. He had only wanted to quiet her, but threatening habits were hard to curtail.

'Come here,' he said, threading his words.

Surprisingly she resisted him – her will was very strong.

'Come with me,' he tried again. 'Take my hand. I mean you no harm.'

Finally his command sank in, taking tenuous root in her mind. He did not think it would last forever. Maybe he could not have made her love him, after all.

He led her out of the room and downwards.

'Do not see us,' he told those who crossed their path. 'Do not remember our passing.'

Out of the castle they went, into the streets, Karrak repeating his mantra to all he saw. As they exited the city via the eastern gate, he heard clinking in the quarry to the south, and grimaced.

A good man would set his slaves free.

Perhaps he would return.

They left the road and set out across flat land dotted by the lights of farmhouses. Karrak put into effect the little trick he'd come up with, to stop Salarkis from tracking him. All night they walked, mostly in silence, and when the sky began to lighten, Karrak knew he had best think about threadwalking. They were far enough from the city now that she could strike out on her own without great risk of running into patrols. Would she try to return to the Plains Kingdom, he wondered? It was still overrun with his soldiers.

'You should head to Althala,' he said. 'It is the safest place in Aorn. Braston does a good job of protecting his people.'

She gave a stiff nod.

'Go, then,' he said. 'You are free.'

'What? This is some trick, is it?'

He marvelled at her resilience – great rulers had proven easier to manipulate.

'*Go*,' he said, 'and forget about me.'

He pressed some coin into her hands.

She glanced back once or twice, frowning, and he knew she would be befuddled for a time, perhaps have difficulty orienting herself, or recalling how she came to be alone in the fields. Maybe she would return to the Plains despite his words, and get herself killed trying to free the Plainsfolk, but that was her choice now, for he had no say over what she did with her life, in this one.

Forcing himself to turn away, he felt a strange sensation prickling at his eyes.

It had been cowardly, he supposed later, to vanish without dissembling his empire, or standing up to his cohorts. He had abandoned a cart he should have set fire to, instead leaving Forger to pick up the reins. But he had been in a strange state that night, and the transition to decency had not been instantaneous. He'd wanted to be good, but for selfish reasons, so perhaps in the hurry to reinvent himself, he had actually failed to do it convincingly. To this day, he was not sure if he really cared for the people he helped, or if he'd worn the mask for so long, he had forgotten what he really looked like. He *knew* the difference between right and wrong, at least, but then again he always had – the Karrak of old had simply chosen to ignore the concepts completely. Maybe he was only acting, trying to fit into the Spell in a normal, mortal way, in hope of one day being rewarded by finding *her* again. If his persona was a facade, he was masterful at maintaining it – *look at me*, he thought, *on the road to join Braston's army, because that's what any honourable warrior would do.*

Or perhaps it was the first chance he'd had, in three hundred years, to prove that he'd really changed.

But did it matter either way? Did the Spell even care, if one could attribute *care* to such an underlying force? Would he ever slip back into its patterns as if he belonged?

And would Braston understand? Would he forgive? Yalenna might, for they had been friends once. Would she remember that?

'Come on, old statue,' said Tarzi, startling him as she took his arm. 'You're falling behind.'

Rostigan blinked – it was true. The group was growing distant on the road ahead.

'Sorry, songbird,' he said.

'Tired?'

'Just . . .'

Well, why not?

'Yes,' he said. 'A little tired.'

Her grip tightened. Following her gaze, he saw what she saw: a dappled butterfly flitting along gaily, rising and falling on a gentle breeze – backwards.

OLD FRIENDS

'Enter,' said Yalenna to the knock at the door.

She was grateful for the distraction. For some days she had been waiting for Braston to seek her out, ever since he had promised to do so. She would not go to him – he knew where she was, and she understood why he had trouble facing her. She reminded him of his fears, and he was enjoying playing ruler too much to face them.

Still, she could not wait forever. This room, plush and cheerful as it was, with its fat curtains and four-poster bed, was beginning to feel like a cell. She did not like to venture out, she had found – did not like the amazement and worship that greeted her everywhere she went, as she might once have done. The trouble was, the joy she lent people was all a lie. She was here because something had gone very wrong. She hoped, if she cloistered herself, she would limit the damage caused by her never-abating blessings. While the other Wardens ran about the world doing whatever they chose, it seemed.

'I said enter!' she repeated, rising from her chair by the window. It wasn't Braston, for the knock was far too timid.

The door opened to reveal Captain Jandryn. She had commandeered him, in a way, made him promise to report to her every day. Still nervous in her presence, however, he entered clutching his helmet to his chest.

'Thought you'd set down roots out there,' she said tersely.

'Apologies, my lady.'

This wasn't like her. She should go to Braston and wring his thick neck for making her wait this long. She would have done so already, she told herself, if she hadn't needed the time to think. What did she want Braston to do, anyway? What was their first step? She did not know, could not appeal to him until she'd figured out what she expected of him.

After what I talked him into, no wonder he doesn't want to hear my ideas.

It made her stomach turn to think of it.

'What news?' she asked.

Jandryn cleared his throat. 'From Tallahow,' he said. 'It seems that Forger has taken back his throne.'

That got her attention.

'Forger? Oh, that is fine, is it not? Braston and Forger both shifting things about, taking thrones that aren't theirs . . . I'm sure it won't have any affect on the Spell *at all.*'

She slumped back in her seat. From there she had a view through a window over the city, and the makeshift camp beyond its walls, where multitudes who had answered Braston's call to arms were being housed and trained.

'They offered *me* my old temple back, you know,' she said, 'and what did I tell them?'

'Um . . .' said Jandryn.

'I said no, of course! They already *had* a Priestess! A rightful one, come to the position by her own path! A rightful path!' She rubbed her eyes. 'Your oafish ruler had better work up the courage to visit me soon, or I am going to bless his buttocks with my foot!'

In the face of her anger, Jandryn dried up completely.

Yalenna tried to calm herself. She was the serene and peaceful Lady of Blessings, after all.

Eventually Jandryn found his courage. 'Do you wish me to take a message to the king, my lady? About you wanting to see him?'

'The *king*,' she answered, 'knows where to find me, and you can wager he hasn't forgotten I'm here.'

She ran her finger down the spines of piled books, which she'd had brought to her from the castle library. Histories, mythologies, spell books . . . none containing any hint of what she must do.

'That will be all,' she said.

Jandryn mumbled his thanks – for what, she wasn't sure – and left.

She let her head fall to her hand. Fighting the corrupted Wardens, she and Mergan had pointed Braston in many directions. Perhaps he was simply fed up with her.

Mergan – finding him was something she needed to do, at least that was certain . . . but even that she could not begin, for where to start looking? She still did not know where he had gone. Surely if he lived again, he would make his way to Althala? Yet there had been no word of him at all.

'Ah,' said a voice, and her head jerked up.

Salarkis sat grinning in an armchair opposite, wearing nothing but a belt of daggers round his waist.

'That's better,' he said. 'Let me see the one pretty face amongst us all.'

Yalenna's blood quickened. Was he here to avenge himself? She found herself both afraid, and strangely glad to see him.

Did the blessing she had given him still hold sway?

'It's good to see you too, old friend,' she said, and he chortled in a way that was not at all amiable.

⁓

Before his transformation, Salarkis might have been the best of all of them. He had a touch of wanderlust about him, and travelled the land helping people as best he could. A rare sort not driven by personal gain, but by deep-seated kinship with his fellow human beings. It had taken a while for Mergan and Yalenna to track him down, for he preferred the edges of things, where folk were most vulnerable, and souls most lost, but once they found him, it had not taken long to convince him to join them in bringing down Regret.

After the change, scant remained of the Salarkis who had been. Chaos became his entertainment, and he revelled in discovering the names of important people and sending knives to find them. Then, after the deaths of Forger and Despirrow, bodies stuck with his blades had mysteriously ceased to fall. Yalenna and Braston hunted him anyway, for it was not just his crimes he had to answer for. After a year of searching, rumours had brought Yalenna, alone, to a small village on the cusp of Dapplewood. Here she found the people afraid, for though the wood was cheerful and sunny, no one had ventured into its interior for months.

'Haunted by a black ghost, ma'am,' said one man. 'It hates the living – jealous I reckon – so best not to gain its attention.'

Into the wood Yalenna had gone, quietly and carefully, expecting only more dead ends and false trails. Instead she came upon a stout, sturdy hut in a once-cleared area that was growing overshadowed with encroaching canopy. Scattered about were family things – an outdoor table, a high chair, a wooden ball and other toys, all looking as if they'd been left to the elements for some time. Beside the hut was a thick-trunked tree, one branch dangling with a rope that had maybe once been used to swing out over the beautiful, clear pool beside the house. Now the only thing swinging from it was a man's body, cuts showing in his desiccated flesh, the blood that had spilled from them now dry stains on the tattered rags that had been his clothes. And sitting on a rock at the pool's edge was a dark figure, his feathered tail swishing in the water.

She moved towards him, bare feet padding across the grass. She did not wish to startle him, yet it became inevitable as she drew closer and still he did not notice her. One of her blessings bounced from him, unable to penetrate his scales, and his head snapped about, his snarl deepening when he saw who it was.

'Please,' she said, spreading her palms, 'can we not speak a moment? We both know you can fade at whim, and I can do nothing to stop you. But I'll go on searching for you forever if you do not hear me out.'

His eyes slid across the foliage behind her. 'Where's Braston?'

'I don't know,' she answered truthfully. 'Looking for you, yes, but not with me. We thought it best to split up to cover more ground.'

'How enterprising of you. Perhaps, though, you should leave me be. You have already dispatched the others, and I,' he glanced at the slowly turning corpse, its mouth a yawning O, 'have lost my claws.'

'It does not look like that to me.'

'Why, because of him?' He gestured at the body. 'I am not evil for killing this man.'

Yalenna wondered how long ago the deed had been done. Weeks, at least, by the state of decay – so what was

Salarkis still doing here, staring into this pool with distant eyes? She dared to hope it was a good sign.

'Who was he?' she asked.

'Nobody. A woodsman. I did not even know his name. Nor did I use magic to kill him. Those wounds I gave him with my own hands, while looking in his eyes.'

'I see. That's better, is it?'

'Yes!' Salarkis snapped. 'He was a villain – a small one, compared to some, but how badly he treated his pretty wife and little children. The tyrant of his own pathetic kingdom, and like no father should ever be with his daughters.'

Yalenna frowned. 'And where are they now, this wife and family?'

'Gone.' He gave an idle flick of fingers. 'Fled. They cried for him, that was the worst thing. But fear of me is stronger than grief, and so, gone.'

'So, you rescued them?'

'Don't go painting me in that fashion. I could have killed the bastard cleanly, but you see the marks, see how many? A slow bleed it was, nothing peaceful. So don't skip gaily down that path.'

'I wasn't about to declare you a paragon of light, Salarkis. However, Forger said something before he died – something about you getting tangled up in the web of your past.'

'Quiet about that.'

'Have you started to remember? Please, I only want to help you. We are old friends, aren't we?'

He turned back to stare into the shimmering water.

'Has it come back to you?' she pressed. 'Your former life? Was this you trying to help somebody? In your own way, in this quiet corner of the world, where no one else could see it? How long have you been sitting here, trying to make sense of this death?'

He did not answer.

'Regret touched us all,' she said, 'but perhaps, for all the ruin he caused, his latent curses did some final good. There are things you *should* regret, Salarkis.'

He got a look on his face then, which, for just a moment, made him seem like his old self.

'It's no good,' he said. 'These eyes don't cry, Priestess. This heart is cold.'

'That's not true.'

'Despirrow had his moment of Regret, and Stealer too. They saw the lives they would have led, save for the change. Yet the experience passed them by, leaving not a scratch! So why must *I* endure this torment?'

Yalenna wanted to hug him then, hard in her soft hands – but she dared not.

'Maybe because you're better than them,' she said. 'The best of all of us, with the farthest to fall.' She sighed. 'When Mergan and I asked you to come with us and kill Regret, what was it you were in the middle of doing?'

The scales of his brow kinked.

'You were helping villagers whose crops were yellowing with disease. You were initially reticent to join us, to save the world from wider evil because you could not differentiate it from what beset those farmers. Pain is pain, and theirs was yours.'

'Thank the Spell,' he spat, 'I am not so afflicted anymore. To go through life *feeling* every last thing, when there will always be pain, always misery. The moment you heal one hurt, ten more spring up, as if healing actually planted the seed! To think,' he flung up his hands in disgust, 'that I believed I could make a difference!'

'But you do still care. I can see it, *sense* it.'

'Your senses do not penetrate me.'

'I'm not speaking of threads and patterns. I can see you with my eyes, hear the quaver in your voice.'

He looked up at the sky.

'You see what is happening to the world,' she said. 'The newborns with their twisted limbs, the rents in the earth, the strange winds and the scents they carry! You know that all is crumbling – soon it won't be saved for anybody, whether they be good or evil. You do not want that.'

His shoulders slumped. 'What can I do?'

Yalenna took a deep breath. 'Let me bless you.'

He searched her face for a trick. 'You can't,' he said. He reached for one of her little bundles in the air, and it glanced off him. 'We cannot affect each other – that has always been the nature of our gifts.'

'Not without assent,' she said.

'I don't believe you.'

'Then there's no harm in letting me try.'

'What blessing would you bestow, if you could?'

'Peace,' she lied. 'I can give you peace.'

He was hesitant, and yet he wanted what she offered. The chaos he spread had spread inward also. He was a broken thing, a fragmented hybrid of all his selves.

'You cannot harm me with a blessing,' he said slowly. 'Else it would not be as named.'

'How true.'

'How do I . . . let you in?'

'Just like that.'

'Just like what?'

'By deciding to.'

He considered her offer. 'Very well,' he said. 'Bless me, then. But, if you are deceiving me . . .'

Yalenna did not wait for him to finish. In that moment of acquiescence, he was open to her powers. The blessing she had moulded for him while they talked, she sent at him. It hit him full in the chest and he jolted as if electrified, as the threads she had fashioned integrated with his pattern. He slid forward off the rock, to his knees on the grass.

'What . . . what have you done?' he gasped. 'This is not peace!'

'Empathy,' she told him. She moved to him, reaching down to set a hand on his stony brow. 'I have given yours back to you. *May you feel what others feel.*'

'No.' His eyes crinkled. 'I told you not to trick me! This will not make me the Salarkis of old!'

'Perhaps not, but at least it's something.'

'It's not a blessing, it's a curse!'

'It is not a curse to gain enhanced perception and understanding. Perhaps now you will care about your fellow man disappearing down a sinkhole of Regret's making.'

Salarkis clutched his chest. 'All I've done . . . it's all coming down on me at once.'

Yalenna kneeled before him, shedding tears for both of them.

'I'm sorry, my friend. It isn't your fault. You aren't the person you've become. Believe me, for I knew you.'

She did hug him then, and he clutched her, unwittingly crushing her shoulders in his stony hands. She pushed that pain to the back of her mind, thinking instead of what she must do. How she wished she could speak with him further and convince him of it voluntarily. He was right, however – he was not the Salarkis of old, blessing or no. He still enclosed a chaotic centre, and who knew how long until a wild mood took him, until he disappeared from her grasp. The time of the Wardens had to end. She could not take any risks.

As he leaned against her, she felt for a dagger at her waist. He did not notice her draw it free, not even as she ran it in lightly down the interlocking scales of his chest, until it notched in a crevice between them.

'Forgive me,' she whispered. He blinked at her, and she slipped the blade through his protection, into his heart.

His grip on her shoulders tightened, grinding her bones.

'You . . . you . . .'

'I love you,' she said, tears now running thick and fast.

'You bitch!' he gasped, and toppled sideways to the ground.

Quickly she set about the messy process of slipping the blade between the scales of his neck, to sever his head. That done, she watched his threads fading, until they passed beyond her perception.

Back to the Spell, she thought, with relief.

~

Now he sat in a falsely casual posture, horny legs crossed and tail swishing lazily.

'Lovely view,' he said, waving at the window. 'All Braston's new minions scurrying about. You know what makes a view better, I always find? Tea! Maybe you could tell a servant to bring some?'

'Salarkis . . .'

'I'm serious.' He smacked his lips. 'Karrak gave me some curltooth, which lingers in my teeth. Do they still make those fruity ones? Raspberry and whatnot? I warrant that would be delicious.'

'You've seen Karrak?'

'Or apple,' he went on. 'Unless, of course, something has happened to the taste of apples. But then, how could it? Surely everything is set to rights, nothing at all strange going on – not since I died *to save Aorn.*'

Yalenna sighed. 'Are you here to take revenge?'

Salarkis leapt to his feet. 'Do not contrive to sound so bored, Yalenna! After what you did to me, won't you even accept rebuke? Some modicum of distemper, that you killed me for no reason? That you were wrong – the great and wise, kind and fair Priestess of Storms was wrong? Have the decency to show some humility.'

'Yes,' said Yalenna icily, though inwardly she felt the sting of his words. 'I was wrong. I have sat here, knowing I was wrong, for days, and I certainly don't need you to clarify it further. Whatever the problem is with the world, it was not solved by killing us all.'

'By the Spell! She admits it.'

'What I was not wrong about, however, was killing you.'

Salarkis froze, save for a claw tip-tapping along the edge of a dagger. 'What?'

'You are a cowardly murderer, Salarkis. From afar you send blades to find good and decent people, revelling in the misery and tumult that you cause. So don't come bursting in here expecting an apology, unless you aim to reduce me to laughter with your indignation. You needed stamping out, and I would do it again.'

Salarkis flung the dagger at her face. With a mental flex she thickened the air in its path, slowing the blade until it dropped gently into her hand.

Salarkis sank back into his chair. 'I suppose you're right,' he said.

'So,' said Yalenna, setting the dagger on her armrest, 'why are you here? Spying for Forger, or do you bring some threatening message?'

'Neither.'

'What then?'

'I told you,' he said, his expression darkening, 'I want some damned tea!'

'Salarkis.'

'*No*, I am not here for Forger, or Karrak, or any of you. I'm here for *me*.'

'But you are in cahoots with Karrak. You said he gave you curltooth.'

Despite the situation, Yalenna found herself thinking longingly of the herb for a moment.

'And that means we are bonded allies, does it?' asked Salarkis. 'Yes, he gave me curltooth, but you won't know the reason from my lips. Suffice to say, I am not joining him in some crusade to rule the world.'

'You are still . . . conflicted?'

'Oh, yes, mightily. On the one hand there are urges to kill, to destroy . . . but, on the other . . . well . . .'

'You still remember who you were?'

'You didn't need to do it, you know. I would have come with you, would have listened to you.'

'I could not take that risk.'

'You never even asked what Regret's curse showed me.'

'I would like to hear it now.'

Salarkis stared at his hands. 'It was strange. I was alone, getting drunk, in a tavern in Galra. Empty after the invasion, just me and the rats and endless barrels. And there, in the bottom of a mug, I saw what I would have been. Nothing remarkable – a farmer!'

'You?'

'Yes. Can you believe it? It was my wife's idea – or she who would have been my wife. She did not hold with my constant wandering, but knew my love of growing things and doing good. So we bought this big farm together, took on many people to work it happily. I used my talents to make sure the corn grew tall, the strawberries fat. I became mayor of the local town. It was a quiet, peaceful life, but fulfilling. I saw it all at once, living through it in a few moments. Do you know what that does to a person, Yalenna? To remember something that never was?'

'I do.'

'You saw something too?'

Yalenna shrugged. 'A long life as Priestess. Perhaps it did not affect me as it did you, for I knew what I did instead was *still* worthwhile.'

'How nice for you,' Salarkis snarled, 'to have remained so *perfect*. Though can you really claim . . .' He seemed to catch himself, and grow a little sad. 'You must excuse me. You were not twisted beyond recognition. I did not choose this.'

'But you can choose to fight it.'

'Yes.'

Again Salarkis stood, this time without menace.

'The blessing you gave,' he said, 'did not survive rebirth.'

Yalenna stared at him in surprise. 'You want it back?'

'Empathy is what I remember most about my old self,

though as a phantom thing I cannot quite grasp hold of. Hurry and put me in reach of it, before I change my mind.'

Yalenna bit her lip. 'Not so fast.'

'Don't pretend you won't. You know I'll find it difficult to be malicious, if I feel that way again. You *want* to bless me.'

'I think you've come a long way on your own.'

'Yalenna!'

'I ask something in return.'

His tail thumped the chair behind him impatiently. 'What?'

'You say you've seen the others.'

'I will not help you fight them. I no longer care for this conflict.'

'I'm not asking you to fight them, just tell me where they are.'

Salarkis frowned. 'That sounds like a good bargain for you. Castrate me *and* track the others? I don't think so.' He flexed a sharp finger. 'I'll tell you what – you give me a thing, I'll give you a thing. That's fair, isn't it? I'll tell you where *one* of them is.'

Yalenna thought hard. Four great threats – Forger, Karrak, Despirrow and Stealer – all roamed the world. Forger was in Tallahow, that she knew . . . but the others? Yet she already knew who she would pick.

'Mergan,' she said.

'Of course, Mergan. Your old ally, your leader, in a way – and yet he left you, without word or trace. How that must have stung.'

'Are you going to tell me where he is, or not?'

'He never died, you know.'

Yalenna sat up straight. 'What?'

'You thought that he and Karrak killed each other? Wrong, I'm afraid.'

'Where is he?'

'The blessing first. Come, you know I will fulfil your request once I have it.'

Yalenna dared not argue further. In truth she wanted both things very much – Salarkis defanged and Mergan back. Between her fingers, she concentrated on weaving a potent bundle.

'You're ready?'

'Yes.'

So, as she had done before, she sent Salarkis a blessing. As it sank into him, he went taut, but his soul was prepared for the effects this time. His eyes took on a faraway look, and she let him have a moment for it all to sink in.

'Thank you,' he whispered.

'Now,' she said, 'where's Mergan?'

Stony as they were, Salarkis's eyes seemed to glitter. 'Trapped.'

'Where?' she demanded.

'In Regret's tomb.'

'Regret's tomb?'

'It's in the Roshous Peaks. When he first went missing I tried to travel to him, and appeared outside the door. Not inside, thank the Spell, but I know he's in there.'

'How?'

'There are threads about that place the likes of which I've never seen. I imagine Mergan thought he could best them, and entered. Instead, they must have enclosed him. When I was reborn, and sought everyone out, using his name took me back there again. He's still inside.'

Yalenna was horrified. 'For three hundred years?'

'For three hundred years,' said Salarkis, and winced. 'I only just realised how awful that is.'

'But why?'

'I don't know. Ask him yourself.' He shook his head. 'I was going to tell you about this before you killed me. You could have saved him from such long internment, if you'd not been so hasty to stick me.'

Yalenna felt sick. 'How do I find the tomb?'

'East of the Spire. There's a path.'

He began to unravel.

'Salarkis, wait!'

He cocked what remained of his head. 'Why?'

She could not think of an answer fast enough, to spit it out before he was gone.

Braston sat on the throne, listening to so-and-so the noble explaining his perceived border issue with such-and-such the neighbouring lord. It was a part of being king which he had somehow forgotten – to actually *sit* on the throne, and make himself available to a litany of suggestions and complaints. Orchestrating the army's growth had been his main focus thus far, so the queue of folk wanting his ear had grown quite long.

He barely heard the words being spoken. Rather, he let his vision slide to the realm of threads, to the between-depth where he was most perceptive, of which other threaders were mostly unaware. String-thin bands ran hither and thither between people and away, a glowing network of interconnectedness with every soul at the centre of a hub.

'Your judgement, your majesty?'

Braston realised the noble had finished speaking, and everyone was watching him intently for a response. He removed the fist he had been resting his bearded chin on, and gave an idle wave.

'You have already argued this case once before, yes?' he said to the noble. 'Loppolo gave you his answer and declared the matter closed. You have chosen, however, to present the case again as if it were fresh. A sneaky ploy indeed.' He raised his voice for the benefit of all. 'Hear this – I am not here to countenance opportunists seeking to re-air every grievance they did not enjoy the settling of. Now, does anyone have any *real* business to attend to?'

He let his gaze travel past the open-mouthed noble. When the man finally realised he was being summarily dismissed, he spun about, trying to pass off the reddening of his cheeks as an outraged huff.

Chortles and whispers rippled around the fountains and paths of the throne-room chamber, an amused susurrous above the trickling water. The stir met another coming from the opposite end of the room, and Braston sat up to see what had caused it. His first thought was that Loppolo had arrived, which always caused a bit of discomfort, but from his raised position, he instead saw Yalenna moving through the court, a sight which made anxiety flutter in his heart.

Although he could not see her connective threads the way he could in others, she may as well have stood in the middle of a rippled, tangled web, for all the complicated emotions she stirred in him. He knew he should not have left it so long to see her, yet he had not been able to muster the courage. He was not angry, exactly, about what she had convinced him to do – her arguments had made sense at the time, and seemed the greatest hope for setting the world right. Certainly, at the least, they had been born of good intentions. More recently, her annoyance over him taking the kingship also resonated – perhaps he *had* been too hasty and should have resisted temptation – yet her indignation was sullied by what had come before, making it something to be rejected, even when he suspected she was right. He was determined, this time, to be less of a follower and heed his own counsel, though unfortunately his instinct was not to think too hard about anything. *Tomorrow*, he had told himself every night, *I will go to her tomorrow*. But tomorrow, it seemed, had come once too often. He was ashamed, and probably rightly so, that he had left her waiting so long.

As she entered the space before the throne, it was hard to read her expression – deliberately mild, which was never a good sign. He noted she had traded her Priestess's robe for a shirt and trousers, her snowy hair tied back in a long plait. She looked ready to travel, and he wondered if he had alienated her sufficiently that she now meant to leave. The thought inspired a moment of panic and he made up his mind then and there to forgive her, for whatever it was he needed to. Giving up grudges made life easier, and although Braston did not suffer from the delusion that things could ever be simple, at least he preferred them plain.

'King Braston,' Yalenna said.

Her formality made him realise he had no wish to constrict her to the niceties of a public arena. He trotted down the steps of the dais, holding out a hand to indicate she should accompany him, and led her around the throne to a place where light spilled through tall windows, which was free of other people.

'I'm sorry,' he said immediately. 'It's unforgiveable. I should have come to you. It's just . . .'

You want to talk about the Spell, he thought. *You want to conjure up theories, and wonder what it is we should do, and chastise me, and I've no wish for any of those things. I am no better than a child.*

'I know,' she said, touching his forearm, her tone bereft of the acid he'd expected.

'You do?'

'Of course. I don't blame you for not wanting to see me. If anyone, I blame myself.'

Old, protective habits sprung to the fore. Suddenly it did not matter what Braston believed. It was more important to correct the notion that the two of them were at odds, which was nothing he desired.

Maybe *that's* what he had needed time to work out.

'It's not your fault,' he said.

Yalenna laughed bitterly.

'I mean it,' he said. 'You were just trying to make things right.'

'Yes,' she said, folding her arms to stare out the window. 'Trying.'

'Well, it worked, in a way. Didn't it? Without us in the world, by all accounts, the corruption mostly ceased.'

'Then why did the Spell bring us back?'

Braston shrugged, though he thought about the Wound.

'At any rate,' Yalenna said, 'I haven't come here to force you into conjecture.'

'No?'

'There is something of more immediate concern.'

'What is it?'

She blinked and Braston suddenly realised she was trying to hold back tears.

'Yalenna? What's wrong?'

She dabbed the corner of her eye, and sniffed. 'It's Mergan,' she said.

ENLISTMENT

Every footstep towards the walls of Althala seemed harder to take, heavier. Rostigan still could not quite believe that he approached the city voluntarily. Events seemed to have swept him along a natural course – the good warrior would surely answer the call, and so long had he played the part, he could almost avoid second-guessing himself. But he also could not help but feel that somehow, a joke was being played upon him.

Braston lurked inside the white spires, and Yalenna too, if rumours were true. What would they make of him? Did he care? They were children compared with him – *all* were children compared to him – but somehow he did not think they would consider him wise and venerable.

He toyed with the idea of not even making himself known to them. Would they recognise him, after all this time? Of course they would – it had not been 'all this time' for them, he reminded himself. They did not have the years behind them to render his face a clouded memory. Neither was it a simple matter of donning a heavy helm, or disappearing into the ranks to become one soldier amongst thousands. His name, false as it was, was well known, and Braston, with his liking for warriors, would no doubt wish to meet the great Rostigan Skullrender. Besides, he had to admit, a part of him was . . . eager? . . . to see them. Perhaps they would be impressed with the changes he had wrought in himself. Perhaps they would listen to his story, which he had never told anyone before. Perhaps he had been a man alone too long, teetering on the brink of giving up on a dream, and these two represented the nearest thing to kin that he could ever hope for.

In contrast to his introspection, the mood of the group grew increasingly lively the closer they got to the city. Young people were spreading out along the road, mixing with others who had journeyed that way. Rostigan lost sense of who was with them and who wasn't, not that it mattered anymore. They would all be absorbed into Braston's army, and any claim he had over them, for buying them bread and boots with a handful of herbs, was already forgotten. They had never been his army. He had only done as Tarzi asked.

Cedris, perhaps, would remain a visible part of his world. The young man had been keen, ever since they had met him, to ingratiate himself with them both. He looked up to Rostigan, that was plain, but his interest in Tarzi was less clear. Obviously he must know he couldn't have her, yet that knowledge would probably not diminish her allure.

Or perhaps Rostigan diminished her himself, by thinking of her in such simple terms, when actually it was the role she had played – a catalyst who had plucked Cedris from his normal life – that bound him to her. Watching them now – Cedris chattering excitably while Tarzi nodded and smiled – made Rostigan wonder if he had ever been so happy and fresh.

Cedris turned and saw Rostigan looking at them. 'Almost there!' he said with a grin.

'Yes,' said Rostigan, as the great white walls spread wide across his field of vision. 'I can see that.'

Traffic condensed through the southern gate. Guards seemed to have forsaken their usual habit of demanding to know everybody's business, instead calling out instructions for those who came to join the army. From what Rostigan heard, they were all to report to the castle square, and it was likely they would then be assigned to a camp constructed outside the walls to the north. How many had come, that the city could not hold them? Did they flock from other directions as thickly as what he saw here? He was surprised, despite what he had seen on the road, that Braston's call had proven so effective. Was it the threat of the Unwoven that stirred people to action? Or were the Wardens really so well remembered that their heroes remained so appealing, their villains so fear-inspiring?

Tarzi slipped her hand in his, which for some reason startled him. He supposed he had minstrels like her to thank for keeping their legend alive.

If 'thank' was the right word.

'Here we go,' she said.

Bumping shoulders in the throng, they made their way into the city. As expected, most people were headed toward the castle square. Tarzi suddenly seemed as if she wasn't in a hurry, her eyes darting about at the many taverns and stores that lined the road. She had wanted to visit Althala for a while, before war had become the motivation, and Rostigan could see her interest piquing.

'I find myself wondering,' he said, 'what you intend to do now, songbird?'

'What do you mean?' she replied, eyeing off a display of crispy-fried lizards on skewers.

'You are not actually going to join the army yourself, are you?'

'Why not? You've taught me how to handle a sword.'

Rostigan smiled, recalling their play-fighting, two figures sweating as they danced about each other in the wild. Still, while Tarzi was healthy and fit, there was also a buxomness to her that he could not imagine an opponent being intimidated by.

'You can strike that look of concern from your face,' she said, pinching his cheek. 'Armies aren't comprised of soldiers alone – they need entertainment too, for good morale. I can be of service in my own way.'

'I see. So, once we get to the castle, you shall inform them of the official minstrel position you've chosen to fill?'

'No, I won't talk to them at all. I shall simply hang about.'

ENLISTMENT

Rostigan chuckled and gave her buttocks a slap. 'You have it all worked out.'

'Indeed. Now, hold on a moment – I want to buy a lizard.'

At a leisurely pace they made their way to the square. Here, hordes gathered in the shadow of the castle, many voices clamouring across the white stones. To the left of the castle was the barracks, a series of connected buildings with fenced-off training areas. In front of the barracks was a wooden platform, on which stood an officer flanked by soldiers. On either side of the platform were tables, behind which carts stood heaped with weapons and armour. Long lines ran from the tables, as people waited to be questioned by the officers manning them. Rostigan watched as farmers and peasants were given equipment, young men and women who had never before handled a weapon now showing them off to each other, as they were steered by soldiers back out of the square.

The captain on the stage was speaking, trying to be heard above the tumult.

'. . . see the captains for your troop assignment. Anyone who has military training or relevant experience, line up to the right. If you are a new recruit, please join the left line. You will be given what you need for your training, then report to the northern camp unless otherwise specified. King Braston is pleased by your willingness to fight those who would destroy our way of life! We must end the threat of the fallen Wardens, for even now Forger and Karrak build their armies, even now they plot our downfall! If you have served previously in any army, please line up to the right. If not, you will be given training. Braston thanks you, Althala thanks you . . .'

'Braston,' muttered Rostigan, shaking his head.

'Come on,' said Tarzi. 'Let's line up.'

'I thought you were just going to hang about.'

'I need to make sure you don't undersell yourself. I want a good room in the barracks, as is only befitting a hero. Let these others sprawl about in the muck.'

Sighing, Rostigan allowed himself to be ushered into the lines.

After hearing several more variations of the officer's speech, he was about ready to smash the man in the mouth.

'Surely, the lines should lead *away* from the stage, as a reward for our patience . . . rather than towards this booming fool.'

'Mmm,' said Tarzi. 'Very well, my statue – let us bypass the rabble.'

'What?' he said, as she pulled him from the queue. 'But we'll lose our place!'

Three hundred years might have taught him patience, but he did not fancy needlessly starting again from the back.

'No,' she said, 'we will gain it.'

Approaching the tables, she spotted an officer standing apart, supervising some of the regular soldiers, and planted herself in front of him.

'Excuse me.'

ENLISTMENT

The officer favoured her with an up-and-down stare, while Rostigan felt a little uncomfortable with her boldness.

'The officers at the desks can answer your questions, miss.'

'What kind of hero's welcome is that?' Tarzi asked.

The officer frowned. 'Pardon me?'

'This,' said Tarzi, standing aside to 'reveal' Rostigan lurking resignedly behind her, 'is Rostigan Skullrender, champion of the Ilduin Fields. Do you think it right that the man who turned back the Unwoven, who quite possibly saved this city, who now offers his services once more, should really be made to wait –'

The officer blinked under her deluge, then held up a hand for quiet. He stared hard at Rostigan.

'You claim to be Skullrender?' he asked.

'Not claim,' said Rostigan.

'He does look like the paintings,' said one of the soldiers.

'If you speak the truth,' said the officer, 'then you are indeed most welcome. But, I am afraid to say, I cannot take your words at face value.'

'Summon Loppolo, then,' said Rostigan. 'He will remember me.'

'The king . . .' The officer winced. 'The former king is not mine, or yours, to summon at will. We have heard rumours, however, of Rostigan being seen on the road from Silverstone . . . and, even wilder, that he killed Stealer and fought Salarkis!'

'It's true,' said Tarzi.

'You really did?' asked a young soldier. 'You killed her? What happened?'

'Hush,' said the officer. 'Either way, King Braston will wish to meet the one who makes such claims. If they are true, Althala is indebted to you.'

'I would myself like to speak with Braston,' said Rostigan.

'Unfortunately the king is not presently in the castle.'

'Oh?'

'He's been called away on a grave errand.'

'What errand?'

'The king's business is his own . . . but, the way I heard it, he won't be gone overlong.'

'Perhaps,' said Tarzi, 'you should assign us quarters in the barracks against Braston's return, at which point Skullrender looks forward to being welcomed by him with open arms.'

The officer gave a slight smile. 'You are an audacious one, miss.'

'I've been called worse.'

'Please do not mistake my wariness for disrespect. I hope you are Rostigan, I truly do. These are strange times, however, and we must all be on our guard. That said, I will give you the benefit of the doubt. To deny you, and be wrong, would be a greater crime than to believe you and be proved a fool. And *I* have been called worse than that.'

Tarzi gave the man a grin. 'I like you,' she said. 'You have a nice turn of phrase about you.'

'And, may I ask, who might *you* be, miss?'

'I am Rostigan's minstrel, Tarzi.'

A couple of the soldiers sniggered and Tarzi raised an eyebrow at them. The officer, however, gave a serious nod.

'That fits. My sources tell me he travels with such a one. A beautiful woman, they say.'

'You have accurate sources,' said Tarzi.

'Cease your noise,' snapped the officer at his soldiers, and they fell silent. 'You have your orders – see to the new recruits! We must imbue them with sufficient skill to keep them alive for at least a few moments on the field. Go!' He waved away his underlings. 'And now, if you would like to accompany me, Rostigan and Tarzi, I will show you where you can stay . . . against the king's return.'

'Against the king's return,' echoed Tarzi, and gave a little curtsy.

The officer led them through the crowd towards the barracks. There, sitting on long benches before a fenced-off archery range, a number of regular soldiers sat regarding the throng with everything from amusement to disdain. Rostigan was glad Tarzi had shoved him in this direction, for he also found the wide-eyed enthusiasm of the greener recruits misplaced.

'Getting a lot in,' he observed.

'Aye,' said the officer. 'We –'

The man froze in mid-step. All noise – the chatter, clanking, footsteps, everything – ceased. Rostigan bumped into someone ahead of him, who stood as still and solid as a statue. The jagged crumples in the fellow's shirt scraped his skin, as hard as iron. Glancing about, Rostigan saw a frozen Tarzi looking at the archery range, where arrows in flight hung suspended in the air. Everything was motionless.

'Ah,' Rostigan growled. 'Took you long enough, Despirrow.'

He had been wondering when this moment would come, had in fact expected it sooner. Perhaps Despirrow had been trying to delay confirming his presence absolutely, yet finally it seemed that some need had won out. Across the whole of Aorn it would be like this, for everyone except Rostigan and the other Wardens, immune as they were to Despirrow's talent for halting the passage of time.

Where is he? Rostigan wondered. It wasn't a question he could answer – Despirrow could be around the next corner or a hundred leagues from here, and there was no way to tell. Only one thing was certain – whatever Despirrow's purpose was, it boded ill.

He started being very careful about where he stepped. With this many people in the square, a lot of dust had been kicked up. Tiny, unyielding particles hung in the air, capable of cutting through him from stomach to spine should he try to pass through them. Well did he remember the pain of moving about in frozen timescapes, but as long as he chose his path well, the wounds would be so small that he could handle them. Consciously he maintained his balance in a way he would not have normally thought about. A trip into a frozen dust cloud would be like falling on a thousand fixed needle tips.

'How long do you need, Despirrow?'

Even when they had been allies, Rostigan had not liked the man. All his charm, his easy smile, the well-groomed, prideful appearance left over from his days as court threader to Braston, all of it covered an animalistic lust, a mindless baseness that Karrak had never admired. Despirrow had ridden his and Forger's coat-tails, desiring nothing more than for life to be full of food and song and women. Didn't sound so bad, Rostigan supposed, unless one considered how Despirrow went about acquiring such things. Did he lie with some poor wench now, exempted from tableau by a strategic touch as the spell was cast?

He thought about what he would do if Despirrow ever came near Tarzi. The man scared her most, he knew, out of all the Wardens. She had told his tale recently, in fact, at one of their tavern stops on the journey here.

'After Regret,' Tarzi said, stalking before the fire, 'Despirrow and Braston returned to Althala together, but it soon became clear that the mindful and conscientious Despirrow of old had been replaced by as selfish a man as you could ever hope not to meet. Not only that, but the change had given him a most incredible gift for tying knots in the very threads of time – he could halt the world for everyone else, while he moved about freely.'

Tarzi held up a wooden ball. 'Anyone who catches this, I'll share a bed with tonight.'

Surprised men sat up straight, eyeing off the ball. Tarzi turned, and threw it in the fire. There were groans of disappointment, and a husband or two had his arm squeezed for letting one slip.

'If you had been Despirrow,' said Tarzi, 'you could have been there in time, by stepping out of it. He used his gift to hunt pretty flowers, and took them wherever he found them, even if her betrothed, or mother or father, was standing right beside her on the street, their unseeing eyes frozen as she mewled piteously, asking why they didn't help, as Despirrow set about her.'

The briefly jovial mood departed, and the women who had squeezed their husbands did it again, this time out of fear.

Tarzi shook her head as if coming out of a daze, and Rostigan wondered if she had affected herself with her own words.

'Braston sniffed out Despirrow's new nature soon enough, for the king had been through changes of his own. He was able to *see* where there was wrong in the world, and it became his obsession to remove it. And although he could not read Despirrow's threads directly, he *could* see them in the women Despirrow raped. Thus he learned the terrible truth, that he had lost his friend to a disfigurement of the soul. He went after Despirrow, but Despirrow sensed the danger and fled. It was not until years later that Braston managed to finish the job. But how?'

She cast around at blank faces, and it was the innkeeper who answered.

'Poison,' he said, while pouring into a cup.

The old man the cup belonged to shot him a scowl. 'Whaddaya say ya given me?'

'Poison,' nodded Tarzi. 'Braston went to a whorehouse Despirrow liked to visit, and left a standing order to slip a packet of powder into Despirrow's wine when he next appeared. Paid handsomely by Braston, with the promise of more if they succeeded, the whores did as they were bid. Despirrow drank the wine, and, by the time he sensed what was happening to him, it was too late. Stopping time didn't help him, since he was still his own poisoned self. He tried to reach Braston – what else could he do but try to discover what was killing him, and get the antidote? – but he could not summon the concentration to threadwalk, through the fug of pain.'

Rostigan thought of Stealer's eyes, opening even after he had split her head in two. Wardens were hard to kill – so what rare strength of poison had Braston used on Despirrow?

Nothing known to the wider world, that was certain.

Time unfroze, and immediately someone barged into him.

'Sorry!' said a youth, backing away. 'Didn't see you there, sir.'

'Rostigan?' came Tarzi's voice. 'Where did you get to?'

He had moved a little from where he'd been before the freeze, so hoped no one had been looking directly at him – if they had, it would appear as if he had blinked out of existence. Thankfully the officer was still weaving through the crowd ahead, having noticed nothing.

'Here I am.'

'Come on,' Tarzi said. 'We don't want to fall behind, lest we lose our new quarters!'

'No,' said Rostigan. 'I'm sure they will be splendid.'

'What's gotten you all grouchsome?'

Rostigan frowned. 'Nothing,' he said, in an entirely unconvincing tone.

THE LAST VASE

Great chunks of orange stone rose and fell on either side of the winding path, making for a jagged horizon. It was as if, Yalenna thought, there were hills at the top of the mountains. A strange place and unsettling, too close to the sun to support any greenery. The vegetation that did exist was thorny, dark, and gave the illusion of being dead.

Ahead of her, Braston squinted into the sky.

'What is it?'

'Thought I saw a silkjaw.'

She glanced around warily. There were plenty of monsters in the Roshous Peaks, but she had constructed about them a shimmering haze to mask their passage from eyes above. Already a flock of silkjaws had flown overhead without attacking, so she was confident that it was working. Things on the ground concerned her more.

'Come on,' said Braston, though it wasn't she who had stopped.

He was in his element – happy there was something tangible to achieve, that she had come to him with a mission instead of questions he'd rather not think on. Well, she thought, if he helped with the pieces of the puzzle, even while ignoring the completed picture, it might be enough.

'Why didn't we know about this tomb?' he muttered for the second or third time since they had arrived. That had been back down the path, towards the Tranquil Dale. They could only threadwalk to places they had already visited, and had chosen a plateau overlooking the Dale and Regret's Spire. Above the Spire, the Wound was clearly visible, its red, ugly edges framing a view of the great threads beyond. Braston had turned away from it quickly, and she had followed, and not mentioned it since. Far from being healed, it looked like it could be growing worse.

'How could we?' she replied. 'Regret planned to live forever, so why would he even build a tomb?'

'I suppose he was simply being thorough,' said Braston with a scowl.

'What I don't know,' said Yalenna, 'is why Mergan didn't tell us about it, or ask us to accompany him. Maybe he thought he was protecting us from some risk, or something equally arrogant. And what did he think he would find in there?'

'Maybe it's not really a tomb at all, but a store of Regret's foul devices and artefacts.'

'Let's just find it,' said Yalenna; this guesswork was starting to annoy her.

Ahead the ground dropped away into a gaping ravine on one side of the path. As he reached it, Braston gave a stifled exclamation and fell to a crouch, peering over the edge.

'Careful!' he hissed. 'Get down.'

She did so, creeping up beside him to peer over the edge, to see what had ruffled him.

For a moment she wasn't sure what she was looking at. At the bottom of the ravine, hidden between mountains, was something like a white lake. It wasn't water, however, but silk, cobwebbed thickly from mountainside to mountainside. The surface moved as strange lumps quivered, and here and there a long bone stuck out, or a weakly flapping wing – then a snout broke free, opening to reveal fangs. The silkjaw worked to free itself of the netting, using clawed wing tips to haul itself along the surface until it reached the edge. There it clambered up the rock face to a ledge where others were perched, testing their wings and swinging their heads about to peer at each with hollow eyes.

'By the Spell,' murmured Yalenna. 'This must be where they come from.'

'Regret's breeding ground,' agreed Braston disgustedly.

'You think he created this?'

'He must have. No other had the skill to subvert the natural order this way. No rutting, no birth . . . just *things*, coming together.'

'Come, let us away.'

'We should do something. This evil cannot be allowed to continue.'

'We have a task, Braston.'

'Maybe it would burn? Silkjaws have a weakness for fire, and this is the very stuff they're made of. We should set the whole thing ablaze.'

One of the silkjaws seemed to look up at them, though it was hard to tell from its empty gaze. Still, the effect was unnerving, and Yalenna began to inch back from the precipice.

'We have no means to make fire,' she said. 'We aren't prepared.'

He kept watching, bristling.

'Braston, don't be a fool! We will stir them against us if we remain.'

'Look!' He dropped from a crouch to lying flat. On the other side of the crevasse was an outlook, which evidently led to the Dale. Unwoven were appearing there, dragging large sacks, which they upended over the edge. Bones went tumbling down to bounce across the surface of the silken lake, until the webbing caught them up.

'They're carrying on Regret's work,' said Braston. 'Giving the silkjaws what they need to form!'

'Where did they get so many bones?'

The two of them exchanged a glance.

'The raids,' said Braston. 'They've been carrying off their victim's bodies.'

Yalenna frowned. 'I'd been imagining that was to eat them.'

'My guess also. Remarkable how that now seems preferable. This further travesty ... well, how could anyone know?' He shook his head. 'Would that someone had wiped the Unwoven out while we were gone. Or that *we* did, before going.'

She wasn't sure if there was accusation in his voice or not.

'Well,' she said, 'that's why you raise your army, isn't it? Part of it, anyway?'

He grunted.

Across the way the Unwoven had emptied the last of their sacks. They started to chant, raising their hands to the sky and dancing about.

'Now what?' said Braston.

'Who knows? Now come, please – maybe when we find Mergan, he'll help us deal with this birthing ground.'

Reluctantly Braston complied.

No sooner had they moved away from the ravine than the sound of many wing beats came from all around. Yalenna felt her skin turn clammy as white bodies rose on mass from the mountainsides. She flattened herself into a boulder's shadow, pulling Braston after her.

'Stay hidden! We cannot fight a sky full of them!'

'Calm yourself – it's not us they're after, I think. Look.'

The creatures swirled to a massive flock, biting and buffeting each other excitedly as they continued to rise.

'There's so many,' she said. 'More than existed in our time.'

'It's still our time.'

On the other side of the crevasse, the Unwoven stopped their chanting and gave a single clap. As a group the silkjaws dove, disappearing behind a mountain-top.

'Do you think,' said Braston, 'the Unwoven are controlling them somehow?'

Before Yalenna could answer, all heat went out of the air, though the sun still shone and the rocks glowed orange.

'Did you feel that?'

Braston sucked his finger and held it up to test for a breeze. Then he bent to a thorny plant that stuck up through a crack and carefully prodded it.

'Time's stopped,' he said.

'Despirrow.'

Braston nodded darkly. He looked around as if the man would leap out of hiding.

'He isn't here,' she said.

'I know.'

For a while they trod carefully as they moved on, lest some usually slight but now fixed thing in their path trip or slice them.

Eventually time started again, and Yalenna wondered what their enemy had been up to.

At the top of the path they reached a vast plateau, on a level with the surrounding peaks. At the far side was a building, a crumbling block set against a spurt of mountainside, its columns framing a doorway that led into darkness.

'Not exactly austere,' said Braston.

A drier, dustier, deader place, Yalenna could not remember. Birds had long ago abandoned these mountains, and not even twisted thorns grew here.

'Careful,' she said, as they approached the building. 'There's some strange threads about it.'

'Isn't that what we were expecting?'

Braston drew to a halt before the ominous doorway. The structure was wrapped in some kind of protection, a mesh of barbed, tightly interlocking threads that pointed inwards, keeping whatever they held inside.

'Easy enough to pass in,' Yalenna said, 'but not out?'

It was a formidable trap, the threads like none she'd ever seen, shiny and metallic to her senses. They had not been fashioned in any natural way – more of Regret's abominable work.

There was some odd refuse scattered about the entrance too – a wicker basket full of decaying bread crumbs, a bunch of flowers withered to stalks, a small knife, a few stains on the rock.

'Hello?' called Braston, making Yalenna jump. 'Are you in there, old man?'

'Braston!' she cautioned.

The threads rippled gently as his shout went through them, yet no echo returned from the dark interior.

'What?' he said. 'It's why we're here, isn't it?'

'Yes, but . . .'

Maybe Mergan was standing right there on the threshold, calling for help, unheard. The thought made her shiver.

'We have to get in,' she said.

Five thousand, four hundred and sixty seven . . .

That was the number of tiles on the floor, if he counted broken ones and corner ones as whole.

Five thousand, two hundred and twelve . . .

That was if he only counted intact ones.

Five thousand, three hundred and seventy.

That was if he matched broken ones to count as whole ones, putting together halves or thirds as best he could.

Sixteen.

That was how many vases had been in the entry corridor.

Two thousand, three hundred and fifty one.

That was how many pieces the vases now lay in, including the only whole one remaining, which counted as a single piece.

Sixteen.

That was how many stands for the vases. Or maybe they weren't vases, but urns? Perhaps the vessel was defined by what it contained, and since these contained nothing, or *had* contained nothing, it was hard to tell which they were, or had been.

Urns or vases, urns or vases . . . urns or vases . . . URNS OR VASES?

Panic seized him.

THE LAST VASE

One.

A dead spider – or, at least, there had been one, a long time ago . . . dust now, not even a mark on the ground where it had been, so maybe it did not count anymore. He pressed close, inspecting the place . . . was that still a tiny hair there, the last identifiable piece of the animal?

One.

That was the number of coffins – a sunken stone troth that had never seen Regret's corpse, its heavy lid resting against the wall beside it. There were little dents and imperfections in the lid, but they ran into and crossed over each other, so it was difficult to tell where one ended and the next began, and thus he had given up trying to find a way to count them.

He watched the last standing vase, tall amongst the broken shards of the others. He could break it too, he thought. He could change the number of pieces on the floor, give him something new to count. The temptation was great, especially when the rage came, yet this last vase he revered. There wasn't much he could affect down here, not much he could change, except this last vase.

Saving it for a special occasion?

He giggled, and the sound of his own voice frightened him.

Maybe he feared that when the last vase fell, he would truly be gone, his tenuous grasp on his sense of self finally broken. Maybe the fact that it remained proved he still had some control. Maybe it was important to know there was still a decision he could make. He could keep making it too, keep deciding to leave the vase alone – whereas, if he smashed it, there would be no decision left. Although sometimes there seemed to be another – he could decide to try and escape Regret's maze.

Not much of a maze, he would laugh, or cry. Just one corridor, really, running in a circle. Enter, and it seemed like there were two, one to the left and one to the right, but they curved towards each other and met at the entrance to the coffin room, enclosed by them in the tomb's centre. Sometimes he would see how fast he could make circuits of the corridor, around and around and around and around – but when time had no meaning, how could he measure speed?

He could still see out the entry door, could see the sun rise and set, so there was that. How many circuits could he do in one day? He never kept going long enough to find out – he would always forget what he was trying to achieve, and dwindle down to rest, only to realise later that he had failed again in his meaningless task.

Sometimes he would lie at the door looking out, but the view was the same bleak piece of rock. Sometimes he saw silkjaws or Unwoven out there, but that was an infrequent break in the monotony.

One.

That was how many bodies he had, and currently it was crawling into the coffin room. He could still make its arms and legs move, slowly getting about in his endless prison.

Was he going to get into the coffin? Not today, though sometimes he did.

Why won't you die? he screamed.

Like the other Wardens, he had stopped ageing. And if starvation was going to kill him, it was taking a really, really long time.

How he cursed his resilience as the years crept by. He had tried to kill himself in every way he could think of. A couple of times he had charged headfirst into a wall, and while he had blacked out for a time after that, his eyes had eventually opened again. These days, he barely had the strength to gain a running start.

He had tried using pieces of vase to dig around in his chest, but stabbing his heart never did any good. While he was unconscious his body would always push out the shard, and he healed and woke again. Perhaps, he had thought, if he could actually get his heart *out*, get it away from him . . . but as soon as he cut enough flesh away to attempt gripping it, he would always pass out. Then he would dream of throwing it away to bounce across the floor, until he woke up healed.

If only he still had his magic. He had been powerful, once, especially after the change. Unlike the others – what were their names? – he had not acquired any new talents, though his native skills had grown remarkably in potency. Time and again he imagined using them to rip himself apart, yet that option had left him at the door. He had parted the barbed threads to make his way inside easily enough, yet as soon as he'd crossed the threshold, his abilities had become stifled, somehow unusable. The threads had snapped closed, and he had not been able to affect them since. He tortured himself thinking that there must be some way, that his magic was still there, buried somehow . . . he went on living, after all.

After a while he had stopped trying to kill himself. There was no point. While a period of blankness seemed enticing, the fact was, it made no difference. He would always awaken to the same circumstances. There was no actual break for him, just because a few days had passed in the world without him knowing it.

His greatest hope was that the threads which trapped him would one day lose their strength. Surely they wouldn't last for all time! They had shown no signs of losing their potency, but he hoped nonetheless – if someone was to heal the Great Spell, maybe they would finally fail.

He had given up thinking that his friends might come to rescue him.

Why hadn't they come?

He had not told them where he was going. What a fool. When he had discovered this place, he'd thought perhaps there was some clue here, to help him heal the Spell once and for all, and, in his impatience, he had entered alone.

Impatience.

It was a strange word now, for one who had lived centuries in the dark.

Even though he had not told them where he was going, surely his friends would have searched for him? If either

Yalenna or Braston had disappeared, he never would have given up trying to find them. So, had they given up on him? Or had they died? Did Forger and Karrak rule out there now?

Sometimes he saw things that weren't really there. Beautiful Yalenna and courageous Braston, at the front door, finally come to set him free! Then he would wake, and how he would have wept every time, had he any moisture left in him. Sometimes he thought he saw markings on the walls, but when he looked at them, they faded away. Sometimes he imagined that the smashed vases were restored, standing proud, all *sixteen* of them.

Maybe he would go and look at his precious vase now.

He moved along the floor, running his fingers over the tiles. If he cracked some more of them, it would make for new counting. The thought made him angry, as mostly everything did. Along the corridor he went until, there, some ten paces away, the last vase stood. He sighed, relieved by the sight of it, and slumped against the wall.

Light shining through the door from outside rippled, as if something moved out there. He thought he heard voices, and grinned. More ghostly company, more illusions. He would not believe in them, but at least they broke the monotony.

A figure moved into the corridor, feeling her way.

Here she is again, he thought. *What does she have to say today?*

'Mergan?' came her sweet voice. 'Where are you?'

Always here, dear Yalenna.

A piece of vase cracked under her foot. It was a big piece too, one of the biggest left. She gave a little cry, took a stumble forwards, and knocked the stand where the last vase stood. His eyes opened wide as it tumbled, seeming to turn forever in the air. Then it smashed against the ground, into a hundred pieces – or maybe a hundred and three?

No, no, he told himself, clutching his arms, *it hasn't really dropped. Hasn't really dropped because, if it really dropped, she would really be there. I still have my vase, my precious last, it's still there. I'm just imagining that it dropped, but it hasn't really.*

'Everything all right?'

Braston's voice, from somewhere outside.

'Yes,' she answered.

Everything all right, he laughed. *My friends are here, my good old friends.*

She stepped over the debris and came a little closer, squinting down the dim corridor.

'Is someone there?' she said.

He gave a faint croak, all that he could muster from his bone-dry throat. It did not matter. Words spoken in his head were as real as the ones he heard from her.

Yes, yes, I am here. For the rest of time, I am here.

He laughed to himself, idly tracing the edges of a tile with his fingertip. It was a good one – one of his favourites.

Suddenly she was standing over him.

Sit down, he said irritably. *Don't loom! Sit down and we'll talk about old times, if that's what you wish.*

'Mergan?'

She reached for him, *touched* his shoulder. *The illusions never touched, they never touched him!* He gave a strangled gasp.

No, no! Ghosts of tears formed behind his eyes. *I cannot stand it, do not touch me! It is false!*

'He's here!' she called back down the corridor.

'Do you need help?'

'Don't step beyond the threshold!'

He slid upwards against the support of the wall, as she stared at him with amazement and horror.

Go away, torment!

'Can you talk? Mergan, you must come with me.'

She reached for him again, and he gave a little cry and tried to twist away. It was no good – she caught hold of his arm and he was too weak to resist, nothing but skin stretched over bone.

'I'm sorry, but I have to get you out of here.'

Now she was dragging him as he struggled lamely.

You will not get the better of me, spirit! I do not believe in you!

As they passed the place where the last vase had stood, he willed it to appear back on the stand. Then he realised, with growing despair, what had really happened – in his hallucinating, *he* must have smashed it! It really was gone!

A cracked expulsion trying to pass for a wail parted his lips, and still she dragged him, cutting his feet on the other vase pieces, carefully laid out in patterns he'd arranged.

No, no!

Towards the door they went, where Braston stood, holding the threads open for them from the outside.

It's not true!

Panic seized him as Yalenna thrust him towards the opening – how he hated bouncing off the barrier that trapped him here, hated knowing how strong and impenetrable it was – but suddenly he was through, falling to his knees in the blazing light, trying to blink away the pain it brought to his eyes.

'Mergan!' exclaimed Braston, coming down by his side. 'By the Spell, what has happened to you?'

And then Yalenna on his other side, weeping and trying to gather him up. He felt the realness of her, her bosom heaving against him, her arms soft and enveloping. Her tears fell upon his cheeks, ran down to slip into the cracks of his lips, bringing the sting of salt. He spluttered as if he had swallowed a river.

Were they real?

Were they real?

Summoning all his concentration, he worked his lump of a tongue, trying to form sound.

'Wa . . .'

'What's that, Mergan?' said Braston, taking him by the shoulders. 'What are you trying to tell us?'

'Wa . . . ter . . .' he managed.

'Water!' Braston near-shouted, the sound piercing Mergan's ears – so close, so real! The next moment a skin was being held to his mouth, and before he knew it water was pouring down his throat. He coughed and gulped messily.

'Be gentle!' said Yalenna, but Mergan seized Braston's wrist and didn't let go, not until all the water was squeezed into his mouth or down his front. He had never tasted anything so fresh.

He would wake at any moment, he knew, back in the dark, as parched as ever.

He released Braston's wrist, weeping piteously.

WHERE THEY WENT

Soldiers sat along wooden tables running the length of the barracks' dining hall, the buzz of their conversation filling the air.

'Standards have gone down,' muttered the man next to Rostigan, letting brown stew slop from his spoon back into the bowl.

'It's the new camp,' said a woman opposite. 'Supplies are stretched and some of the cooks have gone over.'

'Bah,' said the man. 'All these clean-eared kids.'

'You might be grateful for them soon enough,' put in Tarzi, from Rostigan's other side.

She had respected his request so far – to keep a low profile while they took in the situation, and certainly not to make a big song and dance about him being a hero – but it seemed she could only hold her tongue so long.

'And who are you?' said the man. 'You don't look like a

soldier, and certainly I haven't seen you in here before. I'd remember,' he said as he leered at her.

'Careful,' said Rostigan, staring ahead while he wiped his mouth. The man took in his stony face, went to say something more and thought better of it.

'It's not just kids, as you call them, either,' said Tarzi. 'There's plenty of people from all walks of life, come because they care about what happens to Aorn.'

'Ha!' said the man. 'Fairytales and fantasies have made folk crazy. I'll tell you this – Wardens or no, I'd like to see the army that could take Althala!'

Outside, screaming began. First one voice, barely audible . . . then two, three, more joining in, all of them sounding like murder.

'Wind and fire,' said Tarzi fearfully, 'what is that?'

Soldiers rose, glancing around uncertainly. An officer moved towards the doors that led to the square outside. They banged open before he got there, and another soldier stumbled in, his helmet hanging half off his head, blood running down his face. A white monster shambled in after him, swiping him across the back with its clawed wing-tips.

'Silkjaws,' muttered Rostigan.

'To arms!' someone shouted, and soldiers swarmed the creature. It opened its wings full-span, beating them to send forth blasts of wind. Rostigan raced to the fireplace at the end of the room and reached in for a flaming brand. Ignoring the blistering of hot wood on his skin, he leapt onto a tabletop and hurled the brand at the silkjaw. It bounced off the creature's chest with a fiery puff, and the creature reared as it began to blaze. Soldiers hacked at it, their swords cutting easily where the silk turned black.

Rostigan joined them as they spilled past the smouldering body, out into the square. There waited a sight which, in all his long years, he had never seen the likes of before.

Ghostly shapes wheeled in the sky as people fled every which way. Nearby a 'jaw landed on a frantically dashing woman, and arced back up into the sky with her struggling in its claws. Another advanced towards a courtier, who backed away with trembling hands held up pointlessly.

'No!' he cried as the creature surged forward to bite down hard with fanged maw. Blood poured from the courtier's neck into his fancy clothes, and the 'jaw raised him up to shake him savagely. Red lines spread from its mouth to soak into its silk.

The woman hit the ground with a crunch, having been dropped from a great height.

Looking upwards, Rostigan saw a 'jaw land on the side of the castle, clinging on like a bat, and batter its head against a window. The window smashed and three more 'jaws flew through it into the castle.

A pair of threaders appeared on a high balcony carrying torches, from which they sent glowing threads jagging thinly upwards, like orange lightning running from earth to sky. Far above, the 'jaws they hit burst into flames.

More soldiers poured from the barracks and castle out into the square, looking for an enemy to fight – but the surprise attack was spread over the entire city, only a few of the 'jaws within swinging distance.

'What do we do?'

It was Tarzi, beside him.

'*You* get inside.'

'No. I follow you.'

Soldiers charged at the silkjaws that had landed nearby, which stomped about gnashing their teeth in various states of redness. Rostigan watched as a group closed in on one, which seemed to realise it was surrounded and took off.

The officers present were too flustered to give any real orders. Rostigan found himself disgusted by their weakness. *Almost* without thinking about it, he unstoppered his power.

'Ears to me!' he bellowed, threading his voice so all it reached would surely pay attention. 'They are not attacking any singular place, so we cannot muster our strength. Form groups and spread into the city! Watch one another's back!'

Soldiers leapt to obey, squads of them running out of the square in different directions. Rostigan pounded after them, arriving on the street to see a cart overturned, a silkjaw crashing down on a fleeing merchant and breaking his back. Rostigan charged the beast, swinging so hard he almost took himself off his own feet. The blow sliced through bone and silk alike, and the tattered creature collapsed.

'Someone needs to get word to the camp!' said Tarzi.

So, she followed him still. Well, he could not spare the time to argue.

'I'm sure they know what's going on.'

On he ran, trying to judge where the silkjaws were landing, with streets or buildings between. He came to a tavern with the front wall wrenched open, where someone had evidently fought with fire, for the building now belched smoke. He ran inside, reached for an upended chair, broke it across his knee, and handed the legs to Tarzi.

'Get fire,' he said. 'Use a rag and cooking oil.'

As she ran behind the burning counter, a sooty tavern keeper stumbled into view, waving his own fiery brand at the sky. 'That's right!' he yelled. 'No free drinks for you!'

Tarzi returned with two chair legs, each holding a fat ball of flame. The one she handed to Rostigan consumed some kind of checked cloth.

'Dead man's shirt,' she said, her eyes a little blank.

'Keep yours with you,' Rostigan said, and headed into the street again, sword in one hand, brand in the other.

He rounded a corner to find three blood-spattered silkjaws ripping someone apart like squabbling seagulls. A gasp came from above, and he looked up to see a woman who had somehow managed to get herself onto the flat roof of a two-storey building. She backed away from a silkjaw stalking towards her, tightly holding an infant to her chest. The child began to mewl, and the three 'jaws on the ground swivelled their heads towards the enticing sound, dropping appendages from their mouths. Rostigan took in the whole situation at a glance, and knew there was no way he could get to the woman in time. He felt a twang of remorse play on his heartstrings . . . and, for a moment, it stopped his feet as he experienced a moment of sharp realisation.

He *cared*.

Here was a classic victim, the kind he would have laughed at during the height of his power. Mothers who protected their young with all their will, even if they stood against overwhelming odds – such as Karrak and a group of his leering soldiers – were to be mocked. And yet, standing here now, he experienced a sadness that he would not be able to save this woman, a feeling that would never have occurred to Karrak.

The woman backed to the edge of the roof, and sent a terrified look at what lay below. The three 'jaws on the ground craned their necks, spread their wings, and took off. Rostigan gave a shout that he hoped would distract them, but it came out dispirited, for while he might divert one or two, it was a very dim hope indeed that all four might turn about and suddenly find him the more tempting target.

Before his shout even reached them, however, his leading foot crunched against something hard, and he stumbled with a grunt. As he fell he dropped both brand and sword to put out his palms and catch the ground. He winced as cobblestones dug into his skin more severely than expected. Glancing back at whatever obstacle had felled him, an abandoned rag doll smiled her stitched smile at him.

When his foot had hit it, the doll had felt like stone.

Time had stopped.

Carefully Rostigan lifted his palms from the ground. The extra cuts and bruising had been caused by small pebbles and grit that would, under normal circumstances, have given way. He picked up his sword and the brand – having had them in his hands when time had frozen, they were now here with him in this *other* place. He was interested to see that the brand did not burn; its plumes were motionless and giving off no heat.

On the roof the woman's back foot had shuffled halfway over the edge. The 'jaw facing her was tensed to pounce, and the three that had taken off from the ground were now suspended below her at different heights.

Sometimes you have your uses, Despirrow, thought Rostigan.

He took a running leap towards the 'jaw closest to the ground. He landed on its back and it held firm underfoot. He took a short run across it and jumped up to the next one, which was angled more sharply, so he dug his feet into the nook where its wings met its shoulders, lodging and steadying himself. Then he clambered upwards, reached its neck, and inched out along its snout. The third silkjaw was more over than up, so he bent his knees for a spring. Over the gap he went, heavily onto the 'jaw's back, and kept up momentum for the last leap to the roof. He landed next to the woman and saw the stark horror in her shining eyes.

It will be all right, miss.

Now that he found himself here, it was not so clear what next to do. With no idea of how long the freeze would last, he considered the attack from each direction and wondered if the woman would keep her balance into the bargain. Then he remembered the frozen fire he carried, and smiled.

The silkjaw closest in the air had its jaws wide open, ready to snap on the woman. Taking careful aim over the short distance, Rostigan tossed the brand to clatter perfectly into the creature's gaping mouth, the fiery end furthest inside. The creature's silk was somewhat reddened, but hopefully there would be enough dry material there to set it quickly alight.

He took off his belt and tied it to his pants, then knotted the other end around the women's free wrist, attaching her to him firmly. He positioned himself before the 'jaw on the roof, raising his sword. When time came back, it would happen without warning, so he had to stay ready.

As he waited, thoughts began to swirl. He had used his powers, hadn't he, back in the square, on the soldiers. For so long he had kept them dormant – with the one necessary exception of convincing Loppolo to march to the Ilduin Fields – and then, without any hint of internal debate, he had gone ahead and unleashed them. Why? Because of the other Wardens?

His reason for stifling his own abilities had always been to go on existing without causing any harm to the Spell. That was happening now anyway, with or without him, as the others were doing whatever they pleased. If he intended to weather their presence, perhaps it was foolish to think he could do it as a mortal. Yet that was not entirely the reason, either. The situation itself was extraordinary, and so perhaps called for extraordinary actions. If he was to save as many people as possible, was it natural to do so by any means necessary? It did not mean he was going to abandon abstinence entirely, but there had to be exceptions.

. . . save as many as possible . . .

He chanced a glance at the sky. Were there crows about? Probably they had taken to hiding, if they were there at all. He could not feel them out while time was frozen, his magic as static as the fire.

He would just have to wait.

At least Tarzi would not see him blink from ground to rooftop, for she had not yet run around the corner. She had been close on his heels however, so there was every chance that seeing him suddenly up here would rattle her. How long was he going to be able to keep his secrets from her?

All at once, everything unstuck. The 'jaw in front of him, formerly intent on lunging at the woman, was thrown off by his sudden appearance in its way. The woman yelped as he dragged her away from the edge with his momentum as he swung, slicing the silkjaw across the face, cracking the bones that gave shape to its head. There was the sound of an impact, and he spun about, manoeuvring the woman behind him with his free hand. The leading silkjaw clung to the edge, its mouth working furiously as it tried to spit out the fire that consumed it. One of the others that followed crashed into it and they fell together, leaving a trail of glowing filament. The last one managed to dodge past them, to land clumsily on the roof.

The woman was in a panic now, pulling at Rostigan as she struggled to be free. With one hand holding her baby, and the other tied to him by the wrist, she was having some trouble.

'It's a simple knot!' snapped Rostigan. 'Get it undone and get off the roof!'

A moment later the belt fell against him loosely, and he knew she had succeeded. As the final 'jaw advanced, he heard her retreating down a flight of stairs.

On the street below, Tarzi skidded around the corner, stopping to take in the scene with surprise. The two fallen 'jaws were not yet dead, as the blood that streaked them meant some silk remained to hold their rickety bones together. As a combined mass of wings and limbs, they began a lurching, entangled crawl towards Tarzi. She steeled herself and ran forward to meet them, clubbing them with her torch, dancing in and out of range of their dangerous bits, and stamping hard on grasping wing-tips.

Rostigan dealt with the final 'jaw quickly, executing double downward sweeps on each of its shoulders to break the framework of its wings. He gave it a decent kick, sending it backwards off the edge, to land in Tarzi's pile.

'Finish that one off for me, will you?' he said, leaning

over the edge with a grin. He could not help but admire the pluck of his minstrel in that moment.

'How did you get up there so fast?' she asked, between hits.

'Jumped,' he shrugged.

'I can hear the lyrics now,' grunted Tarzi. *'As he fought the monsters city-wide, he scaled buildings in a single stride.'* She put her boot through the last opening jaw.

'Nice,' he said.

Her rhyming made him think of Stealer's power. He'd tried to forget about it – it was simply another talent he dared not use – but now he'd opened the gates. He was dubious about it working – the threads of Regret-made creatures had never been easy to affect. Like the Wardens, they had their own set of rules, many of them unknown.

May as well see.

He spied a 'jaw hurtling downwards some distance away, and intoned words.

Silkjaw, no more.

His poetry found no target, and his voice did not echo out of the air. The 'jaw dove out of view, whole and unaffected. Just as he'd suspected.

From his vantage he could see parts of the camp over the walls. With plenty of fires burning in the open there, he suspected the 'jaws had mostly avoided it. Now its soldiers, some with less than a day's training, were spilling through the city gates, calling to one another as they flooded the streets.

'Are you coming down from there?' called Tarzi, a note of worry in her voice.

A couple of people pounded along the street, skirted wide of Tarzi, and banged loudly through a door into a dark house to hide. Both he and Tarzi looked back the way they had come, but nothing seemed to be in pursuit.

'Hold a moment,' he answered.

At least some of his talents might still prove useful.

He stepped back from the edge so she could not see him, and raised his arms.

Hear me.

In the night, for leagues around, hundreds of dark little minds stirred.

Take to the skies.

His crows were doubtful – their master had not spoken to them in a long time, and they were forgetful of him. Also, they knew that the skies were full of threat.

The white ones must fall! he thundered.

Why? they seemed to reply. *Why, why, why . . .*

Never mind why! You will do as your lord commands!

Near and far, from all around, he felt them taking flight, their cawing filling the sky.

They have not eyes, as you know them, but shred their wings and they will fall.

Various images began to reach his mind's eye. Against a background of stars, several crows converged on a single silkjaw, their beaks tearing bundles from its wings. They could only pluck small amounts at a time, but, as they worked together, the 'jaw had trouble staying aloft. It tried to fight them off but fast became tattered, and soon it whorled downwards, one wing beating frantically in ever-increasing circles.

Some of his crows were getting hurt, or killed – buffeted by larger wings, their own snapped, and little heads became concussed . . . but they were faster and more mobile than the silkjaws, and attacked in groups. More and more of them arrived, and the 'jaws wheeled about, trying to work out how to deal with this unexpected new enemy.

Do well, said Rostigan, *and there will be reward.*

Excited by his words, the crows went about their task with renewed vigour. He did not like to promise such things, but the birds would earn their due. If the city had a tomorrow, its corpses would be cleared away – but there should still be time for an eye or two.

'Rostigan!' came Tarzi's voice, containing a note of worry. 'Where are you?'

Quickly he went down the stairs and through the building, seeing no sign of the woman he'd rescued. Hopefully she had crawled into a cupboard or some such, if she had any sense.

He burst out onto the street, where Tarzi was relieved to see him.

'Thought you were going to leave me,' she said, a hint of tears about her.

'I did suggest you stay inside,' he offered back a little begrudgingly, though he took her and held her close.

Several 'jaws passed overhead, aiming for a neighbouring street, and they heard someone calling orders. Moving towards the sound, they came upon a squad of soldiers led by a threader, who was springing sparks from a torch to light their arrows. One of the 'jaws went down flaming and crashed into a house, while the others arced back up into the sky.

'Stay inside, citizens,' came shouted words from somewhere. 'Lock your doors and bar your windows.'

It seemed that, following the initial surprise, the army was finally getting organised.

Rostigan let his mind go back up to his crows, taking in a bird's eye view of the city. The streets were emptying of commoners, and variously sized groups of soldiers moved about. Others still funnelled through the northern gate from the camp, spreading into the city quickly. Fires were dotted about, such as the one blazing on the roof where the flaming 'jaw had just now crashed, and some of them were growing larger. White shapes whizzed past, or fell, abandoned by the pecking crows once they started to plummet. Crows fell too, amidst a rain of black feathers. He blinked back to his own vision and saw feathers falling around him. More feathers than bodies, at least.

'Crows!' he heard someone yell. 'What curse is upon us now?'

'This must be Karrak's doing!' answered somebody else. 'He sent silkjaws first, now his crows!'

Tarzi's grip on Rostigan tightened. 'Do you think that's true?'

Rostigan scowled. 'No,' he said. 'No one but Regret could command silkjaws. And look – the crows are not after the people.'

He pointed at a silkjaw trailing loose strands, dogged by cawing attackers.

'They fight the silkjaws?' said Tarzi in amazement.

'Maybe they're just being territorial?' said Rostigan lamely. *Lord of Lies*, he had been called, but what he offered up now by way of explanation felt like a poor excuse for falsehood.

A threader reached up towards the burgeoning fire on the nearby roof, and, with a flick of his wrist, wrenched apart the flames to twining twists. There would be others working similarly, and though it had been scorched, Althala would not burn.

In the sky, the silkjaws seemed to be climbing, others taking off to join them.

'They're leaving!' someone shouted.

It was true. With fire and sword waiting for them, no large groups of unprotected townsfolk left to dive upon, and the crows attacking too, it seemed the bloodthirsty and opportunistic attack was over. All over the city, cries of defiance chased the departing silkjaws up into the air . . . but there were many dead as well, and Rostigan knew the morrow would not be a joyful one.

Feast while you can, he sent his crows.

REUNION

It was much cooler now, the fall of night having robbed the Roshous Peaks of heat. On the plateau, some distance from the tomb, Yalenna and Braston sat watching Mergan eat all the food they had brought with them. Braston was eager to threadwalk home, but he was making an effort to be patient. Mergan was not ready – even he could see that.

Yalenna found it hard to accept the state they had found Mergan in. She remembered a strong and lively old man, and would not have recognised this bedraggled, grey, painfully thin fellow on the street, even without the wild beard and long hair tangled down his back. His clothes were threadbare rags, amazing they still clung to him after all this time, and he smelled of ancient dust. At least the water and food were having some effect, returning a speck of colour to his cheeks. His body might heal quickly . . . what really concerned her was his mind.

He muttered and sent them darting glances, still uncertain if they were really here. He was not even convinced that *he* was here. To see him this way broke her heart – to know that, while she and Braston had slumbered peacefully, he had been trapped in living anguish.

We should have kept looking. Oh, we should have.

He was turning a small piece of bread in the air, hovering it just above his finger. He gave a flick, and it sped into his mouth, where he snapped it up.

'Magic,' he whispered, and she nodded.

Only briefly had she felt what he had endured for centuries. Upon entering the tomb, her blessings had evaporated, and all threading ability with them. It had been odd and uncomfortable, as if she had forgotten how to breathe, and she had deeply feared that it would last – even though, as she thought about it now, losing her blessings was the very thing she was trying to do.

'Ah,' Mergan said, smacking his lips, 'is there any more bread?'

'Not here,' said Braston.

'What about those berries?'

'My friend, once we return to Althala, I will throw you a feast to rival anything your imagination can conjure.'

'My imagination?' echoed Mergan worriedly.

Braston looked to Yalenna for help.

'Do not fear.' She laid a hand on Mergan's knee and he stared at it in confusion. 'You will be well again.'

Was it him she tried to convince?

He took a deep breath. 'How long?' he croaked.

'Pardon?'

'How long inside?'

'Oh.' Yalenna almost could not bring herself to tell him. 'Some . . . three hundred years.'

She thought this would shock him, but he gave no immediate reaction. Instead he picked his teeth, producing a berry seed, which he quickly returned to his tongue.

'We thought you dead,' said Braston. 'And . . . well . . . so were we, for most of that time.'

'What?'

'We thought we were helping,' explained Yalenna sadly. 'By killing the others and then ourselves . . . we thought we would heal the Spell, by returning the threads we had taken.'

'The Spell,' echoed Mergan.

'It didn't work. We have, all of us, returned. Only some few days ago.'

'The Spell is not healed?'

'No. In fact it seems, with our return, to be getting worse.'

Mergan dug around in the bottom of Braston's satchel for crumbs.

'Did you find anything in the tomb?' asked Braston. 'Any clues as to what Regret did, or how he did it? What we need to set things right?'

Mergan's expression darkened. 'There's nothing in there. Nothing . . . five thousand, four hundred and . . . nothing.'

He shook his head. 'You say that the others . . . yes, I can see their faces . . . they have returned from death?'

'Yes,' said Braston, 'and we must once more put them down! You'll help us, now that you're fighting fit again, won't you old boy?'

Mergan stared at him for a bit. Then his eyes slid sideways. Yalenna shot Braston a reproving glare, and he shrugged in confusion.

'I'm so tired,' Mergan sighed. 'My mind has been so stretched, for so long. I tried to keep it busy, in the beginning. Thought about how to escape – tried to discover the locks in my mind that stopped me using my magic. Thought of what I could shout at Unwoven if ever they came near, until I learned they could not hear me. They saw only a wretched old man soundlessly screaming in a dark doorway, seeming like a ghost no doubt.

'I tried to keep myself company, talking to myself, until my throat dried out. Pain kept me occupied for a while, as my body withered, my stomach blackening to a nut . . . and then, after a time, pain smoothed out to a kind of fuzziness. Only my eyes grew sharper as I learned every corner of my prison in what little light the days brought, trying to find anything to assist me. At one stage I became obsessed with the notion that I could not see colours or shades in the dimness, that there might be something written on the walls, or the coffin, but I had no means of making light to read it. I ran my hands over every surface, trying to find paint, or ink, or any slight change in texture that might indicate words. I wondered if I could taste what I sought, and wrote the words I hoped to find with my arid tongue upon the stone.

'Sometimes I slept. Maybe years without moving. Drifting, dreaming of better times . . . of you two coming to rescue me . . . of my granddaughters, waking to realise they must be old women, judging by how many days I'd seen go by. Sometimes I dreamed of myself as I really was, lying there, imprisoned in both dream and life. And then . . .'

He put his head in his hands. 'Ah! Ah!'

A wracking fit took him, bending him forward over his crossed legs, to rock as he wept.

'Oh, Mergan,' said Yalenna softly, placing a hand on his back. 'I cannot ask you to forgive us.'

Braston looked close to tears himself, his head sinking to his chest. 'Sorry, dear fellow. We really let you down, didn't we?'

'Yes,' sobbed Mergan into his lap. 'Yes!' And then, 'No.' He raised watery eyes. 'It's not your fault. Why didn't I say where I was going? I was too impulsive.' He screwed up his eyes. 'What a fool.'

'You were trying to help Aorn,' said Braston.

'Yes.'

'But you're free now!'

Mergan gave a sad smile, and rested a finger on his temple. 'I don't think so.' He crumpled the satchel he still clasped. 'Is there any more bread?'

'Plenty of bread, back in Althala,' said Braston.

Mergan shook his head. 'It's no use.'

'Tell us what you need, old friend.'

'Peace,' he said. 'Peace I will not find in life.'

His plaintive look made Yalenna tremble.

'Please,' he said. 'You can't understand, so I beg you to trust me, beg you to help me in this way. Death is my only hope of release. I have tried to find it for myself, but I heal, always. If *you* do it for me, you could make certain that I shall never wake again!'

Yalenna shuddered at the thought, for she wanted no more friends' blood on her hands – but did she owe him what he asked?

'We are proof,' she said sadly, 'that death won't solve your troubles.'

'I do not care!' he hissed, his sudden vehemence making her start.

He blinked as if seeing her for the first time, then wiped his eyes and gave a sniff.

'Can't tell you how much I needed a good cry,' he said. 'Tear ducts, hot and full – I can't begin to describe the sense of release! Even my running nose is welcome.' His giggle frightened her. 'Do you have any more of that bread?'

Braston frowned. 'We told you, not here.'

Mergan grunted and rose to his feet, his eyes taking on a hard look. Uncertainly, they followed him up.

'But what,' he said, 'is this talk of death?'

'No talk,' said Braston quickly. 'Unless you mean the deaths of our enemies!'

Mergan rounded on him in anger. 'No! I care not for enemies. I've done enough! I've lived too long without choice or decision. I met my fate because I lived only for others. From now on, *I* decide what I do!'

Yalenna spread her palms, trying to calm him. 'Yes, that's fine, of course. It's all right, Mergan.'

'Think how comfortable it will be,' tried Braston, 'to sleep in a real feather bed.'

'Not enough to tide me over. You think I owe it to you, is that it? That I will once more *work* and *toil* in a manner of your choosing?'

'That is not how it was,' said Yalenna, growing slightly annoyed, 'nor is it what we ask of you now. We have always been a team. By the Spell, Mergan, you were the one who assembled us!'

'That I will strive and sacrifice,' he continued as if he had not heard her, 'for the good of a land that forgot me? That I will join you, *you* who forsook me so absolutely, who left me to languish and decay?' He rounded on Yalenna. 'You think I want to die? You are mistaken! What I want is to *live!*'

He stabbed twin fingers at them, and whorls of compacted air smacked her and Braston in the foreheads. She flew backwards, limbs trailing, as blackness took her.

Sometime later she awoke, sore and a little stunned. Braston was nearby, leaning on his sword, staring out at the lightening of the sky. Dull streaks on the horizon were slowly melting with the encroachment of sunrise.

'Mergan?' she asked.

Braston glanced down at her, then turned back to the coming dawn.

'He's gone.'

Yalenna's instinct was to search, though she knew there was no point. Mergan could be anywhere, having had ample time to threadwalk while they were out cold.

'Yalenna,' said Braston softly, 'he will come to us. He's simply confused – he still thinks this is all a dream. No doubt a few days will convince him otherwise.'

She wasn't so sure, but gave a little nod.

'He doesn't really hate us,' said Braston.

Again, she wasn't so sure.

Together they concentrated on threadwalking back to Althala. As she tried to focus, her mind kept slipping back to Mergan's angry, twisted face. Forcing him out of her head, she squinted southwards, until the world started to seep. Light oozed past like streams of honey as her undone threads sped across the Ilduin, towards the amorphous white mass of Althala. She made for the square but somehow it rejected her, buffeted her, and she swirled. Although she had no real consciousness at that moment, she followed Braston's similarly affected threads, as they doubled back to a different familiar landmark. Then, together, she and Braston re-formed on the road leading through the northern gate.

Braston glanced around. 'Why did we arrive here? I was envisaging the square.'

'Me too.' She was addled, disoriented. 'This happened to me once before,' she rubbed her temples, 'when there was an unexpected obstacle standing where I aimed. Maybe there are too many people in the square?'

'Why? There is no special occasion today.'

She held her quivering stomach, still a little queasy as her pattern reassembled.

'Something's wrong,' he said.

Off the road sprawled the recruits' camp, but amongst the smouldering fires and strewn belongings, there did not seem to be many people. On the outer edges, where the newest arrivals had been setting up, tents were standing half-erected, a horse or two wandering untended. No Althalan officer would ever let such tardiness descend unless there was good reason. Meanwhile folk were trickling through the gate, moving to and from open plains to the south where mounds were burning. A cart appeared, piled with human corpses, the driver shooing away crows that continuously tried to land on it.

'An attack!' exclaimed Braston. Yalenna, still a little dazed, followed him as he took off towards an officer directing traffic. The man's eyes widened as he saw Braston stomping towards him.

'My lord!' he said, and hastily bowed.

'Enough of that!' snapped Braston. 'Tell me what has happened here!'

'Silkjaws, my lord. They came in the night. We –'

Braston was already moving past him, into the city. Yalenna, trailing behind, heard the man finish.

'– have been looking for you.'

The streets of Althala were a terrible mess. Bodies lay here and there, though efforts were being made to remove them, if not yet the stains they left behind. Many buildings had been marked by fire, some of them damaged badly. A bloody, smoky smell hung in the air and bits of silk blew about, and black feathers. Crows cawed and supped on the dead, squawking angrily as they were chased away. They were bolder and more plentiful than seemed right.

Yalenna caught up to Braston as he inspected the tattered carcass of a silkjaw, which soldiers had been about to heap onto a cart with other white remains.

'If I had known,' he growled, 'that this was where they headed . . . instead,' he kicked the 'jaw angrily, 'we sat idly feeding bread to a madman!'

'Braston!' chastised Yalenna, surprised he would undermine what they had done, even in the face of such tragedy.

He ignored her, staring at what he'd revealed on the underside of the 'jaw – two dead crows, tangled in its silk.

'Were the crows present *during* the attack?' he asked a soldier.

'Indeed, lord. A great many of 'em, came up out of nowhere. They're making the clean-up damnable too.'

Braston turned to Yalenna with rage smouldering in his eyes.

'Don't leap to conclusions,' she said in a low voice.

'Why in Aorn not? This has Karrak's taint all over it.'

'Perhaps . . . but do you not also think the Unwoven could be responsible? You suggested yourself that the chanting, the dancing, might be some form of control. What if they were saying to the silkjaws, *go and stab Althala in the heart*? What if Regret's people have inherited the knowledge of how to set their pets on targets from afar?'

Braston was looking everywhere but at her. 'See, they're all over the place – more crows than is natural, that's for sure.'

'Braston –'

'I heard what you said.' Angrily, he turned away.

They arrived at the castle square, from which much of the clean-up was being organised. Groups of soldiers waited to be given orders and silkjaws were being heaped in piles ready to be carted away. Before the castle entrance, a collection of officers, courtiers and threaders stood, listening to someone speaking. As the Wardens drew closer, they saw it was Loppolo.

'. . . Threaders, I want word sent to Sortree, Ander, Brightrock and all settlements within distance of the Peaks, to warn them of this menace. Make sure to include the Plains Kingdom, for they are much closer to the mountains than we. They may have been attacked already, for all we know.'

The threaders nodded and headed into the castle. They would travel up to the highest points, from which messages could travel the furthest distance.

'We must make preparations in case they return,' continued Loppolo. 'Double the guards on the city walls, and make sure they have fire on hand at all times. Also –'

He stopped as he saw Braston.

'Ah,' he said loudly, 'so good of you to join us, *my lord*. I trust your expedition went well? While the city burned . . .'

Braston turned a dark shade of red. 'You have the situation in hand?'

'Indeed,' said Loppolo. 'After all, you, who have ruled us well for *several days*, were nowhere to be found.'

'And I am thankful,' said Braston, 'to have had such an able stand-in on hand. But now I'm back, and I'm not going anywhere.'

There followed an uneasy standoff. Yalenna imagined that, in Braston's absence, it had been natural for the people to look to Loppolo, and rightly so. Now that they were caught between the two leaders, uncertainty ran rife.

Loppolo scowled and turned on his heel, marching into the castle, followed by his courtiers.

Trouble brewing, thought Yalenna. If only Braston had not acted so rashly to begin with! He should be working *with* the king, instead of in his place.

'Now,' said Braston, 'I want a full report.'

The remaining officers glanced at each other, but Loppolo's deferral was evident in his retreat. They went on to give various accounts of the night, which Yalenna found greatly disturbing. Again she thought about the chant the Unwoven had performed over the silkjaw nest . . . certainly such control would explain why, in the past, Unwoven and silkjaws had attacked together.

What was it, she wondered, that the Unwoven even wanted? Something specific, or was it all simply part of Regret's damnable legacy, as the creatures he'd created mindlessly struck out at the world, instinctively carrying on his work? Trying to carve out ruin because *that's* what they'd been made for, their function intact despite their maker long turned to dust?

Do they sense the growing corruption, perhaps? Has it stirred them to action, a taste of the reality they were built to populate?

The officers finished their reports. It was evident that the work necessary to restore Althala was already being carried out, leaving Braston with little more to order than 'carry on'. As the officers departed, however, one man lingered.

'My lord,' he said, 'there is something else you should know about.'

'Yes?'

'A man claiming to be the great warrior Rostigan Skullrender arrived yesterday. He earned his name at the Ilduin Fields . . . forgive me, but my lord has been informed of the battle that took place there?'

'I have, and of Skullrender's hand in the victory.'

'Quite. Well, having seen this man in action last night, there's no doubt he is an able fighter, Rostigan or not. I am sure, of course, my lord will be able to verify the truth of the matter. He also makes a further claim of undoubtable interest.'

Braston gave a wave of 'continue'.

'My lord . . . he says he killed Stealer.'

That got both Braston and Yalenna's undivided attention.

'Really?' said Braston. 'I had heard rumblings, but, well, if that is so, it is welcome news indeed.'

'Yes, my lord.'

'Where is he?'

'Last I knew,' answered the officer, 'in the barracks. There has been much activity today however, so I'm not sure if he still remains there . . .'

Braston turned slowly to view the buildings at the square's edge.

'Well,' he said. 'I shall have to meet this good fellow. Right away.'

⁓

Rostigan sat in the dining hall, poking at a bowl of stew. He had helped himself to an untended pot that had been sitting on the fire all night, and did not think the long cooking time had harmed the food's flavour.

The barracks were quiet. Everyone who wasn't outside cleaning up or yelling at crows was asleep after a hard night. Tarzi was among them, slumbering deeply in their room. He had tried to sink alongside her, but could too much sense his crows' dissatisfaction to rest easily. Many of them had been injured or killed doing his bidding, and the survivors expected what they had been promised, yet the people of Althala had recovered too quickly and had already cleared away many of the bodies. In the old days Karrak had always made sure his birds were happy, treated as sacred and left undisturbed as they savoured the fruits of battle. Perhaps crows were simply not tools appropriate to him anymore, demanding a payment Rostigan could not provide.

Why? he wondered angrily. There was no right and wrong as far as the dead were concerned. The crows had helped the people of Althala more than would ever be known. What harm if they tore at a little corpse flesh in recompense? People wanted their dead treated with respect, of course, and didn't like to be reminded of their own inner workings, but it was a small price to pay for the service the crows had given.

Of the two sets of double doors on the square side of the room, the ones furthest from him opened. He hoped whoever it was did not plan on staying, for right now he desired solitude, such as it was, with hundreds of little minds cawing discontentedly at the edges of his own. He stared into his stew, not wishing to invite company.

'Hello there,' came a deep, familiar voice. 'I'm looking for a fellow by the name of Rostigan.'

Slowly Rostigan raised his eyes, to favour Braston with an even stare. Beside the king, Yalenna stood with an equally shocked expression. Strangely, Rostigan found himself pleased to see her. They had been friends before the change, and maybe a little of that returned to him now. He remembered the amiable jousts and long talks they'd had, on their way to the Peaks, back when he had been charming and she had been happier. He found himself giving her a little smile and a nod.

'I knew it!' thundered Braston. 'They *are* your crows, aren't they, Karrak? This was somehow your doing!'

He reached for the table beside him, long enough for ten soldiers a side, and flipped it to crash against the next one along. Striding into the aisle Rostigan sat in, he drew his sword.

'Wait, Braston,' Rostigan said, rising to show empty palms. 'I no longer go by that name, nor by his habits.'

Braston wore a mask of rage which Rostigan's words failed to penetrate. The man bellowed and charged, and Rostigan vaulted over the table, putting it between them – until Braston's sword came down upon it, splintering it to a collapsed V and smashing Rostigan's bowl into the bargain. Some of the stew spattered Braston's face and he gave an angry flinch.

'Braston!' said Rostigan, backing away. 'I do not wish to fight!'

'Listen to him!' said Yalenna, approaching from the far end of the room.

'No!' shouted Braston. 'He has a snake's tongue, twisting words as adroitly as he twists through the mire on his belly!'

He kicked through the table pieces and Rostigan darted sideways, narrowly avoiding another great swing. *Short-sighted fool*, he thought as he ran, reluctantly pulling free his own sword. He spun about and found Braston close on his heels. The Warden's blade crashed against his, with all of Braston's legendary might behind it, and Rostigan's entire body juddered. They had never fought man-to-man before, and Rostigan had thought them an equal match when it came to brute strength – but that blow made him think again.

Another came, driving Rostigan's sword downwards, and Braston followed through with a mighty punch of his free hand. Rostigan stumbled, his eye and cheek throbbing. Groggily he raised his sword again, but his wrist snapped painfully as it was turned aside. The next moment he was being lifted, as Braston shoulder-charged him into the wall. Winded, he slid to his knees.

There came the sound of running feet in corridors, the commotion having roused some of the barrack's denizens. Yalenna waved at the doors on either side of the room, weaving them together to become continuous with the wall.

'Let them in!' shouted Braston, hovering his sword over Rostigan's heart. 'I would have them see their king kill the Lord of Crows!'

Yalenna reached out as she advanced, and Braston's sword fell to pieces in his hand. He blinked at it, scowled, and flung the hilt away in disgust.

'Stop that this instant!' said Yalenna, but Braston seized Rostigan under the chin and dragged him up the wall by his throat. In his foggy mind, Rostigan could not believe that he had been beaten so soundly.

'Listen,' he wheezed, 'please . . . I have been living as a good man . . . I have tried to make amends . . .'

'Amends!' guffawed Braston. 'Amends you can make for certain things – for breaking a heart or stealing a pig, and much worse than that besides. But your crimes are too great for *amends*, Karrak.'

Rostigan kicked him hard in the balls and Braston winced. Sweat broke out along his forehead, but he grinned and squeezed harder. Rostigan saw spots, his vision closing in.

'Enough!' roared Yalenna.

Rostigan fell, the pressure on his windpipe gone, blood gushing painfully back into his throat. Meanwhile Braston slammed against the adjoining wall, and slid downwards into a similar position. His expression became one of hurt and shock, seeming for a moment like a chastised child.

Yalenna stalked forward, a hand held out towards each of them.

'Now,' she said, 'will you cease behaving like such a raging lunatic, Braston, or must I rap your thick skull again? Aren't you even a little curious to find out if he really killed Stealer?'

Braston opened his mouth, and for a moment said nothing. Then, 'I had forgotten about that.'

Rostigan rubbed his throat. 'Some show of gratitude,' he said. 'I came here to join your army.'

Yalenna gave him a hard stare. 'Besides,' she said, 'we can always kill him later, should we choose.'

WITHOUT FEAR

From a high balcony Forger looked out over the tiers of Tallahow. His city was sensible and grey, streamlined and efficient, well planned and well executed. For all its sleek, stepped design, however, he had always found it to be a bit of a dull stone amidst his glittering empire. Or what would be his empire, again.

'My lord,' said Threver, 'some of our citizens flee the city. It isn't an unusual occurrence, when rulers change, yet there are more this time than normal. I feel my lord may have scared the populace with the mode of his ascension. Do you wish the guards to lock down the walls?'

Forger glanced at Threver sidelong. The old advisor had been trailing him ever since he'd taken control, quick to see that his orders were followed. He did not mind, for now – the crossbow wound in his side was taking a little while to heal, so it was nice having someone making sure he was fed grapes, and brought randomly chosen victims to suffer his attention. Their pain helped him heal all the faster.

'And you, Threver?' he said. 'Do you wish to remain?'

'Pardon, my lord?'

'It's just,' Forger gripped the rail of the balcony, 'you were very fast to side with me. Surely you must feel for the suffering of the people?'

Threver cleared his throat. 'I do not judge, merely advise. Indeed, I take my role very seriously. I am not, however, advisor to *this* Lord of Tallahow, or *that* Lady of Tallahow. Simply to the ruler of Tallahow, whomever that might be.'

'I see. And your advice, then – is it consistent?'

'My lord?'

'Would you furnish Elacin with the same wisdom as you would furnish me?'

Threver gave him a flat stare, which actually impressed him with its boldness.

'No, my lord. Although I always strive to present the facts untarnished – even if I fear they will not be to the listener's liking – my advice is, of course, always tailored to a ruler's specific aims and desires.'

'How flexible of you.'

Forger turned back to the city, running his eyes along the grey wall that encircled it.

'Well?'

'Lord?'

'What do you advise?'

Threver cleared his throat. 'The people have heard stories of my lord, and are naturally afraid.'

'Is no one *proud* of the heritage I endow Tallahow with? In my day the people were glad to follow me, glad of Tallahow's glory!'

'There are some who are hopeful of glory's return. My informants tell me the mood is mixed.'

'Ah. You have informants.'

'Of course. There are those who speak fondly of the old days, when Tallahow *was* the east and riches flowed into our coffers. There are nobles who would see their holdings expand, who have in the past counselled war with our neighbours. And there are those in the army to whom battle appeals, when there has been no battle for many years. It is one thing to reminisce, however, and dream of glory, quite another to be faced with a unknown king who fills the keep with screams.'

Forger gave Threver a discerning look. 'You think I have been too anonymous, is that it?'

'Perhaps, my lord.'

'Hmm,' said Forger. 'Hmm, hmm and hum.' He scowled. 'If only Karrak were here, he could speak to the people on my behalf. Ah well, I shall have to do this in my own way.' He reached a decision. 'Summon anyone of note to the great hall. Officers, civic leaders, nobles, that kind of thing. Anyone with influence, anyone who stands to profit from war. You can do this?'

'Of course, my lord.'

'Good. This evening then. Tell them there will be a feast to welcome and meet me.'

'And then, lord?'

'Leave that to me.'

⁓

That evening many collected in the keep's great hall, a cavernous room lit by many clusters of candles. They entered to find a magnificent spread – food heaped along tables, stacks of plates waiting for any who wished to pile them high, and servants running about eager to refill any slightly empty glass. There was an excess to it that most had not experienced for some time, for Elacin had been a frugal ruler. Thus, despite an underlying air of nervousness, soon everyone was eating and drinking, and talk and laughter began to echo off the walls. Where, though, was the man who had sent for them?

When Forger entered, all fell to a hush. He strode up the centre of the room, Threver hopping along in his wake, towards a table raised on a dais by the side of the raging fire. He stepped up to it and rounded, to stand looking out over the sea of expectant faces. Half-chewed legs and pastries were set down, glasses lowered.

'The Lord of Tallahow will speak,' announced Threver, from before the dais.

'Hello,' said Forger brightly. 'How very nice to see you all! Looks like some good grub – my compliments to the kitchens. Threver, if you wouldn't mind . . .'

Threver glanced at him with confusion, until Forger gestured impatiently towards one of the tables.

'Well, it is a feast, is it not? Fetch me some food!'

There were some chortles as Threver set about his menial task in a stiff and embarrassed fashion.

'I trust we are all having a pleasant evening?' said Forger, and there were a few hesitant murmurs of assent. As Threver set a plate on the table beside him, 'Ah! Excellent.'

He picked up a sausage to munch, waving it at his audience while he chewed.

'This reminds me of how the great hall used to look. A worthy outlet for an overflowing larder, everyone eating and carrying on. This is how it should be!'

The answering murmurs were more enthusiastic this time.

'This is the Tallahow of my youth,' continued Forger, a sentimental twinkle appearing in his eye. 'Some time ago now, as you probably know. I was born elsewhere, nothing more than a blacksmith's son, set to become a blacksmith too, until my . . . parents . . . saw me controlling the flames at will. "Our boy", they said, "must be built for grander things than we had hitherto imagined!" Thus they sent me here, to train with the finest threaders Aorn had to offer.'

He swallowed and wiped a greasy hand on his chest. He had not thought about his parents for some time, and for a moment almost saw their faces . . . blurred, as if they lay on the other side of misted glass. What had been their names?

He frowned, pushing the thought of them away.

'That's one thing,' he continued, 'that I've always loved about our fair city. Some places are ruled by tradition, and a fat king hands his crown to a fat son, or a useless pig of a daughter. But here in Tallahow, rule has always been decided by strength. Nobles can be made, not born. Thus an outsider, a lowly blacksmith's boy indeed, can rise to the very top, if he has the right kind of mettle.'

He grinned at what he thought was a very clever joke, which unfortunately no one else seemed to get.

'I have returned,' he went on, 'from the dead, to restore us to our former grandeur!'

Some cheers sounded.

'There are a few problems, however.' He picked up a quail and popped it whole into his mouth. The people fell silent again, waiting for him to crack its bones.

'Crunchy,' he said approvingly. 'One problem is that I remember a hard people – a strong people, a proud people – yet who do I return to find, holed up in the shadow of the Roshous Peaks? People who talk, yes, people who claim to remember the good old days, yet here they stay, within borders *I* remember breaking. We still have an army, do we not?'

He singled out a man in well-polished mail, evidently some kind of high-ranking officer.

'You, sir! How many in Tallahow's forces?'

People edged away from the man.

He cleared his throat. 'My lord, it is something like ten thousand.'

'Ten thousand!' said Forger. 'By the Spell, that is a few. No wonder none has ever dared attack us!'

Pride from the crowd at his words.

'But then,' he grew more sombre, 'why do we dare not *attack*?'

He let his words hang for a moment.

'If *I* had to guess,' he stalked across the dais, 'I would say it's because of pain – the one thing in the world worth fearing! Fear of pain is what stops us from fulfilling our potential. Not just pain of the body –' He gestured at the officer, who went down wailing. The crowd backed further from him as he writhed, fear rising from them palpably, '– but pain of loss, pain of guilt. Fear of failure, fear of change! Frustration, anguish – are these not tied up with pain? How to overcome, then, these hindrances, these barriers we dare not try to cross, which render us inert? With the threat of *greater* pain, as punishment?'

He flung out his hands. Threads rippled from him, a web-like network of invisible lines expanding outwards. In a wave people collapsed before him, their bodies wracked by indescribable torment. Forger laughed – he had reached equilibrium, the effort of his outpouring matched by the rewards it garnered. Growing neither stronger nor weaker, he could now *maintain* as long as he wished.

A table tipped over as people fell against it, splattering fine food on the floor. He saw folk trying to stagger from the hall, and with a wave slammed shut the distant doors.

'My . . . lord . . .' choked Threver, from the floor. 'For . . . what . . . purpose . . .'

Forger ignored him, stepping down to move amongst the prostrate throng.

'But what if,' he called, 'someone could take your pain *away*? What if you never had to feel this, or anything like it, again?'

He snapped his hands to his chest, recalling all threads. As they retracted to him they brought little bundles, torn from the patterns of every person present. He drew them into himself, squirrelling them away, as the screaming died down.

'I would prefer,' he said, treading carefully amongst the upwards stares, 'that those who fight with me do so because they are loyal, because they know the rewards for standing at my side. Save the pain for our enemies, friends, for I have taken yours away!'

He summoned a carving knife, and flung it into a noblewoman's arm. She stared at it curiously, unflinching as it dangled from her soft flesh.

'You all had ailments,' Forger said, 'as various as your pleasures. You, sir – a bung leg, forever throbbing, never distant from your thoughts. You, miss – an unhappy marriage, but no courage to leave it, for *fear* of what? Destitution, loss of standing, *pain*? You, little man.' He stopped by a child. 'You were angry, for what reason?'

'Parents,' the boy murmured.

'His parents, dead!' crowed Forger. 'Keeping him up at night, their faces ever in his thoughts! But now, little man, you will sleep soundly. And if your mean old uncle,' he turned to the noble lying beside the boy, 'hits you again, will you feel it, will you *care*?'

'I won't hit him anymore,' said the man.

'What's that?' said Forger. 'Why?'

'I . . . I don't know.'

'Perhaps because he no longer reminds you of your beautiful sister, who died giving him life? Who you, in truth, used to share a bed with? And do you care that everyone now knows this?' He cast his eyes around. 'Does the guilt of this terrible secret linger, the constant fear that foul incest will be posthumously revealed?'

The man checked himself, then met the eyes of his peers. 'No.'

'No!' shouted Forger. 'Who cares about her? She's dead! Life is for the living – and a life lived in pain, in fear, is no life at all. Wouldn't you agree?'

People were beginning to rise.

'That's right!' said Forger. 'Get up! Get back to the feast! Eat more than you need, for no rumbling gut will burn your bowels in the middle of the night! Drink all you like, for no sore head will cloud the morning, no unfortunate words spoken in the fug will return to haunt you!'

People were laughing now, poking at each other experimentally with forks. Forger gave an encouraging whoop of joy and shovelled a handful of meat into his mouth.

'Come, my loves! Let us usher in a new era for our beloved Tallahow. For without pain, there is no fear. And without fear,' his voice grew stronger, *'no one can stop us!'*

The next day, despite his words, Forger himself felt quite sore-headed. He must have drunk a *lot* to not be fully healed. He sat on the throne, fingers to his brow, reflecting that it would be nice if he could take away his own discomfort. However, even if he could have, he knew it would be dangerous to do so. Pain, after all, had its uses, something that those he took it from forgot all too quickly. He would have to watch them closely now, control them well, in case they grew too reckless, or fell to tearing one another apart. But they were *his*, of that he was sure.

'Lord?'

He had not heard his advisor enter.

'Good morning, Threver.'

'That was very interesting last night, lord.'

'You enjoyed it?' Forger peeked from behind his fingers. 'I hardly had to take anything from you, you know.'

'Remorse is not something that ever burdened me overmuch, lord.'

'You surprise me. Maybe you're a worthwhile advisor after all.'

'I certainly hope so. I have a question, though.'

'Yes?'

'If Tallahow's leaders no longer fear you – as I, even now,

find myself less guarded in this very conversation – will they obey you?'

Forger gave a dismissive wave. 'It's a tricky thing. I don't pretend to foresee the exact effects of the gift I've granted. I do know, however, that once unfettered by fear, *desire* comes very much to the fore. Sometimes dark desires, yes, which the person has never dared speak before, let alone acted upon, but everyone is different, aren't they? If someone becomes a problem, they can always be dealt with. I just hope I can point them towards things they want, and they'll obey because they desire what's on offer.'

'I see. It strikes me as similar to what was done to the Unwoven.'

Forger frowned, not liking the comparison. It was true that Regret had created the Unwoven by taking away pain and fear, amongst other things. And perhaps it was even true that whatever threads Forger had inherited from Regret were the very ones that had allowed him to mete out such transformations himself – but Forger did not turn people into stupid, ugly brutes.

'What *they* desire,' he said, 'is very dark indeed. A person does not forget themselves when I take their pain, Threver. Indeed, the kind may become kinder, or love may become freer. What I am pinning my hopes on,' he jerked his thumb in the direction of the great hall, 'is that all of them down there were a bunch of greedy, grasping little weasels in the first place. I find this is normally the case, with leaders.'

Threver nodded. 'Can I have anything brought to you? Water, perhaps, if your head is troubling you?'

'Yes! Bring me a lot of water.'

Threver made some motions at an attendant by the door, who darted out.

'If only Karrak was here . . .' muttered Forger.

'I have heard my lord express this wish before. Can I ask why?'

'He has a way with words. Good at getting people to do what he wants, without all the mess.' He perked up a little. 'Though admittedly, I *like* the mess.' He drummed his fingers along the arm rest. 'Or Salarkis – why hasn't that rotten little bird come home to roost? Or Despirrow, or any of them! What I wouldn't give to know what they're up to.'

'My lord, there is something that may be of interest to you.'

'Oh?'

'It will require a short journey to a lower level.'

'Very well.'

They made for the double doors just as the attendant returned carrying a pitcher of water.

'Ah! Give me that!'

Forger wrenched it from the cringing man and upended it all over himself.

'That's better! Now, lead the way.'

A trip down a flight of stairs brought them to a quiet corridor, lined by barred doors manned by statuesque guards.

'This looks interesting,' said Forger. 'What's in all these rooms?'

'Treasures, mainly,' replied Threver. 'Most of them useless, simply requiring to be kept. But in here . . .'

The guards at the door he stopped at parted as he fumbled with some keys. Swinging it open, he stood aside, and Forger had to stoop to enter – had he grown even taller?

Inside was a cool, empty room, save for a silver-framed mirror hanging on the wall. Hesitantly, Forger went to look at himself – flexed his muscles and inspected his face, which seemed bulgy in an odd kind of way, as if there were rocks under his skin. He looked deep into his own blue eyes, for a moment lost in the notion that *this was him* and *he was really alive right now.*

'Well,' he said, rounding on Threver, 'this is all very fascinating, but I trust you did not bring me here for self-reflection.'

'Ah . . . no, my lord. This mirror is special – part of a set.'

'Oh yes?'

'Yes. Its siblings are much more elaborate, the frames each carved with a thousand tiny flowers, I'm told.'

'And where are they?'

'Hanging in the corridors of Althala Castle. They were a gift to the Queen of Althala a hundred years ago, from our own Lord Dregan. He gave them under the guise of admiration, but, in truth, his intentions were more underhanded. For while we have long been at peace with Althala, it still pays to garner all possible knowledge. The mirrors are threaded, subtly and skilfully enough to have never been discovered for what they really are – spy-holes, linked to this one, through which we can see.'

'Oho!' Forger clapped his hands. 'How delicious.'

'I must warn my lord that we had no control over where Dregan's gifts were hung, and later moved about. One of them even sits in a store room, covered in a cloth, and therefore shows little.'

'I see. Well, enough of your disavowal. How does it work?'

'I cannot say for sure. Until recently there was a threader stationed here, well versed in their use and watching at all times.'

'Where is he?'

'You killed him.'

'Ah.'

'Still, I expect that one as skilful as my lord can easily figure the trick to it.'

Forger rubbed his chin as he considered the mirror. This kind of magic was not really his strong point. Yet, like the other Wardens, he retained the native threading ability he had been born with, as something separate from his Spell-given powers. He reached out to the mirror with his finer senses, inspecting its threads.

'Ah,' he said. 'It is as if this one is the brain, from which branch out the eyes. Ingenious. Now, all I have to do, is prise open the lids . . .'

The reflection on the mirror rippled, replaced with a view of an empty corridor, a vase in the foreground filled with slightly wilting flowers. In the opposite wall a flight of steps led upwards, and to the right was a heavy oak door, which was closed.

'That is the chamber,' said Threver, 'which Braston now inhabits.'

'Really? Interesting.'

'A mirror hangs inside it too.'

'My goodness.'

With a mental blink, Forger moved to the next view. It was a well-appointed bedroom, the large bed looking unslept in.

'Well, at least I can watch him slumber,' scowled Forger. 'I'm sure that will prove exciting.'

'Try the next one, lord.'

Now the mirror showed the chamber of indoor streams and high windows that was the throne room. A few harried-looking guards moved through, and a small group of nobles sat by a fountain.

'I can hear the water gurgling!' said Forger excitedly.

'I cannot, my lord. Must be to do with your gifts.'

'You mean to tell me that the lords and ladies of Tallahow have been eavesdropping on the Althalan throne room for a hundred years, and no one has ever realised?'

'Yes, lord.'

'Dear me. Threaders must have passed this mirror many times!'

'Dregan was adamant that his gifts not be detected for

what they really are. The threaders who crafted them knew that if they failed him they would pay a high price.'

'I admire their skill! Next!'

Forger changed to the next mirror. This one, again in a corridor, looked upon a door hanging from its hinges, across which savage claw-like scrapes showed in the wood. The room beyond was plush and obviously belonged to someone noble . . . yet the bedding was sprayed with blood, ripped to shreds, and a couple of soldiers were lifting a fat body onto a stretcher. Another noblewoman watched on, dabbing her eyes.

'What's this?' said Forger. 'A murder?'

He strained his ears as sounds issued strangely from this distant view, somewhat distorted and muted.

'I think I heard someone say something about . . .'

A third soldier appeared through the door, dragging a large sack, from which poked a bone wrapped in wafts of silk.

'. . . silkjaws!' finished Forger.

'My lord?'

'Ssh!' He listened hard. 'They are talking about a silkjaw attack. Saying there were . . . hundreds of them. Have we heard anything about this?'

'Not yet, my lord. The day is young, however. I have threaders up high looking out for messages.'

Forger was a little disturbed.

'If the Althalans have been weakened,' said Threver, 'it will only further our cause.'

'Perhaps. Have there been other attacks like this since I've been away?'

'There was an incident on the Ilduin some years ago. Since then, the Plainsfolk sometimes complain of silkjaws, but nothing on the scale of hundreds. Are you sure – forgive my impudence – that you heard correctly?'

'I think so.' Forger rubbed his eyes. 'On the Ilduin, it was Unwoven and silkjaws attacking together, is that right?'

'Yes, lord.'

'Why were they not put down in my absence?' He was angry with the world for a second. 'Does no one do anything around here?'

'There has not been a unifying need,' said Threver. 'Until recently the Unwoven have mostly kept to themselves, locked up behind the Pass in the Roshous –'

'I know where they are! Think who you are talking to.'

'Apologies, lord.'

'The question is, is their continued existence a symptom of the Spell's upheaval, or a cause?' He rounded on Threver. 'I can't kill off Braston's army with impunity if they stand between us and hordes of Regret's cursed monsters! Piss and fire, why does everything have to be so complicated?'

'There is one more mirror, lord.'

'Oh yes? And what does it show, another empty corridor?'

Not another corridor, but a large sitting room, in which a group of nobles sat on purple couches, silent as a servant set down a tray of tea and biscuits.

'Loppolo's chambers,' said Threver. 'The king who Braston supplanted.'

'Ah, yes,' said Forger. 'What a hypocrite Braston is. Well, this would be a useful view if Loppolo was still in charge, wouldn't it?'

'Indeed. And maybe still.'

The servant left, and low conversation begun. Forger strained his ears.

'. . . is your right, my king,' a plump, grey-haired man was saying.

'Yes,' said a young woman. 'I agree with Tursa. Warden he may be, it does not mean Braston can ignore you.'

Loppolo stood up, moving over to glower directly into the mirror.

'And how would history remember me,' he said, 'if I was the king who killed the Lord of Justice?'

'They speak of felling Braston!' said Forger. 'Oho, imagine that – if I need not raise a finger and yet it were so!'

'The threader who watched here witnessed similar meetings,' said Threver. 'Those are Loppolo's closest allies, who urge him to take action.'

'And yet he procrastinates?' said Forger, staring into the former king's eyes. 'Come, Loppolo – take back what is yours!'

'And the people,' said Loppolo. 'How could I possibly explain it to them without getting lynched? They love their legendary king, more dismissive of me than I have earned!'

'That's right!' said Tursa. 'How easily they forget that *you* are a hero too, who rode to battle against the Unwoven! They must be made to remember.'

'We could figure some way to make it look accidental,' said the woman.

Loppolo laughed bitterly. 'Braston is no ordinary man. He does not fall down a flight of stairs and break his neck.'

'But –'

'Enough!' snapped Loppolo. 'Who knows the extent of a Warden's powers? Even now we could be overheard.'

His allies grumbled, and sipped their tea.

'Hmf,' said Forger. 'This Loppolo is a ditherer.'

He turned away, the mirror rippling back to its normal reflection.

'I thank you for making me aware of this object, Threver. While it is somewhat random in its use, perhaps we shall glean something pertinent from it. Find another threader to watch over it, and report anything of interest to me.'

'It will be done, lord.'

'Now,' said Forger, 'I think it's high time I inspected our army.'

HAND IN HAND

'Get an axe,' said a soldier. A moment later he jumped back as the previously immovable dining hall doors flew open, to reveal the Priestess Yalenna looking irritated.

'Yes?' she said.

'Er . . .' His eyes slid past her, to a table lying broken on its side. 'Everything all right in there, my lady?'

'All is well,' she said with a tight smile. 'The king and I simply have need of this room for a while.'

'Ah . . . well, very good, my lady. We shall . . . leave you, then.'

'Thank you,' she said, and closed the door.

She headed back to where Braston and Karrak sat across from each other at an intact table, glowers in full effect. Despite the relatively calm demeanour she had presented to the soldiers at the door, her head was still spinning from learning that Karrak had been alive for the entire time that she had been dead.

'And yet do you see an empire behind me?' Karrak demanded, stabbing the tabletop with a finger. 'Do you see how I have crushed the world in your absence, as I could have done, ten times over?'

Yalenna slid in beside Braston.

'No,' said Karrak. 'Though it would have been easy, with no other Wardens to oppose me. I could have run amok, but instead I've been leading a peaceful life – before *you* all decided to come back, of course.'

'We did not *decide*,' growled Braston.

'The Spell brought us back,' said Yalenna. 'Our threads did not return to it in death, and thus the degradation continues.'

'How can you know that?' said Braston, turning on her angrily. 'It could be that the damage persists because Karrak here never died! His presence in Aorn has ensured a state of ongoing corruption.'

'I told you not to call me that. Karrak is gone. My name is Rostigan.'

'You cannot escape your past so easily.'

Rostigan thumped his fist on the table, hard. 'Now listen to me, you pair of *children*. Ever since forsaking my empire, I've kept my power sealed up tight, sworn an oath never to use it . . . and never *once* during that time has the sky turned black, or the ground shaken, or beetles fallen like hail. Yet you have both flaunted your magic from the very moment you awakened, recklessly and with abandon – your blessings like a cloud of toxin Yalenna, and Braston, pulling at the threads of justice, as you call them, deeming to change the natural order by imposing *your* will upon it, what *you* think is right. You *dare* to blame me, you *dare* esteem yourself higher, better? You do as much damage as Forger, as Despirrow. Even the Unwoven, in all the centuries they have lingered, have had no worse effect on the world than you have brought about in *days*. The one time,' he knew he was lying, but did not care, 'that I used my gift to call down the crows, was to save *your* city Braston, in exchange for nothing save a few dead eyes – and the thanks I get? To be mindlessly struck down, accused of being the root of it all, by an oaf without the subtlety or patience for comprehension. You think if I wanted to do you harm, I would be sitting here, waiting under your roof, without allies, ready to accept the blows levelled at me? Would I not be off with Forger, plotting your downfall?'

Yalenna felt herself reeling under the torrent of what she knew to be the truth. She had never tried to deny that she was part of the problem, yet Braston would not talk to her about it, Mergan was mad, and there was no one else. The only one speaking clearly was this man . . . this *Rostigan*.

Braston stared darkly at his hands, clasped on the tabletop. 'I may have acted brashly,' he muttered.

'I *walked* here,' said Rostigan, 'on my own two feet, because I know that, despite your flaws, you two will try to do what's right. In the hope that somehow, together, we can end Regret's legacy once and for all. Have you not heard of my doings at the Ilduin Fields, where I helped the –'

'All *right*,' snapped Braston. 'You have made your point.'

'Where did you go?' asked Yalenna quietly.

'What?'

'You disappeared around the same time as Mergan. We came to believe you had destroyed each other, yet evidently this was not the case.'

'No. I do not know what happened to Mergan. Have you seen him?'

Yalenna gave a small nod, though she did not want to get into it just then. Braston, however, came straight to the point.

'He stayed alive, as you did, though locked in a prison of Regret's making.'

Rostigan's eyebrows went up in surprise.

'We freed him,' said Braston, 'but the experience has left him . . . affected. We do not know where he has gone.'

'He just needs a little time,' said Yalenna.

'I see.' Rostigan's expression softened a little.

'But what of you?' she pressed. 'Where did you go?'

Rostigan sighed. 'It was troubling for me, you must understand. I was a monster beginning to remember my old self. I had a great need to deny, escape, to turn my back on all I'd done.'

'Forger carried on your work.'

'I know. If I had my time again, I would not have left everything so neatly set up for him.' He snorted humourlessly. 'If I had my time again, I would have done everything differently. And I'd be a happier man, long dead.'

He tapped the tabletop. 'We all are victims of Regret. By the Spell, Salarkis used to sing to children and help farmers grow strawberries. Forger wanted nothing more than to save his family from ruin. Despirrow was your best friend, Braston. If you'd asked any of them then if they wanted this, what would they have said?'

Yalenna bit her lip. 'Salarkis remembers himself, somewhat. I do not think he is . . . well, either the old Salarkis, or the monster anymore, but caught between. I do not know what he intends. I blessed him, again. He came seeking it, actually.'

'Then hopefully,' said Rostigan, 'we need not fear him. Nor Stealer.'

'Yes!' said Braston, sitting up, some of his fire finally returning. 'Tell us of that! My officer said you claimed to have killed her, but when I thought you a mortal man, I admit I doubted the story.'

'Nay, it is true. Stealer is no more. By sheer luck I was near Silverstone when she took it. I saw her there, fleeing her crime. I was able to act swiftly, before she knew who I was or what I wanted. Snuck up on her in the night – not much more to it than that.'

'Are you absolutely sure she's dead?'

'I split her head in two and burned her to cinders. I am sure.'

He thought about the other reason why he was sure, but hesitated to share it. Meanwhile he caught Yalenna staring at him.

'What is it?' he said.

'Nothing. You just . . . you reminded me of the old . . . of your old self, for a moment. That fretful look – I remember it.'

'If she's dead,' said Braston, 'why hasn't Silverstone returned?'

Rostigan sighed. If they were going to be allies, he supposed he should tell them everything.

'I do not think the Spell wants its threads disappearing again,' he said. 'Now that it knows the deaths of their possessors do not return them to it.'

'What do you mean?'

'When I killed Stealer, it was like on the Spire, after we slew Regret. The threads she had from the Spell left her, did not disperse with the rest of her. Instead they came to me.'

'Came to you?'

'Yes. Became part of my pattern. *I* house Stealer's powers now. And she, I think, truly sleeps, having passed her curse to me.'

The other two were very still.

'I suppose I will have to show you,' said Rostigan.

Braston tensed.

'Settle down,' said Rostigan, 'I'm not going to rhyme about your underbritches. I shall pick . . . how about that table?' He gestured at one Braston had smashed. 'I daresay losing it will not be a burden.'

'Very well.'

Now that he was on the spot, all creativity left him.

'What rhymes with table?'

'Rabble?' suggested Braston.

'Don't be silly,' said Yalenna.

Together they tried to think.

'Able,' said Yalenna, after a fashion.

Rostigan nodded, and spoke.

A sad thing is a broken table
To hold up food, no longer able

As he finished, the table faded, and the others gasped. His words began to whisper, very softly, in the air.

'Well may you look at me in horror, Braston,' said Rostigan. 'If you had killed me just now, you'd probably have both mine *and* Stealer's threads in you – *your* soul the keeper of the city of Silverstone.'

That made Braston blanch. 'What of the others?' he said. 'If we kill them . . .'

'I believe the same will happen.'

'I wish,' said Yalenna, 'the Spell could make up its damn mind about what it wants done with its own damn threads! And stop changing the story on us.'

'Maybe the Spell has no control,' said Rostigan. 'Maybe it's the threads themselves, trying different ways of finding their path home.'

'So what way are they trying now? Accumulating in us obviously hasn't solved their problem.'

'I suspect,' said Rostigan, 'since they cannot seem to penetrate the veil, they must be returned to the Wound itself.'

'Is that based on anything?' asked Braston. 'Because I, for one, am nervous of that place.'

Rostigan shrugged. 'I am open to suggestions.'

None were forthcoming.

'Whether I am right or wrong,' said Rostigan, 'at least we can hunt the others knowing that, when we put an end to them, we can take their threads into us. Use them or, better yet, choose not to use them. We can be the Spell's goatherds, collecting what it's missing.'

He let this sink in.

'I do still hope,' said Yalenna, 'that Salarkis and Mergan will join us. That we will not have to *collect* them.'

'As do I, but what you've said of Mergan does not instil me with confidence. I have spent three hundred years becoming a good man. Perhaps he has spent them turning from one.'

Yalenna flared at his words, and Rostigan spread his palms.

'He was my friend too, remember,' he said, 'but I cannot imagine any man going through such an ordeal unscathed.'

'He was not unscathed,' said Braston, shaking his head sadly. 'And that's a meek way of putting it.'

'He will come to us,' said Yalenna firmly. 'He will remember he is loved, and come to us.'

'What about Despirrow?' said Rostigan. 'Have you any news of his whereabouts?'

'No.'

'I take it you noted the recent stopping of time?'

'Indeed.'

'Your royal threaders haven't reported anything unusual?'

'There are more unusual things reported every passing day.'

'Anything of his particular smell, though?'

'I shall ask.'

'Good. Make sure you keep an eye on Saphura especially – it always was his favourite place. In the meantime, I have a favour to beg of you both.'

They looked to him guardedly.

'Nothing too strenuous,' he assured them. 'I travel with a woman, a minstrel named Tarzi. She is precious to me, yet she does not know the all of who I am. I wish to keep it that way.'

'Is that fair?' said Braston. 'If you love her, why can't you –'

Rostigan cut him off. 'She is the one who dragged me here, singing loud to all who'd listen about rallying against the evil Wardens. How do you think she'd react if she learned my old name?'

'Come, Braston,' said Yalenna. 'It is unimportant to grant him this.'

'What will she make, then,' said Braston, 'of the attention you receive from us?'

Rostigan smiled. 'Oh, she will take it in stride. I am the great Rostigan Skullrender, after all.'

DESPIRROW

The tavern was cool and quiet, the sun making scattershot forays in through small windows. Despirrow sat next to such a one, a bar of light glancing off him on its way to explode against an empty table in the middle of the room. The only other patrons present were a pair of sour old drunks, whiling away the hours as the rest of the village went about its daily business.

He must look out of place, he knew. This was a farmland area, its people stocky and simply clothed. He, in comparison, was pale and thin, and wore a sheer blue shirt that plunged deeply at the neckline to reveal a silver chain resting on his chest. His fingers were adorned with a dazzling collection of rings, clinking together as he raised his mug, drawing attention to themselves and amusingly annoying the drunks. It was not quite the resplendent fashion of his days in court, but he'd had to strip back a little, for, in theory, he was trying to pass unnoticed.

'Can I get you a fresh mug, sir?'

The barmaid was a healthy auburn-haired girl, the only spark of life in the place. He favoured her with a handsome smile.

'Please, my dear. Thank you very much.'

He'd had a few mugs already, and was beginning to feel the effects. This home-spun ale was not quite the clear, refreshing wine he thirsted for, but it did the trick.

As the barmaid moved away, he watched her posterior with some interest.

'So what're you supposed to be, eh?'

One of the glaring drunks had finally found the courage to address him, while the other sniggered.

'Just a humble traveller, sir,' he answered airily. 'Out and about seeing the world.'

'Look like a wayward lord to me. One who's lost his king!'

They laughed, and he gave them a tight smile.

'May be some truth to that,' he said.

'I'll bet!' The drunk slapped the table. 'I'll bet!'

Despirrow didn't want to encourage them too much, lest they become overly familiar. He became very interested in inspecting his nails.

'Sorry about them, sir,' the returning barmaid said quietly. His eyes flickered over her bosom as she bent to place a mug before him, back up to her face before she had a chance to catch him ogling. She, however, wouldn't have noticed, for she was, in turn, sneaking a glance at his glittering rings.

'That's quite all right,' he said. 'I expect they won't remember me tomorrow, and I'll endeavour to return the favour.'

His wit seemed to pass her by. She gave a little nod, but failed to produce the chuckle he had hoped for. He could tell she was impressed, however, by his garb, and no doubt his good looks.

'What is your name, miss?'

'Veysha,' she said.

'Tell me then, Veysha – such a pretty name – are there any sights to behold around here? Any crumbling old temples, or maybe a stream between trees that catches the starlight, a good place for a midnight picnic?'

She reddened a little.

'Not much to see around here, sir,' she said. 'My beau and I sometimes take a walk, but once you've seen one field, you've seen them all.'

She retreated, and he gave an internal sigh. Mention of a 'beau', whether he existed or not, was obviously meant to convey a clear message.

Had he been too forward?

There was a time when he'd been better at this. He'd had women aplenty flocking to him, well served by his reputation as a lover. Charming in a way that did not feel forced, as it had done recently – ladies falling over one another for a chance at a 'midnight picnic'. Life as a court threader, best friend to the king, had been good. Now he could not even pique the interest of this plump farm-grown tavern wench.

Well, no matter. He had been curious, that was all, to see if he could still cajole interest willingly. The effort bored him quickly, however, and there was always the easier way. One little 'halt!' in his mind to stop the passage of time, while he was touching her of course, and he would bring her with him into limbo while the rest of the world went still. Then he could hike up her skirt and bend her over the bar, and she could scream for her stupid imaginary *beau* all she liked, while he crushed her breasts against the wood, under the dull stare of the drunks . . .

'Everything all right, sir?'

He realised he had been baring his teeth as he imagined the sweat running down her thighs.

'Oh . . . yes.' He smoothed his expression. 'The ale is just a little cool on a sensitive tooth that I happen to have.'

Perhaps raping her would be easy, yet he managed to control himself. All his life his lust had been great, even before the change. He did not want to leave a trail of breadcrumbs, however, marking his whereabouts for cursed Braston and whoever else. He had already broken his rule, effectively announcing to the other Wardens that he was at large, but this Veysha wasn't pretty enough to warrant the risk.

'Are there any whores in this backwater?' he asked, all friendliness gone from his demeanour.

'Er . . .' Veysha didn't like him at all anymore. 'No, sir . . . the men round here stay true to their women.'

Despirrow barked a laugh. 'What's that got to do with it?' He chugged the rest of his ale, flung some coins across the table and stalked out of the tavern.

Outside, the sun hurt his eyes and made him feel woozy. How long had he been sitting in there? How drunk, in fact, was he?

It didn't matter. Nothing really mattered. As long as he stayed out of sight, he could do what he liked. They wouldn't come after him first, would they? Forger and Karrak were much worse than him. Those two were focused, grandiose in their actions, while he was happy keeping out of everyone's way. He could always seek his old comrades out later if he needed to. In the meantime, mystified as he was to have returned from the grave, he wasn't complaining.

He moved down the packed mud street, levelling contempt at the village's small dwellings.

I don't belong here, he thought. *I need a proper town. A city.*

Once outside the village, he found a secluded spot under trees, and sank down in the shade. Time to threadwalk, but where to go?

Saphura, came the answer.

Dare he?

He tried to summon an image of the place, to envisage the line between him and it, but drink made it difficult to hold a steady thought. He was in no state for the complicated process of threadwalking.

Just close my eyes for a little, he thought.

When he got to Saphura, there would be wine and whorehouses aplenty. As he leant back against the trunk, he hoped his dreams would be of them . . .

'It just doesn't feel right,' said Braston, as they made their way toward the throne room. 'I should be marching with the army.'

Despirrow gave a sympathetic smile. Well did he know the depth of Braston's desire to be with his people as they journeyed north to the Ilduin Fields. Aorn's great powers – Althala, Sortree, Galra, Ander, Tallahow and others, had pledged to combine, and throw everything they had at the Pass. It was a desperate plan, and Despirrow foresaw a massive loss of life.

'You know my objections,' he said, 'to such a funnelling of forces. It matters not how many of us cooperate, when a handful of Unwoven can defend the Pass against a thousand.'

Braston frowned. 'I see no other option – no matter the cost, we simply can't let Regret continue with his experiments! Truly, I wish there was another way.'

'Why wish it? It is precisely what Mergan offers.'

Braston got a pained look, which came when his heart was at odds with his head. 'You really think his plan can work?'

'I think,' said Despirrow, 'it has a better chance than heaping the slain at the foothills of the Roshous.'

Braston sighed. 'I ask my soldiers to fight, to die, for me. How will they react when they learn I don't stand with them?'

'My friend, you'll do them greater service if you end Regret once and for all. The sooner he dies, the more of them you'll save. Trust me, they will thank you for it.'

'If we succeed.'

'If we succeed.'

Braston made a vexed noise. 'Would that I had not been born a threader, just a simple king instead.'

'Your commanders are worthy,' said Despirrow, 'and there will be other leaders on the Fields. Have some faith, Braston – it will not fall apart for lack of your gaze.'

Braston grunted.

They entered the throne room, which was unusually empty. At a fountain near the entrance stood the sole occupants – Mergan, with the band of threaders he had scoured Aorn to assemble. Despirrow recognised only one of them – Karrak, prince of Ander, had visited Althala during more peaceable times. Approaching with Braston, Despirrow took in the rest.

There was a bald fellow dressed in leather, his skin a little sooty. A slight girl in a flowery dress tugged nervously at her auburn hair. A soft-faced man in travelling clothes had a serene, unfocused gaze. And a young woman in a white robe, with startlingly white hair, could only be the Priestess Yalenna. Despirrow found his gaze lingering upon her, but he forced aside any lustful thoughts. This was a serious group, put together for serious reasons. There would be plenty of time for romance once the world was safe.

'Ah,' said Mergan, 'Braston, Despirrow – welcome. Let me introduce you to the rest of the Wardens.'

'Wardens?' said Braston.

'It seems a fitting name,' said Mergan, 'given the purpose for which we've come together.'

'And how did you go about finding these fine folk?' said Braston. He moved before them, bowing slightly to Karrak, who returned the gesture. 'What was the standard by which the best threaders in Aorn are judged?'

Although his tone did not imply disrespect, Mergan stood a little straighter. Braston was still king here, and it seemed he was not letting anyone forget it.

'Well,' said Mergan, 'perhaps I should let them show you.'

―

Despirrow awoke with a stiff neck in the afternoon, the last doldrums of ale still curling in his veins. *Wardens indeed*, he thought, annoyed by the dream. That name had lost all original meaning, replaced these days with the hate and fear the likes of him had imbued it with. The Despirrow who had given Braston patient counsel, and silenced his own desires at will, was long gone. Thinking about him now was like trying to remember the details of childhood – a few disconnected images, some vague impressions, and not much else.

He wanted water, badly. In his mind's eye he saw the crystal surface of the Lumin River, bubbling happily under the bridge into Saphura.

Damn it. I have to get out of this nowhere.

He stood and, with a flick, banished all dirt from his clothes and skin. He tried to recall where he was – somewhere between the Temple of Storms and Althala, not that far from Saphura by foot, really – and forced himself to go through the mental preparation for the move. Some minutes later he was on his way, the hot fields fading past him as his threads realigned to the distant point.

He felt nauseous as he stepped out of the air, onto a path hemmed by trees and waxy ferns. A quick scan of his surrounds showed no one about to register his arrival, which was good, because he didn't feel like being delayed by any killing. Before him a bridge hung over a ravine some twenty paces deep, through which the Lumin ran. The bridge swung slightly as he stepped onto it, enjoying the coolness that issued from beneath. On the other side, the path continued on and disappeared around a low hill, which housed a gaping cave mouth he didn't remember.

As he walked towards it, he saw something strange. On one side of the path, before the cave mouth, was a clear, rocky area. There, some of the groups of smaller rocks were rattling together, as if something beneath them was trying to dig out. Suddenly the rocks took off, floating directly up into the air. He waited, watching, until they grew to distant specks.

Things quieted down.

The Spell ails, he thought.

He knew that he was partly to blame – corrupted, as it were. That was what made his enemies so righteous about hunting him, beyond the simple drive to stop a villain. Despirrow understood that was what he was, what he had become, but it didn't bother him – he enjoyed being him. And if the world was coming undone, he was damned if he wasn't going to enjoy that too, while he could.

He felt bolder as he approached Saphura, more inclined to squeeze the town for honey. He followed the path around the hill, and down the slope ahead. Along the Lumin, blue-tiled buildings smiled at him. White froth milled about stone wharves that broke the river's flow, and the doughty little boats tied to them.

It was a relief for Despirrow to see a place so familiar, a place he sentimentalised. He'd had some good times here.

Had that been before the change, or after?

He frowned, not quite sure. Maybe both.

With a shrug and a jolly bounce in his step, he made his way down the hill. As he neared the edge of town, a sight stopped him in his tracks.

'Ah,' he said.

A little way off the path, across grass, nestled between copses of trees, colourfully attired locals gathered around a makeshift stage. Upon it stood a beautiful young woman in a flowing green dress, the groom beside her beaming his fool head off. Between them was a white-robed priest bearing the lightning insignia, listening to them speak their vows, and making the breeze whistle about them.

My weakness, my joy.

Of all things that were hard to resist, weddings topped Despirrow's list. To take the bride in full view of her friends and family – rutting at her would-be husband's feet, his ears unhearing of her pleas, and then leave her there, weeping, as time came back, bloodied and bruised and sullied – oh, there was no greater thievery! So ultimately selfish, such an act of pure *taking*, debauchery divine.

He stepped from the path, all thoughts of whorehouses forgotten. His encounter with the Spell had made him reckless – time was ticking by, and who knew when he might be presented with such an opportunity again?

'Despirrow.'

The voice froze him even as he'd been about to freeze time. One more moment and it would have been done. Instead, coldly, angrily, he turned to take in the equally chilly eyes of his old comrade, who stood under a tree, camouflaged in the shade against the sight of others.

'What are you doing here?' spat Despirrow.

'Saving you from yourself, it seems,' said Salarkis.

'Find me later if you want to talk. I am occupied.'

'I see what you're about, Despirrow. Don't you think *they* might be closely watching, waiting and listening for any sign of us?'

'I do not fear Braston.'

'How about he and Yalenna both? Don't you think they'll hear about a strange happenstance, in which a bride claims to have been raped during her wedding ceremony . . . or simply disappears, if you planned to kill her once you're done? Don't you think it will bring them to you like wasps to maggots?'

'I can be gone from here afterwards.'

'Before you even step foot in Saphura? Don't you wish to see her streets again, drink her wine?'

'I'll let you have a turn!' hissed Despirrow. 'After me, you can have what's left of her!'

Salarkis chuckled. 'It would not appeal to dip my fish in the sop of your handiwork, even if I had the fish . . . which I do not, or have you forgotten?' He grew steelier. 'It's not just Braston and Yalenna after us, Despirrow. It's Karrak too.'

Longingly Despirrow stared as the couple leaned in for a kiss to seal their union. As the onlookers cheered and cried, he knew his precious moment was lost. Oh, he could find her later, but it would not be the same – she would just be another woman then, no longer the bride on her wedding stage.

Salarkis's last words finally trickled into his brain.

'What?'

'Karrak. He is no longer one of us. He has gone over, joined *them*.'

'No.' Despirrow couldn't help but laugh. 'Karrak? Turned good? I don't believe it.'

'It is, however, true.'

'Why? How?'

'He has been alive the whole time we slumbered. Time has changed him, for better or worse, depending where you stand.'

The couple stepped down to move between their guests, who showered them with petals. Despirrow scowled.

'That is unwelcome news.'

Though he had never liked Karrak much in the first place, it was still difficult to believe they were now true enemies.

'Take heart, comrade. You can still have your fun. Just choose wiser victims.'

'I am not some weasel slinking in dark alleys! I take,' Despirrow thumped his chest, 'who I want!'

Salarkis shrugged. 'If you wish. Meanwhile I shall threadwalk far away, for Saphura will be ruined for us all.'

Despirrow's shoulders sagged.

'Come, my friend,' said Salarkis. 'You have gold, do you not?'

'Of course.'

Briefly he remembered the fat-pursed merchant he had met on the road, and his beautiful daughter. That had been the first instance of stopping time since he'd been back, the double reward too much to resist.

'Saphura still has whores, no doubt,' said Salarkis. 'Ease your lust in a common way, just this once, as a favour to me. When you have done so, in the aftermath of clarity, you will know that I was right. If not, curse my name, and do as you will.'

Reluctantly Despirrow knew that he was being given sound advice.

'What about you?' he said. 'Are you still Forger's errand boy, come to counsel me to return to his side? I will get there, in the end. I'm just taking my time.'

'No,' said Salarkis. 'I'm no one's lackey.'

Despirrow scoffed.

'I guess you could say,' Salarkis continued, ignoring the slight, 'that I am taking my own time too. Which doesn't mean I can't look out for my comrades in the meantime. Stealer is dead –'

'So that is true.'

'– killed by Karrak –'

Despirrow grimaced.

'– leaving only you, I, and Forger as . . . allies. The odds are not stacked in our favour as once they were, Despirrow. I only hope that Mergan is mad enough to be no help to our enemies.'

'Mergan? Mad?'

'He was locked in Regret's tomb for three hundred years.'

'How do you know all this? Have you been having any conversations I should know about?'

'Sometimes,' said Salarkis with a wink, 'when I listen, people do not know I'm there.'

He gave a mocking little bow, and unravelled.

The commotion from the wedding grew louder, and Despirrow realised they were heading towards him, no doubt to carry the festivities into town.

He turned away, not wishing to look upon what had been denied him.

As Yalenna made her way through the castle to her quarters, Captain Jandryn emerged in front of her, heading in the same direction. She drifted along behind him for a while, her soft shoes making no noise on the carpet. For some peaceful moments all other thoughts left her as she found herself admiring his well-turned calves. Then he glanced around and saw her, and the tweak of a smile on her lips vanished.

'My lady,' he said, stopping to wait.

'Hello, Jandryn.'

He fell into step beside her. 'I was just on my way to see you.'

'Oh, yes? What should I know?'

'Er . . .' He glanced about. She wondered if reporting to her made him anxious, as she was not officially part of the castle hierarchy. 'I just wanted to see if you . . . wanted anything done?'

'As a matter of fact,' she said, 'I wonder if there's been any word of Despirrow? We are hoping to track him.'

'Nothing I know of, my lady.'

'Braston has already instructed his threaders to keep their ears open, but if you hear anything, come to me first.

Especially anything about strange rapes and assaults on women.'

Her words made him uncomfortable. 'I will, my lady.'

'Good. Now, if you will excuse me, I'm quite tired.'

'Of course.'

They were halfway down a corridor without an easy exit, though it was clear to Jandryn he was being dismissed. Awkwardly he turned and went the other way, trying to make it appear that he had some purpose in that direction. Yalenna smiled a little at his discomfort, finding it somehow endearing.

She reached her quarters and, upon entering, found Salarkis sitting in her armchair by the window.

'Hello,' she said.

Salarkis gave her a wan glance. 'Despirrow is in Saphura,' he said. 'Thought you'd like to know.'

As seemed to be becoming his infuriating habit, he disappeared.

A SWIRL OF LEAVES

Braston led the way onto the bridge. It was important for him, thought Rostigan, to go first, to be bold. Or maybe he did it naturally, instinctively. Either way, *let him*.

Underfoot the Lumin gurgled along happily, somehow putting him in touch with the deep place – with all the rivers he had ever crossed, as if water was a continuum. His skin prickled, and he felt alive; the sun on his skin, the cool vapour rising from beneath, the smell of trees, all simple sensations combining to form a moment of near-painful connection. It was comforting to know that there were forces in the world greater than he, older, outside his control.

'Are you coming?'

This from Yalenna, spoken softly, and he realised he had been loitering at the end of the bridge, as if the final step would change things. He took it, and it did. Peace left him, as he remembered what they were here to do.

They moved along the path, past a hill in which a cave mouth yawned. Curious, Rostigan went to look inside – he didn't remember seeing it before. It was not very large or deep, and he thought it seemed man-made. What had someone thought they would find in there?

'Come on,' said Braston impatiently.

Around the bend the path sloped down towards the town. Saphura was a pretty place, its shiny blue buildings and white cobbled streets hedged in by wood and river, so closely that town and nature were almost intermixed.

Tarzi was fond of this city, he remembered. They had come here once together and spent several days doing not much of anything. He wished that she was here now, that they were heading to the riverbank together, where he would smoke his pipe and watch her fish, eventually snoozing in the shade. There was something about the constant sound of running water that already made him feel half-asleep.

The town itself, on the other hand, was quite noisy. The streets were full of bustle, and there was plenty of activity around the docks. They approached from the lesser travelled direction, and on the other side of town to the north the snake of a wider road was visible, wrapping around hilltops to jaggedly follow the river.

They moved down the slope and drew level with the town. Although the Wardens were dressed modestly – the other two had shed priestess's robe and king's cape for more commonplace garb – they still attracted a number of stares.

Rostigan did not think it was because they were strangers, for Saphura's fish trade and decadent reputation brought visitors from far and wide. Perhaps the three of them – he grim with a large broadsword slung across his back, she beautiful and smooth and sure, and Braston a tower of muscle – simply made for a striking group. The thought did not warm him, for they did not want Despirrow noticing them first. He quickened his step and caught Braston by the arm. Braston, whose eyes had been sweeping back and forth across the street, snapped around, tenser than Rostigan had thought.

'Have you spotted him?' Braston asked intently.

'He will spot us, if we continue charging down the middle of the main road.'

'We should split up,' said Yalenna. 'He can avoid us less easily that way.'

Braston gave a fierce nod.

They turned from one another to go separate ways.

⁓

As she slipped through the crowd, Yalenna hoped Salarkis had not tricked them into coming here – that she hadn't led Braston and Ka— . . . Rostigan . . . on some kind of distractive chase, or into a trap.

I do trust him, she told herself, *if only because I want to.*

Lacking a method to zero in on Despirrow with any certainty, she thought it best to start by checking the brothels. Unlike with some towns, Saphura's brothels were not all cloistered away in some district of ill-repute. Here they were attached to taverns, or stood proudly amongst other businesses displaying their names on signs carved with suggestive silhouettes. There were more of them than she remembered, and she wondered how the local fishermen avoided running into their daughters . . . but then again, many daughters had probably escaped their families elsewhere, to come here. Sons, too, she thought, as she eyed off two muscular youths accompanying a pair of older women dripping in gems.

On the other side of the road she saw Rostigan going through a swinging doorway into a plush-looking den. Inside she caught a glimpse of scantily clad girls on tabletops, around which men sat drinking from silvery mugs. Plush, but not plush enough – and there she found her method. She needed to locate the best, most expensive place there was.

She stopped at a street stall where dried fish hung on ropes over bowls of shiny berries. They looked quite delicious, though there were a half a dozen stores just like it within sight. The storekeeper, who seemed ill kept and sweaty under his freshly laundered clothes, watched her with hopeful eyes.

'Can I help you, miss?'

'I need some information,' said Yalenna.

'Oh,' he said, evidently disappointed. A blessing sank into him – *rats will never steal from your larder* – but he would not guess that he was far richer for the interaction than he would be from any simple sale of produce.

Besides, Yalenna flipped a couple of coins onto his counter.

'Well, miss,' he said, swiftly palming the money, 'that is very generous. What would you like to know?'

'Have there been any assaults in the last day or so?'

'Ah . . .' the man frowned. 'Couple of fellows beat each other pretty bad over at the Curdled Sow . . .'

'Involving women.'

'Hmm? Oh, nothing like that. Saphura may have a colourful reputation, but there are plenty of well-paid guards around to make sure nothing happens to its folk! No matter what line of work they're in.'

'In that case, where's the best whorehouse in town?'

His eyebrows only went up slightly.

'That depends. What kind of . . . taste . . . needs to be catered for?'

'A man's taste for beautiful women.'

'I see.' He eyeballed her in a different way now – perhaps he thought she meant to seek employment. 'That would be The Silken Glove. It's a little further on, on the right – look for the sign, you can't miss it.'

'Thank you,' she said, and popped some berries in her mouth.

True to the storekeeper's word, The Silken Glove wasn't far at all. The sign was a beckoning hand with the name in silver, the door an elegant steel frame carved with spirals, and there weren't any windows on the ground floor. She approached the heavyset doorman who stood outside, a crossbow on his back.

'May I enter?' she asked.

He looked her up and down. 'The mistress does not currently seek any more ladies – though one of your quality shouldn't have trouble finding work elsewhere.'

'I'm not here for work – I'm looking for a friend of mine, maybe you've seen him? He dresses very well, like a courtier –'

'People dress all kinds of ways,' he interrupted, 'and we do not disturb our clients in their rooms for any reason, social visits included.'

His tone had turned a little nasty, and she did not feel he deserved his blessing – *may you never get sick again.* With a subtle flick she seized hold of his boots, and he grunted in surprise as, seemingly of their own accord, they marched him out of her way.

'What?' he said, then realisation dawned. 'You're a thr—'

A little wave, and his lips snapped shut.

'Just you stay out here a while,' she told him, 'and be silent.'

Moving past, she pushed through the door.

Inside was a dim area lit by lanterns and candles, lined with soft couches where men sat meeting prospective partners. Overseeing it was a high desk, behind which sat an older woman in a frilled violet dress, still with a touch of glamour about her, though painted lips and cheeks could not disguise her sagging skin.

Her eyebrow quirked as Yalenna approached. 'Hello. You're not one of ours?'

'I'm looking for a man.'

The madam frowned. 'Why did Gosk let you in? He should have explained that we do not cater for –'

'A particular man,' said Yalenna. 'A tall fellow, thin, probably well dressed, with a taste for fine wine.'

The madam's eyes glittered – she knew something. 'I must ask you to leave,' she said, and glanced towards a dark corner where another brute waited. Yalenna slipped a hand over the desk and seized her by the wrist.

'Do not summon him,' she said in a low voice. A blessing transferred to the woman – *may you never feel the cold of your morning bath*. 'Listen to me. I am a powerful threader. If you do not tell me what I wish to know, I will cause you a great deal of trouble.'

If the madam was afraid, she hid it well.

'There are threaders in the town guards, you know,' she hissed. 'You cannot do as you like just because you have magic.'

'I doubt they'll be here in the time I need to collapse this musk-smelling hovel.' Yalenna released the woman's wrist. 'Come, this is only one man. He isn't a good man, either – trust me when I say that your establishment is better off without him.'

The madam tried to rally. 'We pride ourselves on the privacy we provide.'

'There won't be much privacy to be had when the town dogs wander freely through the rents I'll leave in your walls.'

'Everything all right here, ma'am?'

This from the brute, who had wandered over.

'Er . . . yes, Terrik.' The madam was growing spooked now. Yalenna did not like having to use force, but there was an urgency to her task. 'Please leave us.'

Terrik withdrew, back to his post.

'Well?' said Yalenna.

'All *right*. I think I know what fellow you mean . . . though in truth, the description you gave could fit many round here.'

'He wears lots of rings.'

The madam sighed. 'First floor. Room sixteen. Are you his wife?'

Yalenna gave an unladylike snort and made for the stairs. At the top she found a well-groomed landing, carpet plumped up and lewd tapestries hanging. *Do they want to think they're in a castle?* she wondered disdainfully, as she moved swiftly along the corridor to the door marked sixteen.

She flung it open.

A naked girl tangled in sheets sat up with a gasp, as an open window banged in the breeze. From the street below came the sound of commotion.

'Who are –' the girl said, before time froze.

Despirrow had woken with a start. As one in tune with the threads of time, he'd felt a vibration he knew all too well – a warning, of bad things on the way.

He sat up, causing the girl beside him to groan. He could have groaned himself, for he'd had much wine the previous night. As his eyes fell on the sleeping whore's rising bosom, there came an insistent urge to set about her again – but the feeling that put him on edge superseded it. He rose, and opened the window.

Voices came from the street below.

'. . . a friend of mine, maybe you've seen him? He dresses very well, like a courtier . . .'

Despirrow flattened against the wall. All too well, he knew that voice. Had she come alone, or did she have company?

Carefully, he peeked through the window again. She was in the process of moving the doorman, and before he could summon the focus to bend her skull inwards, she departed from view into the brothel.

He ran to his pile of things and pulled on clothes and boots. Back to the window he went and, as he hastily fixed rings onto his fingers, he scanned the street.

There.

So, it was true – Karrak had gone over to the enemy. He saw his old ally only for a moment, entering a tavern across the way. Hatred suffused him, but there was fear also, enlivening his body and clearing his groggy head.

Yalenna was somewhere beneath, and Karrak nearby, but for a moment the street was clear. Scrambling through the window, Despirrow dropped feet first, sending influence ahead of him to soften the cobblestones to mush. He landed, feet sinking into the street as if it were mud, and people who saw him blinked in surprise. With stinging soles he spun about, spied the doorman standing rigidly with his mouth firmly shut.

'She worked you over, eh?'

He noted the crossbow on the man's back. He might have use for such a thing, for, if he had to stop time, neither he nor anyone else could use their magic. An actual weapon might not go amiss.

"Scuse me,' he said, moving behind the fellow to pull the crossbow free. The man, stuck as he was to the spot, could still move his arms, and tried to grab at Despirrow.

'None of that, thanks,' said Despirrow, and with a waggle of his fingers, ripped the man's throat out. Blood arced across the thoroughfare, splashing people nearby.

'Murder!' someone shouted, and people began to scramble in a panic.

On the opposite side of the street he saw Karrak dash out of a tavern with sword drawn, looking about wildly for the source of the commotion. Despirrow smiled at him, waiting to be seen, scraping mashed cobblestone off his heel.

Rostigan saw the body first, led there by a trail of people dashing away. A man stood next to it, under the shaded eaves of a whorehouse, and Rostigan recognised the cruel, angular features, the sunken cheeks, of Despirrow. The Warden grinned at him, reached out – and Rostigan readied himself to unthread any spell flung at him – but instead Despirrow attacked nearby townsfolk. A merchant fell with blood squirting from his ears, his head misshapen as if hit by a hammer. Further away in the crowd – far enough for the attacks to seem random, to confuse everyone – two women suddenly smashed together as if crushed in an invisible vice. People began screaming, fleeing.

Rostigan ran towards Despirrow, and was instantly caught up in the frightened crowd. He ducked and wove as best he could, elbowing and pushing when necessary. The next moment all went silent, as everywhere people froze in place. A man who would have moved out of the way if time had been running naturally instead remained, and Rostigan charged into him. The impact was hard and jarring, akin to smacking headlong into a tree. Despirrow laughed as Rostigan staggered backwards, and time started again. As Rostigan appeared unexpectedly to those around him, people ploughed into him from different directions, knocking him to the ground.

Time stopped again, and he opened his eyes. Through the sea of statues sauntered Despirrow, raising his crossbow at Rostigan as he gained line of sight. Rostigan raised a hand instinctively, but threading was impossible in the suspended world. The bolt whizzed through the air, and went straight through his palm.

'Despirrow!' came a voice from above. It was Yalenna, standing at a window in the whorehouse above street level. From somewhere else in the still town came a raging roar.

'Ah,' said Despirrow. 'So dear old Braston is here too?'

He loosed a bolt at Yalenna. She ducked from sight, and it bounced off glass that it should have shattered.

Despirrow dashed away, and Rostigan tried to rise. Time unfroze and again the crowd closed in, trampling him as he appeared under their feet. A boot landed square on his chest, its owner crashing down after.

'Keep away from me!' he wheezed, loudly as he could, threading his words. The crowd began to recede, leaving him an island in the turmoil. Then a firm grip took his arm and hoisted him up.

'Where did he go?'

It was Braston, looking wild. He shook Rostigan, though he probably didn't mean to do it so savagely.

'Damn you, Karrak, where?'

Rostigan held out his punctured hand, the dripping bolt still lodged there.

'That way.'

Braston released him so suddenly he swayed, taking off in the direction he'd pointed.

Steadying himself, he took hold of the bolt, and pulled it out with a grunt.

Yalenna appeared. 'Are you all right?'

'Fine.'

He began to move after Braston, wondering if he could yet break into a jog.

'Come on – he's getting away!'

⁓

The crowds thinned as people ran for cover, and Despirrow ducked into a deserted side street lined with moulting trees. Where did he want to go? Briefly he wondered if he could take on all three of his pursuers, and end the threat to himself here, today. The thought was tantalising – if he succeeded, there would be no one to stop him doing whatever he wished for the rest of time, however long that ended up being.

Instincts of self-preservation quieted the fantasy. Much as he admired himself, his foes were formidable, and to be respected. He needed to get away, and find somewhere he could hide long enough to threadwalk. He decided to make for the southern path back up the hill to the bridge, where woods and caves would provide good hiding spots.

'Despirrow!'

The bellow followed him up the street, and he felt a chill at the anger it contained. Braston would always hate him the most, for they had been friends, once. After the change, they had gone back to Althala Castle together, and Despirrow had thought he could hide his new self from the king, and have his way with all the prissy, stuck-up noblewomen who had previously refused his advances. He did not *have* to stop time in order to rape them – just seal them in their rooms against intrusion and, afterwards, kill them, or tangle their minds until they could no longer speak sense. He had not counted on Braston's new talent, however, to *see* the lines of injustice wavering from Despirrow's victims, and understand that his old court threader had taken a sinister turn.

'Can you catch me again, oh King?' he called over his shoulder.

The answering roar was closer now.

Subtly Despirrow manipulated the air, sending up a breeze.

Leaves began to lift behind him.

⁓

Rostigan picked up speed as he followed Yalenna, his body gradually correcting some of the hurts he'd garnered from being stomped and winded, his stubbornness overriding the rest. The pain in his hand was the worst and would probably take some days to heal, but as long as he had his legs, he could run.

Ahead Yalenna was spry and sleek, and further on Braston tore into a side street. Rostigan entered after them to see trees along the pavement swaying slightly, fallen leaves on the ground stirring. Behind the fleeing Despirrow more leaves swirled, as if he'd kicked them up behind him.

Rostigan realised what was about to happen.

'Yalenna,' he tried, but breath was short – maybe he was still a little winded after all. He reached out, attempting to take control of her boots, and instinctively she undid his influence. She did stumble a little, however, and she turned to jog backwards for a moment.

'What?'

'Stop,' he wheezed.

Braston pounded the cobblestones, eyes fixed on his fleeing adversary. Mocking cackles bounced back to him off buildings, maddening him further. Despirrow could not be allowed to exist, his presence in the world was a mocking insult – a grave *injustice*. There was nothing left of the person who had been Braston's friend, the familiar face naught but an illusion to cover the foulness that now possessed him. Braston sent spells after the man, but each and every one was adroitly unthreaded before it reached him. Despirrow was the better caster, whereas Braston preferred strength. If he could just get the little rat in his hands, he could break him like a twig . . .

A leaf stuck to Braston's forehead, and absently he brushed it away. How to halt Despirrow, how to get close enough to seize him? Maybe he could use the wind that whistled down the street, channel it to slow Despirrow. As he reached out to harness the breeze, though, he realised it was not a natural one.

Time froze.

Leaves hung in the air all around, immovable and razor-thin. Braston, already moving at speed, ploughed into them directly. They sliced through him smoothly, his flesh offering all the resistance of warm jelly. One passed through his arm, half-severing it, while another caught him on the neck, barely affecting his momentum as it cut muscle and artery with equal ease. He tried to stop, but had little control as his legs were shredded underneath him. A leaf scraped along his shin, peeling bone like curled apple peel. He fell upon more leaves and slid downwards. A bright agony blossomed as one passed through his gut. As it was about to reach his spine, he slowed to a stop – not all the leaves lay at cutting angles, and a few now cradled his doubled-over torso, so that with knees bent and arms hanging loosely, he could not make it all the way to the ground.

His anger became muted, as if it poured from him with his blood. The leaves embedded in his body were sickening presences, tearing him further every time he shuddered. If only he could lift himself off them, but with so many nerves and muscles damaged, so much flesh hanging from him loosely, he could not make his body respond.

Yalenna stopped, ashen-faced, on the edge of the cloud of leaves.

'Careful,' said Rostigan, arriving by her side.

Braston was bent over and sagging in the air, though something had stopped him from collapsing entirely. It had been so fast and brutal, and already an impossible amount of blood was pooling around him, and dripping from nearby leaves that had been showered in the spray. Beyond it all, Despirrow disappeared around a corner.

Carefully Yalenna made her way into the leaves. At one point she had to get down on her hands and knees to crawl, under the swirl and into the warm redness. Grunting from behind told her Rostigan followed, but she paid him no mind – all her thoughts with Braston.

Is he alive? Please, let him be alive.

Tears threatened to prickle forth, and she blinked rapidly, willing them away. He *must* be alive, she told herself, though at best he would be terribly, terribly hurt. Closer up the damage that ravaged him was all the more shocking. She crawled underneath him, to see if the eyes in his head would open.

'Braston?'

After a moment they did, moving towards her slightly.

'Get . . .'

As he tried to speak, a slop of blood spilled from his mouth, drowning his words.

Suddenly, mercifully, time started again. Braston pitched forward as the leaves supporting him went back to weightlessness. She narrowly avoided his bulk as he hit the ground with a thud, and rolled onto his side.

'Despirrow's on the move,' said Rostigan grimly.

Yalenna did not care. Braston needed help.

His face twisted with pain. He worked his tongue, trying to clear his mouth.

'Don't . . . let him get away.'

'But you –'

'Leave me! I will . . . live.' He sounded like he was trying to convince himself. 'We might . . . not get this chance again.'

'Braston –'

'Go!' The effort of speaking made him wince. 'Please!'

'Come,' said Rostigan, pulling her to her feet. The wind was gone, and all around leaves were landing in the scarlet tide. 'We must do as he says.'

Yalenna tore her eyes away.

'We'll return for him,' Rostigan promised. 'Now come, Yalenna . . . come.'

~

He got her moving, and they cut through streets in the direction he'd last seen Despirrow heading.

Find a man running, he sent out, and several dark presences stirred nearby. They were lazy to his call, however, rustling their feathers but settling again, trying to ignore him.

Find him!

The crows remained reticent, and he sensed their displeasure with him. They had taken umbrage with the last task he'd given them, the survivors not even allowed to eat properly for their troubles.

He had no time for their reluctance. Focusing in on one young male, he made himself big in its mind.

Into the sky with you.

The crow obeyed, lifting from the roof of a nearby house. Through its eyes he saw the town from above, saw people moving about trying to work out what had happened. Guards were inspecting the bodies on the main street, others setting out to patrol. Then he spied a figure with blue shirt flapping, sprinting through alleys on the edge of town.

'He's making for the southern road,' he told Yalenna.

'Hold!'

Two threaders stepped into their path.

'Leave us alone!' ordered Rostigan, and they nodded in agreement and turned away.

The break in concentration made him think he'd lost the crow, but a moment later he found it, still circling overhead. Despirrow was heading up the hill, and behind he saw himself and Yalenna from above, in pursuit through the town outskirts. As they emerged and reached the hill, Rostigan lost connection to his reluctant minion. A glance upward with his real eyes showed him a distant black dot spiralling downwards, losing feathers as it went. His spy, it seemed, had been noted. Meanwhile Despirrow disappeared around the bend of the top of the hill.

Rostigan gave a knowing grunt.

'What?' puffed Yalenna.

'We'll see.'

Up the hill they went, around the bend to the stony area. A couple of vague scuffs on the path led towards the bridge.

'Looks like he tried to cover his tracks,' said Yalenna.

'Or he wants us to think he has,' said Rostigan quietly. 'Send us into the woods, where we could search for hours to no avail.'

He could *feel* the cave over his shoulder, as if it were watching him. An obvious hiding spot, too obvious for Despirrow to trust it, unless he really believed they would fall for his misdirection. Or it could be a trap – Despirrow could be standing just out of the light, waiting for them to approach, so he could stop time and come at them with his crossbow.

Rostigan spun about and seized the overhanging lip of the cave mouth. He wrenched it downwards, and rocks and roots cascaded to block up the entrance.

Yalenna raised an eyebrow. 'You think he went in there?'

'Could be. We'll know more if we collapse the roof.'

Moving around the settling rubble, they clambered up the pinnacle of the hill, which was flat at the top.

'Stand here, at the edge,' said Rostigan. 'We might be all right here.'

'If he's in there, he'll just stop time.'

'Yes, but what's his next move?'

Yalenna shrugged. 'Very well.'

Together they sent influence down into the roof of the cave, seeking out keystones and places where the earth was tightly packed.

'We want to do it all of a sudden, together,' Rostigan told her.

She nodded and tensed.

'Now.'

They tore at the supporting structures, loosened earth that kept larger rocks in place. In answer the hilltop trembled, and began to collapse inwards at the centre.

Time stopped.

It made for an interesting tableau. Before them, beyond the remaining ledge of solid ground they stood on, the hilltop hung in a state of suspended half-collapse. Light shone through holes into the cave interior, where rocks hung at various levels.

'Get down,' warned Rostigan. 'He may have sightlines to us.'

'Are you in there, wretch?' shouted Yalenna.

A bolt whizzed from the darkness and smacked into her shoulder. Rostigan pulled her down with him lest she stumble backwards off what remained of the hilltop. Once they found their balance, she glanced at her wound through watering eyes, and groaned.

'By the Spell!' she growled. 'When I get hold of you, Despirrow . . .'

'Steady,' said Rostigan.

'I *am* steady,' she replied irritably.

Somewhere beneath, Despirrow chuckled.

'I don't know what you're so happy about,' called Rostigan. 'What are you going to do now? You can't start time again without being crushed, and if you clamber up a staircase of falling debris, we'll be here to greet you.'

'You're right,' came the answer. 'I'm in a bit of a quandary. Or, maybe a better way to put it, a bit of a quarry!'

Rostigan gave an unamused snort.

'And how are you, Yalenna?' called Despirrow. 'I hate to admit that I'd deliberately try to destroy such beauty, but really, it was your face I aimed for.'

Yalenna tried to leap to her feet, but Rostigan kept a firm hold on her.

'Don't let him rile you,' he whispered. 'He's just trying to trick you into sticking your head up.'

She scowled at him, but nodded. 'Well, if it's taunting he wants.' She raised her voice. 'How many bolts have you left, Despirrow? Can't be many, if any.'

'No, not many, I admit. One, maybe two. Two would be convenient, don't you think?'

There was a scuffling in the dark, and it sounded like he was moving about.

'Is there a way out?' said Rostigan.

'Not that I can see. I'll look a little longer, though, if you'll forgive me.'

'Take your time.'

'Ha!'

More scuffling, then silence. Rostigan knew, having inspected the cave himself, that it did not extend into the greater hill beneath.

'Let me ask you something, Karrak.'

'That is not my name.'

'Don't be ridiculous. Oh, don't get me wrong – I appreciate the use of a false name when anonymity is preferable. I haven't been going about telling everyone that I am Despirrow, of course. But among those who know you, my friend, you will always be Karrak.'

Rostigan felt his brow grow heavy, as if it wanted to force his eyes closed. 'Go on,' he said. He had to hear Despirrow's arguments, if he were to stand against them.

'Why,' continued Despirrow, 'have you joined these e'er-do-wells? You were the worst of us all, and you want me to believe that you've turned *good*? You're a murderer, a tyrant, a thief, a tormentor . . .'

Rostigan gritted his teeth, and Yalenna's touch tightened on his arm.

'Don't let him,' she said. 'Don't hear it.'

'I need to.'

'Do you remember that night in Sortree when we made the nobles dance like puppets? Their living flesh hooked on barbed chains that we fastened to the roof, screaming as we made them pour our drinks.'

Rostigan closed his eyes, as if that could shut out the images issuing up from the deep place.

'And yet now you've taken up with Yalenna and Braston? You must be playing some trick, surely, taking some deceitful angle? Yalenna, do you really trust him? You should have seen him smile as he made Lord Bayflower mop his own blood from the tiles, jigging about as the fat of his arms worked loose. What has he told you, to secure your confidence?'

Rostigan saw himself, all those years ago, grinning at the suffering he caused, the fierce joy that his power had given him. And then he saw *her* face, hateful as she sat on the bed with her damp hair, waiting for him to come and take her.

'Lord of Crows, they called you,' said Despirrow. 'And what else, I wonder? Oh, that's right – Lord of Lies! What is your plan, Karrak? What is your true intent?'

'He was more convincing,' spoke up Yalenna, 'than your desperate attempt to sow discord. Why don't you come up and join us too, Despirrow, if you really believe Karrak so unchanged? We promise not to *rip out your heart*.'

'So spirited, Yalenna,' said Despirrow. 'And beautiful too, always so beautiful and young. How old are you really, though you look no more than twenty? I always felt sad that we never had our time together.'

'I'd sooner let a worm crawl into me.'

Despirrow barked harsh laughter. 'Well, at least I penetrated you with something – how is your shoulder feeling, anyway? Throbbing a little?'

All at once the cave was collapsing as time started again, but rocks blasted upwards rendered to grit and chunks, peppering Rostigan and Yalenna as they flung up their hands to protect their faces. A second blast sounded as the cave mouth unstoppered, the rubble that blocked it spinning clear.

Wiping his eyes to see Despirrow sprinting out of the cave towards the bridge, Rostigan took a running start along what remained of the hill, and leapt. As the rocky ground rushed up to meet him, he reached out to melt it for a kinder landing. Casually Despirrow gave a flick over his shoulder, undoing Rostigan's spell, so he cracked down hard on the flats of his feet. He tried to continue onwards, but his body had other ideas. Apparently something in one of his ankles had given out, and it dragged behind the rest of him.

'Don't let him get away!' Yalenna was clutching her dribbling shoulder and coming down the hill.

Despirrow reached the bridge. If he made it to the other side, he could dart into the wood, and it would quickly become much harder to find him. Hauling along his injured foot, Rostigan made up his mind not to let that happen. The pain was there, but he forced it away, and tried to quicken his step.

It was no good. Pain and willpower had nothing to do with it. His foot simply wasn't working properly.

He sensed Yalenna threading past him, towards a tree on the opposite side of the ravine. No doubt she hoped to crash it down and snap the bridge apart, but Despirrow saw what she attempted, and with a wave undid it. Yalenna gave an exclamation of frustration.

When Rostigan reached the bridge Despirrow was already halfway across, the gap between them growing ever wider. He put his hand on the rope, forgetful of the hole through his palm, though the rough surface quickly reminded him. Despairingly he knew there was no chance of keeping chase.

As though it had been shocked into him, he had a sudden thought.

Stealer.

Multiple throbbings stole his concentration as he tried desperately to think of a rhyme . . .

The swaying bridge
From ridge to ridge

As he spoke the last word, the bridge vanished.

Despirrow gave a yelp as he hurtled downwards to the gurgling river. He would be swept away, to safety, if Rostigan did not follow . . . so Rostigan stepped off the edge and plummeted after. Below the whistle of the wind in his ears, he heard his own voice whispering the words he had just spoken.

Below, Despirrow hit the river with a splash, his shirt ballooning around him as he bobbed in the current. He blinked water from his eyes to see Rostigan falling after him, and Rostigan guessed what might happen next. He did all he could to prepare himself for it, making sure he led with his good foot . . . and a moment later, crunched against the hard surface of the river, sprawling roughly along little waves and pockets of froth. A few paces away Despirrow's head stuck out of the motionless water, looking at him.

'I'd say that hurt,' he said. 'Hmm. I've never stopped time in a river before. I thought it might keep running, since

I'm in it, but evidently not. Actually, I'm quite encased!' He waggled some fingertips that broke the surface, through which he could not raise his hand.

If he could find the strength, Rostigan could lop his fool head off.

Despirrow's eyes went up to where the bridge had been. 'It just disappeared,' he said. 'Only Stealer could do that, and I daresay I heard your voice just now, speaking some *snatch* of poetry.'

Rostigan wheezed, trying to elbow himself up onto his knees.

'You killed her, didn't you? Salarkis told me about it.'

'I will . . . kill you too . . . Despirrow.'

'I don't think so. Look at you – you're all cracked and broken.'

Rostigan made it to kneeling, his quavering hand reaching to his back, for his sword.

'So you killed her,' frowned Despirrow, 'and now, apparently, you have her power. That is *very* interesting.'

Rostigan grunted as he swung the sword, and instantly icy water swallowed him. He plunged, thrashing for purchase, though it was difficult with most of his limbs damaged. Water flowed through the hole in his hand as he tried to swim, and the current dragged on his leaden foot. It was all he could do to stay afloat as they were carried through the ravine, out into woodland. The river gurgled and frothed in his nostrils, choking him as Despirrow swam ahead easily. With a great effort, Rostigan raised his sword from the water and flung it after him. It hit the water behind Despirrow with a dull slap, and sank.

'See you soon, Karrak!' Despirrow hooted.

Rostigan struggled towards the shore, grabbing at reeds he found there to haul himself along. He was too badly hurt for further pursuit, his lungs too full of water. At the bank he clawed through the mud until he was clear of the water. Downstream, Despirrow was a bright-blue speck swirling in the crystal flow, racing past curious spectators on boats. The river bent, and he was carried out of view.

'Damn you,' Rostigan muttered, and let his head fall.

A GOOD MAN

Tarzi jigged about the semicircle of recruits, who sat on the grass watching her perform. Cedris was there too, tapping his foot in time and beaming. Others off amongst the tents paused in their work to cast curious looks towards the music and song.

> *Did you ever hear the tale*
> *Of the man who thought up ale?*
> *Everyone who heard him thought him mad.*
>
> *'You're going to make a drink*
> *With the ingredients from bread?'*
> *Is what they shook their heads at him and said.*
>
> *But he laboured on a hunch*
> *That to liquefy his lunch*
> *Would produce the most amazing of results.*

THE LEGACY OF LORD REGRET

And he waited and he watched
His barrel of strange broth
Until his greedy mouth began to froth.

'Time to try some!' he declared
And his friends, they came and stared
As he scooped up his creation in a mug.

He let it touch his lips
Just the tiniest of sips
That's how it starts, as we all know, of course!

For soon he was a-guzzling
And his head was fizz-and-buzzing
'By the Spell, it's the most wonderful a thing!'

'It makes me want to dance!
And to seek out wild romance!
I have never felt this good before today!'

And his friends they could not help
But be curious to try
So up they lined to quaff at his supply.

Soon they laughed and slapped their knees
All as drunken as you please
And cried 'This man's a clever man, it's true!'

Into the night they drank
'Til the barrel was a drought
And all began to vomit and pass out.

And when the morning sun
Came to touch them one by one
They woke with groans and sorely pounding brows.

'You poisoned us!' they cried.
'There's no other explanation
For this rotten ruddy ill-feeling's causation!'

And the man had to agree
For it seemed to him that he
Had a flock of sparrows living in his skull.

All crawled home to their beds
With their aching sodden heads
And each and every thought that they would die.

Said 'we shan't do that again!'
And rose many times and peed
And felt very sorry for themselves indeed!

Until the day went by
And the evening did arrive –
The people, they were sound and still alive.

'Let us celebrate!' they called.
From his house the man they hauled.
'What's this?' he said. 'I thought you swore no more?'

'That was yesterday!' they said.
'But here and now it seems quite plain
You must mix up that poison once again!'

She strummed the final notes, and the soldiers laughed and jostled each other. It seemed the silliness had taken their minds off the grim tasks of the previous day. For herself, she was glad to have an audience, for sitting around waiting for Rostigan to return made her restless. She had said she'd be the army's minstrel and, as it turned out, she meant it.

'Storm and sleet, that song made me feel like a drink!' said Cedris, and a fellow next to him slapped him on the shoulder.

'You'll have to wait 'til dinnertime, and then it will be just one mug!'

Cedris screwed up his face in mock disgust. 'Best you take our minds off this sad fact, minstrel – sing us another!'

'Another?' said Tarzi, raising her eyebrows as she ran her fingers over the lute strings. 'Another, you say?'

'Another!' came the happy chorus of voices.

'Very well – how about the old lady who could not understand why her cow gave no milk?'

There was some hooting from those who already knew the answer, and everyone egged her on. Tarzi adopted an air of grave seriousness as she began the nonsense song, as if it were a dramatic ballad indeed.

After she finished that one, there were requests for another song, and another after that. Eventually she held up her hands and protested she could sing no more, a proclamation met with good-natured disappointment. In truth, Tarzi could have kept going for hours, but she had noticed that the sun was low in the sky, and Rostigan had expected to be back before dark. Waving goodbye, she promised that she would return soon – a fairly vague and nonbinding claim as far as she was concerned – and slung her lute over her shoulder to head towards the edge of camp.

Rostigan. Her feet quickened at the thought of him. She felt a bit silly, and a tinge showed on her cheeks, not that anyone noticed, or could know what put it there. How long would he do that to her? It was not as if he even tried very hard – certainly he did not fawn over her, or pay her many compliments. Yet, still and stoic as he was, his thoughts ever withheld and mysterious, he brooked no threat to her person or honour, and his embrace always felt warm and safe. It used to be her fear such moments were only borrowed, that one day he would turn around and say, 'That's enough, be off with you', but that day had never come, and she had gotten out of the habit of worrying about it.

She was proud of him too, extra proud today. Braston himself, and the Priestess Yalenna, had *sought him out*, impressed by his past deeds – and asked him to accompany them on a dangerous mission to kill Despirrow! They had even taken him threadwalking, which was a strange thing to contemplate. She had never heard of non-threaders being transported that way before, but supposed that Wardens were powerful enough to do fairly much whatever they liked. Half of her had wanted to ask if they would take her too – but when she thought about it again, she realised this was one adventure she would rather avoid. She was well-versed in tales of Despirrow, after all.

She knew she should be scared for Rostigan, and she was, a little, but somehow she managed not to think about it much. Her warrior would come back to her.

He always did.

***

'Rostigan!'

He paused and waited for Yalenna to catch up. Truth be told, he could use a moment of stillness. He coughed, spitting up more water.

She arrived at his side and put a hand on his arm. It was an odd sensation – her touch, given freely before the change, was now unexpected and foreign. He was struck by the concern on her face. Concern for him?

He remembered an instance of her bandaging his shoulder, a day or two into their journey through the Roshous. They had been attacked by a couple of silkjaws, and he had caught a nasty gash from a flailing wingtip. None of the group were overly gifted at healing – an oversight of Mergan's, perhaps, too concerned had he been with the aggressive side of threading – and yet Yalenna had done what she could to fix him. Her hands had been gentle but firm as she wound the bandage tighter, making some small admonishment about how he should keep his eyes open next time, smiling as she did, for they both knew he had been the one to warn of the danger, and if he hadn't the outcome could have been much worse . . .

'Are you all right?' she asked, breaking him from reverie.

'I will be.'

She slipped a hand under his arm for support. 'We need to get back to Braston.'

After a few steps, he felt her aid was really more of a hindrance than a help, and subtly retrieved his arm while forcing himself to pick up the pace.

'Lost my sword,' he murmured, almost embarrassed.

Not for the first time, came a stirring from the deep place. How many swords had he been through, over the years? Enough so he was not overly sentimental about any of them in particular.

Down the path, Saphura was abuzz. The murders on the street had shaken the populace, and people gesticulated excitedly as they gave their accounts to the guards. Suddenly the ground shook, and a great crack burst open along the main road, to jag off under storefronts. Yells accompanied sounds of collapse, and several roofs disappeared from the skyline.

'Wind and fire,' groaned Yalenna.

'The corruption spreads,' said Rostigan.

'It's infuriating! Despirrow uses his power so flagrantly. Surely stopping time all over Aorn puts great strain on the Spell – threads that should be moving all stuck in place.'

'Yes,' agreed Rostigan. 'Infuriating.'

'And, by the tides, he does not care a wink! Oh, how I wish we had killed him, curse him, the slippery eel!'

Rostigan did not voice his thought that it was not necessarily Despirrow to blame. He knew Yalenna understood that well enough – she was just frustrated.

Quick as it had appeared, the crack rumbled and closed, leaving barely a line behind. Little comfort for the owners of collapsed buildings, or anyone who had fallen in.

In moody silence Rostigan and Yalenna retraced their steps to Braston. They found him slumped against one of the trees whose leaves had cut him so deeply, pale and horribly damaged, with a few concerned people standing around him.

'We need a healer here!' said a man. 'Someone fetch a healer!'

'They're spread all over – more than one person needs healing right now.'

'How is he even still alive?'

'Make way,' said Yalenna. Despite the softness of her voice, every head turned. Then, in mystified reverence, the people did as she bid. Although they could not have guessed who she was, Rostigan knew how she must look to them – beautiful and angelic, her skin almost seeming to emanate light, her majesty close to tangible. How fond of her he was, again, he realised. Strange, when they had been enemies so long.

She knelt by Braston, whispering to him. Dried blood

across his eyes cracked as he opened them. His mouth quivered, and he seemed to be trying to form a question.

'He got away,' said Yalenna, delicately stroking his brow. 'I'm sorry.'

Braston seemed to deflate, though it might have been the life leaking out of him.

'We have to get him home,' said Yalenna, as Rostigan crouched beside her.

'I don't think he can threadwalk.'

'I . . . can,' Braston breathed. 'I must.' He reached out, though with his arm badly lacerated about the elbow, it was less like reaching and more like flinging out a fishing line. 'Help me.'

'I don't know how,' said Yalenna. 'I cannot threadwalk for you.'

'Send them away, please.'

He spoke of the onlookers, and Rostigan understood. He would be very surprised if Braston could manage to threadwalk at all, but getting rid of distractions was a start at least.

'Away with you,' he told the people, and reflected that, unlike with Yalenna, it was not because of great beauty that they obeyed *him*.

Soon they were three hunched figures alone on the silent street, down which the breeze was turning cold.

'You go first, Braston,' said Rostigan. 'And Yalenna, start preparing too, for he will need you at the other end. I will remain here in case he cannot do it.'

'Where do you want to try for?' Yalenna asked Braston.

'The square,' said Braston. 'Hopefully no . . . 'jaw attack . . . has filled it with people, this time.'

'The square, then.'

They closed their eyes.

Rostigan watched their faces. Concentration took them, minutes began to pass. Rostigan's crouching position was not the best for his injuries, it became apparent, but he held himself steady, daring not to move lest he disrupt them. Sounds came from the surrounding streets – loud talk, feet clomping, and he willed their owners not to turn in this direction.

Then Yalenna unravelled.

Braston did not seem to note her departure. He must have gone somewhere very deep inside himself, thought Rostigan, to find a place where he could ignore his pain. His pattern wavered slightly, and Rostigan dared not breathe – and then Braston was gone too.

Rostigan let out a sigh. He had not enjoyed contemplating the long way back if Braston had not been able to threadwalk. To succeed, in such a state . . . well, he could not help but admire the man's constitution.

Standing up, he stretched a little. Glancing at his hand, he saw how skin was already showing the first hints of growing back. He would have to put his own hurts aside now too, if he was to rejoin his allies in Althala.

Why did she love him so much, Tarzi wondered? Not because of his bravery, not because he was a hero. That was nice to know, of course, and made him worthy of a woman like her, but 'hero' was really just an idea. The person himself was grey, stony, and occasionally Tarzi even thought him apathetic. Yet sometimes a smile would crack his lips, just for her, seeming almost painful for him to give away. Warmth would show through that crack, and in his intermittent humour. He protected her, listened to her, and more often than not deferred to her wishes. His actions showed that he cared, even if the actual words seldom crossed his lips. Besides, she had never found the flamboyant gift-bearing and flowery declarations of the foppish love-makers in her stories personally appealing. Her statue was better than that – ever driven to help, despite himself, when he would much rather sit and stare at a field, pipe smoke wafting around him.

He was a good man.

She heard commotion as she reached the square, and her step quickened. A figure lay sprawled on the ground amidst a crowd of people.

Not him, she told herself, against a rising fear, for the man was much too bulky. Closer, and she saw it was Braston – horribly cut, some of his flesh missing in chunks, multiple wounds pulsing. Yalenna was there too, shouting orders, and Braston was loaded onto a stretcher as healers came running. Fear returned to Tarzi quickly, for Rostigan was nowhere to be seen. She pushed through the throng, heart beating fast. Had they left him behind? Where was he?

'Easy, big fellow,' Yalenna was saying. 'You've been through worse.'

'No I haven't,' mumbled Braston through barely open lips.

'Priestess,' said Tarzi urgently, and for a moment Yalenna glanced at her without recognition.

'Oh,' she said. 'Tarzi, yes?'

'Is Rostigan with you?'

She tried to keep her distress contained, though some of it must have slipped out, for Yalenna's face turned kinder.

'He will be,' she said. 'He's just a little slow to arrive, but he's on his way.'

'But don't you have to travel together? He's not a threader! Doesn't he need you to, I don't know, steer him?'

Tarzi felt that panic was making her stupid, but she couldn't help it – of course Yalenna knew that Rostigan wasn't a threader.

'Well,' said Yalenna, 'taking normal folk thread-walking . . . is a tricky process to describe . . .' Her eyes flickered past Tarzi's shoulder, and she broke into a relieved smile. 'Look, there he is.'

Tarzi spun and, sure enough, a short distance away Rostigan was forming out of the air. She hurried to him, arriving in time to lend him balance as he stumbled forward.

'Songbird,' he said – and there was that smile she loved so much. He gave her a squeeze, which also made him wince.

'You're hurt!'

She grabbed his wrist, turning his hand to inspect the bloody hole through his palm.

'Settle, girl. Nothing time can't fix.'

'Did you get Despirrow?'

He grimaced. 'No. Now, help me to a seat – or better yet, a bed.'

He draped an arm over her shoulder, turning her towards the barracks.

'Where are you going?' she said. 'We need to get you to the infirmary, to a healer!'

'Everyone will be busy with Braston for a while. I prefer to be away from the noise. Please, Tarzi? It's not as bad as it looks.'

'It looks like there's a hole in your hand!'

'I just want to lie down.'

She frowned. She would clean his wound and patch him up – wouldn't be the first time either – but then, she promised herself, it would be straight into the castle to demand a proper healer, that was certain.

Sighing, she let him steer her. As they went, she settled into his body, and snuck a look or two upwards at his handsome face.

Such a good man.

TO KILL A KING

Yalenna took a last look over Braston, satisfied she had done all she could. He was installed in his own quarters, thankfully unconscious, with the best healers in Althala fussing over him. They could not click their fingers and make him well, but at least they could speed along the process. She was confident that, with or without their help, Braston would eventually recover. All he really needed was a safe place to convalesce, and his constitution would do the rest.

She left his rooms feeling tired, her own wound a persistent ache. It had been looked at too, a healer having moved around a few of her threads to facilitate a quicker recovery. The Wardens did not make easy subjects for normal threaders – their patterns were complicated, and stubborn, for the threads stolen from the Spell were impossible to affect. She suspected that she, too, would probably have to rely on time to patch her up completely.

As her feet led her towards her own quarters, she toyed with the idea of visiting Rostigan. No, she decided, there was nothing urgent to discuss. Despirrow had escaped, and each and every one of them had suffered for the experience. A good night's sleep was the best thing for everyone.

She opened her door tentatively, half-expecting to find Salarkis there, but the seat by the window was empty.

'My lady?'

An attendant was hovering behind her in the corridor.

'Yes?'

'Would you like anything? Tea, food, fresh sheets? A fire laid?'

'Some dinner would be welcome.'

The attendant ducked his head, and off he went.

Inside she thought about getting changed, decided she couldn't be bothered, and slumped into an armchair. Through the window she could see the lights of the camp outside the walls, and sighed.

Why must it always be war?

Her eyes closed and, for a moment, she may have slept.

A knock at the door roused her. Begrudgingly she rose, wondering if it was dinner. She wasn't sure if she was hungry or not, though she knew she *should* eat. Moving slowly, she opened the door.

It was Jandryn.

'Ah,' she said. 'You're not food.'

'Sorry to disappoint, my lady.'

He seemed more jittery than usual.

'Please have a seat,' she said, as she retreated. 'I'm so tired, I don't even want to look at someone standing up.'

Obediently he took the armchair opposite as she sank into her own, though he sat on the very edge of the seat, as if still at attention – as if it would be improper to relax. She could not help but smile. Half in dreamland as she was, she found she took pleasure in looking at him. He was a handsome young man, after all, and captain already in his early twenties (through noble birth or bravery? she wondered) about the same age as she looked herself.

'My lady?'

'Hmm? Yes, what has brought you to me?'

'I . . . er . . . I am torn, my lady, but I feel I must report. I don't know if it is something, or nothing, but –'

'Spit it out, Jandryn.'

'I . . .' He summoned his courage. 'I have overheard talk, in the . . . in Loppolo's chambers. Only a snatch, but it was about Braston. Loppolo retains loyal followers, and they have heard of Braston's condition. Some of them still support Loppolo as king, and counsel that now may be the right time to attempt removing his . . . usurper.'

Yalenna blinked. 'What?'

'I did not hear Loppolo say so himself, my lady, so it may be nothing . . .'

Relaxation evaporated. It should not be a surprise, she supposed, yet somehow she had not considered that Loppolo would go so far as to consider assassination a possibility. Short-sighted of her, maybe?

'That is troubling,' she muttered.

'I've had guards put on Braston's door,' said Jandryn. 'Guards I trust.'

For once his voice did not quaver, and he seemed sure of himself. Yalenna watched him closely, wondering what she had done to earn him as an ally.

'I thank you for that.'

'Just a precaution,' he added. 'Loppolo might listen to bad counsel, but that does not mean he will act upon it. I have seen him swayed by others before, however, and do not feel it is in Althala's interests to lose one such as Braston. Or you, my lady.'

'What do you mean?'

'Well, I imagine if Loppolo succeeded in doing something stupid, you would turn your back on us. And that would be tragedy upon tragedy.'

'Ah,' said Yalenna. 'I appreciate your concern, but I don't think I could escape so easily. I do not stand for Althala, Jandryn, but for the world. One man's actions will not turn me against all humanity.'

Perhaps he feared he had offended her, for he was quick to shake his head. 'Of course not, my lady!'

'Which is not to say I do not care for Althala,' she added.

There was another knock at the door.

Jandryn stood up, hand going to his sword.

'It's just dinner,' said Yalenna with a chuckle.

'Ah. I should . . . that is to say, it would be improper for me to be seen at such an hour in a beautiful lady's chambers.'

He used the word *beautiful* matter-of-factly, as if it went without saying that that was what she was. It was nice to hear, for people did not often compliment one as striking as her, as if it wasn't necessary to point out the obvious.

'I'm sure no one is going to leap to conclusions,' she said wryly. 'Unless, of course, it would be prudent that you aren't seen reporting to me, with the potential of split loyalty in the castle.'

'Er . . .'

'You can go and hide in the bedroom, if you wish.'

The idea seemed to make Jandryn even more uncomfortable, as he turned quite pink.

'Thank you, my lady. I will touch nothing.'

She opened the door to the attendant waiting with a tray of food. When she saw the steaming vegetables, and steak, and wine, she knew she *was* hungry, after all. The attendant set the tray on the table, bowed deeply, and was gone.

'All is well,' she called into the bedroom. 'Your presence is not suspected.'

Jandryn emerged looking sheepish.

'I don't want to have to keep telling you to sit,' she said, setting herself down in front of the food. 'Are you hungry?'

'Er . . . no, my lady.'

'I am.'

She began to heap food onto her plate. As she did, the shoulder of her blouse slipped, revealing the bloodied bandage there. Jandryn stared at it in horror.

'My lady, what has been done to you?'

'What? Oh. Don't worry, I'll be fine. I earned it during my run-in with Despirrow.'

'That dog!'

His sudden anger was a little over the top for her right then.

'He should be flayed alive!'

'I completely agree,' she said. 'Flayed alive, boiled in oil, decapitated . . . it hardly matters as long as he ends up dead.'

After she had eaten a bit, he cleared his throat.

'My lady, is there something we should be doing?'

'Hmm?'

'About Braston?'

Yalenna dabbed her mouth with a napkin. 'I'm not sure. As you describe it, we do not even know if Loppolo seriously entertains what has been suggested to him. I can't really go storming into his chambers demanding an explanation.'

'Why not?'

'Well, for a start, it may give you away.'

'My lady does not need to worry about me.'

'Oh, but I do. What if I can use you to find out more? It's doubtful they will speak again in your presence if they suspect you are my agent.'

'I was not really in their presence. I was outside the room – they did not know I was there.'

'You said you put guards on Braston's door?'

'Yes, but guards on doors are no guarantee of safety.

There are other ways into rooms. Windows and . . . well, I do not know all the secrets of the castle.'

Yalenna sighed. She found, strangely enough, that again she had an urge to talk to Rostigan.

'Maybe,' she said, 'the guards should stay *inside* the room, then.'

'Won't they disturb the king's rest?'

'I don't know. Are they particularly chatty guards?'

Perhaps she should be taking this more seriously, she thought. Why didn't she? Maybe she didn't really believe that Loppolo would attempt such a bold move, or maybe she was simply overtired. But if there *was* an attempt made on Braston's life, and she had done nothing to try to avert it, how would she feel then?

She put down her fork with a sigh.

'All right. Let us go and check on Braston.'

As they walked the corridors, Yalenna thought Jandryn seemed troubled by what he was doing – his eyes darted left and right, though there were few people about to note their passing. He had been a king's man, Loppolo's man, and she had not really thought about how easily she had appropriated his loyalty. She was simply used to having people obey her, and the Wardens – the good ones, anyway – had always found followers easily. Yet, when she thought about it, Jandryn owed her nothing at all, and perhaps he struggled with the choices he had made.

She found herself curious – this man had spent long enough in her presence to become blessed, but she had never checked the nature of that blessing. She squinted at him now, searching out her influence. It was not as obvious as in those freshly blessed, having had some days to settle into his pattern, yet when she put her mind to it, she could always find what she looked for.

There.

She gave an audible intake of breath as she discerned this most singular blessing.

May you be lucky in love.

'Everything all right, my lady?' he asked, his brown eyes soft.

'Oh . . . yes. Lead on please, Jandryn.'

As they continued, she wondered about the nature of such a powerful blessing. It did not, she knew, mean that he could make people fall in love with him against their will. It was, perhaps, more subtle than that. To be *lucky* in love . . . maybe it simply meant that he would do well around the object of his affection? That she would see him at his best, notice his finer qualities.

Had it affected *her* in any way, she wondered? Certainly she thought him a handsome fellow, but that was merely passing admiration. Or was it? So long had she served Aorn selflessly that recently a niggling feeling had come, that she wanted something for herself, something out of *life*.

She bumped into him, finding him frozen in time.

Once Despirrow was well away from Saphura, and had really begun to feel the chill of the river, he decided that he considered himself safe. He left the water and walked up the bank, his sodden clothes keeping him in cold's embrace. As he moved into the trees, he gave a wave, expelling moisture from his garments.

How had they found him?

He hadn't done anything to draw attention. The only one who'd known where he was, could possibly have known, was Salarkis.

He thought hard about their last exchange. Salarkis had given the appearance of wanting to help, but Despirrow was not foolish enough to take that on face value. Unfortunately, either way, he knew the best thing to do was go to Tallahow, and Forger. His enemies would baulk at pursuing him there, at facing both him and the Lord of Pain together.

Where, then, in Tallahow, did he remember best? Surely the keep remained – in fact he knew it did, for he'd heard of Forger taking it back. Concentrating hard, he pictured the square in front of it, and soon enough he began to unravel.

He surprised a couple of soldiers, appearing out of the air on the square's grey cobbles.

'I am Despirrow,' he told them. 'Take me to my old friend, Forger.'

Pale at his name (how good it felt not to hide it!), they nodded and gestured towards the keep entrance. Under the archway they checked in with a superior, who looked Despirrow over with a mix of fear and caution.

'If I'm not who I say I am,' said Despirrow coolly, 'then the mighty Forger will no doubt kill me. What do you care? Take me to him.'

As they travelled upwards through the keep, the doors he passed returned pleasant memories to him. Many a night he had spent here, taking wine and wenches as he pleased – perhaps coming back here was not so bad after all.

They reached the throne room, and heard a whimpering coming from within. Without waiting to be announced, Despirrow banged open the door and strode inside.

At the room's far end Forger sat on the throne, watching with interest as a burly torturer cut strips from a man chained to the wall. The torturer looked bleary-eyed, as if his efforts wore at him, and there seemed a halting reluctance to his movements. Next to Forger stood a grey-haired old man in a brown robe, reading a scroll.

'Despirrow!' Forger exclaimed, clapping his hands with delight as he stood and descended from the dais. 'I was beginning to think I'd done something to offend you.'

'Of course not,' said Despirrow, trying to echo Forger's warmth. 'I merely wanted to take in some of the world before seeking you out – you know how it is.'

'Ah, yes, of course.'

Forger loomed over him, at least two heads taller – at peak strength, by the look of him. He clasped Despirrow by the shoulders.

'Let me look at you! My, you're a bit tattered.'

'I had a little run-in.'

'Threver!'

The old man appeared by Forger's side.

'My lord?'

'Organise some quarters and fresh clothes for my friend Despirrow here. Make sure that the clothes are noble – he does enjoy dressing the part.'

'Right away, my lord.'

The man bowed to each of them, and Despirrow was pleased to have respect accorded to him.

'Now,' said Forger, rounding on the torturer, 'Yoj, get out! Despirrow, you must tell me everything.'

˜

Soon Forger was loping back and forth, covering the room in frighteningly long strides. Despirrow sat watching him from the throne, reclining as if it were his.

'No!' said Forger furiously. 'I cannot believe it.'

Despirrow shrugged. 'I'm only telling you what I saw with my own two eyes.'

'Karrak would not turn against me!'

'Salarkis visited and told me he had, and then Karrak showed up and tried to kill me. That's about as much proof as *I* need.'

'Salarkis! And where has that stony bird been? Appeared to me once, acted all, I don't know . . . aloof, unfriendly . . . and hasn't bothered to seek me out since!'

The man chained to the wall gave a low moan.

'Oh, shut up,' said Forger, and the man jolted as his backbone ripped out, to dangle from his waist like a bone tail.

'Idle pleasure?' Despirrow arched an eyebrow towards the quivering corpse. 'Or foe?'

'A fellow I met in the dungeons,' said Forger. 'I released him, and he shot me with a crossbow. Not that I bore him any ill will, for it was just a silly mistake, but he served as well as any to help me stay strong.' He shook his head. 'This doesn't fit. Why would Karrak . . . why would he . . .' He had a thought. 'Come with me.'

Despirrow slid off the throne to hasten after the loping Forger. He led them down a level, along a corridor, through a guarded door, and into a room where a threader sat gazing into a mirror.

'You,' said Forger. 'Seen anything?'

'Yes, my lord – I was about to send word. Braston is badly injured, back from a failed expedition to kill . . . er . . .' she paused, noticing Despirrow standing by Forger, openly eyeing her off, '. . . Despirrow. There is further talk in Loppolo's chambers about killing Braston, trying to make it look as if he died of his injuries.'

'Have you seen Karrak?' demanded Forger, and for a moment she was transfixed by the intensity of his stare.

'I . . . don't know what he looks like, lord.'

'Of course you don't,' growled Forger. 'Run along then.'

She beat a hasty retreat, and Forger went to look in the mirror.

'What is this thing?' asked Despirrow, joining him.

'Look into it, and you will see what its friends in Althala Castle see.'

Despirrow was surprised. 'How remarkable.'

'Shh. I want to listen.'

Despirrow stared into the mirror as the view it showed changed. It was as if he looked though a window into another room – and the room was Loppolo's chamber.

'The people will never stand for it,' growled Loppolo, his voice somewhat muted. 'They will storm the castle and have my head on a pole!'

'Braston's on the brink as it is,' said a fat, aging fellow. 'We could have a healer deliver him poison, under the guise of *tonic*, and it would appear as if he had merely succumbed to his hurts.'

'Don't be a fool, Tursa,' scowled Loppolo. 'You think you can kill Wardens so easily?'

'Braston used poison on Despirrow,' said Tursa evenly.

Ah, that's right, thought Despirrow. *How could I have forgotten? Oh, yes – I didn't.*

'Yes,' said Loppolo, 'but that was some kind of special brew, something potent and arcane, and nobody knows exactly what.'

'Some think it could have been a common poison, but laced with curltooth, my lord.'

Curltooth, thought Despirrow. *That makes sense.*

The wine had been sweet, the best he'd ever had – but how it had twisted in his gut, deadened the pathways of his body, and shot pain through his spasmodically beating heart.

'When again,' Tursa said, 'will Braston be so weak, I ask? This is the perfect – maybe the only – opportunity to finish him.'

A door banged somewhere, and the nobles glanced at each other nervously.

'Who's that?' called Loppolo.

A muscular young man emerged into view.

'Ah, Captain Jandryn.'

'You sent for me, lord?'

'Yes. I wonder if you have reported to Yalenna, yet?'

'Not yet, my lord.'

'You have been keeping an eye on her, though?'

'When it is appropriate to do so.'

'Well find an excuse to go and visit her. I want to know all I can about what went on in Saphura.'

Jandryn nodded. 'As you wish, lord.'

When he had gone, Loppolo leaned forward.

'Curltooth, yes,' he said. 'I have heard that theory before, but only as the guesswork of storytellers. No one really knows for sure.'

'The minstrels' tales make sense, lord. Curltooth would enhance the qualities of a poison, bring out its worst, as it were. And even if it did not work, no one would have to know it came from you.'

'This is pointless,' said Loppolo. 'We don't have any curltooth.'

'Ah,' said Tursa, reaching into his pocket. He produced a small vial, inside which clung a few brown specks. 'But we do.'

'But how? There hasn't been any in years!'

'It's very rare, that is certain. This cost me a great sum to procure, but I would gladly sacrifice a pleasant meal to see the kingdom restored to rights.'

He held out the vial to Loppolo, who took it gingerly.

'I have a man in my employ,' Tursa continued, 'blessed with an absence of scruples. He waits outside, and will deliver to Braston, should I ask, a pleasant tonic, looking much like lily water – yet mixed with heartsorrow.'

Loppolo turned the vial thoughtfully in his hands.

Forger stirred beside Despirrow. 'Perhaps this is better than seeing Karrak,' he murmured.

'Can we find Braston himself with this thing?'

'Maybe.'

The view changed to an expansive bedroom, and there, sure enough, was Braston. He lay half under the sheets, the exposed parts of his body a stitched mess, bandaged in various places, scabby and bleeding, his skin pale and his eyes closed.

'I do enjoy seeing the fruits of my labour,' said Despirrow.

'You did this to him?'

'Yes.'

'Impressive. You must tell me the story in great detail.'

'Gladly.'

'It's a shame you didn't finish him off.'

Yes, thought Despirrow. *Especially now that I know what happens to our powers when we die.*

They watched Braston for a few moments, then the mirror changed views again – Forger was controlling it somehow in a way Despirrow couldn't quite work out – and they saw some other places around the castle, but nothing of any consequence. Eventually they cycled back to Loppolo's quarters.

A man now stood amongst the nobles and ex-king, wearing the robes of a threader. In his hand, a tall cup made popping sounds, as Tursa sprinkled in the curltooth.

'They've decided to do it!' said Forger excitedly. 'I didn't think they would, I thought Loppolo too timorous!'

'Succeed in your mission,' Loppolo said dully, 'and you will be generously rewarded.'

The 'healer' nodded, and departed with the cup.

'This is miraculous!' said Forger. 'They're actually going to do our work for us!'

Despirrow's mind began to tick. If Braston did take the poison, then he would die – Despirrow was sure of it, sure that was what had been done to *him*. What, then, would happen to Braston's threads? Who would inherit his Spell-given abilities?

'Look!' said Forger excitedly. The view changed to the passage outside Braston's door. Two guards stood there, their eyes turning to a flight of stairs as the 'healer' emerged. He approached the door, nodded to the guards.

'I'm here to attend the king,' he said, and swirled the cup. 'I bring a healing tonic that will see him back on his feet in no time.'

The guards apparently did not suspect a thing. They stood aside and one of them even reached to open the door.

Despirrow knew a moment of agonising indecision – and, as the guard's fingers touched the doorknob, he stopped time.

The view in the mirror froze, and it took Forger a moment to realise what had happened.

'What – why did you do that?' he exclaimed, turning angrily. 'Yalenna is in the castle, Karrak too, if you're to be believed. This will give them a chance to notice what's going on! To save Braston!'

Despirrow really did not want to tell Forger why he had stopped time, but staring into those blazing eyes, he could not think of any explanation other than the truth.

'Listen to me,' he said. 'You said you wanted to hear the story of what happened in Saphura. Well, here's one part of it – Karrak has inherited Stealer's power.'

'What?'

'He killed her, and now he can do what she could.'

Forger frowned. 'Are you sure?'

'Well, he didn't used to be able to make bridges disappear with rhymes. I think the Spell's threads must be acting again as they did that day on the Spire, when they leapt at us out of Regret.'

'You think Stealer's threads are in Karrak?'

'Yes. And I think that when Braston dies, his power will go to whichever one of *us* is closest.'

Forger's frown grew deeper. Then he shrugged.

'What of it? I don't want to be able to see damned *injustice* wherever I go – nor do you, I daresay. It would probably drive us mad.'

'What about Braston's monumental strength? Do you really want to see it go to Yalenna, or Karrak? To make our enemies more powerful?'

'I have not decided yet if that's what Karrak really is.'

'Even so, why take the risk?'

'What are you suggesting then?'

'One of us has to be on hand when Braston is finished.'

Forger shook his head. 'There's no time. We can't threadwalk while the world is still. And if you start things moving again, it will take too long – Braston will be drinking the poison before we can hope to set off, and heartsorrow works swiftly.'

'Your thinking is limited. Certainly we cannot threadwalk there quickly enough . . . but we could *walk* there.'

'What?'

'No time is ticking by. No Wardens have any of their powers. Braston is sealed in his room, will receive no healing beyond what his own body can muster. And without food or water to fuel his recovery, he will likely lie in torpor for the weeks it will take us to journey on foot to Althala.'

'I don't know. That is a very long time to hold the world steady, and it *will* do damage.'

'Don't be so weak,' said Despirrow derisively.

Forger took him by the shirt and hauled him up off his feet.

'I may not have my powers,' he said, 'but I'm still bigger than you, Despirrow.'

'Release me,' snarled Despirrow. Forger let go, and Despirrow tried to make his landing as dignified as possible. He took a moment to straighten out his ruffled collar and smooth his front.

'I can go alone,' he said, 'if you do not wish the journey. Once Braston is dead, I can return far more swiftly.'

'You do intend to return?'

'We stand a better chance against them united, don't you agree? That is why I came here in the first place.'

Forger got an odd look then. 'Yes.'

'What have you been doing here, anyway?'

'Tallahow's army is making ready to begin the march to Ander. We leave tomorrow morning . . . well, once "tomorrow" stops being such a relative term.'

'You intend to conquer afresh?'

'Of course.'

'Well, let me play my part.'

'It is many leagues to Althala.'

'I will make it. And I shall win for us advantage.'

Forger turned away. 'Very well. But be as swift as you can manage. While none of us will starve, we will indeed go hungry.'

Despirrow nodded, and departed quickly lest Forger change his mind.

THE LONG WAIT

Even though Yalenna knew that Despirrow could be anywhere in the world, it also felt as if he could be just around any corner. She glanced at Jandryn, decided there was no need to worry for him, and quickened her pace towards Braston's quarters.

Maybe Despirrow had come back to finish the job.

She arrived to find the guards Jandryn had mentioned, one of them reaching to open the door. Waiting patiently to be let through was a healer, carrying what looked like lily water. As for the door itself, it was closed, and there was no way she could presently budge it.

She bent down to peer through the keyhole. In the room beyond a closed window let in a trickle of unwaning, unwaxing moonlight. Braston himself was a battered lump in the bed, and there was no one else in there, and no sign of any danger.

She straightened.

Well.

Despirrow was probably just up to his old tricks, taking out his ire on a poor girl somewhere, and time would return once he was done.

She decided to seek Rostigan. She had wanted to speak to him anyway and, with her own bed suddenly as hard as rocks, it may as well be now. Making her way through the castle, she sometimes had to change her path to avoid immovable obstacles. Eventually she emerged into the square, and crossed it to the barracks. It was after dinner, however, and the dining hall doors were closed.

Sighing at the inconvenience of it all, Yalenna picked her way around the building. It had been a warm night, so many of the bedrooms had their windows open. She checked one after the other, observing soldiers in varying states of consciousness or undress, and more than once felt like a peeking intruder. She hoped Rostigan's window would be open – if not, he would be trapped just like Braston. It was a disturbing thought, that she might be the only Warden able to move about – but even if it were the case, it wouldn't be for long.

At the fiftieth or sixtieth window, she finally discovered Rostigan's room. It was wide open, thank the Spell, and he lay abed with Tarzi next to him. He was sleeping soundly, ignorant of the fact that time had frozen. Perhaps there was no need to disturb him, she decided.

With nothing better to do, she sat down under the window to wait out the duration of Despirrow's spell.

Despite the hardness of the ground, she found her own eyes closing, and sleep coming upon her.

―

Salarkis had been riding a horse when the freeze snapped in around him.

He wasn't quite sure why he rode one. There was no need, not for a man who could travel anywhere he wished in the blink of an eye. Perhaps it was *because* of that, because he wanted a taste of the man he had been – a man who had loved galloping through fields with the air whistling in his ears. Perhaps he hoped that repeating the experience might put him further in touch with his old self.

Unfortunately, it had not proven even remotely satisfying. The horse was skittish, as if it sensed the strangeness of its rider. Either that, or he was just too heavy. In annoyance he'd kicked the beast onwards, increasingly desirous of speed, and the frightened horse had done its best. For a moment he'd felt bad – who was he, to torture this creature for the sake of melancholic recollection?

Then came the freeze. The horse entered the still world with him, for he had been touching it, and stumbled immediately. *Blades of grass*, he would later think, with little amusement.

The beast screamed as grass sank into its hooves. Its front legs buckled and it crashed headlong into the sea of waiting stalks. They caught it fast like meat slapped on cactus, and made it a corpse in an instant. Salarkis flew from its back, wondering what had happened as he turned in the air. His first reaction was to blame himself for pushing too hard, and breaking the creature's back.

When he landed, he knew differently. Daggers from below crunched into his scales and, where they found joins, slid through into flesh beneath. Painful as it was, his hard exterior mostly saved him from ruin. There were a few places where agony welled, but nowhere life-threatening.

He lay as still as he could so as not to make it worse, staring up at the star-prickled sky.

'By desert and storm and sea, when I find you, Despirrow . . .'

What to do next? His instinct was to threadwalk, but of course he could not. Maybe if he was careful he could get up and walk on the grass, but he had no idea how far he was from any road, or bare ground, or rock that he might stand upon. Perhaps it was best simply to bide his time, as Despirrow went about whatever mischief had caught his fancy.

Trying to ignore his hurts, he settled in to wait.

~

Mergan had been in a tavern when the freeze had come, at a table to which he had welcomed all and sundry, as he continuously ordered more food from the kitchens. Now his fellow eaters sat glassy-eyed, the spread before them like a sculpted feast. Even the steam rising from the blackened pig was hovering endlessly in the air.

He waited for what felt like hours, though without day's passing such measurements had no meaning. He had long ago finished the hunk of meat he'd had in his hand when time had stopped, and grew increasingly impatient for his next serve.

In the meantime, he had the opportunity to scrutinise his guests. Plainsfolk, for the most part, for he was in the Plains Kingdom. One lass in particular had caught his eye, and he had been charming her in between mouthfuls, maybe. She had laughed a couple of times at his wit, the warmest sound he'd ever heard. She had also looked at him rather oddly once or twice, and he had tried to force the madness back under his brow, so it did not shine so bright in his eyes. He wondered if, after a good feed and a few wines, she might develop a moment or two's affection for a generous old man. He was not so bad-looking, was he, for his age? *Certainly not for my age!* he thought, and chuckled. The couple of days spent roaming and eating since escaping internment had certainly done him wonders. Though his hair, he supposed, remained rather wild – perhaps he should have it tended to.

But I can't do anything until you release me, damned Despirrow.

He rose with nowhere to go. The tavern door was closed, the windows open but barred, and even the chimney was clogged up with smoke. There was no way to leave what had briefly been paradise.

By the Spell, do not leave me trapped here for too long! I could not abide another prison.

Already his mind was beginning to tick treacherously, bringing him information he did not want.

Eleven people in the room . . . sixty mugs behind the bar . . . how many beams of wood in the floor?

Was he still there? Did he still lie on the tomb floor, having dreamed himself a brief escape, only to put himself in another cell?

He rubbed aggressively at his eyes.

'Wind and fire,' he shouted, 'I don't care how many damn mugs!'

⁓

Yalenna awoke with a stiff neck, to the sound of someone at the window. She looked up and saw Rostigan's face framed by the fall of his dark hair.

'Yalenna?'

She rubbed her neck. 'Mmf.'

'How long have you been there?'

She glanced around. It was still night. She felt rested, and would not have been surprised to discover she'd been asleep for hours.

A quick poke at a pebble on the ground showed that time was still stopped.

'I don't know.'

He clambered out and dropped down beside her.

'What is he up to now?'

'I don't want to guess. Some poor woman still suffers for his attention, somewhere? Or this is his strange way of punishing us – flaunting the fact that he's still out there, making us float in a suspended world for as long as he deems.'

Rostigan frowned. 'How's Braston?'

'Locked in his room. He was blacked out when I last saw him, and probably still.'

'You don't think Despirrow might be here – sneaking about, trying to discover a way to have his revenge?'

'It crossed my mind. Maybe we should have a look around?'

'May as well.'

They rose and set off to search. During a long sweep of the castle and its grounds, they saw nothing move, heard no sound. Eventually they emerged onto the castle roof, to look up at the sky. The fixed stars did not even give the impression of twinkling. They were just dots.

'This is ridiculous,' Yalenna said. 'There has never been a freeze this long. What's he playing at?'

'It can't be good.'

The ghosts of hours must have become days at some point, but it was hard to be exact in the eternal night. The best method Despirrow had to keep track of his progress was noting the settlements he passed. He moved through one now, a grey place with lanterns that made it seem more jolly that it actually was, built in the same uniform manner of so many places close to Tallahow.

Close to Tallahow – that was depressing.

Despirrow tried to recall the names of these places, to see a map in his mind's eye – *come on man, you have looked on Aorn so many times, so many maps on castle walls, and taverns, and tapestries* – and though he felt the knowledge was there, it flitted out of grasp. If only he'd brought an actual map . . . but even a small thaw in the long freeze, all the time necessary to pick up a map from a table, would be long enough for the distant door to open, and let Braston out of his cell.

A map and a horse, that would be ideal . . . but no, a horse would need to eat, drink and rest, unlike him. Of course he felt hungry, but he knew he would not starve. He was thirsty too, but he'd had practice at that, for he was always thirsty. Sleep was but an unnecessary comfort. As he kept on, his body went through cycles of wearying and recovering, and the recovering part was actually quite pleasant. If ever he became truly tired, he could always lie down in the middle of the road for a bit. He had to stay on the road, for the grasslands were deadly, and the woods a maze.

If only he had realised he would be making this journey before fleeing all the way to Tallahow. Saphura was so much closer to Althala.

He kept a lookout for places where maps might hang in plain sight. He spotted a tavern with an open door, and ducked inside. A quick glance about showed that he was out of luck, though his eyes lingered over a buxom barmaid. There were others too – nice girls in this place.

Stay on, he told himself, turning away. *Keep on.*

Whenever he found his focus waning, or desirous thoughts queuing up to be had, he pictured Braston's hateful face, and it pushed all else away. So unforgiving the man had become after the change. So quick to dismiss the years of service Despirrow had given the court of Althala, just because he'd developed a few little quirks. All those evenings spent together as young men, sipping wine and discussing the kingdom, had meant nothing in the end. After helping rid the world of Regret, Despirrow should have been allowed to do anything he wanted, and yet his old friend had made it a personal mission to kill him off.

Thus Despirrow moved past barmaids, and farmhouses likely full of innocent young daughters, and roadside campfires, and whores standing outside whorehouses with a moonlit shine on their naked chests . . . and he stayed on, kept on.

Braston had not used a fast-acting poison on Despirrow, oh no. He had wanted, Despirrow was certain, for Despirrow to know what had been done to him. With cloudy vision and swimming mind, he had fallen out of the whorehouse bed, not able to summon the concentration necessary to threadwalk to Althala, where Braston had probably been laughing at him.

No, not laughing. Staring sternly with that righteous expression, satisfied that *justice* had been done.

Satisfied. That was worse than laughing.

In those last moments, before Despirrow could do nothing at all, he had killed every whore he could lay his eyes on – punishment for drugging him, for doing Braston's will.

Was that justice, you endless fool? So happy you were to spend the lives of others, if it but cost me mine.

No, he didn't need to sleep, not yet. Imagining Braston meeting the same end as he had gave him renewed energy. *That* would be true justice. He didn't care as much about stealing the magic, as he did about seeing Braston's face, once he realised what had happened to him.

So he kept on, stayed on.

⁓

'It must be weeks now,' said Yalenna.

'Aye,' said Rostigan. 'Longer, maybe.'

They arrived at Braston's quarters, and she crouched to look through the keyhole.

'Are you all right, Braston?'

There was a moment's silence, followed by a groan. The lump in the bed sat up.

'Piss and fire,' she heard him mumble. 'What is taking so long?'

'We don't know.'

'Has he died? Has he stopped time, then somehow got himself killed, and consigned us all to limbo forever?'

She glanced worriedly at Rostigan – it was something they had discussed, but neither really knew what would happen if Despirrow died while the world was frozen.

'We don't think so,' she said. 'Surely his death would start things again. Besides, how would he die?'

'Who cares?' said Braston, and collapsed back into bed.

'Are you healing?'

'Taking a while. Fighting infections too, now. Would be better if I could eat, or drink!'

Yalenna glanced at the frozen healer, still poised to enter the room. At least Braston would get a drink as soon as time came back, but she didn't think it was worth telling him that now. It might torment him, knowing it was on the threshold, so close and yet unreachable.

'We will check on you later,' she called.

They walked away, though without anywhere in particular to be, it was a rather aimless meander. They had wandered the castle many times already – where they could get to, anyway – and the city itself as well. They had even climbed the platforms of water that issued up from fountains in the throne room.

At least Rostigan and Braston had soft beds, as both of them had been in them at the time of the freeze. Yalenna had suggested that she might borrow Rostigan's, but he was too worried about what would happen if time started and Tarzi woke up to find her there in his place.

His counter-offer had been to stay in the room and watch over them both as they slept, so he could wake her if the world unfroze, but she had been uncomfortable with the notion somehow. Not that there was much need to sleep, beyond a way to break the boredom. They were hardly burning energy, and were both, in fact, growing extremely restless.

'Perhaps we should have a race,' she had suggested at one stage, 'around the square? Or from castle top to bottom?'

He had given her a rueful look. Not much one for frivolous fun, it seemed, even in the face of such monotony.

They'd had many conversations, about many things. About what was happening to the Spell, about the damage Despirrow was surely doing with this prolonged use of power, about what should be done with Loppolo.

'It is only a potential danger,' Yalenna had said, gazing out across a tableau of courtiers from her perch on the top of a water font. 'We don't know for sure that Loppolo will act.'

'No reason for us not to,' Rostigan replied from further down, kicking at colourful fish below the water's surface.

'I don't know that we should tell Braston about it. He will demand retribution.'

'Retribution for retribution?'

'He is blind to justice when it concerns himself. He refuses to think that he's part of the problem. Who knows – perhaps Loppolo is even being driven by some need of the Spell's, to restore things to rights?'

'Braston did raise an army, which we will need should Forger march, or the Unwoven. Surely the Spell does not object to *that*.'

'He could have raised it anyway. He did not *need* to be king.'

'Well then, what do you suggest?'

'I will talk to Loppolo. Try to . . . I don't know. Smooth things over.'

'It's a big bump to smooth,' Rostigan had said glumly.

Now they reached the castle roof, and instantly Yalenna could tell something had changed. Her eyes went to the sky, and what she saw made her miss a breath.

Rostigan followed her gaze.

'Huh,' he said.

From star to star in a great line, light crept, like a fissure opening between pressure points. Meanwhile the moon, which had been brightly fixed in place, now seemed duller, almost as if it were fading from existence.

'The world is straining in place,' she said softly, with a heart full of dread. 'It knows the night should have passed.'

Rostigan sighed. 'For so long I held my power close.'

The look he shot her made clear it was not only Despirrow's presence he begrudged.

'You aren't the gatekeeper,' she said in annoyance. 'This is not Rostigan's Aorn, you know.'

'No,' he said, turning away. 'It isn't.'

Seventeen.

It was flames in the fireplace now, the number of distinct tips reaching up the chimney.

Mergan slumped back on someone's lap. It was so unfair – he'd only had a few days, a tantalising taste on the end of his tongue, of life after his long winter. This was *worse* than the tomb, sometimes, maybe . . . to have these listless companions with him, to see food on the table he could not touch.

Enough to drive a man mad, he thought, and gibbered.

Ugly thoughts reared their ugly heads, and his eyes wandered over sharp objects – a sword strapped to someone's belt, the edge of the bar, even the dangling cloth the innkeeper used to polish a glass. Maybe if he took a run at them he would do a better job of caving his skull in than he had with the flat wall of the tomb.

And then what? What if these others finally wake, to find me lying apparently dead – if they bury me, will I open my eyes inside of the earth, prison after prison after prison?

He shook his head. He was not going to succumb this time. Despirrow would have to release him eventually. In the meanwhile, he knew how to do this.

Of all things, I know how to do this.

Twenty-five chairs . . .

⁓

Forger was bored. He could not even be bothered to chastise himself anymore for allowing Despirrow to depart on his ridiculous errand. So what if Yalenna inherited Braston's power? She was high on the list of people Forger wanted to kill anyway.

He sat on a swing in someone's yard, watching a mother and father play with their little girl. Love was plain on their faces, the girl caught in an embrace between the two of them as they hoisted her into the air. She was laughing, her little hands reaching skywards.

Ah, how simple it would be to reduce them all to tears.

'If I could,' he muttered.

He had grown shorter again, which added to his bad mood. He could not cause pain to the impenetrable, and thus, as he waited for the world, his power had diminished.

Nothing he could not quickly correct.

As he daydreamed about things he could do to the small family – more inventive than simply killing one of them, though that was ever-effective – he thought he heard something. He cocked his head, wary that his mind might be playing tricks on him – but there it was again! Somewhere in Tallahow, someone was calling out.

Excitedly he slid off the swing onto the little garden path. Careful to avoid the grass, he made his way to the gate, and clambered over. In the street all was still in the odd light of the faded moon and bright cracks in the sky. He listened, trying to make out the voice, and what direction it came from.

'Hello?' he shouted. 'Who's there?'

He began to jog, no echoes sounding from his footfalls. Up towards the keep, that was where the voice sounded!

'Hello!' he called. 'Hello, hello, hello!'

'Is that Forger?'

This time he heard the words, recognised the voice. As fast as he could, he bounded up through the tiered city towards the rising cliff face, until he reached the keep. There, in the square, he found Salarkis waiting.

'Thank goodness!' Forger said, halting before the stony Warden. He patted his chest affectedly, as if he needed to catch his breath. 'I was beginning to think I'd be alone forever.'

'Hello, Forger.'

'How did you get here?'

'I was away to the west somewhat, when this,' he waved a hand about, 'occurred. Had to pick my way amongst grassland to the road.'

'Oh dear.' Forger seemed genuinely concerned. 'That must have been painful.'

'I have good balance. I was able to keep to the flats of blades, mostly.'

'Well, I'm very happy to see you.'

'And I you. Assuming, of course, you can explain to me what the *blood and piss* is going on!?'

Forger blinked, taken aback by Salarkis's ire. He still did not know where the Warden's loyalties lay, he realised, though he hoped for the best.

Mustn't be too hasty, he decided. *You'll fall victim to your own good nature.*

It was even possible that, once time started, Salarkis would whisk away and try to stop Despirrow, even to *save Braston* . . . that was, if he found out exactly what the plan was.

'Despirrow has an errand,' Forger said vaguely. 'I'm not sure what.'

'Then how do you know he has one?'

'Isn't it obvious? Look around you.'

'So, you haven't seen him?'

'No one has visited me.' Forger pulled a remorseful face. 'Not you, or him, or Karrak, or Stealer.'

'Stealer is dead,' said Salarkis flatly.

'I heard the rumours, and feared them true.' He sighed. 'Come, we have much to discuss, and nothing but time to do it. Let us enter,' he gestured at the keep, looming above him, 'my humble abode.'

Despirrow glanced at the sky uneasily. He knew he could not keep this up forever, or even much longer. His cycles of recovery were coming more slowly, and did not last as long before heaviness returned. His hold on time felt slippery, and sickening, as if he'd gripped something slick and rotten. Soon he would have to let it go.

And he would.

Ahead loomed Althala's towers. He could not believe that he had made it. For so long he'd held them in his mind's eye, hoping to see them over every hill, around every bend, and finally, here they were.

With the sky cracking above him, Despirrow stole up the road, into Althala.

A NEW DAY

He slipped along carefully, hugging walls, for his movement amongst the statues would stand out to the other Wardens. He saw no one on the streets, however, and soon reached the open square before the castle. Here was where the real danger lay – Yalenna and Karrak were most likely somewhere nearby, for what would be the point in venturing anywhere else? And if they happened to be overlooking the square – not that he expected them to be maintaining vigil, as such – but they might just happen to be looking . . .

He loitered under the leaves of a tree on the square's edge. He wished he could trust the dark of night to cover him, but the cracks in the sky were growing larger, spilling out the light of day – or even several weeks' worth of days! Even Despirrow had to fear what he had done, though he told himself it was just concern that the world would be ruined before he had a chance to enjoy it.

A NEW DAY

Then he noticed movement on the castle roof – two figures, one of them pointing upwards. He smiled with relief, for it was easier to avoid them now that he knew where they were. Once they receded from the edge, he broke into a run across the square. Through the open archway of the main entrance he went, past guards, making straight for Braston's quarters. Being all too familiar with this place, he found his way easily, and indeed a touch of nostalgia tweaked him as he went. Castle Althala had been his playground for many years.

One room in particular gave him pause as he passed it, recalling it from his final night here. He had *undone* the lock, snuck in upon a sleeping Lady Jariss while her husband was away, and proceeded to have his way with her for hours. He had stoppered her voice so she could not cry out while he pinched her hard in all the wrong places, and took her upright, mercilessly thumping her posterior against the wall until it was bruised all over. How woeful, to have been interrupted in the midst of such pleasure – to sense someone outside reversing the changes he had wrought on the door. He had flung the lady aside and stalked into the wardrobe, where he had parted wooden backing and the stone beyond to escape the room. As the wall closed up behind him, he had heard Braston bursting in, and known there would be no hiding what he had become, anymore. If Braston had previously suspected foul play, now he would know for sure. Despirrow had been forced to flee, and had never seen the horror of realisation in his old friend's eyes, because abhorrence had so quickly replaced it.

You leapt so quick to condemnation, Braston. You didn't even try to understand.

As he entered the corridor that led to Braston's chamber, a growing excitement threatened to make him giggle. He passed a silver framed mirror on the wall, admiring it briefly as he went. All this time it had hung there undetected, a gift that was no gift at all. Would Forger be ready to watch what happened in the next few minutes? He had no way of knowing that Despirrow had finally arrived.

The treacherous 'healer' and guards stood outside Braston's door, one of them on the verge of turning the knob. Despirrow briefly inspected the healer, and the cup he carried. It did not look suspicious at all, but in fact, quite inviting.

By the Spell, he would toast Braston's memory with lily water soon enough, and laugh.

Suddenly the door's keyhole seemed like an eye, and Despirrow experienced a horrid worry that Braston, with nothing better to do, had taken to watching from it. He hurriedly withdrew around a corner into a stairwell, but after a few moments he relaxed. No sound came from inside Braston's room to indicate that Despirrow had given himself away. Just his anxious mind, making him jumpy. He slumped down on a stair.

Well, here he was. All he had to do was let time flow again.

Strained as his grip had become, now that it came to releasing it, he found it to be difficult. It was as if he'd held a hand in the same position for too long, and now it was unresponsive, and bent out of shape. Concentrating hard, he took a deep breath, and forcefully let go.

Out of view down the corridor, he heard the door open, followed by Braston's exclamation of surprise.

'My king,' came the healer's voice. 'Excuse me, I did not mean to startle you.'

The healer coughed a little – no doubt it smelled truly ripe in Braston's quarters.

'You didn't!' came Braston's reply. 'It's just . . .'

Don't try explaining it to him, thought Despirrow.

'Never mind. Suffice to say I am glad to see you! To see anyone, indeed.'

'My lord is looking better than I expected,' said the healer.

Not too much better, I hope.

'Don't shut that door!' barked Braston.

Despirrow could well imagine that he did not fancy being trapped in the room any longer.

Come on, give him the damned drink.

~

To Braston, the fresh air entering his room through the open door was more welcome than he'd even imagined.

Healing had been slow, due to the deprivation he had experienced. Nonetheless he felt like he had passed a certain point, that the worst was behind him and he could at least stand. His body still ached, but he rose determinedly from the tangle of fetid sheets. His eyes found the cup the healer carried, and, had he any saliva left, his mouth would have watered. Thirst had been the most vocal of his needs, and he had dreamed of lakes and rivers as he lay, mouth as dry as paper.

'I have brought you some lily water, lord,' said the healer, extending the cup.

Strange light played into the room. Braston turned to the window, which had remained closed all this 'time', and wrenched it open. Across the heavens, great lines rippled with the brightness of day, pulsing as they tried to dispel the night. Meanwhile he heard distant gasps, saw people below pointing and staring.

'Despirrow,' he muttered. 'What have you wrought?'

He turned back to the healer. His instinct was to ask what had happened while he'd been locked away, but of course the man could not answer that.

He needed to find Yalenna.

The healer stared past him out the window in amazement, as did the guards at the door.

'My lord,' said the healer, 'what is happening out there?'

There was something about him, Braston realised – something in the network of threads wavering about him that seemed important, to do with justice.

'You're going to do something, aren't you?' Braston asked.

The man paled. 'Pardon, my king?'

'You have something planned, don't you? Of great consequence.'

The man seemed to shrink back into himself. 'I . . . I'm not sure what you mean, lord.'

Braston frowned. 'Maybe you don't even know it yet, but the Spell likes you.' Sight of the cup reminded him of his thirst. 'Now, give me that – my tongue is dry as tinder.'

He took the lily water from the healer's unresisting fingers and raised it to his lips. Oh, he was thirsty, and, as he gulped the drink down, he was amazed by how sweet it was. It tingled in his mouth and danced down his throat, so thick with deliciousness that it made him, for a moment, forget every other thing. Then, slowly, he lowered the cup.

'What was *that*?' he asked.

'Er . . .'

'What manner of tonic? Answer me, man!'

'Just lily water, lord . . . although, by order of Loppolo, there was some curltooth added.'

'Curltooth!' Braston smacked his lips. 'Well, that explains it. An odd gesture, but perhaps he seeks peace between us – I will thank him for it when I see him.'

Pain coursed along his ribs.

'What . . .' he gasped, clutching his chest, but got no further.

The pain converged on his very core, burrowing into his heart. He cried out, hardly recognising his own voice. *I do not sound like that*, he thought distantly, so full of fear and horror. He always hid his hurts well, gritted his teeth, carried on.

He went to his knees, to the floor, onto his back, where a surreal upside-down view of the doorway greeted him. The guards were falling, blood spraying from their throats... and past them into the room walked Despirrow, slamming the door behind him. The healer, trapped as well, backed away into a corner.

'Well,' said Despirrow, grinning malignantly, 'how does poison feel, Braston?'

'You...'

Even if he could have choked them out, there were no words to convey the measure of his hatred. The heat of it mingled with the heat running through him, and he tried to rise, tried to ignore the deep burning within.

Despirrow cackled and booted him in the side.

'I dearly wish,' he said, 'that I could stand here and bathe in the joy of this circumstance. Unfortunately,' he raised a sword, taken from one of the guards, 'your friends are no doubt on their way to save you.'

The light of the maelstrom outside flashed over the blade as it travelled downwards. Braston tried to raise a hand, but his strength no longer matched his will.

On the roof, Rostigan and Yalenna watched the cracks breaking over the world, as day struggled for supremacy over night.

'This,' whispered Yalenna, 'is so very bad.'

'It will settle,' said Rostigan, trying to sound certain.

'Braston!' Yalenna exclaimed.

They turned and ran to the stairs down from the roof. In the corridors below doors were opening, disconcerted occupants emerging in their bedclothes.

'Have you seen the sky?'

'The end has come!'

'The Spell is broken!'

'Priestess! Tell us what has happened!'

'Not now!' said Yalenna, pushing through.

They arrived outside Braston's door, where they saw the bodies of his murdered guards.

~

Despirrow drove the bloodied sword through Braston's chest.

'Don't look at me like that,' he told the man's severed head. 'I'm trying to do you favour – stopping your heart from pumping poison through you.'

He gave it a kick, so it wasn't looking at him anymore.

Impatiently, he waited for a sign that beheading, stabbing and poison had proved enough. Braston was a stubborn bastard . . .

There! Braston's pattern began to unwind, his threads lifting to fade into the air – except for one twisting bundle, which hovered above him, as if in indecision.

'Here I am,' said Despirrow, holding out his hands in a gesture of embrace.

The bundle flew toward him, heading for his arm. It curled around the limb like smoke, and he felt the foreign threads suddenly dig in, breaking his pattern as they wriggled into place. For a moment it was uncomfortable, and felt very wrong. His vision flickered . . . and then new strength flowed through his veins.

Laughing, he reached to grab the cringing healer by the neck and haul him to his feet.

'This is wonderful! You did a good job, sir, poisoning the king!'

'I . . . I didn't . . .'

'Come now, you don't have to lie to me! I am glad you did it – don't I seem glad? Long live Loppolo!'

He sensed someone trying to undo the spell he'd set on the door – *just like old times*. Shoving away the healer, he glanced around. He did not really fancy taking on Rostigan, Yalenna *and* whoever else they had at their disposal, especially whilst trapped in this confined space.

He went to the window and poked out his head. Only a few slivers of night now remained, the day very close to winning. The ground was some hundred paces below, but there were other windows nearer than that. As he clambered out, he summoned the sheets from Braston's bed, lengthening them to form a fabric rope. He sent one end to knot around the bed frame, then lowered himself down to a window beneath. Once there, he wrenched out glass and frame with one swipe of his hand, and swung into the lower room.

He found himself in a noble's quarters, deserted with the door lying wide open. He wasted no time dallying, and ran out into corridors filled with frightened, gabbling people.

It would not be difficult, he imagined, to disappear into the turmoil.

Salarkis rested his hands on the rail of one of the keep's high balconies, watching the display in the sky.

'Despirrow has put us all in danger,' he said.

'We were already in danger,' replied Forger.

'Well, then, he's made it worse. I shall go and find him immediately.'

'I don't want you interrupting his mission.'

'Ah. So you *do* know what he's doing!'

'I admit, I do.'

'Why didn't you tell me?'

Forger sighed. 'Come, Salarkis. There's something I want to show you.'

He stepped aside and held a palm up through an archway.

Salarkis dithered for a moment but, 'Very well,' he said, and allowed himself to be ushered through.

Something heavy smashed across the back of his head. He pitched forwards, bruised under his scales, bright lights flashing before his eyes. As he fell he turned, tried to use his tail to catch himself, but it scraped along the floor and he landed unceremoniously on his buttocks. He blinked rapidly, trying to clear his vision.

Forger stood over him, a broken length of stone – some of the balcony railing? – in his hands.

'Ah,' he said thoughtfully.

'What do you mean, "ah"?' snarled Salarkis. 'So we *are* foes, after all? Is that what you wanted to show me?'

'More or less,' said Forger. 'People think I don't pick up on things, but I'm not stupid, you know. Even before we died, we were growing distant from each other. And I've heard the stories – didn't you think I would – about you and Yalenna. About how she blessed you, before killing you. Are you still blessed, Salarkis?'

'You might call it that.'

'Besides,' said Forger, 'you have such wonderful gifts. I admit I got a little greedy, wanted them for myself.'

'What?'

'Never mind.'

'You know what's going to happen now, don't you? I'm going to disappear.'

'Yes, I know.'

'How could you even think there was any point to hitting me like that?'

'Well, I don't know!' said Forger exasperatedly. 'I just thought maybe, if I could knock you out for a moment, you wouldn't be able to threadwalk, and I could finish you off in the meantime.'

'Well, it didn't work.'

'I *know* it didn't.' Forger rolled his eyes. 'I can see that, thank you very much. On the other hand . . .'

'What?'

Salarkis waited, itching to be off, but also wanting to hear this last thing Forger had to say.

'WHAT?' he shouted.

'All right, all right. Well, I was just going to say . . . this one more very important thing, before we part ways . . .' Forger smiled. 'On the other hand, at least I have bought Despirrow some time.'

Salarkis scowled as he unspooled.

⁓

As Yalenna burst into the room, the sight that greeted her almost made her reel. She wobbled in place, just managing not to collapse.

Entering after her, Rostigan looked about grimly.

A sword stuck proudly out of Braston's barrel chest; his head, in a corner, was facing away; there was a smashed cup on the ground; and in another corner a quivering healer held his knees to himself.

He will pay for this. The words began to run repeatedly through her head. *He will pay for this, he will pay for this.*

Rostigan approached the healer. 'What happened here?'

The man started to stutter. 'My . . . I was . . . Despirrow . . . that is . . .'

'We don't have all day for your gibbering,' said Rostigan.

'All day,' echoed Yalenna, staring out the window. The light that shone through it was now constant and strong. Day had taken hold.

'Tell us what happened,' said Rostigan, spinning persuasive threads into his words.

The healer blinked, powerless to withhold his secrets. 'I came to bring King Braston poison,' he said.

Yalenna spun around. 'What?'

The healer nodded. 'On the order of the true King Loppolo. Heartsorrow, mixed with curltooth.'

'And did he drink it?'

As Yalenna stalked towards him, he swallowed.

'Answer her,' said Rostigan.

'He drank it. Then Despirrow came, and . . . well . . . Braston was not able to fight back.'

Yalenna was almost nose to nose with him now. 'So you killed him together.'

'Er . . .' The healer's face was full of fear – speaking under Rostigan's influence seemingly did not change the fact that he knew he was in a lot of trouble.

'I should bless the skin right off you,' growled Yalenna.

'By the Spell!' This from Jandryn, who had arrived at the door. 'Lady Yalenna, are you all right?'

'Take this man,' she said, thrusting the healer at him with eyes blazing, 'to the dungeons. He has poisoned King Braston.'

'Poisoned?' echoed Jandryn, glancing at the headless body.

'And send out guards,' said Rostigan, 'to search the castle. Despirrow is here, somewhere.'

Jandryn paled. 'Right away.'

'We should search for him too,' said Rostigan. He touched Yalenna's shoulder, and she started. 'Yalenna? Don't you want to find him?'

'Yes,' she said. 'I do.'

⌒

Salarkis appeared out of the air somewhere between Althala and Tallahow. A quick glance confirmed what he already suspected – he had not made it to Despirrow in time. Either Despirrow was threadwalking himself, or dead.

Sighing, he sat down in the middle of nowhere to consider what he should do next.

⌒

Despirrow appeared back in the square outside Tallahow Keep. This time his sudden arrival was hardly noted, as everyone present was pointing at the sky – here, like elsewhere, the middle of the night had fast become day.

He paused to look upon a person or two, to marvel at the new sense he had acquired. He could see a new kind of thread, of which several wavered from each and every individual – not part of *their* pattern, but part of *the* pattern. It was something to do with how everything was connected – he didn't pretend to understand it – but evidently it was how Braston had been able to discover where justice and injustice lay.

He made his way into the keep, feeling so powerful that he almost hoped guards would try to bar his way – yet they simply bowed and let him pass.

Already I am known here, he thought, oddly disappointed.

'Look at you,' he said to one of them. 'Your mother raised you all by herself, and you don't even visit her anymore! Shame on you.'

The guard blinked in surprise, and Despirrow moved on. Having Braston's power was going to be fun!

He tracked down Forger to the mirror room. The Lord of Tallahow was staring into the mirror, chortling and rubbing his hands together.

'Oh, my!' Forger crowed. 'You should come and see this, Despirrow! They are running about the castle like little ants, still looking for you . . . and I have seen, *have seen* your work!'

Despite his ambivalent feelings towards Forger, it was hard not to glow at such enthusiastic praise.

'And you have acquired Braston's powers?' Forger asked.

'I have.'

Forger nodded. 'Well, that is something, at least.'

'What do you mean, *at least*?'

'The prize is won at terrible cost, my dear, you must know this. When the world can't decide if it's day or night, that is a bad state of affairs.'

'It has cleared up now. The day shines true.'

'Mmm. But who knows what the lasting harm may be? Anyway, I should not be maudlin, for these are exciting developments! Braston dead, and you with his talent.'

'I'm so glad you approve.'

As he watched the mirror, Forger's eyes widened. 'By the Spell!'

'What is it?'

Forger didn't shift from whatever he saw. 'Come, look for yourself!'

Hesitantly Despirrow went to the mirror. He found himself staring at the view into Braston's room. The door was still open – had in fact been wrenched from the wall – and a healer was supervising Braston's remains, having his neck wrapped so that it stopped trickling. It warmed Despirrow to see it, though he could not immediately ascertain the source of Forger's excitement.

'What am I looking at, precisely?' he said.

His body jolted, and there came a cold sting in his chest. He looked down to see the point of a blade sticking from his breast. Turning slowly, he found Forger staring intently into his eyes.

'What . . .'

Forger punched him hard, sending him staggering.

'Forger,' he rasped, grasping for purchase at nothing. 'Don't do this.'

'I'm sorry, my dear,' said Forger. 'You are simply too irresponsible to wield such power.'

'But we are . . . friends.'

Forger shook his head sadly. 'No, not really. You only came here when you got scared, not because of any true loyalty. I have realised, much as it grieves me, that I must stand alone. It's not the way I'd choose it, but you, Salarkis, Karrak . . . all have abandoned me.'

Despirrow tensed, trying to take hold of the strength so newly acquired. It was there, he knew it – he reached for Forger, who moved smoothly backwards, and Despirrow pitched forward onto his hands. The strength was there, but he could not rise to use it. He stared down at his splayed fingers, feeling the hopeless spasms of his punctured heart.

'You . . . just want . . . my powers.'

'Maybe,' said Forger. 'I'm not sure. I don't really enjoy the stopping of time, athough maybe I will when it's something I control, rather than an inflicted annoyance. I already have strength to match Braston, as you can see.'

Forger's heel on his back drove Despirrow to the ground, pushing the sword backwards out of him. Forger seized it and pulled it free.

'It's a shame,' he said, 'that I have no use for the pain I cause another Warden. Good for you though, I suppose, else we could be here a long time.'

Despirrow shakily raised his head and saw Forger with the blade in one hand, a sputtering candle in the other. Where had he got a candle? Despirrow wondered vaguely.

'But I don't want to die again,' he pleaded.

'Who does?'

Scorching lines leapt from the candle. Despirrow tried to unthread them before they reached him, but he was too enervated. Fire touched him, and he screamed. There was no place to retreat, except maybe . . .

Desperately, he stopped time. The flames spilling from the candle ceased, and those on his body fell away in hard red shards.

'You want to prolong this?' said Forger. 'Make me hack you to bits instead?'

'If you kill me now,' Despirrow forced the words through scalded lips, 'how can you know that time will ever start again?'

'Because *your* threads aren't frozen,' said Forger, 'so they will come to me.'

And he set about Despirrow with his sword.

The story continues . . .

The Lord of Lies
BOOK 2 in the STRANGE THREADS DUOLOGY

The world is crumbling.

Having joined the Warden Priestess Yalenna, Rostigan must face those Wardens who remain bent on steeping Aorn in ruin and, somehow, heal the world by closing the Wound in the Great Spell.

Standing in his way is a superhuman army commanded by a madman, a sky full of silkjaws and, worst of all, an old friend, once betrayed, whom he must now convince to join him again.

There is only one thing for it – Rostigan must break an ancient oath and use powers he has dared not touch – powers that could tip the balance in favour of the spreading corruption.